TWO QUEENS AND A CHRONICLER

Two Queens and a Chronicler

A NOVEL

Alta Ifland

www.openendspress.com. email: editors@openendspress.com

Cover design: Peter Selgin

Portrait of Queen Marie by Philip de Lászlo, public domain

Photograph of Queen Elisabeta from 1882, public domain

This is the first paperback edition.

Manufactured in the United States

ISBN 979-8-9917990-4-1 (paperback)

"… by virtue of her pen she has
won her freedom. She is no longer
a royal queen in a cage. She ranges
the world, free like any other
human being to laugh, to scold, to
say what she likes, to be what she
is. And if she has escaped, so too,
thanks to her, have we. Royalty is
no longer quite royal. Uncle Bertie,
Onkel, Aunty, Nando, and the
rest are not mere effigies bowing
and smiling, opening bazaars,
expressing exalted sentiments, and
remembering faces always with the
same sweet smile. They are violent
and eccentric; charming and ill-
tempered; some have blood-shot
eyes; others handle flowers with
a peculiar tenderness. In short,
they are very like ourselves. They
live as we do. And the effect is
surprising."
—from "Royalty," Virginia Woolf's
review of *The Story of My Life* by
Marie, Queen of Romania

"Recollections may vary."
—HM Queen Elizabeth II

Author's Note

During the span of several years when I was writing this chronicle, some of the princes and princesses mentioned by the queens and their chronicler became kings and queens, received other titles, or in some cases had their titles withdrawn. I decided to use the titles and the styles they had at the time the conversations took place. This is why you will see the same person referred to in different ways, depending on when the conversations happened (thus, Prince William is in some instances called "the Duke of Cambridge" and in others "the Prince of Wales"). In most cases I used the Romanian spelling of localities (Balcic instead of Balchik, or Dobrogea instead of Dobruja); in other cases, I used the spelling most familiar to the speaker (Elena for Helen of Greece). The reader will need to notice that there are several characters with the same name: several Helens, Alexandras (abbreviated as Alix) and Nicks. Sentences in italics are literal statements or utterances made by the queens. These are to be found in their correspondence or other bibliographical material listed at the end of this novel, some of which I have read in Romanian and therefore had to translate into English.

Main Characters

Maria or Marie
(1875-1938)
Queen of Romania: former Princess of Edinburgh, granddaughter of Queen Victoria; called Missy by her family; wife of Ferdinand

Ferdinand
(1865-1927)
King of Romania (1914-1927): former Prince of Hohenzollern-Sigmaringen; called Nando by his family; nephew of King Carol I

Elisabeta
(1843-1916)
Queen of Romania: wife of King Carol I, former Princess of Wied, writing under the pen name Carmen Sylva

Carol I (Rom.) or Karl I (Germ.)
(1839-1914)
Former Prince of Hohenzollern-Sigmaringen, domnitor of the United Principalities of Moldova and Wallachia (1866-1881); King of Romania (1881-1914)

Carol II
(1893-1953)
Crown Prince, King of Romania (1930-1940): eldest son of Maria and Ferdinand

Elena

Pet name Sitta, former Princess of Greece, wife of Carol II,
Queen Mother after Carol's abdication

Mihai (Michael)
(1921-2017)

King of Romania (1927-1930; 1940-1947): child of Carol II
and Elena (Sitta)

Elena Lupescu

Also called Magda; mistress, then wife of Carol II

Elena Văcărescu

Lady in waiting of Queen Elisabeta

The Chronicler

A contemporary, Romanian-born American writer

The dialogue between the two queens and the
Chronicler takes place in the present.

A Chronology of Historical Events Discussed in this Book

1866 Prince Karl of Hohenzollern is chosen by the Romanian political elite as Romania's ruler (*domnitor*). At the time, the country was called the United Principalities of Moldova and Wallachia (the Eastern and Southern regions of today's Romania). Transylvania (the North-Western province) was part of the Austro-Hungarian Empire.

Prince Karl/Carol arrives in Romania in May; in June, Romania's Parliament adopts the 1866 Constitution, according to which only males can ascend to the throne.

1869 Marriage of Carol of Hohenzollern with Elisabeta, Princess of Wied

1871 Birth of Princess Maria (nicknamed "Itty"), the couple's only child

1874 Death of Princess Maria. Elisabeta will suffer numerous miscarriages, incapable of having other children, and, as a consequence, other members of Carol's family will be considered as heirs.

1877 The Independence War against the Ottoman Empire, in which Carol I is an active participant

1878 Romania's independence is acknowledged officially.

1880 Elisabeta starts publishing under the pen name "Carmen Sylva."

1881 Carol I is crowned King of Romania. Queen Elisabeta becomes a member of the Romanian Academy.

1886 Ferdinand becomes heir presumptive to the throne of Romania, following the renunciation of his father, Leopold (brother of Carol), and older brother.

1891 Queen Elisabeta/Carmen Sylva is exiled to Venice with her lady in waiting, Elena Văcărescu, following the queen's unsuccessful (and unconstitutional) plan of marrying the latter with Ferdinand of Hohenzollern.

1892 Queen Elisabeta is exiled at her mother's residence, near Neuwied.

1893 January 10: wedding of Marie, Princess of Edinburgh, to Ferdinand of Hohenzollern

October 15: birth at Sinaia of Carol II, Maria and Ferdinand's eldest child

1894 Queen Elisabeta's exile ends.

1913 Romania gains Southern Dobrogea from the Bulgarians, a multiethnic region beautifully described by Queen Marie in her writings. This is where she will build Balcic Castle.

1914 October 10: King Carol I dies and is succeeded by Ferdinand.

1916 March 2: death of Queen Elisabeta

Under the influence of Queen Marie and against his own pro-German feelings, King Ferdinand enters the war on the side of the Allies against the Austro-Hungarian Empire.

1918 September: Prince Carol deserts from the front and elopes with Zizi Lambrino whom he marries in Odessa despite his family's wishes and against constitutional rules. Eventually, he returns and observes a light punishment in a monastery.

November: the Allies cross into Romania, whose military joins them. The defeat of the Germans, until then difficult to imagine, becomes a reality. Kaiser William abdicates. Queen Marie receives the medal of the Croix de guerre from the French ambassador, Count Saint Aulaire. News that the Tzar and his entire family were murdered.

November 29: Bukovina's General Congress proclaims its union to Romania under the rule of King Ferdinand.

December 1st: the Romanian Royal Family returns to Bucharest from its exile in Iași, being welcomed with huge enthusiasm by the entire population. On horseback, dressed in military uniforms, King Ferdinand, Queen Marie and General Berthelot lead the parade on Calea Victoriei, to the cheers of the population.

1919 Queen Marie is sent by the Romanian government to attend the Treaty of Versailles. Thanks to her charm and diplomacy, Transylvania becomes part of "Greater Romania."

Prince Carol's marriage to Zizi Lambrino is annulled, but several months later, a child, Mircea Lambrino is born. The child's paternity is acknowledged by Carol but rejected by the Royal House of Romania.

1921 Marriage of Elena/Helen of Greece with Crown Prince Carol, future King Carol IIBirth of Prince Mihai, future King of Romania, son of Elena and Crown Prince Carol

1925 For the third time, Crown Prince Carol renounces the throne, this time for Elena (Magda) Lupescu, with whom he leaves the country under the name of Carol Caraiman. King Ferdinand summons the Crown Council, names Mihai as his successor and a Regency of three people (Prince Nicolae, Patriarch Miron Cristea and the President of the High Court of Cassation and Justice, Gheorghe Buzdugan) to lead the country until Mihai comes of age.

1926 October 18: Queen Marie begins her visit to the USA.

1927 King Ferdinand dies, and Mihai becomes king at less than six years old.

1928 Carol divorces Princess Elena/Helen.

1930 Carol returns from exile, dethrones his own son and becomes king. Consequently, his former wife is exiled to Italy in Florence, where Mihai sees her once a year, per his father's wishes. Due to Carol's jealousy of Queen Marie's popularity, the Queen is also encouraged to move away, and she settles in Balcic (today in Bulgaria).

1938 In the context of Germany's Nazification and of the fascist (*legionar*) movement in Romania, King Carol II establishes a royal dictatorship, cancelling the 1923 Constitution and abolishing the political parties.

1940 Following the Molotov-Ribbentrop Pact, half of the region of Moldova (also known as Moldavia) is annexed by the Soviets. This region is in the Eastern part of Romania and includes Bukovina and most of Basarabia (Bessarabia). Today there are two Moldovas: Eastern Romania and the Republic of Moldova, which was part of the Soviet empire until 1991 when it became independent.

King Carol II is forced to abdicate by his Prime Minister, General Ion Antonescu, a Nazi supporter. The King barely escapes alive by leaving the country in a train containing some of his assets, followed by the *legionari* (Romanian fascists), who are shooting at the train. Mihai becomes King again.

1944 August 23: coup d'état of 22-year-old King Mihai against his Prime Minister; following the King's orders, the Romanian army joins the Allied forces against the Nazis, a move supposed to have shortened the war by six months and saved thousands of lives. Later, the Communist regime will cynically appropriate this date, and August 23 will become Romania's national holiday, generations of Romanians being indoctrinated into believing that the Communists saved the country from the Nazis. Even today most Romanians wrongly associate this date with Communism.

1945 March: under pressure from the Soviets, King Mihai appoints the Communist Petru Groza as head of the government.

August-January **1946**: King Mihai goes on a "royal strike" against the Soviets.

1947 November: King Mihai attends the wedding of Princess Elizabeth (future Queen Elizabeth II) with Prince Philip of Greece and Denmark, an event where he meets his future wife, Princess Anne of Bourbon-Parma.

December 30: King Mihai is forced to abdicate by the Soviets.

1948 January 3: King Mihai and his mother, Elena, leave Romania with a few pieces of luggage. During his exile, Mihai will be the poorest of all exiled royalty.

June 10: King Mihai marries Princess Anne of Bourbon-Parma in Greece. The couple will settle in Switzerland and will have five daughters: Margareta, Elena, Irina, Sofia, Maria.

1953 King Carol II dies in Estoril, Portugal. His son, King Mihai, is not present at the funeral.

1989 December: the anti-communist Revolution; dictator Nicolae Ceausescu is killed.

1990 December 25: King Mihai enters Romania for the first time after his abdication, but after only 24 hours, the regime of Ion Iliescu forces him to leave.

1992 King Mihai visits Romania during Easter. A huge crowd of about a million people gathers to listen to his speech delivered from the balcony of his hotel room. Consequently, the King is forbidden to return to Romania until 1997.

1997 King Mihai recovers his Romanian citizenship and, a few years later, Peleş Castle, Pelişor Castle and Săvârşin Castle. The Royal Family is also granted use of Elisabeta Palace in Bucharest where they can conduct official events on behalf of the state. This becomes the King's part-time residence, together with his residence in Switzerland.

2003 The remains of King Carol II are brought to Romania to the Monastery Curtea de Argeş. King Mihai refuses to participate at the event.

2007 December 30: sixty years after his forced abdication, King Mihai names his first-born, Princess Margareta, as his dynastic successor.

2015 August 1st: King Mihai signs a document removing the title of "Prince" and succession rights from his grandson, Nicholas Medforth-Mills, Princess Elena's son.

2016 King Mihai retires from public life; his wife, Anne, dies and has national funerals.

2017 December 5: King Mihai dies at his residence in Switzerland; his first-born, Margareta, takes the title of "Custodian of the Romanian Crown."

December 13: the coffin with the body of King Mihai is brought to Romania on an official plane and displayed for two days at the Royal Palace where thousands of people come to say goodbye.

December 16: the King is given full state honors and a funeral attended by all of Romania's dignitaries and Europe's royal families. His body is buried at Curtea de Argeş next to those of his ancestors.

Part One

Carmen Sylva
(Queen Elisabeta)

Chapter 1

Woodsong

> "Woodsong, Carmen Sylva is my
> name—the name under which I
> hid myself for so long."
> —Carmen Sylva, *A Real Queen's
> Fairy Tales*

Carmen Sylva: I always believed in Destiny, and now that I am no longer, I believe in it more than ever. After all, death is the ultimate fulfillment of one's Destiny, or, as Mother used to say, death alone brings us absolute happiness. All my life I lived with death's presence by my side. It was my mentor, and I, its devoted student. Yes, some have mocked me as a crazy woman, but haven't all exceptional souls been ridiculed by mediocre minds? Isn't any great artist and poet akin to Baudelaire's albatross, a winged Prince of the Skies exiled here on earth amidst the vulgar masses for whom his wings are but crutches?

> *Le Poète est semblable au prince des nuées*
> *Qui hante la tempête et se rit de l'archer;*
> *Exilé sur le sol au milieu des huées,*
> *Ses ailes de géant l'empêchent de marcher.*

I should remember to hide this page from the King's eyes: he will be furious if he finds out that I am reading Baudelaire again. The masses are under the illusion that a Queen can do whatever she pleases; in fact, if I had been a regular mortal, I would have been able to read Baudelaire with no fear; but, as things stand, I am Queen and therefore, forbidden to read the works of a "dangerous, immoral" mind. I am a slave to my own position and I am being forced to sacrifice my God-given nature for the good of … the good of … well, not even for the good of my people; rather, for the good of the smallest-minded of my people. But what can I do? I gave my word to Carol, and a Queen's word is sacred. A Poet's word, even more so; therefore, my word is doubly sacred.

From my most tender years, I knew that I was destined to fulfill an exceptional Destiny. More than once, Mother told the story how, when I was barely two years old, I arrived one evening in the middle of the salon, uninvited, with my hand extended toward the male guests, expecting them to kiss it. Although Mother never discouraged my tendency to take myself very seriously, she always chastised me for writing poetry, as if poetry were some kind of badge of dishonor. Once, I caught her telling Carol that she'd seen me read an author from his blacklist.

In our daily lives we cannot see ourselves from the outside, we inhabit our own existence, and we take for granted everything that happens to us, good or bad. Before I began to tell the story of my life, it never occurred to me that, as a child, I had been treated with horrible cruelty by my father, Prince Hermann. At the time, it was common to whip one's children in order to instill discipline, and Father, a strong believer in the idea that our moral qualities can only develop through punishment, did not spare the rod. Until I reached puberty and Father took charge of my education, I only saw him twice a day, in the morning and before going to bed, and then, our interaction consisted of my kissing his hand. My education was rigorous, both academically and etiquette-wise, and it was provided by a series of mean governesses, who, having been given free reign from their masters, used corporal punishment on a regular basis as part of their teaching methods. At the dinner table, children were strictly forbidden to open their mouths, and the food was purposely prepared in a dull way, never intended for pleasure, which was looked upon as a decadent indulgence. Food was merely a necessity meant to keep us alive: we ate butterless, dry, whole-grain bread, like monks and nuns in a convent.

When I was thirteen, Father decided that the governesses and teachers I'd had until then were no longer adequate, and proceeded to give me lessons himself. Together, we studied philosophy, history, religion, painting, the French chroniclers, the poets of antiquity. We read Ovid, Horace and Cicero, and I even attempted my first translations into English. Every week I was assigned to read forty pages of said subjects and to write six-page summaries of what I'd read. In our family it was understood that our lives were not ours to dispose of for our enjoyment—the American idea that we are entitled to happiness, that happiness is the very purpose of our lives, would have been seen as pure folly, if not downright insanity, by Father, had he been familiar with it. No, our lives are being lent to us by a Higher Power, which we are obliged to serve by working for a higher purpose, for something bigger than us. At an age when most children are narcissistically focused on themselves, I swore, kneeling in front of the altar, that I would devote my life to helping others: I would serve humanity! It was an oath that tied me to a higher authority, thus turning my life from a mere succession of chronological events into resolute, single-minded Destiny. If one were to look for what all great men of the past have in common, one could easily find a red thread: every single one of them was focused on a goal that transcended his personal interest, as if he were a mere tool in the hands of the Divine. This submission of one's will to something higher is what, in the end, transforms that man from an anonymous individual of the crowd into a Man above the shapeless masses—a paradox, to be sure: greatness out of humbleness. Form out of the un-formed. It's as if Destiny and Creation were, ultimately, the same thing.

From my most tender age I knew that I was destined to be, out of many, One! Unlike most girls my age, I was not interested in marriage, and the prospect of remaining an "old maid" did not scare me. At the rare parties I was allowed to attend, I discussed Schopenhauer and other philosophers to the dismay and exasperation of my dance partners, who complained to Mother. Instead of wasting my time with empty-headed young men I preferred to stay home and learn another new language that I could add to those I already knew: German, French, English. Later, I learned Romanian, of course, and some Swedish; I managed to learn Italian to perfection during just one brief sojourn there.

The Chronicler: Carmen Sylva—Song of the Woods, Woodsong in Latin. You were so very different from my other queen! Both queens of the written word, one in stories and the other in verse, one a gorgeous blond charmer under whose seductive, playful appearance was hidden a determined, no-nonsense *femme du monde*, the other, a severe woman dressed solely in black or white, resembling more a white-haired scholar than a queen.

Carmen Sylva: Indeed, since taking my pen name, I resemble more and more a linden tree. I always identified with the woods—when I was growing up, with the woods in Germany, and later, as an adult, with those in Romania. My white hair is *like the silver lining of the linden leaves—it gives a bright sheen to thoughts otherwise too grave.*[1] I was often asked what it is

---

1. The words in italics are taken from the Queen's correspondence with the King and translated from German into Romanian by Silvia Irina Zimmermann (see Bibliography), and from Romanian into English by the Chronicler.

like to be a queen. For me, a queen is similar to the linden tree under whose protective shadow take refuge the world's sweetest songbirds. As a queen, I endeavored my entire life to offer shelter to those whose workmanship is akin to that of a spider, and to the industrious bees, which would otherwise perish in winter. I have always attempted to be of use to those around me, artists, poets, musicians. They were my industrious bees, and I was the Queen who sacrificed herself for their triumph.

The Chronicler: Indeed, you constantly draped yourself in a veil of tragic romanticism and martyrdom, from behind which you penned yet one more poem, yet one more *adieu* to the world:

> Around me cheers and Amen,
> For them I am an icon
> Who sports a golden crown at night,
> And sitting on my precious throne
> Give gracious smiles all around,
> For I am but a Queen!
>
> Why would you waste your time to read
> My words? In vain is all, a pity!
> And when I'm dead, finally then,
> You'll say: She was like us,
> A mere mortal—almost,
> For she was but a Queen![2]

These were your last written words. You signed your name and, a moment later, you joined Carol in eternity. Your last words were the words of a poet angry with her contemporaries for seeing her "merely" as a queen, when what you really wanted was to be seen as the Queen of Poetry. Of course, when

---

2. Translation into English by the Chronicler

a queen sees herself as someone who is endowed with a merit other than the one given to her by birth or royal alliance, the very commoners who bow before her as before an icon may not be happy because she is usurping their turf. The realm of the genius never belongs to the one holding the scepter, who is seen as an entitled oppressor, while the genius is a poor youngster forced by circumstances to entertain the rich and powerful in order to find the means through which to forge a path ahead for himself. Needless to say, this was a way of seeing against which your entire being rebelled. You were a poet first and foremost, and to be undervalued, or worse, dismissed for the sin of being queen, seemed unfair and unacceptable. Especially if the dismissal came from the King himself. The King of Poetry, that is—not Carol, your husband, who had as much interest in poetry as you in engineering. Yes, the one who is looked upon as the King of Poetry by all the Romanians, and who thought of himself as "the Morning Star" (or "the Evening Star," depending on the translation, his thoughts being, obviously, in Romanian, not English), Mihai Eminescu,[3] finally and reluctantly, accepted an invitation to come meet the Queen.

The day Mihai Eminescu met Carmen Sylva … But maybe we should let her tell us the story. You know that there are several versions of it.

Carmen Sylva: There may be several versions, but there is only one truth. I met Mihai Eminescu on October 30th 1882, a year after Carol and I were proclaimed King and Queen. He was very clumsy and, how should I put it? Socially awkward, as they say nowadays. To begin with, he didn't look me in the eye at all for the first ten minutes or so, and he kissed my hand in such a rushed, perfunctory way that I almost felt insulted. But I told myself that the man must be intimidated, as so many are in the presence of a Monarch, and I did everything I could

3. Romania's national poet (1850-1889)

to make him feel at ease. His voice was hoarse yet tender, his fingers long and elegant, and his childish smile reminded me of Shelley's famous portrait, but his proverbial good looks were considerably less impressive than word-of-mouth had made me anticipate. When I praised his verses, he gestured dismissively and said: "Poetry is being shed from us the way a tree sheds its dead leaves." Note the royal "us," meant to underline who, between the two of us, was the real Sovereign.

I tried to get over the disappointment caused by his grumpy demeanor, but after his repartee about poetry, he just sat there, frowning, his jaws clenched, without saying another word until, eventually, I handed him a sheet of paper with my latest poem. It was a poem I was truly proud of, so, as I gave him the paper, I asked for his opinion. He read it very carefully, deep in concentration, and then, handing it back to me, said:

"Your Majesty, I would advise against sending this out, as it is not yet ready for publication."

"Are you forgetting to whom you are speaking?"

"Your Majesty, you may be the Queen of Romania, but you are not the Queen of Poetry."

These were his exact words, and I won't hide from you that they hurt me so much that for a brief second I wished for the times when a Souverain could send a cheeky subject to the Tower and order to have his head placed where his feet were standing, as the Romanian saying goes. But after he left, I reread my poem and had to agree that he was partially right. Yes, the poem was imperfect and needed more work; still, it was a very good poem, and in the Poet's categoric dismissal I could guess hidden more a rejection of authority than an honest response to an honest question. Looking back, I realized that the only thing that had given him some pleasure during this painful visit had been the cup of tea I had myself offered him, causing in him, I presume, a feeling similar to that experienced by a mortal who is being waited on by a god.

Queen Marie (whispering to the Chronicler): She never forgave him and never invited him again to one of her salons. Aunty was not given to taking insubordination lightly. She was, after all, a German. It's, really, a paradox, because she was, at the same time, very romantic, just like Eminescu; they wrote the same kind of poetry, and they both thought of themselves as tragic, misunderstood heroes. "The madness of poets is unlike any other madness," she used to say. In her notebooks she describes him as a lonely, somber man whose entire being was possessed by a disquieting interior music, a man whose Faustian face was ravaged by pain, illness and wrinkles, although he was only in his early thirties. More than once, she confessed that, although she hadn't managed to trigger in him any curiosity about, or interest in herself, he always remained for her the very image of the Poet.

Carmen Sylva (who didn't hear Queen Marie's comment): Eminescu behaved rudely and most ungraciously. A completely different character than Enescu.[4] It is true that when Enescu started to come to my salons he was almost a child, his mustache was just beginning to show. He too was clumsy, poor boy, but always respectful, in spite of his very modest origin. I would sometimes invite Caragiale[5] and Grigoraș Dinicu[6] in the hope that their presence would make him feel more comfortable, but the poor dear was so in awe of us, the King and me, and so terrorized of a potential faux pas, he just couldn't relax, his anxiety and tension were so thick you could cut them with a … what's the Romanian expression? Cut them with a knife.

4. George Enescu (1881-1955): the most famous Romanian musician (composer, violinist, conductor). As a teenager, he was a frequent guest of the Romanian Royal Family. In 1939 he married Princess Maruca Cantacuzino, a good friend of Queen Marie.
5. Ion Luca Caragiale (1852-1912): the most famous Romanian playwright. He practiced an absurd kind of theater that influenced Eugène Ionesco.
6. Grigoraș Dinicu (1889-1949): Romanian violin virtuoso and composer of Roma origin

Queen Marie: Hmm … You mean with an axe?

Carmen Sylva (visibly annoyed): No, I mean with a knife. There is no Romanian expression about an axe.

Queen Marie: Well, as far as I know, anxiety and tension run high not thick, in which case they should be cut with an axe, not a knife.

Carmen Sylva (clearing her throat): Looks like someone has an axe to grind …

The Chronicler: Or a sword to sharpen. Or a guillotine. If we talk about cutting something from up high, maybe we should bring up the guillotine—but that would be a delicate topic, wouldn't it? So, let's talk about lunch, instead. They say that these lunches were sheer torture for poor Enescu because protocol demanded that the King be served first, and since Enescu was the youngest, he was being served last, by which time he was starved. Punctuality was strictly observed, and at 1 pm sharp, the royal couple, the King's personal aide, the Court Librarian—why the Court Librarian? Don't ask me, ask her! (pointing to Carmen Sylva)—and the guests entered the lunchroom (unless there were too many guests, in which case they used the Moresque Salon) where they occupied their pre-assigned seats at the round table decorated with bronze and glass sculptures, some of which held the cards with their beautifully calligraphed names. Let's see what they ate at these gatherings:

> *Déjeuner du 6 mai 1914*
> *Fish soup*
> *Sturgeon*
> *Poulet au riz*
> *Courges à la crème*
> *Escalopes de veau panés*
> *Salade/gâteau/fromage/dessert*

Of course, the menu was written in French, as the custom demanded, and was designed daily by the Court's most famous artists on fancy white paper with the royal cipher and the symbol of the crown at the top. Like today at Buckingham Palace, the dishes were being brought on platters, steaming hot, via an elevator, from the basement up to the lunch or the dining room. The wine came from the Brătianu[7] wineries, though most often they drank Bordeaux.

Carmen Sylva (suddenly melancholy): Yes, Bordeaux was Karl's favorite wine. He always drank a glass. Never more. Always so … what's the word? *Cumpătat.* Measured. Perfect balance. Never an excess. He was born to be King, my Karl.

Queen Marie (whispering under her breath after rolling her eyes): He was born to torment us, your Karl. And to be tormented by you. Two control … what's that expression Americans from your generation use? Control-something …?

The Chronicler: "Control freaks"?!

Queen Marie: That's it! Control freaks. Two control freaks. Never before in the history of humanity has this expression been more adequate.

The Chronicler (peeks at Carmen Sylva, wanting to make sure she hasn't heard, and resumes the conversation from where she'd left it): The porcelain, silverware and glass sets were divided into three categories: for everyday use, for gala and super-gala. The set they used for gala, that is, for official occasions but not state visits, was made of white Sèvres porcelain with blue floral motifs, the silverware was ordered at Nuremberg, and the crystal was from Bohemia. But their most precious glass set, ninety-three pieces glowing with a coppery-

---

7. The Brătianus: one of the most important families of Romanian politicians. Ionel Brătianu (or Ion I.C. Brătianu: 1864-1927), leader of the National Liberal Party, Prime Minister and Minister of Foreign Affairs on several occasions, had a complicated relationship with Queen Marie. He will play an important part during the unification of Transylvania with the Romanian Principalities.

pinkish shimmer and decorated with leaves in relief, was American and had been designed by Tiffany with the famous Favril method. One can only imagine how out of place poor Enescu or Eminescu must have felt there. In fact, it's very likely because he felt so out of sorts that Eminescu compensated by being rude.

Carmen Sylva: My dear, you speak like one of those "royal correspondents" who have no idea what they are talking about, yet, in order to feel relevant, make up stuff, which they present as reality. My guests were always treated with utmost courtesy and respect—I am sure they felt perfectly at ease, surrounded as they were by fellow artists and the country's greatest minds. They were there not to see a queen, but a soul cut from the same cloth. The fact that I happened to be their queen simply meant that I could offer them the use of my surroundings, a space in which for a few brief hours we could all share our gifts away from the mediocre, maddening world.

The Chronicler: I'm afraid a queen who thinks of herself as misunderstood by the mediocre world is doomed to fail as a leader because the strength of a monarch, that of a consort included, comes from identifying with one's people.

Queen Marie: But Aunty never thought of herself as a "leader," unless hosting a literary and arts salon counts as being a leader! She was a child of her time—as, I suppose, we all are. She saw herself as Baudelaire's albatross, a winged giant floating above the multitudes, which she despised.

The Chronicler: I don't think she would agree with this characterization.

Queen Marie: I'm not saying she despised the Romanian people. She simply did not understand the common people because she thought of herself, first and foremost, as a genius poet, and only second as a queen. I am sure a republican would see in this an enlightened attitude—"She is one of us," etc.—but this would mean to ignore the very greatness of the monarchic principle, that of the communion between the Sovereign and His or Her people. As for myself, I was One with my people, and this communion is … what is the English word? I no longer know my language—funny, that you, a Romanian, should write in *my* language, while I, a Brit, should speak the language of your ancestors. The word in Romanian—such an apt word—is *întrupată*, literally made-body, intobodied, although, now that I think of it, Romanian language has another word, almost synonymous, *întruchipată*, intofaced, made flesh, made-face, that is to say, "represented." While *în-trupată* is identical to the English *em-bodied*, in Romanian, to represent in the flesh is also *to give a face*. Which is what I attempted all my life, especially in my dealings with foreign dignitaries: to give a face to the Romanian people, to give them *my face*.

The Chronicler: I always suspected that your desire to have your heart removed and placed in the Stella Maris Chapel from Balcic—your dream place, as you called it—while your body was placed to rest in the Curtea de Argeş Cathedral, next to your husband and the rest of the Royal Family, was your way of saying that you will be alive forever in the hearts of the Romanians. I also assume that you must be familiar with the Middle Age doctrine of "the king's two bodies," according to which a king has a natural or biological body, which is subject to life's vicissitudes and, eventually, death, and an immortal, celestial body that will go on living forever because a king never dies. Hence, the French "Le Roi est mort !" followed immediately by "Vive le Roi !"—as if a king's successor were of the same essence with the dead king, because there is only one, eternal king made in the image of the divine. And so, you decided to subject your royal body to this duality, to this duplicity, that of being in two places at the same time: your dead body in the royal Pantheon at Curtea de Argeş, and your heart—your divine essence—in the chapel by the Black Sea.

Carmen Sylva (muttering to herself and rolling her eyes): Talk about an over-inflated ego! Phew!

Queen Marie (to Carmen Sylva): I didn't expect this from you! I thought that you, of all people, would understand.

Carmen Sylva: Oh, I do understand. If there is something I understand, it's a queen's vanity.

Queen Marie (whispering in the Chronicler's ear): She could never forgive me for having taken the place of her dear Elena Văcărescu. You know the story, don't you?

The Chronicler: Yes, you did tell me the story. It will be interesting to see what she has to say.

Carmen Sylva: Karl forced me to go into exile after I had made it clear that I despised his judgment and Ferdinand's (Nando's, as he calls him) lack of honor: for the sake of a pathetic throne, I told him, you trampled on the happiness of three people. You robbed me, I said, of the one whom I treated like my own son and the one who was like my own daughter. You gave credence to the most disgusting rumors and plotted against me with my own mother, my mother who dared to insinuate that I was so attached to Elena because I had "unnatural relations with women!" I will never agree to be separated from Elena because to do so would be to accept the triumph of these pigs who have slandered the purest women in Europe. My idea of mixing our blood with that of the local population was brilliant and he, Karl, should have embraced it and pretended it was his—I had and have no ambition of getting involved in politics. I know what I am talking about because I am familiar with all the European princely houses, and I know that they are doomed to perish because all the princesses are idiots! I think it's because they all marry among themselves, and so they live in very narrow circles, which, eventually, can only lead to stupid and ugly people. It's comical that Mother felt that we would dishonor our house by a marriage with a Văcărescu, a very old and respectable princely family, and that a marriage with a Solms would be preferable. What makes the Solms any better? The queen of England is the daughter of a German administrator, Holland's queenie is the daughter of an average Dutchman. That's why all the princesses are vulgar and bourgeois! Oh, but they all have titles—titles to compensate for their brainless heads.

I wrote to Karl: I am sorry I have to leave this for posterity, but I'm afraid it has to be said. I love Nando dearly, I love him as if he were my own son, but he really is a cretin. You know very well, I told Karl, how hard we tried to educate Nando ever since he was elected Crown Prince and heir of the Romanian throne, all to no avail. He is always nice to me, it's really touching, he is quite endearing, but the fact remains that he is not, how should I put this, very gifted. At dinner, he laughs all by himself. The stories he tells, goodness gracious: *at Potsdam I used to have a horse with a thin tail.* And then he laughs. All by himself. You can see it just by looking at his face: its lower part is much larger than the upper—*his brain is getting smaller and smaller* in spite of everything he's learned from us. *The distance between his ears and his forehead is barely a small palm.* You should hear how the servants mock him! At dinner, they say, the King plays with his fork and napkin, and the poor Queen, what can she do? She attempts to have a conversation about books, but in the end, gives up and smiles. *Yes, the Romanians have cruel eyes, fine-tuned ears and biting humor, as biting as the North wind that blows across the ocean.* I think we must resign ourselves, I said, to the fact that our successor is truly *sărac cu duhul,* poor in spirit, he is *like a little poodle walking in my footsteps* and wiggling his tail. It remains to be seen what wife he'll take, I said: if she is as dumb as him, all is lost; but if she happens to be smart or sensuous, she'll be the one in charge and will have to drag him after her. I used to think that only by marrying a very smart woman could he stay on the throne, but look where we are now! Now, Nando has a wife—and what a wife! She isn't dumb, not like him, anyhow, but her problems are no less serious. The entire country can see who was right, in the end. The exiled and maligned Queen or the *mauvaises langues*? What I can't accept is for our lives' work to be destroyed by this irresponsible couple: he, a cretin, whose brains get smaller by the day, and she, a … a … I won't say the word, but the entire country knows that only her first two children were Nando's. The third one was fathered by that syphilitic lieutenant, Zizi, or what's his name, and Missy[8] did everything she could to get rid of the child but was told that the doctor could go to prison for fifteen years and was forced to give birth. And so, she had the child who now passes for royal, while Nando can't stop crying—good Lord, I have never seen in my entire life a man who cries like this! He's pathetic, they both are pathetic! They should get a divorce, but, of course, they won't, because they don't want to lose the throne. As far as I can tell, after their third child, their marriage was a sham, *praf în ochii lumii*, they each took their pleasure somewhere else, and only stayed married for the sake of the damn throne. Nando sleeps with whomever he can get his hands on, even Gypsies, everybody knows this, and Missy gets choked with resentment. They are all unpopular, including little Prince Carol, who is so very full of himself as if, as they say in Romanian, he invented the hole in the macaroni. Whom do you think he takes after? Just look how his mother behaves, oh, look at me, I am Marie the Great, the prettiest, the smartest, look at me, Me, Me, Me! Today, when I hear people exasperated by Meghan, the Duchess of Sussex, or, as some call her, MeGain, or MeMeMe, I can't help thinking: you think there is anything new under the sun? This is how most princesses behave, these empty-headed, pretty faces.

The Chronicler: Don't you think you are a bit biased? You can't believe that Marie was empty-headed! Weren't you the

8. Queen Marie's pet name

one who discovered her artistic gifts and encouraged her to write and paint?

Carmen Sylva: If I am biased, it's only because I want what's best for my country, which I love more than anything else in the world. It would have been a tragedy if this couple had been Romanian! Thank God they weren't! *My Romanian children shouldn't be associated with such depravity, for I love them way too much! My Romanian children are my children, mine only! Je les aime douloureusement, maternellement !*[9]

The Chronicler (to herself): Wow, talk about a martyr syndrome! The Queen-Mother of the nation and her poor children! The martyr-Queen suffering for her children like a martyr-Mother with no hope of recognition and reward in this unfair world.

Queen Marie: *I* was the one the Romanian people called "Mother" and "Mother of the Wounded Soldiers," not her! Jealousy and envy can truly blind one. To compare me to Meghan Markle! A C-list actress who, aside from her looks, enhanced by modern cosmetics, has nothing to boast about, not a single original thought in her life! Every time she opens her mouth, I hear "You are brave! You are beautiful! Don't let anyone tell you otherwise!" Just listen to my speeches and you'll see that never in my life did I speak in this cheesy, syrupy language that could be the death of a thousand flies! Who likes that kind of demagoguery?

The Chronicler: I'll tell you who likes it: Gloria Steinem. I just saw her in an interview in which she defended the Duchess, whom she called Meghan, by asserting that the poor woman is "stereotyped" as a "Princess." I don't know if Gloria Steinem is simply misinformed, or has problems with logic, but to make such a claim about a woman whose official title is (or was) "Princess of the United Kingdom," a title one can see in open records, such as her son's birth certificate,

9. I love them painfully, like a mother (Fr.)

is the peak of absurdity. "The whole idea of a 'princess' is a problem," says Gloria Steinem. "I mean, we had a Revolution to get rid of royalty." In that case, why didn't she tell that to the Duchess when they met? Why didn't she ask her why she kept those titles, which are incompatible with the status of a US citizen, not to mention a feminist? Why didn't she ask her why she signs her brands, her book included, "The Duchess of Sussex," when she could simply sign "Meghan Markle"? Who is Steinem chiding? Is she chiding us, the public, for using a title listed in Meghan's passport, according to UK regulations about the Royal Family? Or is she chiding the British citizens because they have a form of government she dislikes?

Queen Marie: I couldn't care less what this Steamer person says. What I do care about is truthfulness and a fair representation in the eyes of posterity. Whenever I expressed an opinion in my writings about Queen Elisabeta, I did my best to be fair, even when I had reasons to say negative things about her. And, unfortunately, she hasn't reciprocated. How can she compare me to Meghan Markle, who, not only made no efforts to adapt to her new country, but also left less than two years later, accusing the very people who welcomed her and spent a fortune on her global wedding, of racism? I came to my new country as a mere child who knew nothing about life, not even how children come into the world. I left everything behind, comfort and a good life, to devote the rest of it to my adopted country for which I sacrificed my personal happiness. I spent my entire life near a weak man I pitied because I placed the fate of the Romanian people above my personal wishes. Do you think it was easy? Do you think it was easy being a young English woman in a country at the end of the earth where men are so biased against the fair sex?

Carmen Sylva: I know it wasn't easy, and this is the very reason why I took your side at the beginning. Don't you remember? I was sorry for you because I knew more about Nando than the rest of the country.

Queen Marie: You should have been sorry for yourself, for having accepted to live with a man who took no joy in life and did all he could to crush whatever little joy Nando and I had in our lives. If I accepted an invitation to a party, you both looked at me as if I was a prostitute; if I went horse-riding with a friend, there were eyebrows raised and heads shaken.

Carmen Sylva: Horse riding. We have all seen how this type of horse riding ends.

Queen Marie: Oh, you, bloody jealous, pitiful woman! I know you could never accept me because deep in your heart you felt that Nando and I were taking the place of your little Itty. And this, you could never forgive, even though it wasn't our fault. It wasn't my fault that you couldn't have children. And it wasn't my fault that I gave Nando six children while the only child you gave Uncle was taken from you.

Carmen Sylva (to the Chronicler): Did you hear that? Did you hear what this "progressive" woman just called me? A "feminist" of her time. A suffragette proud to travel across the globe without her husband so she could better ensnare other men.

The Chronicler: Your Majesties, ladies, I'm afraid I need to take control of the narrative before you start pulling each other's hair and hitting each other over the head with your purses.

Carmen Sylva (muttering to herself): Listen to this one! She thinks she is witty. Phew! Who does she think she is, really?

The Chronicler: *Who* do I think I am?! (Suddenly pensive, to herself): Who *do* I think I am? (Loud enough to be heard by the queens): *Who* am I, *really*?

Carmen Sylva: You are no one. Nobody cares who you are. Why are you trying to make this about you?

Queen Marie: Well, you are *Me*, of course! You are Me.

CHAPTER 2

ELENA

armen Sylva: Nothing happens without a reason, and even the most painful grief can become fertile soil for future joy. The day young Elena crossed the threshold of my Moresque Salon with her black curls cascading down her white gown, and my eyes met her large, dark brown eyes under those arched, thick eyebrows, *I knew right away*. She curtsied deeply, lowering her gaze, and when she lifted her head, our eyes met. Those eyes! All the wisdom of the world was gathered in those pupils, whose velvet sadness bespoke a maturity far beyond the girl's age. I couldn't help touching her dear innocent face, a light caress, with the back of my hand, and the smile with which she rewarded me brought tears to my eyes. As my hand retreated from her face, she grasped it with her right hand and kissed it. There were four other girls present, my *domnișoare de onoare*—ladies in waiting—, all dressed, according to my wishes, in white, as was I. We sat at the round, solid walnut table, adjusting our eyes to the enveloping darkness of the room whose curtains had already been drawn by the servants. The only two candles that had been left burning a few feet away from us spread a pale light, just enough for us to find our seats and place our hands next to each other on the round table. Everyone grew silent, and for about a minute only the wall clock's tick-tock could be heard. Then, I spoke: "A." Silence. I went on: "B." Silence. "C." I kept on until, when I finally reached "I," the table made a creaking sound, and it suddenly tilted toward Elena. I looked around: in the darkness, our white dresses around the table appeared like six friendly ghosts. "T," I said, and the table tilted even more in Elena's direction. A collective gasp rose. "T," I repeated, and, this time, the table produced such a loud, screeching sound that everyone froze. Then, we all saw, mouths agape, how the table began to dance, yes, there is no other way of putting it, it just began to dance, moving frantically up and down, left and right, until I opened my mouth again and said "Y." The table stopped for a few seconds, as if confused, then, with a wailing like that of an infant in pain, moved all the way next to Elena. Although the darkness stopped me from discerning her features in a clear way, I could see that her eyes were closed and her head tilted back, as if in a trance. Her lips were moving as if of their own accord, and her entire body shook spasmodically. Tears rolled down her cheeks, and a voice that enclosed in it all the world's beauty, a voice sweeter than honey said: "Mommy, mommy!" My child was speaking to me from the netherworld. After countless attempts and séances, my child was, finally, speaking to me. "Itty," I exclaimed, and reached across the table for both her hands, which I held in mine for a long minute with all my strength.

"What in God's name ...?"

Karl had entered and was now standing in the door in a pool of light, frowning.

"Didn't I ask you ...?"

Yes, he'd asked. Meanwhile, I could see that Elena was gradually coming back to her senses. Once awake, she looked around with the expression of a frightened child:

"What happened?"

"Nothing, my child."

And from then on, she was, indeed, my child. My reborn child.

I asked her to be one of my ladies in waiting, and we became inseparable. I found her presence very soothing and allowed her to do things I granted no one else. She could sense my slightest indisposition, and would hug and kiss me on the cheeks, and likewise, I could feel her heart and soul stir when, at night, seated by the fire with my other ladies in waiting, I would read out loud my latest poems, holding my notebook in my right hand and her right hand with my left. Our souls were in such harmony that even when we were apart we could tell when the other was in pain, like twins, so that, after a while, our bodies too fell in sync, our monthly womanly affliction on the same date. Occasionally, we were joined by Ferdinand, who sat a few meters away from us, quiet and pensive, propping his lowered head in his hands, and mumbling incomprehensibly whenever anyone addressed him. He was seated in an armchair, following our conversation with interest but without saying a word, even though Elena constantly provoked him, asking for his opinion about this or that poem I had just read. It was painful to see him struggle to put two words together, and it soon became clear that he was there not so much because of his interest in my poems, but because he had his eye on my Elena.

The Chronicler: You make him sound like some kind of idiot, when in fact, he was a scholar in many areas, in particular botany.

Carmen Sylva: My dear, knowledge and intelligence are two different things—I am surprised you don't know that.

Queen Marie: In fact, according to his own version, he was there because he wanted to please his aunt and Queen, and he knew that the best way of achieving that was by pretending he was interested in her art.

Carmen Sylva: Well, if that makes you feel better! As for me, I know that my intuition is never wrong. There is a higher Truth, a Truth only poets and mediums have access to, because they are both channels of divine wisdom, and this is what Elena and I had in common. I was the Poet, and she, the medium through which God had found a way of speaking to me. And Ferdinand—Ferdinand was a mediocre witness to a divine mystery he was incapable of understanding, but even such a witness cannot prevent the touch of the Angel of Love and its winged feather, and so, very soon, one could see in Ferdinand's eyes the languid look of the one in its power. I, most certainly, did not want to stand in its way, and so I read love poems as often as I could, poems by Lamartine and Eminescu, and, with the corner of my eye, I could see my dear Elena sitting straight, her head half-turned toward the prince, her breathing changed, her face flushed. A miracle was taking place before my very eyes.

The two started to meet regularly at my salons, always in my presence, where Ferdinand was often the only man. His clumsy dark-suited body contrasted with the white, ethereal grace of my ladies in waiting, including Elena's. Like me, they were often dressed in white, although I occasionally allowed them to wear brighter colors with gold thread, and, unlike them, I also wore a flowing white veil. At the time, I was focused on painting an illuminated missal on parchment, and so I was seated in front of an easel. The young women were also seated, engaged either in reading or embroidering silk flowers, two on my left, and the other, together with Elena, on my right, while Ferdinand sat by the window, through which one could see the tall green firs that surround Peleş. Ferdinand was always silent, and when he was addressed, he would first clear his throat, then let out a nervous chuckle and, eventually, begin to stammer incomprehensibly.

Later in the evening, I would let the two youngsters sit next to each other. This is how it happened the first time: all of a sudden, Elena stood up, placed her embroidery on the vacated chair, and then, slowly but deliberately, began to advance toward Ferdinand, her wide open, immense dark eyes fixed straight ahead. When she was next to him, he, his face flushed, eyebrows arched in wonder, got up, offered her his seat, and then brought a nearby chair for himself. After a moment of incredulous bewilderment, the other young women returned to their reading or whatever else they were doing, but I kept watching the couple from the authority of my position, full of maternal love, yet aware of my duty to protect their innocence. From where I was seated I could see their lips moving and hear their whispers. Night after night, I allowed this game to take place, and I am not regretful, not a single bit. One should never regret encouraging the mystery of Love.

The Chronicler (whispers): The "mystery" of fraud. The "mystery" of a calculating young woman, who sensed that this was her opportunity, an opportunity facilitated by a vulnerable, foolish woman who'd lost her child and lived in her own head.

Carmen Sylva: Sometimes we held our salons in the music room, so enchanting with its stained windows and dark woodwork. I thought that this room was more intimate, sunk in darkness with only a few candles here and there, its romantic harpsichord and great organ, which I played while the enamored couple sat aside by the window, eyes locked and souls aflutter. Here, my maids of honor sat at my feet, on cushions placed directly on the ground, their heads resting on my knees, one on my left, the other on my right, occasionally changing places. These young women were maiden in the most literal sense of the word, and were chosen by me from Romania's aristocracy, often from families undergoing some hardship or down on their luck. When they got married, I had to find others to replace them, but they remained my daughters forever and came to see me years later with their children in tow.

After meeting like this for several weeks, the couple received my permission to take a walk in the surrounding woods, ac-companied by me, of course. There isn't a more perfect environment for romance than the forests around Peleş, the foliage's raw green sprinkled with dewdrops polished by furtive sunrays, and the beaten paths under the green canopy leading to the hunting lodge where we always stop for snacks, drinks, to change clothes, or to rest. We walked at a brisk pace in the crisp morning air, with mist hanging from our lips, and when we arrived at the lodge, we were out of breath, cold, and thirsty. Petre, the caretaker, offered us tea with rum, which we drank from tiny porcelain cups, sitting on wooden benches against the walls covered with bearskins, boars' and stags' heads. Afterwards, I retreated to my studio to work on a few poems, and for a while, I heard the lowered voices of the two lovers, who were continuing a conversation started earlier. But at some point, as I raised my head from the page, I suddenly realized that there was deep silence all around. Intrigued and with an ominous sense of foreboding, I got up and walked as silently as I could in the direction of the main room. There, as I stood in the doorframe, I saw two heads, a dark-haired one and a light brown-haired one, pressed against each other in a passionate kiss, as their bodies moved closer until there was no more room left between them, and their respective arms reached for the other body. A strong emotion took hold of me, as I was fighting two opposite feelings: one of pleasure and approval, and another, darker and harder to explain even to myself—a feeling that they had no right to such happiness (if happiness is what they were experiencing), and that this happiness stained the memory of my lost child. They too sensed that they were being watched, and a minute later, the heads and mouths separated. I straightened my posture, cleared my tangled thoughts and said, "It is time for us to go back. His Majesty is waiting."

That night, Ferdinand did not show up at the salon. Elena was seated to my right, as usual, concentrating on her embroidery. She hadn't looked me in the eye all night, and when I'd read

Eminescu's "Lake," a tear had rolled down her cheek and, sighing deeply, she'd said: "Your Majesty's voice is like the murmur of a thousand springs, or like a violin concert on a summer night in a blooming meadow." (Incidentally, I need to mention here that not few are those who have commented on the beauty of my voice. My dear friend, the French writer Pierre Loti, has called my voice "pure music"—"music as delightful and fresh as it is youthful"—and has stated both in private and in public that he has never heard anything more beautiful.) She then took my right hand and kissed it, and I felt her wet tears covering it. An overwhelming tenderness descended upon me: I wanted to hug and console this young girl, whose pure heart was opening to the greatest of all mysteries. I took her chin in my right hand as gently as I could and looked deeply into her pitch-black eyes, and what I saw shook me to the core: it was as if my younger self had taken refuge inside her, she had the purity of a majestic swan arisen from the bosom of the waters. Gently, I pressed my lips on those teary eyelids. As the other girls let out a collective gasp, Elena went down on her knees in front of me and, her face bathed in tears, she began to frantically kiss the hem of my dress and the tips of my white shoes. "Everything is going to be OK, my dear one, my little one," I said. "It's going to be OK." I helped her get up and asked her to sit in my lap, which she did, embracing my body with her young, willful arms. "I will make sure that you will get what you deserve, my dear, my little one," I said. "It is my oath to you: you shall be happy!"

A new chapter began, in which I arranged for the two lovers to meet initially in secret, then at our dinner table, where I made sure that Elena was seated next to Ferdinand, while in parallel I took on the difficult task of persuading Karl. I knew that this was a delicate matter, and so, initially, I simply lauded Elena and her many gifts. Every now and then I invited Karl to our spiritism séances, but not only did he always refuse, he did it spitefully, reminding me that there was no science to back our claims, and insinuating that our spiritual practice was no more than womanly foolishness.

One night, when everybody else was gone and only Karl and I were left alone, I grabbed my heart with my teeth, as the Romanian saying goes, and I said: "I thank the Lord for having sent me this young girl, Elena, who is a blessing to my soul. She is so sensitive, and she masters the Romanian language with such maturity for her age, she is already a true poet! Everybody agrees that she is an angel, even Ferdinand seems to have noticed." Karl, who had been reading his paper, suddenly raised an eyebrow, and, putting the paper down, asked in a rather ominous tone, "What in the world do you mean? Are you telling me that the rumors I have been hearing are true? I silenced all the naysayers, telling them that the Queen would never act in such an irresponsible way, but it turns out they were right. You are creating a constitutional crisis!" He said the last sentence almost yelling, and I felt truly insulted. I told him that I was not a stupid, uneducated woman, that I knew very well what I was doing, that everything I did was for the good of the Romanian people, which was dearer to me than anything else, even you Karl, I said, even you, and through this divinely-ordained marriage, two pure lovers as well as two countries would wed each other. Our blood would mix with the blood of *our* people! I thought that I offered him the best argument possible, yet, upon hearing this, he leaped from his chair and began to scream at me in a way he'd never done before.

And so, very soon thereafter, I was forced to take the road of exile, first to the South of Italy, then to Venice.

Chapter 3

Exile in Venice

Carmen Sylva: We are staying at Hotel Danieli, Elena and I, together with the servants, a whole floor of us. The government has decided that Danieli was luxurious enough for a queen, but not quite as opulent or conspicuous as the Ducal Palace, and honestly, I don't even care. Everything around me—the gaudy "royal" chairs with golden embellishments and design in relief, the high ceilings with enormous crystal chandeliers—is a constant reminder of my tragic and unfair circumstances, of the fact that I have been chased away from my home and my people. Chased away, banished like a thief, or worse, two conspiring criminals, Elena and I, two women in love with beauty and poetry, two women that were too pure for a world of pigs who can only see ugliness, for, in the end, the world seen through our eyes is always, more or less, an image of ourselves. As expected, Ferdinand acted like a coward: he vanished. He stopped answering Elena's letters, of course, he did—he would never dare disobey his uncle and king. But he didn't have the courage to ask Elena for his letters back, nor did he break the engagement in any official way, or unofficial, for that matter. He simply vanished. Silent like a fish. The cat ate his tongue.

At night, Elena and I still host our literary salon, just the two of us and the odd guest. Multilingual wordplay and puns are our favorite pastime, aside from poetry reading, of course. The other night we were playing, as usual, tossing words around with invisible tennis racquets, and after she said in Romanian, "*mut ca un peşte*" ("mute like a fish"), I replied in French "*Le chat lui a mangé la langue*" ("The cat ate his tongue"), and, for the first time in weeks, we laughed. I was happy to see my little one joyful again, her black eyes twinkling, her mouth, which had been contorted for months in a grimace of despair, relaxed again, ready to capture the grim reality with its sparkling wit.

"It's strange that both the fish and the cat are seen as symbols of silence," said Elena. "Depending on the language one speaks."

"Not quite my dear. In this saying, the cat appears more like a silencing creature. Remember: the cat *ate the tongue!*"

We laughed again.

The Chronicler: "Silent or *silenced*?" This reminds me of the (now infamous) interview with Oprah and the Princess. "Were you silent or *silenced*?" asked the American journalist, with a heavy emphasis on the latter. And the Princess—who had started the interview with the word "Finally ...," as if her entire life, including her life as a British Princess, had been merely a prelude to that interview, because, let's face it, when you grow up in Hollywood, there is no bigger queen than a talk show queen—was happy to oblige. Was the Hollywood queen aware that the British queen herself—then, still among the living—kept silent for over seven decades? She may have been vaguely aware of that, no, in fact, she surely was aware of that, because no one ever heard HM Queen Elizabeth II express an opinion in public. But Hollywood queens know that rules don't apply to 21st-century influencer princesses who are accustomed to giving uplifting speeches peppered with the latest buzzwords; they are used to being in control of their PR team, and to being "number one," and, to her dismay, our Hollywood Princess realized that she'd never be number one, because in a monarchy only the Monarch in number one, and one day Catherine would be Queen Consort, and she, Meghan would have to call her "Your Majesty," aside from having to walk a few steps behind her all her life, imagine that, such an affront to our republican Princess! Not that she'd had any problem with other people—British racist people—curtsying to her and calling her "Your Royal Highness." And so, yes, our Princess was silenced, because otherwise she would have regaled us with her influencer opinions, but even in the absence of said opinions, her countrymen awarded her and her Hollywoodized Prince a prize for work on the environment, which consisted in the couple's pledge to have no more than two children. Apparently, having sixteen bathrooms in a Californian desert has nothing to do with the environment.

And so, the Hollywood Princess, the little Mermaid whose tongue had been eaten by an evil queen, found her voice again next to the journalist who'd rescued it for public consumption, the way only certain American journalists know how to. Speaking of which, has any journalist tried to interview Elena?

Carmen Sylva (indignant): Good Lord, no! They know she would never stoop to their level. But this hasn't stopped *them* from filling their dirty rags with gossip. All the European papers are talking about the "scandal" at the Royal Court of Romania. Karl is still very upset and reminds me in every single letter of the work he needs to do to "fix" what I have done. He has never appreciated Elena, even though she's done more for Romania's image in the world than any other young woman her age. Let me tell you a little anecdote: once, when she was in Paris, she got lost, away from her hotel. Scared, she looked around and, hearing a couple speak German, introduced herself as "Hélène Văcăresco, the author of *The Bard of the Dâmbovița. Romanian Folk Songs Collected from the Peasants.*" At this, the German couple responded: "Sure, we know who you are." And they helped her find her hotel. Isn't this a great story?

Queen Marie (sarcastic): Fantastic! A fantastic story in all the senses of the word. Dear Auntie, how can you be so gullible? That couple simply pretended they knew who she was out of politeness.

Carmen Sylva: *Ti-ai dat arama pe față!*[10] I thought you'd have the noblesse d'esprit to acknowledge the qualities of the woman Nando should have married, but you don't. Together, Elena and I raised Romania's profile to peaks never before encountered. My play, *Ullranda,* was played at Weimar and at the Théâtre Français in Elena's magnificent translation. I was so famous throughout Europe that simple people used to stop me on the street to compliment me. Once, a woman came all the way from Australia just to see me and tell me how much she admired me. And another woman from Holland claimed that I was immensely popular there too. But I was never a prophet in my own country, it was always foreigners who appreciated me most. In my own country of birth I am maligned for the sin of having written a novel. As one of Karl's adjutants said, they were abusing a true treasure, a saint!

Queen Marie: (exchanges a glance with the Chronicler and rolls her eyes.)

Carmen Sylva: All I ever had was my pen, my feather and ink. My pen was my hidden treasure that carried me through life's vicissitudes, my sword and my emblem. Elena, who was almost my double, could see this—that's why I loved her so. Karl, on the other hand, never inquired about Elena while we were in exile, and when he referred to Ferdinand it was only to mention some official event they'd taken part in, or some deed or accomplishment the little cretin had done. Yes, I am calling him "a cretin," and I am more than willing to expose myself to posterity's criticism. If he'd had half a brain, he'd have realized he could never find such an intelligent young woman among the idiot princesses of the European royal houses, he'd

10. Romanian expression equivalent to "You showed your true colors!"

have seen that our Elena is more noble and more worthy of him than all those empty-headed, vacant-eyed, blue-blooded blondes. But no, he and the entire Court of Romania wanted a "European Princess"! A granddaughter of Queen Victoria, no less!

The Chronicler: "Half a brain"? What 19th-century woman would use such an expression? You talk like … like me.

Carmen Sylva: In that case, you should have a talk with yourself. Or with the half-brained author of all this. Whatever.

The Chronicler (in disbelief): "*Whatever*"?

Carmen Sylva: That's right. Whatever.

> Whatever is
> Whatever's not
> I am a Queen
> And you are not.
> Whatever is
> Mostly a what
> Without an everlasting
> Plot.

The Chronicler: ?

Carmen Sylva (in deep concentration, with a frustrated air, seemingly searching for a word): Without an everlasting plot … plot … What rhymes with "plot"? (Suddenly victorious): I know! Quack! Without an everlasting/Plot/Quack-quack!

The Chronicler: I think you should stop at "plot."

Carmen Sylva (ironic): Really? You think so? Who do you think you are to tell me when to stop? Eminescu?

As I was saying before you interrupted me, we were staying at Hotel Danieli in Venice when my friend and admirer, Pierre Loti, came to visit me. Like all great writers, he is a generous soul, and, after his visit at Peleş, he wrote most kindly about me, praising my voice, my gifts, the benevolence of my "motherly smile," and my knowledge of "superior things," of which, he said, I spoke "in a superior fashion." In a country of fierce republicans, his praise cost him his reputation, and he was mocked in public by one of the Goncourt brothers. Such is the fate of those with a pure heart these days: to be mocked and trampled on.

The Chronicler: As my math high school teacher used to say: "Modesty to the power of n+1."

Carmen Sylva (confused): What was that?

The Chronicler: Oh, nothing … Just that some people would think that you aren't very humble.

Carmen Sylva: And *you* think *you* are humble? Writing in the voices of two queens? Making "witty" remarks for posterity? My dear, who do you think you are fooling?

The Chronicler: *Whom.* "Whom do you think you are fooling?"

Carmen Sylva: As I said, making witty remarks for posterity. But thank you for correcting my grammar. Do you know what Pierre Loti was most impressed with when he visited me at Peleş? With my impromptu translations from one language into another. I read to him a Romanian ballad, translating it on the spot into rhythmical, poetical French. On another occasion, I read a text translating it directly from German into French, and Loti praised my "harmonious phrases" and "charming voice." In fact, he couldn't stop praising me, and believe me, I can tell fake praise from genuine admiration! After I sang a German lied, he bowed deeply before me with tears in his eyes, saying that he could feel how all the anguish of my soul had passed into my voice. Yes, we artists have a way of feeling, of recognizing each other, like twin souls, and Loti was such a twin soul for me.

The Chronicler: Wouldn't it be more … uh-hmm … correct to say that you found a twin soul in Loti because he was one of those rare beings who bowed before *both* the Queen and the Artist, and that his adoration gave you the mirror you so desperately wanted? After all, he called you "a noble soul," "a genius," "Mater Dolorosa," and on and on …

Queen Marie (smiles and clears her throat): …

The Chronicler (addresses only Queen Marie): Just as you, my dear queen, would have never fallen in love with Barbu Știrbey had he not had that attitude of slavish adoration and absolute devotion to you. A queen needs to be adored.

Queen Marie: I fell in love with Barbu because he was a handsome, intelligent man. And yes, he was entirely devoted to me, which in a country like Romania, is an invaluable gift.

The Chronicler: You mean, in a country of traitors, like Romania.

Queen Marie: Don't put words into my mouth!

The Chronicler: Well, it's too late for that! Not putting words into your mouth, that is. But why not say the truth now, you know it's the truth. Romania is a country of traitors, and the first traitor was your eldest son.

Queen Marie: I never thought of things in this way.

The Chronicler: But *how* did you think of them?

Queen Marie: I always took one situation at a time and tried to make the best of it. Only you Romanians have this bad habit of deciding beforehand how things will end because you have a pessimistic view of life according to which everything is preordained, and things are always stacked against you. With this attitude you can never build anything. You know very well that it is because of my refusal to take no for an answer and because I went to Paris as a victor that, in the end, the Great Powers gave us Transylvania.

Carmen Sylva: Why are we talking again about Missy? I thought we were talking about my exile in Venice—an exile that almost killed me.

The Chronicler: Venice: I can think of worse places to be exiled to. I can see you and your entourage climb into those fabulous, Egyptian-looking gondolas and glide over the waters, alongside those somber, ancient homes with deep-cracked walls. I can see you and Elena spend long, enchanting hours in these gondolas, holding a book in your hands, under a protective sunhat or a parasol, exchanging ideas about your readings, with the serenity of people who don't have to think about making a livelihood. There is silence all around, occasionally interrupted by the splash of oars, and when a gondola gets close to another one, the gondolier issues a warning call, to which another gondolier responds, their calls echoing through the maze of ancient buildings. Hotel Danieli where you are staying, occupying the entire first floor, is one of the most beautiful Gothic palaces in Venice, with marble staircases and incredibly elaborate ceilings from which hang enormous glass chandeliers. This is the "horrible" exile you were subjected to.

Carmen Sylva: My dear, there is something more important than the glitz of a hotel, and that is honor. My honor had been stained by my enemies, and my right to be next to my people had been taken away from me. Besides, you can't understand what an exile entails.

The Chronicler: *I* can't understand what an exile entails?

Carmen Sylva: Some of my most devoted people were taken away and I could never know whom to trust. I was surrounded by smiling faces, but under the smiles I could feel the treachery and the dishonesty. The illness had transformed me into an invalid that had to be carried in an armchair by menservants. My hair had become entirely gray, and I was a shadow of my former self. Even so, I always did my best to present as joyful an exterior to the world as I could: I am of the opinion that one should never look *more unsightly to behold than one can possibly help*. One of my favorite comparisons of a proper-looking person is that of a clean toilet. All this being said, I was still a shadow of my former self, a shadow that spent her time in Elena's company and a very small number of ladies in waiting.

The Chronicler: More like ten or so ladies in waiting. Or almost. All sitting by your feet, the way they used to at Peleş, with Elena never leaving your side, her expression that of a spoiled child. A spoiled child who, for a while, thought she'd hit the jackpot with the Crown Prince. If there is something the Romanians should be grateful for it is that King Carol was not a fool and he had great respect for the rule of law. He didn't bend the law to fit the whims of a spoiled child who deluded herself that she was some kind of genius because an exuberant and eccentric queen had led her to believe so. Even Loti could see through her. He describes her phony, affected expressions, the way she serves her queen from a doll-like cup, as the queen lies down on her favorite Empire couch, as if they were playing mother and daughter, always making sure that this dynamic that exploits a mother's loss of a child is somewhere in the queen's head. A manipulator of the highest class. When the queen is taken to her daily promenade in the gondola, Mademoiselle Hélène, as Loti calls her, is always there, a barrier between the fragile, elderly woman and the world. The gondoliers, in white shirts and black pants, set forth, and the gondola moves slowly on the dark, silent waters, in which are reflected the rectangular shapes of the ancient, crumbling houses. Curious onlookers, who have heard of the exiled queen, bow and wave from nearby windows, and the majestic woman waves back. Elena reads the latest French paper, which informs them that she has committed suicide. "For the third time!" Elena says, laughing, and they all laugh together. Questioned by Loti, Elena scoffs at the idea of suicide as a cheap solution that only vulgar, low-class women chose. Indeed, our contemporary readers may not realize it, but there was a time when suicide was associated with being low class because many young women who worked as salesgirls killed themselves for romantic reasons. A lady never committed suicide: a compromised lady just disappeared. As Elena will, eventually, do.

As the gondola sailed, every now and then a curiosity shop caught Elena's eye, and then, they stopped; the young woman, accompanied by one or two servants, got off to examine the goods, and soon returned with childish cries of joy—"Look what I found!"—holding various tchotchkes (a dolphin, a swan), and causing the queen to greet her with a motherly smile. They returned to the hotel in time for dinner, but only the guests went in to eat; the Queen never ate; she remained in the gondola and waited until they were all back, and then, they started off again, accompanied, this time, by another, much bigger gondola lit up by red lanterns, and hosting a double string quartet, a chorus and two soloists. The two gondolas glided over the dark, shimmering waters, followed by other, smaller gondolas that were seduced by the music, and leaving behind a formation of bubbles like the silver traces of some huge snails. The soloists' voices bounced off the marble walls of the adjacent palaces, lingering in the air in decrescendo spirals that followed them through the canal and the narrow streets. In a short time, dozens of gondolas had gathered behind the queen's, full of ladies reclining on cushions and listening to the echoing music, under a pitch-dark sky on which the glittering stars shone even brighter. The music rose from the waters in a fog of languid notes enhanced by the sound of the violin, until the two gondolas reached the Rialto Bridge and the gondoliers paused in order for the music to be heard with even greater intensity. They all sat and listened to the moonlit sound of the night, and Loti could see a tear glistening at the corner of the Queen's right eye. When they returned to the hotel it was close to midnight.

Carmen Sylva: Yes, that is a pretty accurate description of how we used to pass the time. It does sound like paradise, doesn't it? But this paradise fails to take into account the treacherous actions that happened behind closed doors, for instance, the betrayal of that servant-girl whom I once saved from dire poverty and who, I found out, had been purloining and copying letters of mine, as well as excerpts from my diary. This girl, who would have been on the streets had it not been for me, had chosen to repay me in this way. And God only knows how many of them, those maidens who kiss my hands and flatter me every day, how many of them are doing something similar behind my back! Aside from these miseries, I also suffered because of Nando's silence. Theoretically, he was still engaged to Elena, whose letters and ring he hadn't returned. I kept writing to him, asking him to clarify his position, but the coward never answered.

The Chronicler: You know very well that he was simply obeying his uncle and King.

Carmen Sylva: I know that a man should have honor and courage. And Ferdinand was no man. He behaved in an undignified way. Still, being the woman that I am, instead of succumbing to the disgrace of my situation, I tried to make the most of it and enjoyed the beauty of Venice as much as I could. I went out to watch the dealers of the Piazza San Marco, whose white tents were spread all over under a blinding sun that polished their glassware and jewelry with a coating of celestial diamonds. Elena was always next to me, braving the local telltales, who, informed from the slanderous press, watched us with the curious eyes of those who enjoy hearsays. Maybe it was her youth, but she never seemed unfazed by these gossipmongers; on the contrary, she took pleasure in making fun of them, not of them as individual people, but as symbolic representatives of universal stupidity. Together we laughed at this most human of faults, we laughed and made an oath never to accept the chains of petty mediocrity.

The Chronicler: Loti also talks about the candor of your laughter, both yours, and Elena's, but he also remarks, quite subtly, that it was the singling out of Elena among your other maids of honor that contributed to your downfall. Those beautiful young women, all rescued by you, all eager to please and flatter you, could not have received with indifference the elevation of one of them to a station far beyond theirs. Such an affront is not easily forgiven, all the more so since, initially, your motherly overtures led them to believe that they were all equal as your "daughters."

Carmen Sylva: It's not for nothing that I used to call them "my little monsters," which is what they proved to be, in the end. But I shouldn't complain, for, in the end, everyone betrayed me, even the one I thought of as a saint, my King and husband. I shall never forget the day when he stopped me in the hall to tell me that I had to get rid of my dear child, Elena, who was ruining my reputation and endangering our house. I couldn't believe that the man whom I trusted more than myself had fallen victim to the gossip spread by one of my chambermaids who was horribly jealous of Elena because she was obsessed with me and had been pining for me since God knows when. I had noticed her jealous behavior, but, naïve that I am, I always give people the benefit of the doubt and assume they are purer than they really are, because this is how I am. It's Elena who opened my eyes and made me realize that the maid, a horrible-looking hermaphrodite, was spreading rumors about us, questioning the purity of our relationship, because a woman with impure thoughts imagines that everybody is like her. It was also the same maid who spread the rumor that I was having an affair with a family friend, a composer.

The Chronicler: How do you know that? How do you know it wasn't Elena who was spreading the rumors?

Carmen Sylva: Because Elena was the purest being I ever met. She was so pure she didn't even know how children were made. She thought they were conceived through medical intervention.

The Chronicler: This is what *she* told you?

Carmen Sylva: This is what *I* know. I know that everybody around us conspired against us because they had dirty minds, and dirty minds need to stain everything around them. I know that the chambermaid plotted with the man who had been my biggest enemy since my youth, my stepfather, the ignoble man my mother had married, and who had tried to get his hands on me in my mother's house. Once, he opened my door in the middle of the night, and I could see his erect member showing under his white nightgown, and when I screamed at him to get out, he pretended I misunderstood his intentions. Ever since, he hated me with passion, trying to bring about my downfall through evil gossip, such as my so-called affair with the composer. My mother never believed me, and he's done everything he could to convince her that my "nerves" were "shaken" because of Elena's influence. I understood a lot about female passion by studying how my mother sacrificed her own child for a man.

One day, a servant exclaimed, looking at a portrait of my stepfather that he resembled in an uncanny way my late father, and then I realized that he was like a caricature of my father, that he had very likely been jealous of him and trying to usurp his place. I know that I will never rest until I avenge my father's usurper, because, just like Kriemhild from *The Song of the Nibelungs,* I never forgive. Yes, I am a woman of stone, or of iron, an undecipherable sphinx; my husband and the intrigants around him have made me into one. My volcanic passion, the passion of a poet and a woman in love, have been turned inside out, and now I have morphed into the opposite, an indifferent cold-hearted woman.

The Chronicler: Your stepfather may have been a deplorable man, but this doesn't mean he plotted against you with the maid. You are saying this only because Elena has planted this idea in your head, and, based on many other ideas she planted in the heads of many other people, one has reasons to doubt her honorable intentions. When your husband accosted you in the hall, he didn't do it out of jealousy, he did it because he had been informed by many such individuals of Elena's machinations. She claimed that she'd received a letter from the Princess of Wales, which she never did, and some of Romania's politicians were informed that she was trying to stop a possible marriage between Prince Ferdinand and one of the Edinburgh young princesses.

Queen Marie: Me, to be more precise.

The Chronicler: The list of the many things Elena claimed, and which proved to be lies, is incredibly long. To begin with, she was in the habit of claiming to be friends or acquainted with many famous writers and European aristocrats, claims all debunked as falsehoods. She never spoke in secret with Queen Victoria, as she had asserted; nor with the Princess of Wales, who never said that she "understood" why Prince Ferdinand couldn't commit to one of the Edinburgh girls, given the amazing young women surrounding Queen Elisabeta.

Carmen Sylva: It wasn't her who claimed these things, but her enemies in order to cast a shadow over all her assertions, because they were jealous of her wit and of my love for her. She was a young girl but had the wit and wisdom of an old woman. Once, she told the German Emperor, after having stared at him intensely for several long minutes, and after he, intrigued, had asked her why, that she was admiring Attila II.

The Chronicler: Another proven lie, a claim debunked by the emperor himself.

Carmen Sylva: I don't believe it for a second. He never debunked it in front of me.

Queen Marie: He debunked it in front of your King and husband. People didn't want to hurt your feelings, that's why they pretended to go along with your silliness.

The Chronicler: You interrupted me, and I didn't finish my point about Elena's many lies and deceptions. Her alleged friendship with Loti, Taine, and a few other writers—all lies. Another famous French writer, Paul Bourget, mockingly called her "Mademoiselle Crampon"—roughly and freely translated, "Miss Glue," because she clung to one like glue. But no story is as outrageous as the one narrated by the famous *académicien* Sully Prudhomme, who related how she received the Award of the Académie Française for one of her poetry collections. Apparently, she gave him the manuscript, and because he found it terribly mediocre and full of faults in French—which is funny, because you, my dear Queen, are under the impression that her French was so good she couldn't write properly in Romanian. In fact, it appears she couldn't write properly in either language—he proceeded to correct and improve it. Then, this woman took the edited manuscript and entered it for the prize of the Académie, which, in the end, she received. Lecomte de Lisle made it clear that she was awarded the prize simply out of deference for you, my Queen. Sully Prudhomme refused to vote, but he was also discreet enough not to say why. Only later did he explain that he "couldn't vote for himself." This story made the rounds of all artistic and aristocratic circles in Europe and is one of the reasons many people are questioning your judgment and have come to the conclusion that you must be mentally ill. Or, as the two doctors who have examined you came to the conclusion that you have suffered psychological abuse at the hands of a fraudster and a group of people who had deliberately attempted to take advantage of your gullibility.

Queen Marie: Indeed. Elena and her father were known all over Europe as charlatans, "an Association of Liars," and even the Romanians, whose moral standards aren't the highest, were appalled when they realized the magnitude of the deceit. It is now known that she and her father had conspired to ensnare poor Nando and together had weaved a web of lies. The other expert weaver was the other Helen, Hélène Bibesco, Marthe Bibesco's mother—like mother, like daughter (did I mention that Marthe was one of my husband's many mistresses?)—who was heard stating that "The Queen believes anything." Thus, like in a Greek tragedy, the two Helens put their minds together to fool their queen.

Carmen Sylva: My "gullibility"? My "silliness"? Yes, I am aware that you, as well as my husband, think that my belief in spiritual practices is childish and the root of all my problems, but I happen to believe in a higher order, an order that is only visible to a few elect individuals, and it isn't my fault you aren't among them. My belief in magnetism, hypnotic trance and the power of turning tables to put us in touch with the dead and to predict the future is not the "superstition" of a fool but the result of lifelong study and reflection. My own father was the author of a scholarly work that tried to reconcile science and spirituality. As for the Văcărescus, they are one of Romania's oldest and noblest families, and your spiteful rejection of them simply proves your bias. I've said it before and I'll say it again, the other European princesses are all bourgeois, uneducated and without grace, the result of hundreds of years of intermarriages that have weakened the race. I am one of the very few still left who has race.

The Chronicler: We should probably explain for our American readers that you use the word "race" in the spirit of the times when it was synonymous with "class." But about your father's work: the King was kind enough to read his book in order to better understand where you were coming from, and he wrote you a long letter explaining that you had misunderstood what you'd read, that, in fact, your father warned his contemporaries about the danger of cheap and manipulative spiritism, precisely the kind of spiritism Elena engaged in. When she played the medium through whom your late father and your dead child spoke to you, she engaged in the kind of deceit performed by the worst charlatans, a deceit of Macbethian proportions, and your credulity can only be explained by your emotional vulnerability.

Carmen Sylva: My dear, your interpretation is proof of your being a child of your times, someone with no feeling for a world beyond our senses. You speak of things you do not grasp, and your confidence is proof of your arrogant ignorance. Besides, where is your impartiality? You are supposed to be an impartial chronicler, yet you are siding with Missy against me, probably because you are one of those self-hating Romanians, who always think that Westerners are better.

The Chronicler: My dear Queen, my conclusions are simply based on facts and the statements of many individuals. Your librarian, who accompanied you everywhere, just like Elena, told the King that he'd noticed how Mlle Elena had made the tables turn, how he had personally witnessed her deceit. He never told you this because he didn't want to spoil your pleasure. These were his words. Monarchs are very vulnerable to their subjects' deceit because few people dare to tell them the truth, that's why it is imperative that they do not fall prey to abject flattery, and I'm afraid you were easily persuaded by flattery.

Carmen Sylva (pointing to Queen Marie): And *she* wasn't?

Queen Marie: Whatever I was, I didn't create a constitutional crisis through my behavior. I didn't attempt to convince my husband to change Romania's constitution because only I, an enlightened being, could understand something the Romanians themselves did not understand. I didn't tell my husband, listen to me and I will make you the greatest king that ever was! By orchestrating a marriage between Nando and a Romanian woman, we will create a new dynasty, a dynasty rooted in Romanian blood mixed with ours, the blood of our adopted son, a Hohenzollern with the weakened blood of a fish—*fin de race*—, which will be refreshed through the mélange with a hot-blooded Oriental. I didn't tell him, I don't want to get involved in politics, I prefer to be in the shadows, acting behind the scenes, and you can appropriate my advice as your own idea for your greater glory.

Carmen Sylva: Speaking of Orientals, our Romanian readers may find it interesting to know that in a long letter to me, their adored King Carol I states explicitly that the Orientals are deceitful people, always engaged in political intrigues, that one should never trust them, and that Elena's behavior was simply the embodiment of this comportment.

The Chronicler: For the benefit of our American readers, we should mention that by "Orientals," which is how people in the Balkans were known at the time, King Carol meant the Romanians. And, having spent the first twenty-five years of my life among Orientals, I can only and wholeheartedly agree with him.

Carmen Sylva: As I was saying, a self-hating Romanian …

The Chronicler: I am, rather, an observer of human nature, and I know that this characteristic of the Romanians and, likely, other Orientals, is a survival technique of people from authoritarian societies, a technique observed, for example, by one of the greatest Romanian novelists, Marin Sorescu, when he describes the double language of Romanian peasants. But in the case of Elena we are probably dealing with the case of a sociopath. Besides, aren't you a self-hating German too? Don't you always bash your German relatives?

Queen Marie: King Carol confirmed to me my suspicion that it was Elena who deliberately tried to isolate Auntie from her own family and to make her believe they were her mortal enemies. But the most frightening thing is not that she, Elena, used deceitful rhetoric. Language is one thing, acting is another. Apparently, she went so far as to use some potions and dark magic—witchcraft, in plain English—on her queen. This is the conclusion a few doctors arrived at, that the Queen had been poisoned, and that explained her many bizarre symptoms, her constant complaints of pain all over her body, her overall weakness, sickness and mental confusion following her *tables tournantes* sessions. And that's why the King decided that Elena had to be sent away. Not because he was, supposedly, jealous.

Carmen Sylva: Yes, I was poisoned, I know that, but not by Elena. I was poisoned, first of all, by human stupidity and pettiness. Second, by one of my chambermaids, and by the intrigues of another. This was the reward I received from my "daughters," to whom I had sacrificed everything, spending on them all the money I had, never even buying a dress for myself when I was traveling.

The Chronicler: Why would these young women want to poison you?

Carmen Sylva: Why would Elena want to poison me?

Queen Marie: Do you remember when Nando was so ill before he met me that he almost died, and the doctors were puzzled by his condition? You know that some of them later concluded that he too may have been poisoned by the same hand who had poisoned you.

Carmen Sylva: That may very well be true, but you are dead wrong about the hand. I did my own investigation, at the end of which I fired my chambermaid.

The Chronicler: And in doing so, you placed the King, once again, in a very delicate position, since it was only him who had the right to fire the personnel. You acted without consulting him and, as a result, all the Romanian papers exposed you as over-reaching your prerogatives. The poor King, who had to constantly defend himself against the Romanian nationalists, the Francophiles and the ill-wishers, had to waste his time mending what you broke.

Carmen Sylva: The "poor King," as you call him, was

unpopular because of his own actions, and I had the brightest idea about how to make him regain his popularity, but he was incapable of seeing that. He, who was once a saint to me, had become a tool bent to destroy and silence me. But I have no political ambition, all I am is a poet, and from then on, I decided that I will keep my opinions to myself, that I will embrace the enigmatic silence of a sphinx.

The Chronicler: "*Nemuritor şi rece.*" "Immortal and cold," as in Eminescu's poems. What an incurable romantic you are, my dear Queen! You have created this persona of the misunderstood genius, a martyr, and Elena, who, like all narcissists, mirrored you and mimicked your persona, saw herself as a witty genius too—hence her obsession with proving how adored she was by "the rich and famous."

Carmen Sylva: If you were a true novelist, you wouldn't rush to judgment so easily. You would build your case more patiently and with more caution.

The Chronicler: Are you talking to me?

Queen Marie: She is talking to you but hopes that it will ricochet in my direction. It's with me that she is competing, not you.

Carmen Sylva: "Compete" with you? Don't flatter yourself, Missy. I never compared myself to anyone.

Queen Marie: Not explicitly. But you trusted a woman known all over Europe as an *héroïne de roman*, a Madame Bovary who claimed that Nando had threatened to shoot himself over her, who lied that he'd asked her to commit suicide together with him, that he'd drunk vitriol for her, that she'd smelled sulphur in his room. You became a character in a very cheap novel. So cheap that, after pretending that Carol of Sweden was in love with her and wanted to marry her—he too! See a pattern here?—she faked a trance during a turning table session, in which she said that Nando was a rival of Carol's. This is how she planted in his head the idea of their "love."

Carmen Sylva: If Nando had had any honor, he would have shot himself. A man who gives his word to a woman is obligated to keep it, otherwise he is dishonored.

Queen Marie: He should have killed himself for *that* woman? How can you say that you love him?

Carmen Sylva: I loved him like my own son, but I would rather lose a son than accept a coward.

Queen Marie: You'd rather lose a son than accept *me*.

*

Carmen Sylva: After I had to give up Elena and I returned from exile, I spent more and more time among my books and embroideries. This is when I discovered the works of Charles Howard Hinton, a mathematician who invented the fourth dimension, and who believed that entering it places us in a higher space that allows us to get rid of the self, and of the notions of left and right, and up and down. I found it all fascinating. Missy, you may remember that we had soirées twice a week in which we read his book.

Queen Marie: Yes, I remember. It was, indeed, interesting. Even the men found it captivating.

Carmen Sylva: Yes, I remember now. Prince Ştirbey was always there. In my naiveté I thought he was interested in the fourth dimension, when, in reality, all he cared about were *your* dimensions. Do you remember the Tesseract or the hypercube?

Queen Marie: Of course, I remember. It was all quite complicated. But I seem to recall that you even invited him to give us a lecture. He came, but was unable to give the lecture because he fell ill and two months after he left he was dead.

Carmen Sylva: Yes, the poor man. What did he suffer from? I just can't recall. Was it gout? Or maybe something completely different. He had a very funny smell, he smelled of ... well, death. But he did humor me and, the night of his arrival, participated in one of our séances.

Queen Marie: A year before you invited him, you ordered his kit with eighty-one colored cubes. At first, I couldn't understand anything, but, eventually, I began to enjoy those meditation exercises during which we had to visualize the fourth dimension.

Carmen Sylva: Oh, dear. I almost fainted the first time. It was exhausting staring at those cubes and having to memorize their colors along the edges, two by two, and so on. After about an hour I had a splitting headache and felt that the entire room was spinning. Maybe it was dizziness, maybe it was the fourth dimension itself, I did enter a state in which my ego left my body and I began to levitate. I was light and pure, and from up there, I could see you all, struggling within your brown human broth.

Queen Marie: Our "brown human broth"?

Carmen Sylva: That's how you all seemed from there. You know I always had a penchant for the spiritual realm.

Queen Marie: Don't I know it!

Chapter 4

Immigrant Princesses and Poet Queens

Carmen Sylva: We monarchs are the envy of all, but, in the end, we are the loneliest beings on earth. All mortals are allowed to defend themselves, or, as you say nowadays, to have an opinion. Sovereigns alone are expected to be like God, and give no reply when they are spoken ill of. I've said it before: no man can be a friend of a sovereign, unless one is without passion, without ambition, and without selfishness.

The Chronicler: Hence HM Queen Elizabeth II's motto: "Never complain, never explain." A motto that has worked for a long time, but which the British Royal Family is forced to abandon these days because when one is being publicly accused of racism, what can one do? Prince Charles felt compelled to issue a statement in response to a report speculating about who could have been the senior royal to have made the "racist" remark Prince Harry and Meghan accused them of making in that Oprah interview from March 2021. And since the couple made sure to specifically exclude the Queen and Prince Philip from the guessing game, the circle of the possible culprits was narrowed down to Prince Charles, Camilla, Prince William, Catherine, and Princess Anne—funnily enough, no one is considering Prince Andrew. The man who walked Meghan down the aisle because her father wasn't there (and why he wasn't there is another story) and who, at the end of the ceremony, took her mother's arm in a very unusually warm public gesture, the man who went out of his way to welcome this woman in the family, the man who is known to have been very happy that his second son finally settled down, the ecumenist who has declared that, as King, he intends to change the title of "Defender of *the* Faith," passed on to him by the Queen, to "Defender of Faiths," this man had to answer accusations of racism because of a vengeful son who was seething with anger after daddy "cut him off," leaving him only with the millions inherited from his mother and great-grandmother. A son who, two years later, in the ITV interview with Tom Bradby, denied ever having made any accusations of racism, and blamed once again the media for twisting his words. Speaking of which, just the other day I watched another interesting interview with another woke Princess, Martha Louise of Norway.

Carmen Sylva: Wait, you are going too fast! I can't keep up. First of all, why are we talking about the British Royal Family? I am tired of hearing about them, They behave as if they have invented the monarchy. The oldest monarchy in Europe is the Danish one, and they have a much more captivating royal family. Their monarch, Queen Margrethe II, is probably the most intellectual and artistic member of all contemporary royal families. She has translated, together with her late husband, Prince Henryk, who was French, Simone de Beauvoir's *Second Sex*, she is a theater costume designer, and like me, has created many embroideries, albeit none of them of a religious nature. Between the two of us, I don't think she even believes in God, I think she may be the only European monarch who gives her yearly address on New Year's Eve, not on Christmas, like the others. Maybe the King of Norway does the same too, I am not sure. But what did you say about his daughter, and what does "woke" mean?

The Chronicler: Oh, Princess Martha Louise of Norway? She is engaged to an American man who happens to be black; according to her words in the interview I mentioned, she has been "awakened" by him to her "white privilege." "Woke" comes from "to awaken" and has religious connotations, although, technically, it refers to someone of a certain political persuasion. Poor Princess Martha! If she needed an African American man to make her aware of her privilege, and if she thinks that this privilege is due to the color of her skin … The woman is the daughter of a King, but she thinks she is privileged because of the color of her skin! Of course, this whole discussion took place because the Norwegian media made a big fuss about her lover, and of course, the awakened Princess is accusing the media of racism. The funniest part of the story is that her lover is a … umm, Shaman. He goes by the name "Shaman Durek." The Princess engaged to the American Shaman. Now, this Shaman, who, truth be told, has a striking face, is very special: he believes that he is part "reptilian" and, together with Martha Louise, offers workshops in "healing" under the banner "The Princess and the Shaman," workshops in which they teach that "cancer is a choice." Being attuned to supernatural phenomena, the Princess communicates with angels, but "not with the dead." She has founded a spiritual center in which the students are encouraged to find their "inner truth" by engaging in dialogue with angels. Oh, I forgot: the Shaman is, of course, from LA, the spiritual supermarket that has also given us the humanitarian Meghan Markle and a whole load of other humanitarians. I remember when, thirty years ago, Madonna started the trend of drinking only holy water from Jerusalem in their meditation retreats. Imagine the cost of transporting and bringing this water to these ecologically-minded people! Spiritual seekers, all. Now they've enriched their ranks with the man formerly known as "Prince," who, in a videotaped therapy session—of which I only watched excerpts on YouTube because, aside from not having the stomach to consume the whole thing, I would have also had to pay forty bucks—informed us that he consumes psychedelics in order to have visions that help him "discover himself." Apparently, he does this at the advice of the therapist who was leading the session—one of the many spiritual counselors Harry now has—who also suggested that, if Harry's family was not as open-minded and as "spiritual" as him, there was nothing wrong with cutting them off. One can smell the spirit of these people advising him to keep talking and wash his dirty linen in public from miles off. Oh, what a mighty royal cow to milk, what a golden goose to relieve of its eggs! A little devil tells me that these spiritual people, therapists, ghost writers, publicists, life coaches and documentarists, are hoping that the drugged Prince could end up making some "shocking revelations" that could fill up their pockets even more. Once he is on a spiritual path, there is no end to it. From now on, we can expect an avalanche of revelations, all for the benefit of his "mental health."

Queen Marie: What is wrong with being a spiritual seeker? Speaking for myself, I love the many types of American spirituality! I love that this country is so open to so many ways of being religious. Unlike, I might add, just between the three of us, the Romanian people, who, with crosses on their chests and Hitler in their hearts, have chased my son, Carol, out of the country.

Carmen Sylva (spiteful): Yes, you and your Bahai! A queen who converts to the Bahai religion in her old age! Some spirituality! You have always thought of yourself as superior to the Romanian people. As for your son, Carol, don't get me started!

Queen Marie: You are jealous, jealous because it is I, and not you, that the Romanians have chosen as their most beloved queen of all time. You have always been jealous of me. You are nothing but a bitter, bitter old woman.

The Chronicler: I don't like the direction this discussion is taking. Let's go back to the Danish monarchy! What do your

Majesties think of Crown Prince Frederik and his wife, Mary?

Queen Marie: I like them. Mary is the most accomplished European princess; not only does she have a *je ne sais quoi* about her, but she is the only royal to come close to my role as a bride from a faraway land who has become one with her new country. She learned to speak Danish fluently in a few years, and, unlike the Duchess of Cambridge (now Princess of Wales), who is very beautiful and always perfectly dressed but cannot give a speech longer than four minutes, Princess Mary is a master orator. Did you listen to the speech she gave when Frederik turned fifty?

The Chronicler: Indeed, I did, and I was impressed. It was perfectly delivered, the right tone and intonation, she had clearly rehearsed it many times. But unlike most speeches, it wasn't only empty, uplifting words, it was witty and included even a few original thoughts. Most so-called royal watchers, who are obsessed with British royalty, don't seem to know that there is such a thing as the genre of a royal speech. The members of the British Royal Family were discouraged by the Queen to give a speech longer than a few minutes to avoid making gaffes—the longer the speech, the higher the probability of an error. Still, Prince Charles, now King, has always delivered long speeches on state visits or when hosting other royal families, speeches in which one can recognize the regal trademark: a reference to their common past and unifying ancestors. This style is in stark contrast with that of Meghan Markle, whose eloquence follows the glorious tradition of American celebrity speeches: a mixture of pop activism and "progressive" corporate demagoguery, which finds its dialectical resolution in a stomach-churning stew where ingratiating phrases such as "activating compassion" and "You are brave!" "You are beautiful!" stick their heads out to lick the pathetic egos of their followers. Her husband too is a master blabberer of such nonsense. Princess Mary's speech at the fiftieth birthday celebration of her husband embodied the highest form of the genre of royal speeches, whose perfect manifestations can be found in all the Nordic royal families. The first demand of this genre is the lack of any jargon or stock phrases—through simple but carefully chosen words, one addresses the audience, or, if one gives the speech in someone's honor, one speaks directly to the feted person, as Mary did to Frederick. The second requirement of the genre is the balanced mixture of private and public elements, and Mary struck the perfect balance. "You come in many guises. You are in constant movement," she said, (knowingly or unknowingly) channeling Montaigne. "We never know if you'll come through the door dressed in uniform, a business suit, a wetsuit, or as 'Mamil.'" Smiling, the princess explained that "Mamil" referred to a subculture of "middle-aged men in Lycra, who ride expensive racing bicycles wearing professional style body-hugging jerseys and shorts. Opinions differ as to whether Lycra and men over forty are a good combination." Like any good speaker, the princess waited for the audience to end laughing, and then, continued, provocatively: "But, darling, you still look rather sharp in Lycra." She then invoked the time when they'd met in a bar at the Sydney Olympics, and he was wearing shorts and a T-shirt. And then, very cleverly, she contrasted that image of the Crown Prince with this: "I remember clearly the first time you changed from casual to gala." It was during her first visit to Denmark and the prince went to change for New Year's Eve, then returned in full gala uniform. "If I had known Danish at the time I would have said, 'Wow, I scored high above my league!'"

These are words Meghan Markle would never have used. She wouldn't have used them, first of all, because they are self-ironic, and a Hollywood activist is never self-ironic. Second, because they are the words of a self-confident woman who isn't afraid of being accused of having "clinched" a man "above her league." An arriviste (not to mention an arriviste activist) would never spell out the obvious—that marrying a prince is "scoring high above one's league;" no, an arriviste will make sure to film herself around a chicken's coop so everyone can see how "relatable" she is and will publicly disparage the multi-million dollar wedding an entire nation has given her by calling it "a spectacle." An arriviste never says "I am grateful" because an arriviste always wants more.

Carmen Sylva: Are we talking about that American woman again? The Danish princess is much more interesting, at least she can speak more than one language. And she even ended her speech by reciting a poem, something only Prince Charles and Camilla can do in the British Royal Family. Charles often recites Shakespeare and Wordsworth, and I even heard him declaim Mahmoud Darwish. His wife has more popular taste, she likes bestseller novels, love stories and the like, but at least, she reads. In fact, she even has a book club, "The Queen's Reading Room," started during lockdown. Those who keep comparing her unfavorably to Diana, who didn't read and had no interest in classical music and the arts, are the kind of people who prefer a pretty face to a woman of substance. As for the new generations, they never read. They have no interest in the arts unless it is the latest film or one of those pop songs. That half-wit, Harry, has grown up in palaces that contain some of the largest art collections in the world, yet he can't tell a Vermeer from a Matisse, or a Renoir from a Pollock. What am I saying? I don't think he's ever heard of them. What a shame, to have access to some of the greatest works of art ever created, yet to have so closed a mind and no interest in improving it. But look at me, I am back to talking about *them*!

The Chronicler: Indeed. Obsessing about someone gives them power. But I still haven't told you what I liked most in Princess Mary's speech. This is the part: "You (i.e. her husband) love your country and you have long ago imparted this love to me. So much so that I am deeply moved when I sing 'In Denmark I was born, this is my home,' well aware that, although I am at home and I belong here, I wasn't born here. My own explanation is that our roots continue to grow throughout our lives. We can always find our home."

Queen Marie: I can see why you like this part. I do too. I too "identify" with her, as you Americans say. I too grew new roots in my adoptive country, and I too teared up listening to its national anthem. I think we become our country through our children and the suffering that comes from—

Carmen Sylva: "We become our country through our children"? Are you saying that those of us who weren't blessed with children cannot be faithful to our country?! Are you drawing a direct line from having children to being patriotic?

Queen Marie: No, no, you misunderstood me.

Carmen Sylva: Oh, I understood you too well. I understand you better than you understand yourself. You, the great Romanian patriot with six children fathered by I don't know how many men, and I, the childless, unpatriotic queen. I, the woman who had seventeen miscarriages and had to suffer the spite of the Romanian politicians for it, and the pain of child loss without being allowed to show it. I, who was so selfless I even wanted to die and thought of killing myself in order to free my husband so he could marry another woman. I, who was forced to adopt my husband's nephew, witness the transfer of affection of my dear Romanians to a new, younger couple, and pretend I didn't care.

Queen Marie: Why do you hate me so much, Auntie? What have I done to you?

Carmen Sylva: (long pause) You haven't done it *to me*, you've done it to the Romanian people. You've never considered yourself their equal, you wanted to become a queen for your glory and vanity. I—I and Karl sacrificed our lives and happiness for them. Karl in the most literal sense, on the battlefield, sharing the mud and the trenches with his soldiers, who adored him. For months he lived in a tent with straw on the floors, with the rain pouring in his bedroom through the broken roof. All for the country's independence from the Ottomans. His bravery was so appreciated by the Tsar that the medals he issued became the most popular, even more popular than the Russian ones. He was so brave that once he ordered fire from a trench that was exposed to the Turks' fusillade; half an hour later an artillery corporal was shot dead right on the spot where they'd been together. After this event, Colonel Gaillard forbade him to stay in the trenches any longer. My goodness, if something like this were to happen to a contemporary royal from the young generations, the poor man would undergo counseling for the rest of his life! Just look at the two British princes, Harry and William, all they talk about is "mental health"! In our days, we just called this "life." Karl wrote to me about his fight in the war, but we never spoke about it after he came back. What would have been the point? As for me, I would have loved to fight next to him, but I was not allowed to. While he was fighting the Turks, I knitted his warm clothing, flannel gloves and undergarments, and made him felt shoes and blankets. What have *you* ever knitted for *your* husband?

Queen Marie: I knitted for him more than he for me.

Carmen Sylva: "Knitted." Indeed, you have. You have both knitted so much that you have stitched a net in which not only you, but also the entire Romanian monarchy was caught, taking it down with you in the gutter. And with the monarchy, the entire Romanian nation. My beautiful, *chipeşi*, dark-eyed Romanians! What wonderful people! As I told my dear Karl in a letter: just look at their clever eyes, refined features, sharp judgment and wisdom!

The Chronicler (rolls her eyes): "Refined features?!" "Sharp judgment?!" That's some brown-nosing for posterity.

Carmen Sylva (continues her thought): They didn't deserve this. They, who adored my Karl, they who covered themselves in glory at Plevna, they with their innate sense of justice, didn't deserve to be made the mockery of Europe with the scandalous behavior of their royal family.

Queen Marie: *You* are one to talk about scandals! When I met you, you were in exile, exiled by your own husband for your transgressions against the Romanian Constitution. I, on the other hand, was sent by the Romanian government to Paris to negotiate the Treaty of Versailles. By the time you were back from exile, I already had my second child, Lisabeta. I could have used some help, you know, as a seventeen-year-old bride. But I had to learn everything on my own, including how children are born. At the beginning, I was being criticized for everything, even for the decision of using chloroform to alleviate the pain of childbirth. I endured that torture six times for the sake of Romania, because my children were not even mine, they were *her* children. My husband and I were not allowed to raise and educate them, you and your dear Karl took all the decisions, and then you blamed *me* for their failures. As for your constant insinuations, maybe I was not the kind of woman to knit gloves for my husband, but I made him proud anywhere I went, including to America. I am a woman of a different era than you, Auntie, I was a woman of my time, and you, of yours.

Carmen Sylva: You may have been a woman of *your* time, but I was not one of mine. I was always ahead of my time, that's why I was exiled.

Queen Marie: Well, that's quite an interesting interpretation! Are you maybe saying that you sabotaged the Romanian Constitution because you were a republican rather than a monarchist?

Carmen Sylva (red with anger): Take that back, you … take that back, or … (to the Chronicler): Ask her to take that back! I won't allow her to smear my relationship with the Romanian people, which was sacred.

The Chronicler: I can't ask her to take anything back. It's too late for that.

Carmen Sylva: You can ask her anything you want. (Lowers her voice): Hypocrite!

The Chronicler: It's not a good strategy to upset your chronicler, you know.

Carmen Sylva: Are you threatening me? You think I can't tell you are on *her* side?

The Chronicler: I am on no one's side. I am only the chronicler.

Carmen Sylva: You are not a chronicler, you are a novelist. You make up stories. The first obligation of a chronicler is to respect *chronology*. Look at you and your story: it's all over the place! You start something and aren't going anywhere with it. You keep moving in circles, like a duck.

The Chronicler (ignores her and turns to Queen Marie): Speaking of ducks, I saw a charming photo of you and your sister, Ducky, in your masquerade ball costumes. What year was that when she spent several months in Romania? The two of you were the chic of the chic, taking rides in the *trăsura la șosea,* like two Parisian aristocrats in the Bois de Boulogne. Or like young Queen Elizabeth and Princess Margaret half a century later. (To Carmen Sylva): Wasn't that the ball where you were dressed up as Dante?

Carmen Sylva: I don't remember. Maybe.

Queen Marie: When Ducky came to visit me, we sometimes went out incognito, and that's when we had the most fun. We were rather mischievous—funny, how adults become children again when they are in the presence of those with whom they spent their childhood! We often laughed so hard our mouths hurt. Of course, we had to watch ourselves in the presence of the King and Queen, with their severe, constantly judging demeanor.

Carmen Sylva: "Severe"? "Judging"? Are you thinking of the time when you and Ducky were caught poking with your umbrellas the behinds of fellow strollers on what is now Calea Victoriei? I was told that you were laughing so hard everybody around turned their heads. Do you think your relatives in Great Britain would have approved of your behavior? I really doubt it.

Queen Marie: The British Royal Family may love to follow strict protocol, but they have a good sense of humor. No one in my family ever chastised me for laughing. Even today, the British royals enjoy a good laugh, sometimes at their own expense. Have you ever heard of "It's a Royal Knockout"?

The Chronicler: Oh, yes, Prince Edward's short-lived TV show and film company. I watched it and didn't know whether to laugh or cry. I am not surprised that Sarah Ferguson and Prince Edward took part in that tasteless spectacle, but I am surprised by Princess Anne's part in it, and the fact that the Queen approved it.

Carmen Sylva: What spectacle?

The Chronicler: A TV show in the 70s, I think, in which the actors, among whom members of the British royal family, played medieval characters and were engaged in all kinds of gregarious team competitions against each other. At first, I laughed, because it's hard not to laugh when respectable people place themselves in silly situations, but, eventually, I came to resent it. The show ended up being cancelled because it was thought that it was detrimental to the royals' reputation.

Carmen Sylva: I always despised these oh-so-full-of-themselves royals from the major European royal houses. They act as if *nu le poate ajunge nimeni cu prăjina la nas*,[11] but,

---

11. Romanian idiomatic expression meaning "No one is good enough for them."

really, they have no reason to. They are ignorant, entitled, and, as this example indicates, have no class.

Queen Marie: Auntie, what does it mean to you to "have class"?

Carmen Sylva: It means to behave with dignity and respect for the title you've been given. And to sacrifice everything else for the honor of your position. If I hadn't been a princess and, later, a queen, I would have been celebrated as a poet and a philosopher. In fact, even more than a poet, my vocation had been that of a philosopher; not a few of Europe's serious newspapers and magazines have written at one point or another about my scholarly work. Even after I became queen, the biggest compliment one could give me was to praise my poems and philosophical essays. Do you know that once when I was on vacation in Germany I wrote thirty-two poems in four days, and ninety-five lieder in five weeks?

Queen Marie: No, I didn't know that, but if I were you, I wouldn't brag about it. Being a factory of poems does not make one a poet. But be that as it may, what does being a poet and a philosopher have to do with having class?

Carmen Sylva: I am telling all this to underline the fact that although everything in my constitution and education entitled me to call myself a scholarly woman, once I became engaged to a Crown Prince, and especially after I became Queen, I knew better than that because I had higher responsibilities and it was more important for me to preserve the honor of my husband and of my title than my personal feelings. During the same vacation in Germany when I was introduced to the Emperor and his family, I deliberately downplayed my intellectual qualities and embraced the persona of a young, naïve housewife, which I knew would be looked upon much more favorably than that of a scholarly woman, who, in Kant's immortal words, could only bring to mind the image of a bearded lady. As I told Karl in a letter I sent from there, I showed people that I was neither blue (previous gossip had made me appear melancholy and depressive), nor a "*bas-bleu*."[12] And yet, I was constantly being criticized by the members of my own family and the press of my country of birth for the sin of being a writer, in particular a writer of novels. Maybe some of these crowned heads and brainless princesses were simply jealous, otherwise I can't explain their viciousness and the ugly campaigns against me. As long as I was only a poet, they tolerated my writerly activities, but they couldn't take my being a novelist. To me, that was both incredibly naïve and amusing. I was lucky I was the Queen of Romania where the population appreciated my work as a writer, because, had I lived in Germany, I would have had to fight this idiotic attitude. No one in Germany read my novel *Deficit*, yet everybody judged me for it. I am convinced that one of the main reasons for their negative judgment was that they couldn't forgive me for also being a woman, because, unlike the French, the Germans are much more backward when it comes to the treatment of women. But I kept my mouth shut and swallowed all these insults smiling, for I knew that the reputation of my country and of my husband were more important than my own feelings. In Germany you can live a peaceful, sweet life of leisure as long as you don't stir the waters, keep to your place and, if you happen to be a woman, play the role assigned to your lot.

Queen Marie: And so, you pretended you were someone or something you weren't in order to earn their approval. And you call that "class."

Carmen Sylva: What a spin you can put on things, my dear! I hid my own qualities for the good of my husband and of my country. I vanquished my vanity for a higher cause, something you wouldn't understand. It wasn't easy, believe me, because my greatest desire had always been to be no more

---

12. Pejorative French slang of the time that referred to a scholarly woman (literally, a "blue stocking")

than a philosopher and a poet. But I have been vindicated because some of the brightest and most talented minds of this world, like the French Pierre Loti, Lecomte de Lisle, or Sully Prudhomme, who teared up listening to my translations from Romanian, and my compatriot, Paul Heyse, who later won the Nobel Prize in Literature, wrote me letters of appreciation and even composed poems in my honor.

One of the greatest pages in the novel of my life was my journey to Wales in 1890. I was invited there as a poet, not as a queen, and for this reason, I am prouder of my reception there than of any of my accomplishments. I translated for them my short story "The Poet's Dream" and a few poems from Elena's *Bard* to show to the Welsh, who have an innate gift for song and poetry, what their brother, the Romanian bard, is capable of. I shiver even now with a feeling of awe remembering how Europe was united, then and there, through the power of the Verb. It was the greatest annual gathering of the bards in Bangor, and I felt in my element among my fellow poets, simple people, peasants and folk singers. They led me onto a field, accompanying my steps by ovations and cheers, and a ninety-year-old man gave a speech from which all I understood was Romania, Wales and Carmen Sylva. Then, he began a ritual with a sword above my head, followed by the question "Is there Peace in the world?" To which the others answered in unison, "Peace!" After this, twenty other bards began to jump on a boulder and improvise poems in my honor. Then, the contest began: singers and poets sang and recited, one after the other, some with a harp, others just with their voice, and at the end, they chose a winner, whom they put on a throne. I was asked to place on his head the crown, which was made of dark green velour with a gold ribbon and oak leaves, as he knelt before me. In the end, several bards and a bardesse improvised again poems in my honor, followed by Elena, who recited one of her poems in English, and by me, with a translation from her book. Everybody was charmed and they began to cheer again, irrupting in a series of hoorays. To think that this nation of gifted people with a melancholy soul so similar to that of the Romanians is being oppressed by such a prosaic and tone-deaf people like the English! Speaking of which, an English sir who was present had the idea to introduce physical exercises at these festivities. Imagine that! Physical exercises! I told him that singing was exercise enough. Only an Englishman could have come up with such an absurd idea. Aside from this silly incident. I had a great time, meeting simple, poor people who walked up to me to tell me how much they admired me, and at night came under my windows to cheer and sing. I often heard workers whisper to each other, "She is so sweet!" Their press published daily around fifty articles about me, all praising me, in particular my so-called "beauty," obsessing over every single article of clothing I was wearing. I found this all very amusing, as I never thought I was "beautiful."

The Chronicler: Nor were you ever "sweet," a typical Anglo-Saxon word of praise, which describes much better your English niece. It is in watching the two of you interact that I came to realize that you, Carmen Sylva, a German-born queen, and I, a Transylvanian descendant of miners and peasants, share the same structural temperament. And yet, it is your niece that I admire.

Carmen Sylva (to Queen Marie): I have no doubt that such praise goes right to your heart. *Te unge la inimă*. It *butters up* your heart. (To the Chronicler): Do you, maybe, admire her more because you are very sensitive to physical appearance, and Missy has always displayed a certain shallow prettiness, the kind of "beauty" she herself used to admire in the Princess of Wales? I met the famous Princess of Wales during the same trip, when I stopped at Edinburgh, and she was, indeed, very pretty. The same kind of perfect "beauty" contemporary women who have seen the knife of a surgeon are famous for.

Perfect fake teeth, perfect fake hair, perfect makeup, all bought, nothing natural. Yes, the Princess of Wales was perfect, she even had a certain grace, but her house sported the most horrible taste I'd ever seen, no sense for the harmony of colors. And don't get me started on the stupidity of the entire Wales family, one more idiotic and uncultivated than the other. "I taught my daughters horse riding, not foreign languages," the Princess declared with a certain Sarah-Palinesque pride, after she listened with jaundiced envy to the praise her husband lavished upon me.

The Chronicler (laughing): "Sarah-Palinesque"?

Carmen Sylva: I learned a thing or two from you. As for me, one can examine me under a microscope, they won't find anything fake. It's all natural. I don't look like "a Disney Princess." Nor a British one—which has encouraged the *mauvaises langues*, my own family included, to gossip and spread lies about me. That I am neurotic. Crazy. A nymphomaniac (because of my relationship with Elena). That I take quinine, the way some take morphine and opium. That I am an eccentric with my head in the clouds. That my eccentricity and bizarreness show in my novels. Well, I showed them when I went to Balmoral. I showed them that I am a thousand times more practical than them all because in Romania I learned to walk through dung manure while they walked all their lives on feather soles. Queen Victoria, a dear old lady with common sense, who can see through smokescreen, was very kind to me, and I appreciated her kindness. It was awe-inspiring to touch all those objects redolent of old times, to sniff the powdered silver left on them by history. I was also impressed with the eating habits of the English Court. At five o'clock they served tea with tiny sandwiches, as tiny as rose petals. Generally, their portions are much smaller and healthier than those of the Germans or the Romanians, both of whom have very large stomachs. I learned a lot during this trip, and more than anything, I learned that we shouldn't rush to judgment because there is a lot we don't know about people from foreign countries.

The Chronicler: Apparently, the tradition of those tiny five o'clock sandwiches has survived because even HM Queen Elizabeth used to eat and serve one-inch cucumber sandwiches from which the crust had been removed. Hence, the expression "cool as a five o'clock sandwich." Just kidding. But speaking of sandwiches, there is another American, Julie Montagu, who has married a British nobleman, Viscount of Hinchingbrooke, a descendant of the Earl of Sandwich. A different type of American than Meghan Markle: natural, hard-working, appreciating the chance of being accepted into the British aristocracy and using it to preserve its patrimony. Someone could do an anthropological study of American society just by comparing the two.

Queen Marie: I think we should confine our study to Romanian society.

Part Two

Queen Marie

"Life is like a great puzzle made up of but small bits: at the outset we are little interested in the pattern it makes … Then there comes a moment when all the pieces fit into the puzzle and it suddenly lies complete before us: a picture—We gaze—and understand."
—Marie, Queen of Romania, *Later Chapters of My Life*

Chapter 5

In which We Learn of Kings and Queens of Yore and How Their Lives are Intertwined with Ours

Queen Marie: Seventy-seven years. That's how long it took for my heart to come home. My poor heart, which has survived so much, including my own death.

On November 3rd, 2015, after years of demands and negotiations with the Romanian authorities, the Royal House of Romania was given back the tiny silver box containing my embalmed heart, which had been kept hidden since 1970 in the deposit of the National Museum of History, at the order of the then Communist Prime Minister, Ion Gheorghe Maurer. To avoid a diplomatic scandal, the Prime Minister had ordered the transfer after the mayor of Brasov had taken upon himself two years earlier to open the marble sarcophagus that housed the jewelry box in which my heart had been placed according to my instructions. Like all small men in a position of power who are compelled to bring everything around them to the level of their own smallness, the mayor did not fear God's wrath. He wanted to see a Queen's heart, so he opened the sarcophagus. He thought that by getting so close to royalty some of it would brush off onto him. Funny how the Communists never miss an occasion to ennoble themselves. Well, this indignity has passed too, for everything passes. No one knows what the future will bring, and it is my experience that things usually resolve in the least expected manner. I requested in my will for my heart to be removed from my chest and placed inside a crystal globe, which in turn was going to be put in a golden box adorned with precious stones and the coats of arms of the three Romanian provinces—the box I had received as a gift from the Society of Romanian Aristocratic Ladies upon my arrival in my adoptive country in 1893. I chose as my eternal resting place the Stella Maris chapel in Balcic. My Fata Morgana. I couldn't know at the time that a mere two years later our Cadrilater would be taken by the Bulgarians, and with it, my dream Palace, the dreamhouse I had built there on the shore. The Romanian authorities had to negotiate with the Bulgarians to bring my heart back. It was decided that my heart should be kept at Bran Castle because the latter had been offered to me by the City of Brașov after Transylvania was united with the two big provinces that formed Romania at the time, Wallachia and Moldova.

All my life I was obsessed with the creation of an Ideal House, a house that meant more than a living space, no matter how cozy, and which represented a sublimation of my desire to set roots in my country of adoption. *Creating* houses was an artistic genre of mine, in which I reveled as soon as I was liberated from the authority of King Carol I and Queen Elisabeta. As long as I was under their yoke, all my creative powers had to be contained, even though the Queen was an artist and a poetess herself. Yes, Queen Elisabeta wrote under the pen name Carmen Sylva, and at her court one could meet some of the greatest artists of the time, but also some of the most bizarre and absurd characters I have ever encountered, for Carmen Sylva was, whatever one might think of her qualities and faults, an immensely original woman. She saw herself as some kind of majestic tragedienne, always dressed in white or black, always surrounded by a throng of worshiping women, and the artists she invited to perform were a curious assortment of uneven talents and motley social backgrounds, from princes and royal-blooded characters, to witty, beautiful women from Romania's nobility, to eccentric European aristocrats, to middle-class Romanian intellectuals and artists, to gypsy fiddlers and old crones picked on the capital's streets. For this reason, she often found herself in dubious situations, being taken advantage of by all kinds of fraudulent characters, which made the King furious. One couldn't imagine two people less alike. This was not, however, the cause of our disagreements. The reason we couldn't see eye to eye was because both Aunty (the Queen) and Uncle (the King) had decided that they should be in control of our lives: we were not allowed to have any friends because Uncle was afraid that the constant intrigues that plagued the country's politics would spill into our lives. Later, when we had children, it was decided that the King and Queen would supervise their education, a decision that was at the core of our arguments and which had dire consequences in our lives. True, in all royal households, the Monarch is, in principle, in charge of the education of all royal children, and He is the legal custodian of His descendants in line to the throne. Even today, the British Monarch is said to be the legal custodian of Prince William's children. But this is only on paper. In reality, the royal couples are allowed to raise their children as they please. This was not so in our case.

Please don't misunderstand me. We loved our King and Queen. But life under them was very austere for a Crown Princess who'd come from a different country, had no friends and was judged by unfriendly eyes from all directions. As in a story by Poe, the eyes of the crowds surrounding me followed me everywhere. Oh, how I dreaded those eyes in my youth! It is the fate of every princess who comes as a bride to a new country—it seems that it is more common for a Prince, rather than a Princess, to journey over hill and dale (*peste munți și văi*) to find his fated one. Think of Princess Mary of Denmark (now

Queen), who'd come all the way from her native Tasmania; of Princess (she too now Queen) Maxima of the Netherlands, originally from Argentina; and yes, of the Duchess of Sussex, formerly known as Meghan Markle. By contrast, a male commoner, half-American, half-British, Christopher O'Neal, who has entered the Royal Family of Sweden by marrying Princess Madeleine, is someone no one could care less about. Why this is so I am not sure; my own guess is that women are more pleasant to watch, their clothes more interesting than those of men and their body shapes more appealing. And when the status of a beautiful woman is enhanced by a title, the crowds go crazy with excitement, as if drunk on some magic potion. It is both a blessing and a curse—ask Meghan Markle. In its most extreme form, the adoration of the People is channeled into a new shape, a shape that is eventually turned into its very opposite, Absolute Resentment. This is an Idol's fate: to be a mirror of this perverse dynamic between adoration and hatred. The greater the adoration, the greater the hatred. When in May 2018 the entire globe had become a huge pink candy of lavish, uncontained, sugary praise for the "Disney Princess"—

The Chronicler: "Disney Princess," a term—if I may interrupt your Majesty—certain American tabloids used not mockingly, as one might think, but in earnest, as if any self-respecting woman would wish to be labeled in this way, a term that is a reflection of the young women working for these magazines and of the ideal they hold in their minds.

Queen Marie: Indeed. But what puzzled me the most is that the closest association these Americans have with the institution of the monarchy is Disney. For us Europeans, royalty means tradition and continuity, that is, the very opposite of the values embraced by most Americans, in particular the American Princess.

The Chronicler: Indeed. Remember the cover of the special issue of *Vogue* she curated, called "Change"? For an American, "change" is positive by definition. Americans call this "progressivism," when in fact they should call it "Americanism."

Queen Marie: I was talking about the eyes obsessed with princesses coming from faraway lands, and I digressed in order to make a point. Let us return to the story of the seventeen-year-old princess who was born at Eastwell, Kent, England, in the fall of 1875, to Queen Victoria's second son, the Duke Alfred of Edinburgh, and to a mother of Russian origin, the Great Duchess Alexandrovna, the only daughter of Tsar Alexander II: Princess Maria Alexandra Victoria, the couple's second child—I, Maria. A princess with metallic blue eyes and long, blond hair generously cascading over her shoulders, who had grown up surrounded by love, in the company of her siblings: her older brother, Alfred, who would die at a young age of venereal disease, and her younger sisters: Victoria Melita (nicknamed Ducky), Alexandra Victoria (Sandra) and Beatrice (Baby Bee).

When the princess came of age, young men began to swarm around her, though even as a child, her male playmates had courted and admired her. A freckled eight-year-old Winston Churchill had declared that he wanted to marry her, and her first cousin, George, the future King George V, who served in the Royal Navy at Malta under the command of his uncle, the Duke of Edinburgh, when the young princess herself lived there with her family between 1886-1889, was known by all of Europe's royal households to be in love with her. These are simply anecdotes I now find amusing and believe that my readers too will find entertaining. I, for one, don't believe I have any role in what people call "my beauty"—wherever it may come from, my parents or the good Lord, this beauty is part of me on par with my other traits. I find it strange when women are proud or even full of themselves because of their looks, as if they had any merit in them. I find even stranger the opposite inclination in today's world, of pretending that it is somehow inappropriate to notice one's physical appearance. I should note that this is something happening today in English-speaking countries. In Latin countries, especially in a country like Romania, at the other end of Europe, people are very exuberant and eager to either compliment one on one's looks, or, on the contrary, make fun of them. Like the French, the Romanians are cynical, outspoken, and have no problem telling you what they think. So, when the seventeen-year-old British Princess arrived in their midst, she was constantly complimented on her looks, which, in the beginning, embarrassed her a little, but eventually, she got used to it. The Romanians were proud of their princess's beauty, as if it were a national asset. As for me, I have always been attracted to Beauty in all its forms, whether in nature or humans, and when I couldn't find it around me, I tried to create beautiful objects to compensate for its lack. The most powerful memories from my childhood are of beautiful princesses and princes from our family. I remember wanting to kneel in front of Tante Alix and kiss her hand as a sign of adoration for her beauty. Alexandra, Princess of Denmark, whom we called Aunt Alix, was married to the Prince of Wales—Queen Victoria's second child and future King Edward VII (Uncle Bertie). She was one of the most glamorous and beautiful women of her time, bringing to mind a rare orchid or an aromatic rose, radiating unsurpassable charm, always elegant, with a golden bracelet in the shape of a snake perennially circling her left arm, a fascinating rare stone set in the snake's eye.

I shall always cherish the memory of the Princess of Wales dressed in a long red velvet gown, as she entered our nursery while we children took our bath, a dreamy apparition that left me spellbound. Fascinated by the emerald stone that glared with a snake's hypnotic coldness, I would take the Princess's hand in mine and, like a bewitched lover, would slowly caress my face with it, then, pushing the hand away from me, admire the stone whose shimmer, reflected in the bathwater, it too resplendent with the light coming from the candle, submerged us all in its liquid-green luster. I confess that, in my youth, it is the Princess of Wales I used to style my hair after by curling it on my forehead. Ironically, Aunt Alix would play a role many years later in the failed marriage proposal between me and her second son, George, when she showed herself less than enthusiastic because, apparently, she disliked the German education I had received at Coburg, where we had moved after Malta. I should add that, at the time, I had no idea that George wanted to marry me. We were close, yes, and he had expressed his feelings for me numerous times, but when it came to marriage, young girls were kept entirely in the dark, and the parents, together with the young man, arranged everything behind the future bride's back. Usually, they would set up a "chance" encounter between the two young people, and if the two seemed to like each other, they continued their machinations behind closed doors. What I didn't know at the time is that George had proposed, and Mother had refused. Why would Mother refuse such an offer, which was considered by all a great prospect, is something that has been discussed by many royal biographers, and it is time that I too shed some light on it. There are things one cannot talk openly about for many reasons, mainly because other people are involved in the story and their feelings might get hurt, which is why I never broached the subject until now. It has been said that Mother was strongly opposed to the marriage because the Russian Orthodox Church, to which she was so devoted, forbids marriages between first cousins. There is some truth to this, but as Hannah Pakula points out in her biography, both marriages of my sister Ducky were to a first cousin. The truth is that

Mother was a very proud woman, a woman who had grown up at the most sumptuous royal court of Europe, where she had been treated with a respect and reverence far surpassing those given to royals in the Constitutional monarchies of Western Europe. When she came to England as a young bride, she was very disappointed and had a hard time adjusting. I've heard stories of rebellion among her servants who were forced to treat her with the same deference accorded the Queen. Of course, that didn't sit well with anyone, especially the Queen, who was furious when the Tsar asked her to let his daughter use the title of "Her Imperial Highness" in addition to the customary "Her Royal Highness." (This may, in fact, be the reason why Queen Victoria declared herself Queen-Empress two years later.) There was a constant power struggle between the Queen and Mother, and so, when Mother saw that the Queen wanted me to marry George, she concocted the plan of offering my hand to Ferdinand, the Crown Prince of Romania, because she couldn't stand the idea of letting the Court of England decide my future. One can't help but notice the cruel irony here: out of resentment for her mother-in-law and wishing to prove that her family was worthy of more respect than it received from the English, Mother ended up ruining the prospect of an alliance with the future King of England. Everybody was shocked that she would choose the heir of a minor East-European monarchy over the House of Hanover, and Queen Victoria expressed her puzzlement in no uncertain words: "The Country is very insecure & the immorality of the Society of Bucharest *quite awful.*"

The Chronicler: Speaking of Queen Victoria, may I be allowed to interrupt Your Majesty with these wise words spoken by none other than Virginia Woolf?

> If we want an example of the difference between
> writing and non-writing we have only to compare

a page of Queen Marie with a page of Queen Victoria. The old Queen was, of course, an author. She was forced by the exigencies of her profession to fill an immense number of pages, and some of these have been printed and bound between covers. But between the old Queen and the English language lay an abyss which no depth of passion and no strength of character could cross. Her works make for very painful reading on that account. She has to express herself in words; but words will not come to her call.

Queen Marie: Very clever of you to flatter me like this. As you must know from spending so much time with royalty, praise works. But I was saying: "A minor East-European country." This was the prevalent opinion at the time, and I later found out that everyone pitied the young and pretty British Princess who was being sent to the end of the world by the Black Sea where the Latin poet Ovid had been exiled two thousand years earlier. And what did *I* think? Well, you can imagine what a seventeen-year-old girl who hasn't been taught anything about life could think. I could barely find the country on a map. And yet, I felt pulled in that direction, pulled by an unseen force that rose from the depths of my childhood that had stored the enchanted memories of our Russian escapades. How could I forget those bewitching times among my Russian relatives, the tall blond uncles smelling of leather and tobacco, the fascinating aunts and cousins in their mesmerizing gowns and opalescent jewelry, the enormous tiaras heavy with diamonds, the emeralds around their swan-like necks, the church incense and the baritone voices of the Orthodox church choir suffusing everything with a sense of inviolable mystery? Never before or after have I heard such powerful music, music that grabbed your soul and lifted it up close to the Realm of the Gods. And when the Russian anthem—the most awe-inspiring anthem ever created—was added to all this, you felt carried on a magic carpet among heavenly clouds. This divine mystery, for me, was embodied by "the East," the enigmatic East my mother had come from, and the "minor East-European country" I was being sent to was, to my innocent and ignorant eyes, but a variation on the same theme.

Once upon a time, there was a faraway kingdom ruled with a firm but fair hand by a King and his Queen. The King, Carol I, whose name harked back to all of Europe's royal families, starting with Charlemagne, left behind the German version of his name, Karl, and the land of his ancestors, to start a new dynasty in a land unfurling between the Black Sea and the Carpathians. Soon after he set foot in his new country, the young king went to fetch himself a bride, and returned with Elizabeth of Wied, a German princess full of romantic exaltation, an eccentric soul fed on poetry and lyric dreams, with an uncommon propensity for tragedy, which often left her suspended half-way between the sublime and the ridiculous. The royal couple was blessed with a single child, a daughter, Maria, whom the gods took away when the girl was barely four: little Itty, as she was nicknamed (from "Little," which she couldn't pronounce), and who died of scarlet fever, was "the only truly beautiful poem" Carmen Sylva had ever written. Itty had been baptized in the Christian Orthodox faith, the Romanian national religion, the first member of the new dynasty to share the country's faith. She was also the first to speak Romanian like a native, which prompted this remark by the King upon her death: "Our child's religion and language are now sacred for us, for every Romanian word shall henceforth remind us of the sweet voice we will never hear again." The bereft couple was left not only childless, but also without an heir to the throne, and so, another heir had to be found. After some search, the heir was found in the person of young Ferdinand, the son of Carol's older brother from the same family, the Hohenzollerns, whose dynastic seat was in Sigmaringen. Ferdinand—Nando—my husband, whom the Romanians now call "*Intregitorul*," "the Unifier," or "the Loyal."

Ferdinand's mother, Antonia, who was born Infanta of Portugal and married Leopold, Prince of Hohenzollern-Sigmaringen, one of the wealthiest men of his time, was famous for her beauty, although when we met, I had a hard time finding in her the cause of all the praise I'd heard about her. When Nando and I got engaged, my mother and I went to meet Queen Elisabeta, whom King Carol had sent in exile to Neuwied because she had behaved in an improper way by playing matchmaker between Ferdinand and her lady in waiting, Elena Văcărescu, with whom Nando had fallen in love. With her fanciful fantasy, the Queen, who often held spiritism and turning-table séances in her salons, had decided that the soul of little Itty had migrated into Elena's chest, and a marriage between her and Crown Prince Ferdinand would not only seal a double alliance between their families, but also a spiritual communion between a native daughter and the Royal Family's German blue blood. When the King discovered his wife's foolishness, he was livid with rage and banished her. The Queen was accused of causing a constitutional crisis because the Romanian constitution stipulated that the members of the Royal Family who were in line to the throne could only marry other royals from foreign countries. The goal of this law was to keep the members of the Royal Family above the many and contorted intrigues of Romania's political life, and to strengthen Romania's position in the world through alliances.

We found ourselves in the middle of the German woods before a gray castle, in an atmosphere reminiscent of the tales of the Brothers Grimm. The Queen's mother welcomed us, followed by a cohort of strange-looking creatures, every one of them lacking some part or vital function of the human body: one an eye, another a leg, yet another an arm, one blind, another deaf, women and men limping about in worn-out garments, as the Princess of Wied—Elisabeta's mother—led the way. The Queen herself was dressed impeccably in white cashmere and welcomed us graciously in her room, propped against a row of white pillows. Later, I found out that the Princess of Wied was a psychic healer and that, when she wasn't entertaining her poor and crippled relations, the Queen liked to invite over musicians, writers and artists. I will say more about this when I get to the part about our new life in Romania, as the Queen's salons were famous, and they deserve to be described in detail.

Now I just want to mention the strange ways of our Lord: this woman who was fated to be my Queen, and whom I succeeded to Romania's throne, could have been … my father's wife. Before my father married Marie, Grand Duchess of Russia, his mother, Queen Victoria, had set her eyes on a German Princess who was none other than … Elizabeth of Wied. Queen Victoria and her entourage had decided that Elizabeth was the best match for her son, and she'd sent him to propose. But when Elizabeth, who valued Art over everything else and suffered from an exacerbated form of romanticism, asked the very young prince—who could play the violin in a serviceable way—to play for her outside under the leafy trees, the prince refused categorically and never proposed.

The Chronicler: Your Majesty, are you sure that it was your father that Queen Victoria wanted to see married to Elizabeth of Wied, and not his older brother, future King Edward VII? It is well known among historians that Queen Victoria tried to match Princess Elizabeth with her older son.

Queen Marie: Of course I'm sure. There is even a corollary to this anecdote: years later, after I'd become Princess of Romania, my father came to pay us a visit and an encounter between him and Queen Elisabeta was unavoidable. Meeting him again after thirty years, the Queen welcomed him with the nervousness of a woman who was rekindling an old flame. She really was quite anxious, as she waited for him reminiscing about his blue eyes and "incredible musical gift," while I tried to prepare her for the arrival of a blasé, alcohol-guzzling middle-aged man who cared more about cigars than the violin.

The Queen organized an outing in the woods, dragging all her guests, some of whom had come for the arrival of the Emperor Franz Joseph of Austro-Hungary, whose visit coincided with that of Father, to a rocky formation, and invited them to take a seat on the rocks, which were quite uncomfortable. The majority of the guests were her usual followers, a gang of eccentric sycophants whom the exalted Queen repeatedly invited to express their admiration for the show they were attending—in this case, a musical performance by a man who happened to be among the Queen's favorites at the time: a painter with angry, rebellious whiskers that covered half of his face, and who, curiously, was not there as a craftsman but as a singer. The man claimed he could sing tenor, baritone or bass, according to requests, and entered the open stage from behind a rock, posing with his saber in a heroic attitude, as if ready to be immortalized by an invisible photographer. Needless to say, the performance was a catastrophe, which didn't deter the Queen's cohort from displaying its usual encomiastic responses—sighs, applause, more sighs—but, before the Queen had a chance to raise her arms in her usual gesture of victory, and then clasp her hands near her heart in her customary, adulatory fashion, Father grabbed my right arm and dragged me down the path, as he vented and raged against the impostor-singer.

"Such a talented young man!" the Queen said later that afternoon, when she summarized the events of the day. "He was such a talented young man! Whatever happened to his talent? Such a pity."

I thought she was referring to the unfortunate singer—although he wasn't *that* young—but no, she was talking about Father.

The Chronicler: Well, it appears that Queen Victoria may have played matchmaker for both her sons, and when she didn't succeed with the oldest, she tried again with your father. She really seemed to have liked our Queen Elisabeta.

Queen Marie: *If* the story about Edward VII is true. (Whispering): Maybe *she* spread that rumor.

*

Like all kings of yore, the first thing Carol did after his arrival in the country was to begin the construction of a Royal Palace, and he chose to do so not in the country's capital, Bucharest, but up in the mountains, which reminded him and his bride of the landscape they'd left behind in their homeland. This is how the construction of Peleş Castle was begun a year after the passing of little Itty, at Sinaia, the small town with a singsong name, in fact, a village at the time, named after Mount Sinai, *See-na-ja,* a castle the King came to appreciate so much he almost never left its grounds during the months he was in residence. He stayed there every year during the summer months all the way until November, when he returned to Cotroceni Palace in Bucharest. One might say that Peleş was his Balmoral, but, in fact, it was more than that. The King was enormously proud of his castle, and it's there that he gave his last breath.

When the Princess of Edinburgh came to Romania in 1893 as a young bride, she found Peleş Castle dark and cold, exactly the opposite of what her descendant, Crown Princess Margareta of Romania, declared in 2009 when the Romanian state returned the stolen castle to her father, King Mihai I. "I thought it would be dark and cold, but no, it is quite cozy," Margareta declared. Compared to medieval castles, it may, indeed, be true that Peleş is "cozy," but our princess was hungry for light and freedom, and this castle was a golden prison that a good but austere king had built for the Royal Family.

There were three Sinaias, but only one was close to my heart: there was Uncle's Sinaia, the place where a mighty castle had been erected, a castle full of treasures and invaluable collections, in whose halls a somber and rightful King could be seen pacing to and fro; there was the Sinaia that belonged to the high society, that of the fashionable ladies in colorful hats and fancy dresses, a world of gossip and idleness I had no interest in; and there was the Sinaia of the surrounding mountains, of the thick woods and roaring rivers, a magic realm under whose charm I had fallen, and whose paths I got to know by heart during long, enchanting rides on my favorite horse, either alone or in Nando's company. Sometimes, my solitary rides crossed those of the King, and then we continued together on horseback, a circumstance that contributed to our getting to know each other. Eventually, we both came to appreciate, and even love, one another.

It has been observed that, while I mention numerous times in the three volumes of *The Story of My Life* how desperately in love with me my husband was, I never claim that *I* was in love with him. To make such a claim would have been a lie. I did, however, have great affection for my Nando, and during the time of our engagement, I went, like all young girls, through a period of infatuation. I was attracted to his boyish looks, which, in combination with his intense, almost pathological shyness, triggered in me a maternal desire to protect him in spite of the fact that he was ten years older than me. I had been taught by my mother that the most important skill a woman must possess in high society is the art of conversation, and I had been trained to make small talk, although at the time I got engaged I was so young I hadn't had much chance to practice it, as I hadn't yet made my debut in society. Sitting next to my fiancé at various social events and seeing how much he struggled to express himself, I felt sorry for him. Later, after King Carol's death, I witnessed many a painful scene in which poor Nando stood paralyzed with fear among his guests, diplomats and politicians, incapable of uttering a word, or else, stammered incomprehensibly, and created an embarrassing spectacle for everyone. As you may know, when one is in the Monarch's presence, one is bound by protocol to wait for the Monarch to open his mouth first, or close it last, in the case of official dinners—no one is allowed to eat any more after the Monarch has stopped eating. This can generate rather delicate situations if the Monarch happens to be, like my Ferdinand, painfully shy and socially clumsy.

I remember how once, at some political event where all the ministers were present, I was wearing a splendid violet gown on which I had pinned a tiny bouquet of violets near my heart, and everybody was complimenting me on my attire. We were both greeting those present, who were lined up in two rows, and I was shaking hands with those on the left, while the King was working the right side. I was at the end of my row, with my back half-turned to the King, when I noticed with the corner of my eye that he and the gentleman in front of him were staring at each other, while sweat dripped from the gentleman's brow. I took a closer look and heard the King make some sounds that were barely human, after which the face of the gentleman before him blushed violently, and then the King made another attempt to speak, letting out a hysterical giggle, a sound like a broken mechanism. I hurried up to save the situation, shook the man's hand and, giving him a large smile, congratulated him on his recent success—he had been elected to some kind of important political position for the first time. The man was so relieved to be freed from the embarrassing circumstance that he ended up making an almost ninety-degree bow in front of me, before kissing my hand.

The Chronicler: Ferdinand's extreme shyness was inherited by his grandson, King Mihai I, the last ruling king of the Romanians. After Mihai was allowed by the government to return to Romania in 1997, fifty years after his forced abdication, he could occasionally be seen at various public events together with his wife, Ana, a cheerful, unpretentious woman, who could put anyone at ease, the exact opposite of her husband, who was, like your husband, very clumsy in social situations. However, unlike his grandfather, who had been described as "ugly" by certain ungracious tongues—mostly because of his protruding ears, which were set perpendicular to his head, thus being a constant source of mockery in the press—, Mihai was "as handsome as an actor," even in his later years. Tall and straight, with a posture that could only be described as "regal," he would enter the hall where the event was to take place exactly at the top of the hour, not a minute late—a habit that ran counter everything the Romanians stood for. They say that a few seconds before he entered a room, a thick veil of silence descended over it, as if Divinity itself announced its presence, and once he was there, with his commanding figure, a shiver ran through all those present. It may have been because he had been exiled, it may have been because he was the last king, it may have been a compensation after half a century of Communism—whatever the reason, for the 21st-century Romanians, King Mihai I was a quasi-divine creature. I know at least one famous Romanian artist, who has publicly stated that for him, after Jesus Christ, King Mihai was the most important moral authority. So, everybody stood in perfect, awe-filled silence, while the King, full of divine grace but short on human grace, moved mechanically from person to person, his expression absent, his mouth clenched, like an impenetrable, sublime Sphinx.

Timid and reserved, King Mihai rarely opened his mouth, and when he did, he spoke as if he had some kind of speech impediment, or, as some bad-mouthed Romanians would say, "as if his mouth was full of plums." His impairment was both a question of form—manifested in the physicality of the muffled sounds he uttered—and content. He was the kind of person who was incapable of making small talk, and he only managed to express himself with rigor and clarity when he recounted military actions—his, or those of the Romanian army. Like his German predecessors, he was a military man at heart, a man who had acted with unparalleled bravery when at the age of twenty-two, he ordered the Romanian army, until then fighting alongside the Nazis, to take up arms against its ally. Unlike his father, King Carol II, who had been nicknamed "the King of Culture" because he was a strong supporter of the humanities, a man famous for the ease with which he absorbed the most difficult literary and philosophical theories, King Mihai had no claims to intellectual pursuits, and, according to his own words, had never found any valuable life lesson in any book except the Bible. Hannah Pakula, your most astute biographer, has noted that a characteristic of the Hohenzollerns is that every male crown prince rebels against his antecessor, a rebellion that occurs even at a genetic level: unlike his bashful, introvert and always obedient father (Ferdinand), Carol II was arrogant, overconfident in his abilities, completely devoid of respect for his parents, and incapable of self-control and discipline. By contrast, Mihai I, his son, was modest, self-tempered, a man with his heart on his sleeve, or rather, in his eyes, always dangerously close to shedding tears, especially when one lauded the deeds of the Romanian army or when he was himself praised. King Carol II was a womanizer, a man who had deserted the army for a woman during the Great War; King Mihai I was a one-woman man, a man who banned his own grandson from the Royal Family for having fathered an illegitimate child—a transgression that surely reminded him of his own father. Of course, rumors abound about the "real" cause of the banishment, and the Romanians being big consumers of conspiracy theories, there are those who say that—

Queen Marie: Oh, let us return to our story, the story of the beginning of our dynasty, the Royal House of Romania! You keep interrupting me!

Once upon a time there was a Prince who came from the fierce and orderly realm of the Germans to a charming but chaotic land. Upon arrival, intrigued by the living conditions in his new kingdom, the Prince asked to see his palace, and his men pointed to a rather average mansion in front of which a couple of pigs played excitedly in a mudhole where the road was supposed to be. This was the beginning of the longest reign in the history of the country, forty-eight years devoted by the King to his new kingdom, which started, appropriately enough for someone shocked to be welcomed by a mudhole instead of a road, with the construction of the country's first railway.

Chapter 6

In Which I Talk About
What It Means To Be Queen

"I need to be seen to be believed."
—HM Queen Elizabeth II

"Apa trece, pietrele ramân."
"Waters are fleeting, but stones are
forever."
—Romanian proverb

Queen Marie: On the morning of October 10th, 1914 …

The Chronicler: Exactly 105 years before these words were written …

Queen Marie: On the morning of October 10th, 1914, I was awoken by an unexpected call from Prince Barbu Știrbey.

"You are Queen," he said.

Regină.

The previous night, King Carol I had died at Sinaia. Since then, more than a century has passed, millions of people have died, and millions more have been born. Everything endowed with the gift of life passes. As the Romanian saying goes, "Waters are fleeting, but stones are forever." In Romania, the stones' everlasting life is best embodied by monasteries, edifices of modest size that can usually be found in rural areas and whose original architectural design, a combination of Byzantine and local styles, are a joy to the eye and a balm to the heart.

According to tradition, King Carol was buried at the Monastery of Curtea de Argeş, located in the southern part of the country, a famous monastery founded in the 16th-century by the *Voïevod* Neagoe Basarab. This monastery, whose restoration caused quite a few disagreements among specialists and lay people alike, is shadowed by the famous legend of Manole, a craftsman employed by Neagoe Basarab to build "the most beautiful" monastery ever erected. The legend says that everything Manole and his apprentices built by day was destroyed by a dark force at night, and so, each day they had to start all over again.

One night, Manole dreams that in order for the construction to last, a living soul must be sacrificed: the first woman to appear on the path with a snack for her husband or brother shall be walled inside the edifice itself. Only then shall the walls remain erect; only then shall the stones' eternal beauty shine through the centuries' gray wisdom—when the artist sacrifices what he holds most dear. The next day, Manole sees his pregnant wife, Ana, advancing on the path toward the monastery. He prays to God to bring floods and winds to stop her, but nothing can deter her: she is the first woman to arrive and she will be entombed alive in the monastery's walls, together with her unborn child. After the sacrifice, Manole finishes the construction of the most beautiful monastery ever erected, and when the *Voïevod* who ordered its creation asks him whether he could build another one like it, he proudly answers that he could build another one even more beautiful. Hearing this, the *Voïevod*, who wants to own the most beautiful edifice in the world, orders that the scaffolding be taken away. Manole and his men are left stranded on the roof, so he puts together some makeshift wings with which he attempts to fly. But, like Icarus, who flew too close to the sun, Manole got too close to Absolute Beauty, and his wings cannot save him. He cannot save himself, but his construction shall last forever, like the fountain gracing today the spot where Manole has fallen and died, and where a spring instantly surged from the ground.

According to historians, the legend—which was recorded for the first time by the famous writer and educator Vasile Alecsandri, a regular at Queen Elisabeta's salons—is based on a real event, and every character in it has a correspondent in real life: apparently, Neagoe Basarab, who ordered this construction, may have acted at the order of the Turkish Sultan, Bajazid II. Basarab hired a famous Armenian craftsman called Manolj, who was so envied by his colleagues and the other apprentices and craftsmen working under his orders that all his work was sabotaged by them. As for Ana, it seems that this was the real name of Manole's wife, and that she died in unclear circumstances due to the jealousy of Manole's apprentices. It is suspected that she was, indeed, walled up in the monastery's walls.

Today, the Monastery Curtea de Argeș stands eternal in all its dark, night-suffused glory with its white, laced towers, and Manole's fountain by its side. On its grounds are buried Neagoe Basarab, Mircea the Elder, King Carol I, his wife (Elisabeta), King Ferdinand, myself (albeit without my heart, now placed in the Golden Salon of Pelișor Castle), King Carol II, whose body was brought from Estoril by the Romanian Royal Family and reburied in 2003, Queen Ana—who has never reigned in her husband's country, and yet, in 2016 was given the first royal funeral after my own funeral in 1938—and my grandson, King Mihai I, buried with much pomp in December 2017. As of this moment—October 10th, 2019—, preparations are under way for the repatriation of the body of Queen Mother Elena, Carol II's wife, who died in Lausanne in the early 1980s and will soon take her place next to the other members of the Royal Family. In order to accommodate all the above, a new cathedral has been built next to the old monastery.

Sic Transit Gloria Mundi. In 1990, immediately after the fall of Communism, when King Mihai asked the new Romanian government to allow him to enter the country after his forced exile, he specifically requested permission to visit the graves of his ancestors. After Crown Princess Margareta had a personal discussion with Prime Minister Petre Roman, the request was grudgingly approved, and the exiled King came accompanied by his wife, Ana, Princesses Margareta and Sofia, a French photographer, a British bodyguard (Mihai was too poor to afford his own bodyguards, and this one was being "lent" to him by the British Royal Family) and his personal secretary. He was received with warmth and reverence by the puzzled airport staff, who could vaguely remember from their precarious history lessons that the country had once had a king. On his way to Curtea de Argeş, however, Mihai was stopped by a barrage of three police cars and about two dozen civilian cars filled with angry "proletarians" (the Communist custom of staging proletarian anger was slow to die). The policemen surrounded his car armed with semi-automatic weapons and ordered the King to leave the country at once because he had entered it illegally.

That was a lie, of course. Mihai had entered the country perfectly legally, with his passport on which he was identified as Michael de Roumanie. "The 'former' King has changed his name," declared the Prime Minister, alluding to the fact that during the first years of his exile, Mihai had used the last name Hohenzollern. It may seem somewhat strange to see the name of a country as one's last name, but there is a clear explanation for this. Members of royal families who are in direct line to the throne have no last name, and if the need arises, they use their titles or a geographical location as their name: Prince William of Great Britain was known as William Wales when he worked as an ambulance helicopter pilot, and his eldest child, George, was known as George Cambridge in school. When my own son, Nicolae, was banished from the

Royal Family by his brother Carol, he was given the last name Brana after Bran Castle. And then, Carol himself left Romania as Carol Caraiman, after the mountain peak with the same name. At the beginning of his exile in Switzerland, King Mihai attempted to convince the Swiss authorities that he didn't have a last name, but the republicans would have none of it: he was a citizen like everybody else and was supposed to have a last name. And so, he took the name Hohenzollern, although historical circumstances prevented him from doing so. The Hohenzollerns had cut ties with the Romanian Royal Family when on August 27th, 1916, after two years of neutrality, my husband, King Ferdinand, took the monumental decision to declare war on the Austro-Hungarian Empire, thus becoming a hero for the Romanians and a traitor for his own family. His own cousin, Willy, the Kaiser—

The Chronicler: Or Billy, as you spitefully call him in your war diary: "Billy the Kaiser is strutting around our country, as if through his own property." You are referring to his visit in the summer of 1917 after the country had been occupied by the Germans. Vowing to unseat Ferdinand, who was now his mortal enemy, the Kaiser took the time to pay his homage to Carol I's tomb at Curtea de Argeş.

Queen Marie: Willy or Billy the Kaiser struck Ferdinand's name from the House of Hohenzollern and declared him dead. It was the most difficult moment of Ferdinand's life, he, so obedient by temperament, so fearful of disappointing his relatives, so hesitant in taking any kind of decision. As he put it during the Crown Council, he was first of all King of Romania, and second, a member of the Hohenzollern family, and to do his duty he had to "vanquish himself."

The Chronicler: I dare say that this betrayal by the King of his own family in favor of the Romanian people is the very foundation of the sense of identity of the modern Romanian citizen: the Other (the Foreigner, the Westerner) is not only a part of who we are, he is our *best* part. Used to the constant betrayal of leaders issued from their own ranks, the Romanians, who value family ties above all else, appreciate Ferdinand so much because he put country first and family second. Of course, I am talking here of the urban Romanian, not of those from the countryside.

But to come back to our story: aware that taking the name Hohenzollern was going against history, King Mihai took the decision to relinquish the name of the dynasty to which he belonged, and at some point during his exile changed his name and that of his daughters to "de Roumanie." Thus, the old habit of referring to kings by the name of the region where they came from was consecrated in law by the Swiss authorities. A Hohenzollern by blood, Mihai spoke German with difficulty and obvious displeasure. Like the Windsors, the former Hohenzollerns want nothing to do with their German roots. Aside from the obvious reason—the two world wars—, the Romanian Royal Family became more anglophile not only because of you, but also, in the case of King Mihai, because of his mother, who had been raised and educated in the English tradition.

Queen Marie: On October 18th, 2019, the body of Queen Mother Elena of Romania, former Princess of Greece and Denmark, wife of King Carol II and mother of King Mihai I, was exhumed from the cemetery of Lausanne where it had been buried in November 1982, and, after being brought back to Romania in a military airplane and being offered an official welcome at the airport by government officials, was driven to Elisabeta Palace from where the Queen had left the country on January 3rd, 1948, together with her son, after his forced abdication. From Elisabeta Palace, the official car convoy drove to Curtea de Argeş where the Queen Mother's coffin, draped in her standard and carried on their shoulders by the officers of Mihai the Brave 30th Guards Brigade, was eventually placed in the New Royal Cathedral next to her son's vault. The New Royal Cathedral now hosts the bodies of Queen Ana, King Mihai and Queen Mother Elena, all next to one another, while King Carol II is placed across from them. The body of King Carol II has been itself recently reburied after sixteen years spent in an improvised chapel on the grounds of the Monastery Curtea de Argeș, the old monastery where the first kings and queens of our dynasty are buried. Carol II was repatriated in 2003 from Portugal where he died in 1953 and where he was given a state funeral because of his blood connection to Portugal's Royal Family. I loved Carol dearly, but when all is said and done, he was a bitter disappointment—my heart never stopped loving him, but my mind loathed this man who treated everyone miserably: his wife, by exiling her; his son, by keeping him away from his mother; me, by surrounding me with spies, taking from me all my trustworthy courtiers and friends, depriving me of a royal office and turning the army and the Romanian people against me with evil gossip—thus compromising the work of my entire life, the destiny of our dynasty and our country.

The Chronicler: Speaking of Carol and of your other son, Nicky, I always wondered what conclusions could be drawn from the fact that the two male royal children in line to the throne, the first to be born and raised on Romanian soil, relinquished their duty, and both for a woman—actually, in the case of Carol, for two women. It clearly says something about the way they were educated, the courtiers they were surrounded by, and the teachers they had. It means that in Romania it's impossible to raise royals the way they do it in the other constitutional monarchies because once these imported princes go native, or as they say in Romanian, *se împământenesc*, all the ancestral bad habits come back.

Queen Marie: Maybe what this means is that the males are less apt than the females to do their duty because they are incapable of resisting the sirens' calls. I am not aware of any woman who has abdicated. Even at the British court, King Edward abdicated to marry the American, twice-divorced Wallis Simpson with whom they are now comparing Meghan Markle. Speaking of whom, did you notice how fast she and Harry decided to "abdicate" and move to LA? After they left Great Britain for Vancouver, it took them less than three months to move from Canada to LA—one would say that this was Meghan's intention from the beginning. Why would a bride refuse to invite her own family to her wedding and, instead, invite this famous American journalist, what's-her-name, Opera or something, whom she didn't even know?

The Chronicler: Because she was ashamed of her family, and for someone who grew up in Hollywood, like her (her father was an award-winning lighting director for several television series), the supreme success means being in the company of Hollywood "royalty." We all want to be recognized by those who mean something to us. This is why Meghan wanted from the beginning to return to America: to show who she was to all those who counted.

But let's get back to our story: the repatriation of the body of Queen Mother Elena. As always at these kinds of events—funerals, *pomeni* or repatriations of deceased members of the Royal House—, the former Prince Nicolae, né Nicholas de Roumanie Medforth-Mills and his wife, Alina, were also present. Contrary to the belief of most Romanians, Nicolae was not "born a prince." A grandchild is not automatically a prince unless he is the child of the Crown Prince(ss), which is not the case here.

Queen Marie: This is, by the way, the reason why Prince Harry's son, Archie—who, when the interview with the American journalist took place, was not a grandchild, but a great-grandchild of the reigning Monarch—was not made a prince, and not the deceitful reason given by Meghan, who suggested that it may have been "racism." This rule was established by King George V in 1917, and it is impossible for Prince Harry not to have been aware of it. According to this rule, Archie was supposed to become a prince once Charles became King.

The Chronicler: Which is precisely what happened. Both Harry's children are now princes. On the occasion of Lilibet's christening in March 2023, the Sussexes used the titles of "prince" and "princess" to refer to their children, thus forcing the hand of Buckingham Palace to make the modification on their website. The couple who claimed to start an independent life an ocean away from the British monarchy and never loses an opportunity to voice its criticism of it, has chosen to give these titles to their little children. As everyone knows, the late Queen's daughter, Princess Anne, chose not to accept titles for her children because she wanted them to have a more normal life. Other members of the Royal Family, driven by the same desire to protect their offspring, have chosen to let them decide at the age of eighteen whether to use their titles or not. And what do you know? The couple who invoked the need to protect their children from the media and their desire for privacy among their reasons to leave Great Britain, has opted for precisely the opposite.

Queen Marie: King Charles had the option to take those titles away from the Sussexes' children, which is what most people thought he would do, given his son's behavior, but I knew he wouldn't. Whether he didn't want to be seen as vengeful or whether he wanted to keep the door open for the prodigal son, he chose not to do it.

The Chronicler: Other, more cynical people believe that there could be a third reason. At this point, the Sussexes' conduct is seen as blackmail by most monarchists. Let us use our titles, let us monetize them, or else … more "revelations" are in the works. As everyone knows, Harry signed a contract for more than one book.

But the House of Romania is not the House of Britain. Nicolae was given the title of Royal Highness and made a Prince by King Mihai in a public ceremony at the age of twenty-five, and had the same title revoked by the time he was thirty.

At the ceremony of repatriation of Queen Mother Elena, young Nicolae and his wife Alina were present, having arrived before Her Majesty Margareta, her husband, Prince Radu, and her two sisters, Princesses Sofia and Maria. Some witnesses claim that there are signs that the conflict between the (now former) Prince and the rest of the family may be softening because Ion Tuca, the Director of the Royal House, was spotted talking to him while they were all waiting for the senior royals. They hope that Nicolae has finally realized that the Romanians who have given him advice were misguided, to say the least, if not downright plotting to take Margareta down—no surprise that a misogynist society like my country of birth has a hard time accepting an institution led by a woman—but I believe that this is merely wishful thinking. The Constitution preceding the Communist takeover was based on the Salic Law, which meant that only men could ascend to the throne. All constitutional monarchies with similar laws, with the exception of Japan and the Principality of Monaco, have changed them after WWII in order to reflect societal changes about women, and the countries in which the monarchy has been abolished, such as Romania, would have done the same, if given a chance. But the ambiguous situation of a successor to the throne in the absence of said throne (the throne disappeared quite literally during the Communist regime, only to be found a few years ago) has given rise to all kinds of naysayers who claim that, if we were to follow the Salic Law, it is Prince Nicolae who should be the rightful successor—an absurd and illogical claim, given that Margareta and Nicolae are from different generations, and that Nicolae couldn't be a monarch before his mother, Princess Elena, is Queen. But if Margareta cannot be Queen, neither can Elena, which means that her successor, Nicolae, is equally prohibited from ascending to the throne. If the Romanian Parliament were to reinstate the monarchy in its Salic form, they would have to bring another (foreign) Royal Family—this is what those who claim that Nicolae's place has been usurped by Margareta don't understand. But, of course, reason and logic have nothing to do here. In fact, this is not very different from the circumstances of King Charles, whose detractors would have liked him to be skipped in favor of his son, Prince William. In both cases, many of the detractors simply prefer a new generation of young, energetic, modern, and last but not least, beautiful royals.

Queen Marie: Indeed, *appearance* plays a huge part here: the appearance of beauty, the appearance of honesty, the appearance of identifying oneself with Romania's destiny. I know something about this, having once been the face of Romania. Appearances can be deceiving. Those who are so sure that the prince has been removed from the line of succession through an orchestrated plot should first try to understand how royal houses work. Nicolae was most certainly manipulated by certain jealous insiders, frustrated because they were out of favor with the Royal House, a task easy to accomplish with a Swiss-born, British-educated, inexperienced young man who could barely speak Romanian and understood nothing of the country's complex and Byzantine political meanderings when he came to Romania.

The Chronicler: After his banishment, Nicolae dug his hole even deeper by claiming in at least one interview that King Mihai had designated him "as his successor" in November-December 2007. In reality, at the end of December 2007, exactly sixty years after his forced abdication, King Mihai designated his first-born child, Crown Princess Margareta, as his dynastic successor, after having done the same thing in another public, videotaped event, ten years earlier. In *The Fundamental Norms of the Royal House of Romania*, he also listed the other royals in the line of succession: after Crown Princess Margareta, her sister, Princess Elena, her first-born child, Nicolae, and his sister, Elisabeta Karina.

In fact, during the same interview, Nicolae acknowledged that he had been designated third in the line of succession, which contradicts his point that the King chose him on the basis of the 1923 Constitution,[13] which only accepted the accession of males to the throne. If that had been the King's intention, why did he make so many public declarations that his first-born, Margareta, was his direct successor? Why did he ask the Romanian Parliament in his political testament that in case of a restauration of the monarchy, it should modify Romania's 1923 Constitution and allow women on the throne, according to the principle of gender equality of all European countries, to which Romania also adheres? Clearly, not only is this prince—like another prince from Great Britain to whom he has been compared[14]—ignorant of succession rules, but he also has problems with logic. How can you claim that you are "the successor" because only males can accede the throne, while *at the same time*, acknowledge that you are supposed to succeed two other women: your aunt and your mother?! Aside from this, Nicolae didn't even realize he was shooting

---

13. *"Bunicul meu a considerat, a luat după Constituția din 1923. Un băiat a trebuit să fie succesorul, şeful familiei, cum a fost întotdeauna."* Translation: "My grandfather thought, he followed the 1923 Constitution. A boy had to be the successor, the family chief, as has always been."

14. The comparison was made particularly during the nuptials of the couple Nicolae-Alina, which took place on September 30th, 2018 at Sinaia Casino, a mere four months after the grandiose and much-publicized wedding of Meghan and Harry. It is easy to see why: both couples are physically attractive and about the same age. In fact, Nicolae is exactly the same age as Harry. Although he was born in Switzerland, near Geneva, his father was British, and he grew up and was educated in Great Britain. After Prince Harry's "abdication," the comparison between the two couples is even more appropriate. (**The Chronicler**)

himself in the foot when, during the same interview he stated that he isn't even the only one, or the oldest, of King Mihai's grandsons: there is another grandson, who happens to be a month older than Nicolae—Michael, who is Princess Irina's[15] child. The fact that the line of succession follows the order Margareta, Elena, Nicolae, Elisabeta is the best and irrefutable proof that King Mihai chose his successor irrespective of the child's gender, and for Nicolae to state the opposite is an offense to the memory of his grandfather.

In fact, King Mihai had written a letter to his first-born as early as 1986 letting her know that in the event of a change of regime in Romania, he intends to request a change of the succession order from the Parliament. But this whole discussion is, in the end, ridiculous. To all those who believe in the conspiracy theory that Nicolae was removed through a plot, I say: what Monarch in his right mind designates a successor by whispering his wish into his princely ear? If King Mihai had wanted Nicolae as his heir, he would have made this desire known through a *public document*—that much is certain. But there is no such document. On the other hand, there is a very public document signed by King Mihai on August 1st, 2015, which states the following:

I, Mihai I,

As Chief of the Royal House of Romania,
Bound by my obligation to history and to my Family's
descendants, and acting in accordance with my own free will,

DECLARE PUBLICLY

---

15. Irina, King Mihai's third-born daughter, was herself stripped of her title and of her succession rights in August 2013, and received her title back from HM Margareta, the Custodian of the Crown, after the King's death. **(The Chronicler)**

I revoke the title of 'Prince of Romania' and the designation of 'Royal Highness' given to my grandson Nicolae, the son of Princess Elena. I am also excluding Nicolae from the Line of Succession to Romania's Crown. These decisions shall take effect today.

I have taken the above decisions out of consideration for Romania's future when the reign and life of my daughter, Margareta, shall come to an end. The Royal Family and the Romanian society of the future will need a ruler guided by humbleness, well-thought actions, moral principles, respect and constant care for the others.

With the same affection for my grandson, Nicolae, I hope that in the years to come he will find the appropriate manner in which to serve his ideals and enjoy his God-given qualities.

Mihai (Signature)
Aubonne, August 1ˢᵗ, 2015

Queen Marie: We haven't even discussed the main reason Mihai banished Nicolae: before he met his current wife, a very nice young woman, by the way, he allegedly fathered an illegitimate child, just like my Carol—Carol, the biggest disappointment of my life. We shall come back to this story when I speak about my children. The saddest part here is that, by his behavior, Nicolae has managed to prove the pointlessness of a return to monarchy. So far, a major argument for the country's return to monarchy has been the behavior and moral integrity of the Royal House's members in comparison with Romania's politicians. Leaving aside the lack of ethics on Nicolae's part, the fact that he succumbed to these schemers is proof that if the country were to officially return to monarchy, the Royal House would be suffocated, and eventually compromised, by all those fighting for power and favor from it. This constant series of intrigues that plague Romania's political life has been the very reason why the Romanian Parliament voted to stop the insanity of fratricides by bringing a foreign prince on the country's throne in 1866.

The Chronicler: And here they are on October 18th, 2019, in the old church at Curtea de Argeş, with only three of Queen Mother Elena's five granddaughters—her namesake, Nicolae's mother, who lives in England, visibly absent, very likely out of embarrassment for being caught in the power struggle between her sister-the-Queen and her son, the would-be-King, and Irina, also absent for the reasons mentioned above. Here they all are, holding together the *pomana*, that wheat cake served at Orthodox funerals, engaged in one of those absurd church rituals, all in a circle around the priest who holds the cake and another priest carrying a bottle of red wine, both cake and wine moving up and down according to the ritual, as if mimicking a sexual act, and the members of the Royal House with their arms extended toward the cake, the three sisters, the Prince Consort and the two beautiful trolls, Nicolae and Alina. After the ceremony, the officers of Mihai the Brave Brigade place the coffin on their shoulders again and, followed by the members of the Royal House, begin a short procession toward the New Cathedral where Queen Mother Elena will join her son, Mihai, his wife, Ana, and her once-husband, Carol, who cheated on her, took her son away from her, forced her into exile, and even took from her the title of Queen. Here they are, together in eternity.

Queen Marie: Curtea de Argeş is now a Royal Pantheon, a necropolis where, more than anywhere else, shine in all their glory the unbreakable and inextricable ties between the country's monarchs and the foundational myths and legends of this country. There is no better proof that we, its kings and queens, are now part of the country's DNA than the fact that the place itself where our bodies rest in eternity is the birthplace of a myth that sanctifies the creation of a divine, supremely beautiful cathedral through the sacrifice of its creator. When myth and reality merge in this way, there is always a higher force at work. Maybe because I am an artist I always understood the profound need humans have of myth, and with my writer's flair and my heart's desire of Beauty and Truth, of Beauty *as* Truth, I embraced the country's myths of creation as my own. I literally left my heart to rest inside the most romantic of my creations, Balcic Castle, while my body, separated from my heart, took its place where duty obliged it to be. Thus, in death, as in life, I shall be split between duty and passion.

The Chronicler: It is not by accident that the crown you ordered in 1922 for your own coronation as Queen of Greater Romania, and created by Falize Jewelers in Paris, was modeled on the medieval crown of Despina Doamna, wife of Neagoe Basarab, depicted on the walls of the Monastery Curtea de Argeș. Ornated with Byzantine motifs, the crown has lateral pendants, each with a medallion with the coats of arms of the Houses of Edinburgh and of Romania. From the medallions are hanging three long chains all the way down to your chest, in the shape of wheat stems, a symbol of fertility, and at the end of each chain there is a solar symbol represented by an ancient cross later appropriated by the Nazis and transformed into a swastika. The crown is decorated with precious and semi-precious stones, chosen for their symbolic value: turquoise, rubies, peridot, moonstone, amethyst, the latter said to protect one against trouble of the pancreas, which, ironically, may have been the cause of your death. When the coronation took place, you were forty-seven, and, as in the case of Queen Elizabeth II, your beauty, enhanced by the aura of that gloriously dazzling paraphernalia, projected your image onto the stage of future legends.

If this were an interview, at this point, the interviewer would ask the interviewee, "What did you feel at that moment?" This is the vicarious *question du jour*, a form of vulgar gossip masquerading as intellectual curiosity. Talking about a queen's inner life is a risky proposition. Yet you did even this, in the many books you wrote, you talked about a queen's inner life.

Queen Marie: It is true that to divulge one's soul and mind was a no-no for my relatives in England, where the Royal Family is bound by much stricter protocol rules, and whenever I met my relatives I could tell that they looked at me askance. But don't forget that Carmen Sylva too had done this, albeit in a more indirect and veiled way, as her medium was that of poetry. There is a clear explanation for the reluctance of royal heads to show what "hides behind closed doors," to use a TV cliché. Regular mortals are under the impression that princes, princesses, kings and queens are all privileged beings, which, of course, they—*we*—are; but what the general public doesn't realize, is that privilege is almost always doubled by an equal, parallel vector, which is its very opposite: when one is the exception, when one is One, one is the loneliest being on earth. No one can share a Monarch's worries and demons because no one can identify with her. People may adore or hate a Monarch, but they can never look at her in the same way they look at other human beings, and they hold this against her. The Monarch is considered guilty of her own privilege, as if she had any choice in the circumstances of her birth. "I am the only person in Spain with a Destiny," Spain's King Felipe once said. These words may sound arrogant, but, in fact, they are simply meant to indicate that in a democracy—and today, all European monarchies are democracies—all citizens, no matter how poor or marginalized, have the right *to create* their own destiny by choosing their profession, their spouse, their religion, their political beliefs. The only one not allowed any of these is the Monarch. A future Monarch's profession and religion *are chosen* for him before his birth; his spouse has to be approved by the government, and he has no right to express any political beliefs, which is tantamount to not being allowed to express any opinion whatsoever as long as what constitutes a "political belief" is debatable. "You can be whatever you want," "The Sky's the limit," "Dream big!" This is what children are being told today wherever they might live and whoever they might be—all children, with one exception: the Monarch's eldest child and heir to the throne. A future King cannot opt to be a dancer or a doctor or an architect, no matter how passionate he might be about these vocations. In the old days, he couldn't even pick his spouse, or else, was forced to select her from a very small pool of candidates. Today, members of royal families are still forced to be baptized in the official religion of the respective royal house, if not that of the country. A Monarch is the only one who, in King Felipe's words, *has* a destiny, because he isn't allowed to *create* his own destiny.

A Queen is first and foremost a symbol, that's why talking about a Queen's inner life is undermining the very thing she stands for, the symbol she embodies. A real Queen is careful not to present herself as one of the people, not out of arrogance, but because she is by the nature of her profession the Exceptional One, the One above all. The reason why Queen Elizabeth of Great Britain is universally revered is because she never voiced any opinion of her own about anything and always acted like an entitled Monarch, the kind of Sovereign who believes in her God-given right to be *One*, the One anointed with holy oil. She was a divine cypher, a tabula rasa everyone could project his or her own opinions on, an impenetrable Lady-with-a-hat.

The Chronicler: I once saw an interview with her at Balmoral, in which she talked about herself using the impersonal pronoun One: "One likes to spend time here in the summer and recharge One's batteries for later. One is happy to be surrounded by so much vegetation, and to do things the way things have been done for generations. One is very much constrained by rules, which is what the younger generation doesn't like, but One realizes that these rules are good, and One is saddened that there aren't more people who live their lives according to tradition and continuity."

Queen Marie: I see what you mean, but you have to remember that Queen Elizabeth was British, and the impersonal form is much more common in British than in American English. I wouldn't ascribe her usage of "one" to her relationship with the divine. I think it's rather a way of speaking that has to do with the time when she grew up and her desire to preserve that time.

The Chronicler: Maybe so. But I can think of another monarch with the same majestic aura, King Mihai. There is an interview with him taken some time in the early 2000s in which he refers to himself using the royal "we." When the interviewer tells him that a certain Romanian politician has called him an insulting name, the King's reply is: "We know who We are." He may be the Last Monarch to have used the royal *we*. By contrast, his successor, Margareta, who, after spending her first years of life in Great Britain, was educated in Switzerland where she finished high school, is impregnated with the democratic principles of the republic, aside from being rather shy and reserved, like her father. If we lived in different times, her natural qualities, of which her personal charm is probably the greatest, would suffice to give her the necessary aura for her position. But she is queen in a country that has exiled her father and proclaimed the monarchy unconstitutional, and she holds Court in a parallel universe to that of the elected officials. She depends on the goodwill of the elected officials whenever she needs to use the Throne Room from the Royal Palace for official events, such as awarding medals and hosting diplomatic receptions. She was forced to negotiate a deal with one of the most corrupt governments in Romania's history in order to be able to continue to reside in Elisabeta Palace, which the government had given to King Mihai in 2001 after he was allowed to return, a "palace" that is, really, no more than a mansion on the Chaussée Kisseleff in the center of Bucharest. King Mihai used it as his main residence in the last years spent in Romania; in fact, he'd been forced to abdicate in 1947 in an office of this very palace.

Queen Marie: The building had been bought by my eldest daughter, Elisabeta, who married King George of Greece, brother to my daughter-in-law, Elena. (Yes, the two Greek siblings married the two Romanian siblings.) It is a beautiful, two-story, whitewashed construction, in neo-Romanian style with Moorish influences visible in the soft angles and the inside arches. Elisabeta allowed King Mihai to use the house during WWII because it was very well located, right in the center of the capital, but the house never belonged to him, and he didn't claim it when he asked the government to give him back the properties that had once been his. As everyone knows, his main property was Peleş Castle, which King Ferdinand had given him after Carol's abdication. But because the Communists had expropriated all the objects inside the castle, the Royal Family owns only the adjacent land and the castle's walls, which were returned to them in 2008. For a token amount, the government's Department of Culture rents the castle from the Royal Family and uses it as a museum, guaranteeing in exchange to take care of all the necessary renovations—but that never happens. Just this past winter, the Royal Family had to pay a hundred thousand euros from its own pocket to replace the heating system, which had stayed the same since the inauguration of the Palace in 1875. Once upon a time, this had been the first electrified building in Europe; now, its walls, like everything else in my country, are peeling and beginning to crumble. I could never say these things openly while I was Queen, but if there is an advantage in being dead, this is it: even a queen has the right to free speech, and death has liberated me and given me the right to speak.

One cannot act in a regal way if one is not convinced of the legitimacy of her own election. From the moment I found out I was Queen I knew that this was my vocation. I was born to be a Queen.

For a long time, I couldn't take myself seriously. I was merely a pretty, innocent British princess who found herself trapped in a marriage arranged behind her back by a domineering mother with grand ambitions, a marriage with a man I found nice enough, and with whom, in time, I became close friends. I suppose that a marriage in which the spouses are good friends is better than most marriages, though it's certainly not enough. I was young and I hadn't even had a chance to make my debut in London's high society, young and full of life, married to a pathologically shy man who was terrified of his uncle—an uncle who forbade us to travel and forced us to live without friends out of fear that they would drag us into the country's muddy political waters. Later, I had to admit that his fears were justified. Still, no young person can live in complete isolation. On the rare occasions when Uncle organized social events, mostly for my sake, I was allowed to dance only with old politicians. I felt terribly lonely, and if it hadn't been for my horses, I don't know how I could have survived in spite of the general welcoming attitude of the Romanian population. Upon my arrival in Bucharest, the City presented me with a silver cup engraved with the words *"Bine ai venit, mireasă, de Dumnezeu aleasă spre a patriei cinstire!"* I wish I could translate those words into English because they have the perfume of ancient poetry, but I'm afraid my translator skills don't do them justice and make them sound pompous and vain: "Welcome, bride of ours, handpicked by our Lord for our country's eternal glory!" No, that doesn't sound right, there is a rhyme in Romanian. "We welcome thee, bride divine, our Lord's Chosen One!"

And then, one day we went to Russia. Nando and I were invited to attend the Coronation of Nicholas II and Alexandra (Nicky and Alix, as we called them). It was three years after my arrival in Romania, and I was dying to get out of there. To understand the essence of royal life one needs to have experienced the splendor of the Russian Court, which greatly surpassed any other royal house, England included. Gala costumes for female members of the Russian Royal Family were made of brightly colored velour with a lengthy train, embroidered with golden and silver flowers, and long, large sleeves hanging in the fashion of medieval dresses. On their heads they wore *kokoshniks*, halo-shaped headdresses from which hung a white veil, and when the entire Royal Family walked in procession, dozens of cousins, uncles and aunts, all dressed in gold and silver, one was dazzled by their shimmer, a procession of God-like creatures about to explode into a solar apocalypse.

During my childhood, Uncle Sasha and Tante Minny were Emperor and Empress. I still remember Tante Minny's dress made of gold and covered entirely with silver flowers. On her head she wore a tiara set with sapphires large as wide-open eyes, and around her neck one could see several diamond necklaces and strings of pearls hanging all the way down to her waist. The memory of this splendor had stayed with me throughout my entire childhood and was revived when we arrived for Nicky and Alix's Coronation. Nicky and Alix were young and beautiful, which added to the already overwhelming glamour of the event. Sporting a superbly cold, spiteful face, dressed in gold and adorned with countless diamonds, a *kokoshnik*-shaped diamond fringe tiara on her head, Alix looked like an evil goddess, an undecipherable, impenetrable enigma. This woman, with her lips pursed in a constant rictus of spite, never even smiled at me, never uttered a nice word. Why did she seem so unhappy even now when she was almost deified by her people?

Today, many of the tiaras of the Russian Imperial Court belong to the British Royal Family, whose members bought them from the exiled Russians after the Bolshevik Revolution, or more precisely, entered into their possession in exchange for allowing the exiled Russians to live on their estates. For this reason, Queen Elizabeth II was always cautious in her choice of tiaras at official, state events. Often, when a tradition dies, it is being appropriated by another, sometimes rival institution. What I mean is that the tradition of the *kokoshnik* has been appropriated by the jewelers of the House of Windsor, who have created so-called "*kokoshnik* tiaras" since the demise of their Russian counterparts. At her wedding on October 12th, 2018, Princess Eugenie of Great Britain wore the Grevile Emerald *kokoshnik* borrowed from the Queen, a tiara dating from 1919, featuring a huge oval-shaped emerald as a centerpiece and other smaller emeralds alongside. Even I ordered a *kokoshnik*-like tiara from Cartier when I became Queen.

At the festivities following the Coronation in Russia, I could spot myself dancing in the huge mirrors, in my gold lamé dress and my beautifully styled golden hair, and I have to admit I was pretty content with myself. All those Russian men, cousins, friends of cousins, officers, were complimenting me and asked to dance with me, exuberant, loud, full of confidence, the very opposite of my Nando. It was the moment I realized I had a special kind of power over men, and from that moment on I began to use it to my advantage, although never in the way those inclined to ugly rumors have sometimes implied.

We came back from Russia to our dreary lives under the supervision of Uncle and Aunty. Aunty had returned from her German exile in 1894 around the time my second child was born, and consequently, we christened our baby girl after the

Queen: Elisabeta. All my social life revolved around the Queen and all my acquaintances, including me, were being spied on by her people. I soon realized that in spite of her professed love for the arts and everything beautiful, we had nothing in common. Although at the time I was too young, inexperienced and uneducated to understand that more than half of her guests were, if not impostors, at the very least fools and mediocrities, I was instinctively put off by the slavish adulation of all those young odalisques sitting at her feet during her salons while she played the piano or declaimed poetry, and by the constant flutter of nervous excitement coming from them. True, every now and then a genuine talent happened to come by, like the composer George Enescu, at the time a teenager, but being so used to seeing and hearing only buffoons and pretentious tricksters around Aunty, my antennae were turned off, and it took me a long time to recognize his genius.

The Queen was famous for her histrionics all over Europe, but even so, I doubt anyone could have imagined what an exhibitionist she was. Consider the following scene: the Queen opens the window of her palace (the palace situated on Calea Victoriei, the capital's main road) and prepares excitedly for the gathering of the crowd. Sure enough, within a few minutes, a large gathering of gawkers can be spotted under the window, and the happy Queen proceeds to indulge her audience by taking various theatrical poses: with her hands by her chest, with her arms in the air, shifting her weight from one leg to the other. When she sees an old beggar, she extends her arms toward him like a rescuing Madonna, and orders that the man be brought to her, fed, washed and clothed. At the end, she tells our friend, who is visiting from Germany and is watching with dropped jaw: "Think of the effect this will have on the onlookers."

The Queen and I couldn't have been more different. She was also the exact opposite of her husband, the most cautious, rational and least spontaneous man one could imagine. King Carol I was a man of no vices, almost a saint, in some way. Idle tongues, which in this country are very industrious, have always said that the Queen's "frigidity" was the cause of her incapacity to get pregnant, when the truth is that she had more than a dozen miscarriages. In a country in which having an affair is the norm rather than the exception, and people get remarried multiple times with the Church's blessing, people cannot conceive of a man, in particular a king, with no mistresses. By contrast, my Nando had dozens of mistresses, most of them bland, women of questionable quality, whom he was only interested in very briefly and for strict biological purposes, with the possible exception of Marthe Bibesco, the writer-princess from Romania's old aristocracy who served as a model for Proust's Duchess of Guermantes. Or so they say. Ironically, most of my contemporaries were convinced that it was I who was the most unfaithful in our couple simply because most Romanians are cheaters themselves and cannot imagine that anyone, a beautiful woman in particular, would behave any differently than they do. But the truth is—and God is my witness—that besides the King, there was only one other man with whom I shared my bed. Yes, there were a couple of others who managed to gain access to my heart, and in my youth I was more flirtatious than I should have been—a flaw that led to that horrible scandal with my Aid-de-Champ, Zizi Cantacuzino, about which I shall talk in due time—but I never had much interest in that thing that is on everyone's minds and which these days they call "sex." The thing that was always on my mind and in my heart is the invisible link between our humble selves and a greater whole that encompasses them, the invisible link that united Me with my People and with the Almighty, and it is for this reason that I ordered for my heart to be taken out of my chest and placed away from my body in my spiritual tomb at Balcic. Like the warriors of antiquity or of medieval times who used to take the hearts out of their rivals' chests and throw them to the dogs or eat them, I am not afraid of a little bit of blood. I believe in hungry ghosts and in the need to feed them, and I know that my ghost would be hungry until the day my heart found its way back home.

I was accused by other royals of being too "theatrical," but to these people I say: what else is a monarchy if not theater? If you don't believe me, maybe you can believe Queen Elizabeth II, who used exactly these words to describe the essence of royal life. I often read comments by various Toms, Dicks and Harrys—alas, even *I* am on social media nowadays, if I want to know what's going on—who accuse Queen Elizabeth II of "showing off," which is laughable because it betrays a fundamental misunderstanding of the very essence of monarchy. *"Showing off" is the point.* This is the reason why the Queen filmed her Christmas addresses next to a golden piano in Buckingham Palace—a piano inherited with the palace, and which she wanted to showcase to her People on a special occasion. Of course, those in the business of constantly complaining were offended by the Queen's decision to "show off" her riches, as if the Queen were some newly minted President who made himself rich overnight from tax heavens and fraud and wanted to show his golden fixtures to his G7 rivals.

Theater is the point. I was criticized by some of my relatives for the theater of the 1922 Coronation at Alba Julia to celebrate the enthronement of King Ferdinand and myself after Transylvania's union with Romania following WWI. It is true that instead of using as a model the somber pomp and circumstance of Westminster Abbey ceremonies, I was inspired by the Coronation of my Russian relatives and by the Byzantine crown of a medieval Wallachian princess. If I was going to play in a drama, then it was going to be a medieval drama! It should be added, though, that theater is but the esthetic dimension of a ritual that is as much religion as it is art. The organic link between the Sovereign and Divinity, a link which has been severed in constitutional monarchies, survives in the ritualized theater of contemporary royal life. If you've ever watched a jubilee celebration of Queen Elizabeth with the Prince of Wales by her side on stage at Covent Garden, and you've heard "God Save the Queen" sung by thousands of mouths, including that of Angela Gheorghiu, your hair must have stood on end, like mine, and you too must have felt a bit closer to God. But, dear God, watching all those royals spend their days cutting ribbons and unveiling plaques, one can sympathize with Prince Philip's self-deprecating remark that he is the most experienced plaque unveiler of all times! What sad fate for Europe's royalty, from the days when it led its soldiers on the battlefield to thunderous victory to today's impotent men and women who show up to pull on a rope!

The Chronicler: Indeed. Even Queen Elizabeth II's comings and goings had something absurd about them. On the one hand, there was something incredibly dignified about the ninety-something-year-old monarch simply showing up anywhere, never mind showing interest in what was going on, smiling and shaking hands; on the other hand, seeing the golden carriage in which she appeared alone in her always-bright colors, either with a fantastically-shaped hat or a diamond tiara in her white hair, while throngs of excited onlookers screamed hysterically behind police barricades, holding those rectangle-shaped electronic devices in their hands like some kind of magic talismans, I sometimes wondered whether such rituals are ... well ... any more civilized than some barbaric rituals. I mean: a golden carriage carrying an elderly lady from here to there, while a lot of people scream full of excitement. One can see there is something primitive in all this. Yet, in this very barbarity also resides the divine aspect of the thing. Divinity is, unavoidably, separate from the People, yet it needs to be seen by the People: alone, in a golden carriage. But speaking of electronic devices, the Queen once deplored the presence of smartphones because it prevented her from seeing people's eyes: "I miss their eyes." How truly old fashioned! To prefer the eyes' mirror rather than the phones' screens!

Queen Marie: Humans need a presence that reminds them of something bigger than themselves, someone before whom they can bow and to whom they voluntarily surrender the way one surrenders to a lover. To those who might accuse me of being anti-democratic I say: when the masses don't have a leader able to uplift and remind them of a higher realm, they do not replace him with a more democratic one, oh, no. They replace him with a false idol, *un chip cioplit*, as they say in Romanian, what a beautiful expression, so much more beautiful than "a false idol," an idol who actively labors for their own destruction because whenever a natural impulse is stifled in us—in this case, the need to worship a higher presence— that impulse is being perverted into something else. Yes, *the world has an instinctual need for idols*, and whenever this need is hindered by revolutionary upheaval, the toppled idols are swapped for idols with feet of clay. The masses place their idol on a pedestal, but they end up taking down what they had initially put up. They often do this with wicked delight, *as though avenging themselves upon the unfortunate idol for their own mistaken enthusiasm*. It's as if man felt the childish need to inebriate himself with some kind of magic potion—Kool-Aid, as they call it in your country—only to smash to smithereens the glass from which he'd drunk. The stronger the inebriation, the more numerous the smithereens. The higher the pedestal, the louder the sound of the idol's fall. *I can never understand why man must be so excessive, in both adoration and hatred.*[16] This is the reason why I have always been apprehensive of excessive hero-worship, including my own. I like balance in

---

16. From *Later Chapters of My Life*.

all things and I hate injustice, and so I like to keep a cool head when everybody around me is giddy with excitement; in fact, I believe that those in my position have a responsibility to keep a cool head.

If I look back upon my life as a Queen, I think the adulation of my person reached its peak during and immediately after the Paris Peace Conference in 1919. It is, of course, ironic that the stage for this sentiment was a republic, but not at all surprising. I've said it before: republicans are the most eager to meet with royalty, the most impressionable. But there is always something missing in such encounters, even when the crowds go crazy with enthusiasm. I'd much rather suffer the worship of a Romanian peasant who treats me like a goddess, kisses my hands, the hem of my dress and the ground I walk on, than be the target of the ingratiating compliments of many freethinking bourgeois.

The Chronicler: Speaking of which, are you aware that there is a little black-and-white film of you dressed up in the Romanian national costume, surrounded by peasants, to whom you are offering flowers, and when one of them—a very humble, dirty-looking woman (or was it a man?) in rags—takes your hand to kiss it, you take your glove off and then offer your hand to be kissed? It's a gesture that doesn't fail to impress all contemporary Romanians, this sign of respect shown to such a humble person, but which, very likely, would not impress an American because she wouldn't appreciate the kissing of the hand to begin with.

Queen Marie: Well, there are many such little films in which I appear. Or maybe not that many, by today's standards. But to come back to our republicans, the French were so excessive in their praise that there were times when I felt awkward. They burnt so much incense before my so-called virtues, extoling them and mercilessly rubbing their worship into me, in addresses, speeches, poems, what-have-you, that I was truly embarrassed. That's because power is for them something almost magical. In fact, commoners tend to think of power as something evil and intangible because it's something they want but cannot have. They can only imagine it, and because they are outside of it, they behave like small children behind a high fence stretching their necks this way and that, trying to get a glimpse of a forbidden world. But those of us who live in the thrust of things, those who live inside this world, the insiders, as it were, know that power as such does not exist. We know this because, in many ways, we are just as powerless as the least fortunate. Power is only a projection that the outsiders fabricate in order to explain something they cannot grasp, in the same way Divinity was created by the masses to explain the unexplainable in the universe. But maybe Divinity lives in all creation, maybe Divinity is a throbbing, living thing, rather than some static, oppressive force—this is, I should add, what has attracted me to the Bahai religion. And in a similar way, maybe power is an airy thing, an energy that is summoned between people, through their mental projections and collective imagination. Yes, if I were to define power with my own words, I would say that it is an act of collective imagination.

The Chronicler: Indeed, I can corroborate this definition of power with my own experience when the Romanian Communist regime, which seemed eternal and all-powerful, fell in a matter of days. For those of us who lived through that time it was uncanny to see how the entire state, all its institutions, practically, fell apart, as if they were a torn fabric whose thread kept unraveling until the state was left in its barren nakedness. Then, I understood that power is, really, nothing, nothing at all. It is, as you say, our own projection over those among us who have the audacity to grab it and sequester it within their own inner world, the world of the insiders, while we look on with slavish fascination, abject and powerless. But, to think of it, I am not sure your contemporaries—and that means, you too, of course—would have used this word, "power," the way we use it now. In fact, I am pretty sure no one at the time thought of power in the obsessive way we think of it today. But if this is your definition of power, how would you define then a good Monarch?

Queen Marie: A good Monarch is the one who is able to align his soul with that of his subjects, and a great Monarch is one who becomes One with her people. I will leave it to others to say whether or not I was a good Queen Consort, but I can tell you that Aunty, Queen Elisabeta, was as removed from her people as light is from day.

The Chronicler: Funny that you should use the correct title: Queen Consort. Usually, you and the Romanians seem to forget that Ferdinand was the monarch, while you were only the consort.

Queen Marie: Well, my dear, can you blame me? I mean, poor Nando. Do you know how his servants, or, as they call them nowadays, staff, used to refer to him? "Poor King Ferdinand!" But to come back to Elisabeta, oh, poor Queen Elisabeta! I told you about the episode with her foreign guest and the beggar she invited into the Palace. This whole episode occurred because, you know, she thought of herself as a "Great Queen" and she wanted to see it in the eyes of the beggar, she wanted that poor wretch to bow before her all the way to the ground, to kiss her hands and the hem of her dress as he called her "the Greatest Empress of all Times." She wanted to see her power in the smallness of that man.

The Chronicler: Did you just say "Empress"? Why would Queen Elisabeta think of herself as an empress? You, on the other hand, write in your memoirs that while visiting the wounded soldiers during the war, when approaching their beds to talk to them and to comfort them, more than one replies to you by declaring that his suffering is nothing if it means making you "the Empress of All Romanians." You write this with a certain … what's the word? Pride. Yes, you seem proud that a dying man would think of you and your dreams of grandeur—*Marie, the Empress!*—when this man had, very likely, a family, and he should have thought of that first.

Queen Marie: My dear, you start to sound like your contemporaries, you assume that the beautiful Queen can only be vain, that if she refers to herself using the arrogant words "the Empress of all Romanians," it must be because she is full of herself. You forget that, at the time, the greatest wish of all the Romanians was to be united into a "Greater Romania," which was, indeed, an empire, given that it was made of two countries: Transylvania and Romania (the latter, made of Wallachia and Moldavia). So, "the Empress of all Romanians" simply meant "the Queen of Greater Romania," the Queen of a Unified Romania, and if a dying soldier cannot dream of a great fate for his country before giving up the ghost, well then, I am sorry to say that your generation does not know the meaning of "patriotism."

But your many interruptions have made me lose the thread of the answer to your initial question: what did I feel at my coronation? What did I feel when the newly minted King placed the Crown on my head in front of the thousands of onlookers, *my people*, who cheered us, delirious with ecstatic joy, joy that can be compared to nothing else, immeasurable and indescribable, because how can one describe ecstatic joy? How can I describe the feeling of being One with the sea of people outside of me, One with the Divinity whose symbol I was being called to incarnate? I, the People and God—One in this ecstatic union, e pluribus unum, that uproots one from one's limited, confined self and throws it into the impersonal realm of the gods. I could see myself in my white dress, the flutter of the King's and the Patriarch's long garments next to mine, all of us covered by the fabric of the moving square within which the ceremony took place, and the thousands of hands outside of our sacred square moving like rapturous birds, accompanied by the cacophony of voices, hip-hip-hooray, hip-hip-hooray! You feel that you are no longer contained within the outline of your mortal body, you are spilling outside into a communion with your people, you are them and they are you, all this transfiguration embodied by the crown you now wear on your head. When Nando put the crown on my head a shiver went down my spine and tears began streaming down my cheeks.

The Chronicler: The feeling of being united not only with your people but also with Divinity itself is symbolized by the Crown placed on the Monarch's head—the Crown as the symbolic One. One needs to still feel a connection to this symbolic arrangement in order to be able to experience awe. In the world I live in, this connection and any understanding of a symbolic worldview have been obliterated. I write these words on September 10th, 2022, two days after HM Queen Elisabeth II passed away, the last representative of a worldview in which the crowning was seen as a sacrament between the Monarch and the Divine, and the Monarch and her People. It is this sacrament that was the basis of her Majesty's lifelong sense of duty. We are now living some extraordinary moments, my dear Queen, when for the first time in recent history we can see glimpses of the old symbolic order: the proclamation of Charles as King during the ceremony of Accession in front of all the country's former PMs, in the presence of the Queen Consort and of the future heir. The language used is, according to the script, charmingly archaic: there is, first, the announcement, by the Lord President, of the death, on September the 8th the year of our Lord 2022, of "our Queen of blessed memory," followed by the Proclamation of the Clock of the Council: "whereas it has pleased Almighty God to call to His Mercy Our Queen of Happy Memory," and her heir is proclaimed "our lawful liege-Lord." This, in turn, is followed by the new King's speech in which he refers to "the peoples whose Sovereign I was called upon to be." At the end, the first speaker asks permission from His Gracious Majesty for "the publication of his gracious speech." Listening to this wonderfully obsolete, almost Biblical language, with its amber-like inflections and its honey-sweet drip, I am overcome by melancholy. In a world of robotized influencers and digitalized non-beings that speak a non-language made of synthetic abbreviations, infantile emoticons and fashionable un-words, technology separates us from whatever is left of the divine, placing us in the realm of the Ungracious itself. The world has lost its aura.

Chapter 7

In which I Talk about My Heart

Queen Marie: I found out I became queen while staying at Mogoşoaia, chez Princess Martha Bibesco, whose sister-in-law (that is, her husband's sister), Nadeja Ştirbey, was Barbu's wife. It was Barbu who called: "You are Queen."

The Chronicler: What an incestuous world, my dear Queen! While your husband was having an affair with Martha, you were having an affair with her brother-in-law, Barbu!

Queen Marie: I was not "having an affair"! Barbu was the man of my life. You can't compare what Nando had with Martha to what Barbu and I had. Nando had dozens of affairs, or rather, adventures, because he rarely slept more than a couple of times with the same woman. Martha was an exception. But Barbu … very few women in this world have the luck of being loved the way Barbu loved me. Barbu was an anomaly in Romanian society—his *noblesse de caractère*, his devotion combined with his absolute discretion were unparalleled.

The Chronicler: And yet, in spite of his "absolute discretion," your love story was no secret. Neither then, nor now. Everybody knew about it.

Queen Marie: It's not that they "knew" about it. It's that they guessed simply by looking at us. We were extremely careful, but the Romanians were constantly on the lookout for my so-called "lovers," and whenever I was seen in the company of an attractive, desirable man, there were speculations. And Barbu was one of the most desirable men in Bucharest at the time. Strange, I didn't notice how attractive he was when we were first introduced, probably because I was used to treating everybody with the cautiousness my position demanded! The King and Queen had lectured me so many times on the demands of my role, and I was still so traumatized after the scandal with Zizi Cantacuzino that I handled all the men with the same vaguely superior air, while flirting only enough to appear charming, but never more than necessary. It was only after having attended several official functions where Barbu was present that I began to feel an energy coming from him, the kind of feeling one has when one is being insistently scrutinized. Every time I accidentally turned my head in his direction, there he was, staring at me. No, I misspoke, I never caught him staring, but I always felt the insistence of his gaze drilling into my back. He had the most passionate gaze I'd ever seen, two dark eyes—the eyes later inherited by Mircea—under two thick, equally dark eyebrows! I remember vividly the first time I realized what was happening. We were seated next to each other at an intimate dinner at Martha's. Just the six of us: him, Nadeja, Martha, her husband, Nando and me. Martha was narrating an interminable war love story about a German officer and a Romanian nurse, and when she said, "Isn't this the eternal story of impossible love between a man and a woman who betray their families and nations to satisfy their desire?" I felt a magnetic pull coming from Barbu, who was seated between me and Martha. I lifted my gaze to meet his, but he was deliberately avoiding it, and at that moment, I understood that he was forced to do that for fear of revealing his feelings about me. From then on there was a secret understanding between us, an invisible cord that tied us to each other.

It took him a whole year to declare his feelings. It is true that we were almost never alone, but even when the opportunity presented itself, he refused to take advantage of it. Whenever circumstances forced us to be alone for the span of a few minutes, he busied himself with one thing or another and never looked me in the eye. This was more revealing than anything else, because in his interaction with everyone else, the King included, he was very forward and unafraid to speak up. With his impeccable posture and Roman profile, he gave his opinion only when asked, but then he did it with conviction and in an unambiguous manner. In this, he was very different from his compatriots, who are very opinionated even when they know nothing about a subject, always eager to share their feelings simply because they have them. Barbu, on the other hand, was extremely measured, measured in a way that made him almost … British. His reserve, discretion and tone contrasted so much with the garrulous world in which we lived that I began to have an intense desire to poke the perfect exterior in which he was enveloped to reach for the inner core whose fire was sublimated in his eyes. Whenever he was in my presence, his passion was so palpable and yet so mute that I decided to make him speak.

Once, when we were at Mogoșoaia, I invited him to go horse riding with me so I could ask for his advice on a certain matter. When I made the request, his gaze met mine for the briefest of moments, and he answered, "If this is Your Royal Highness's wish …" It was a canned phrase, but in his mouth, it took the opposite meaning. He seemed to be saying "I wish you didn't ask me this." Before I could think of a proper response, I heard myself utter, "And what is *your* wish?" The silence that followed was so long I began to wonder whether I had really asked the question or had only dreamed about it. He was standing in the middle of the room, hands behind his back, gaze lowered, in stark contrast to his straight, masculine upper body. "Now or never," I thought, getting up from the couch where I was seated and advancing toward him. I was dressed in one of my favorite white dresses, a vaporous design with embroidered violets, and, careful not to step on the hem, I began to walk very slowly around him, outlining a circle with my steps, all the while whispering, "So, *you* have no desire. No desire whatsoever." He continued to stand like a statue, his eyes the only thing alive. At some point he opened his mouth but quickly closed it back. As I finished my circle, I too stood there, silent. "Your Royal Highness is playing a very dangerous game." Did he really say that, or did I imagine it? For about a minute I was at a loss about how and what to reply. "Well, then, if you have no desire, it is my desire that you accompany me horse riding." I walked toward the door, indicating that he should follow me, while the servants prepared our horses. As soon as we were at a safe distance from the servants, I spurred my horse, adding over my shoulder: "Catch me, if you can!" When I had done the same thing with Zizi, many years earlier, I had allowed him to catch up with me, as few people in the entire country could equal my riding skills. Sitting on his horse, Zizi had put his arm around my waist, causing us both to fall down, and there, in the grass, he kissed me. It was the first time anyone else besides my husband had ever kissed me, and I felt a double pleasure: the pleasure of being desired by a young, attractive man, and the pleasure of an illicit kiss. By that time, Nando rarely kissed me, his physical overtures confining themselves to violent acts of sexual intercourse that left me humiliated and disgusted. His desire was so brutal and unrefined that, in spite of the humiliation, I felt pity for him. Zizi was the first man from whom I learned that physical relations between men and women could be different, yet they never went beyond kissing.

But Barbu was no Zizi. "Your Royal Highness likes danger," he said as soon as we paused to catch our breaths, on a tantalizing tone that was half a question, half a statement. "Do I like danger? I don't know. When I am on horseback I never think of danger. It seems to me that if I broke my bones, I wouldn't even feel it. When I ride, I live entirely in the moment, just me and my horse, and everything seems possible." As soon as I uttered those words, I realized that, although I was entirely honest, I was repeating almost word for word Gwendolen's answer to Mr. Grandcourt in George Eliot's *Daniel Deronda*, which I was reading at the time. I asked him if he was familiar with this British author, and to my great surprise, he answered yes. I say "to my great surprise" because most Romanians I know are well acquainted with French or German authors, but not so much with the British ones. He hadn't read this particular novel, however, and so he asked me if I liked it and why. Usually, I have no trouble giving my impressions of a novel, but Barbu's reserve, and the way he preceded each question with a long, thoughtful pause, put me on my guard. I didn't want him to think I was a *gâsculiță* (little goose), so I took a minute to think my answer over. "I think I like it because the heroine, Gwendolen, who is young, beautiful and desired by all, appears superficial and intellectually limited, only interested in being the center of attention" (here, he suddenly turned his head in my direction, and fixed me in a way that made me blush) "and getting the utmost pleasure out of life, but in reality, she is a strong-willed, independent woman who refuses to accept the role the others and society want to force her into."

"And what is this role?" "Well, the role of a woman who knows her place, of course. Everybody wants to marry her, but she doesn't want to get married. Or, if she were to get married, she would want a husband that could give her the independence she craves." "And this independence, what would she do with it if she had it?" Here, I was a bit at a loss about what to answer, and so I adopted Gwendolen's attitude when in doubt. I laughed nonchalantly, just like her, and spurred my horse on.

"I suppose she'd use it to give herself any pleasure she wanted," I said over my shoulder, laughing again. "And do you think a life of fulfilled pleasures is an ideal life?" I heard behind my back. By then, both our horses were running, so I made no reply. But when we stopped, breathless and exhausted, he stubbornly repeated his question, almost defiantly. I felt that a lot was expected from my answer, and I couldn't get out of it by playing Gwendolen. "Well, I suppose a well-lived life should balance pleasure and duty. A life focused entirely on pleasure is probably just as immoral as a life devoted to duty and nothing else." I turned my head to see his reaction and, for the first time, I saw him sporting a large smile. "I won't tell his Majesty that you think of duty as 'immoral.'" "Now, now, I didn't quite say that!" I protested. "Not quite, but almost," he said laughing and showing a row of perfectly aligned, white teeth. He was even more handsome when he laughed, his straight figure projected against the green landscape of fir trees, suddenly wrapped in a cloak of casualness that contrasted with the seriousness of his questions. I kept quiet, and his laughter slowly retreated until it made room for an expression of deep concentration. He began to scrutinize the horizon, ignoring me, or pretending to. "Quite a view, isn't it?" he asked, pointing to the undulating line of trees under the blue sky. "Yes," I said. "I sometimes come here to paint. As a matter of fact, I will come a week from now." (Why did I tell him this? Was I hoping he'd come to meet me here in secret?) Once again, he ignored my words, and asked abruptly: "What matter did your Royal Highness want to talk about?" What matter? As if he didn't know that it was all pretense! Then, why did he ask? Did he want to humiliate me? "Matter? No matter. I had something on my mind, but I seem to have forgotten." I could feel, or thought I could, his breath and the rhythm of his thoughts. Not his thoughts exactly, but the way they formed and moved from his brain to his lips—his lips that, now that I focused on them, made me want to hold his head between my hands and touch with mine. His eyes still fixed on the horizon, he replied in a softer tone: "When you remember, I am at your disposal." The same double entendre. "Are you?" And then, finally, he looked me in the eye. "Yes."

Yes! He said yes. For the rest of the day I kept playing this scene in my mind, imparting it all kinds of meanings. What had happened? Nothing, really. Yet something irretrievable did happen. From then on, he was constantly—well, "constantly" is a way of speaking—on my mind. Looking back, I realize that what made me fall in love with him was, even more than his personal qualities, the way he loved me. Of course, Nando loved me too, but, as I said, his love had something vulgar about it. I did not feel, how should I put it, elevated by his love, while Barbu's love was the kind of love the troubadours had for their intangible ladies.

The Chronicler: Just as I thought. You fell in love with your own idealized image.

Queen Marie: Cynical, as always. No, I fell in love with his generosity. I was surrounded by vultures, all of whom wanted something from me, but Barbu would have adored me for the rest of his life without asking anything in return. This is why I slept with him.

The Chronicler: So, you slept with him out of generosity, not because you had a mediocre husband who couldn't satisfy you?

Queen Marie: If you think that all I wanted was what you call "sex," you are wrong. In fact, my husband's physical overtures disgusted me to such a degree that for a long time I was left with repulsion for this part of life.

The Chronicler: I didn't say that was all you wanted. I think what you wanted was the adoration of a romantic man who could satisfy your body and soul, equally. Your husband was, clearly, incapable of that. Besides, no husband can "adore" his wife. Only a lover can.

Queen Marie: Why do I have the feeling that you are implying that my love for Barbu was, somehow, the result of my vanity? You seem to have a perverse need to taint what is pure.

The Chronicler: I have a perverse need to get to the bottom of things.

Queen Marie: At least, you acknowledge your penchant for perversion.

The Chronicler: Isn't writing a perverse activity by definition? As a writer, you should know.

Queen Marie: Why would you say such a thing about writing?

The Chronicler: Writing places a screen between you and the world. When you ride a horse, there is no screen. You are in the heart of things. But when you write, all you have is their elusive, ghost self. You keep trying to get to their essence by digging deeper and deeper, but the more you dig, the farther you get from their core.

Queen Marie: That's an interesting thought! I never considered things this way. I do feel much more alive when I ride, it is true. Maybe that's why I could no longer ride after the death of my little Mircea. And this feeling, of being intensely alive, is also present when one falls in love. I know that many Romanians thought of me as vain and coquettish because I sometimes flirted with other men, but it is not out of vanity that I was flirting, it's because my soul was dying and I wanted to feel alive.

The Chronicler: Hmm ... Still, this doesn't exclude the presence of vanity, which, insofar as it demands constant recognition from others, is in itself an engine of dramatic effects. You may want to look up this sentence from *Daniel*

Deronda: "for vanity is as ill at ease under indifference as tenderness is under a love which it cannot return." Or this other sentence in which Gwendolen is depicted not so much fond of men as fond of their homage, a trait that, with very rare exceptions, is common to all beautiful women. My dear Queen, why don't you acknowledge it? You were fond of men's homage to you.

Queen Marie: Very well, then. If it pleases you, my dear, I will acknowledge it. But I thought you were interested in hearing my story, not in being proved right. Can I go on?

The Chronicler: Please do.

Queen Marie: After the scene described above, Barbu and I didn't see each other for at least a month. He was abroad on business, and I was busy with matters of state. He returned a day before the anniversary of his birthday, and I made sure that, aside from the official present sent by Nando in both our names—a wooden crate with *Toscani* bottles of wine—, a separate present from me was waiting for him: a copy of *Daniel Deronda* with my inscription. I spent several long, agonizing hours trying to come up with the perfect dedication, something that would allude to our mutual feelings while being expressed in such a way that no other potential reader could guess its secret meaning. "No stronger ecstasy than the one found in the impossible calling. *Marie of Romania.*" I thought that this was ambiguous enough to be interpreted as referring to the calling of a writer or artist, but after I sent it out, I began to wring my hands. What have I done? Weren't all the courtiers and servants already prejudiced enough against me and predisposed to interpret my most innocent remark in a tendentious light? Why was I providing fuel for their fire? Barbu's neutrally polite, cold thank you note only made matters worse. Was he upset with me because I put him in a potentially delicate situation with his wife and servants?

It took another two weeks until we met in person on his estate. We were surrounded by at least a dozen people, members of both our families and servants, so we spent the first two hours chitchatting with our entourage, during which time we never made eye contact. At a certain point, I was engaged in conversation with one of his aides when I had the distinct feeling that he was watching me. I turned my head as discreetly as I could in his direction and saw that he was peeking at me with the corner of his left eye. Throughout the rest of our lives we always could tell when the other was in proximity and were never wrong. Once (this was years later), I was hosting an important state event in the very large Throne Room at Cotroceni Palace, when, all of a sudden, I felt that the energy in the room had changed. I had just shaken hands with the Danish ambassador and was politely laughing at his insipid joke when my head turned of its own accord, propelled by some secret inner mechanism, my eyes fixed on a point at the other end of the room. And there he was, watching me. Always watching me or watching *over* me. All women find pleasure in being desired, but being desired by a handsome man, solid as a rock, is particularly pleasurable. I use the words "solid as a rock" in all its meanings, for he emanated physical strength, but, even more than that, he was, aside from Colonel Boyle, the most devoted friend I ever had. Barbu was both my lover and my guardian angel, a rare combination in a man.

The Chronicler: And Boyle? What were your *real* feelings for him? This man whom you describe in your war diary as the absolute incarnation of manliness. This Übermensch, as you call him.

Queen Marie: Colonel Boyle was a very dear friend and the most extraordinary man I ever met. I was lucky to have met him.

The Chronicler: Many historians believe that you were in love with him. Is that true? Some believe that the two of you had an affair, others think that your relationship was platonic. What's the truth?

Queen Marie: You are indiscreet, as always.

The Chronicler: Colonel Boyle was a very strong, physically impressive man. You were attracted to men who could dominate you physically but chose to devote their lives to you and worship your royal persona. Am I right?

Queen Marie: Is it very important to you that you be declared "right" by a queen? Is that your ambition?

The Chronicler: Well, I seem to remember that in the journal you kept during the war (1916-1918) you confessed that, as a young girl, your vision of love was very naïve and romantic, and your ideal man was someone you could look up to and obey. And, as the chronicler of your majestic life, I am supposed to get things right, aren't I?

Queen Marie: My "majestic" life?!

Carmen Sylva (who appears out of nowhere and vanishes again after giving her reply): *Sarcastic.* Our Chronicler thinks she is being sarcastic. The lower classes get particular enjoyment from bashing and dragging down the upper classes. They feel this imperious need to take what is up and pull it down to their own level.

Queen Marie (a look of surprise on her face at the sight of Queen Elisabeta, quickly replaced by a vaguely melancholy air): Yes, I am beginning to see that. (Turning to face the Chronicler): Does it give you pleasure to mock my heart, to take my relationships with Barbu and Boyle, and sprinkle them with witticisms meant to emphasize your superiority, all the while showing how pathetic this queen was, how much alike, in the end, to a common shopgirl who falls for a sailor?

The Chronicler (taken aback by the Queen's outburst, tries to avoid giving a straight answer): A sailor? Are you saying that

I was implying that Colonel Boyle was a sailor because he was always engaged in some kind of heroic deed that took place at sea? Honestly, this isn't what I had in mind. But I suppose you could call him a sailor, although I think the word "adventurer" describes him better.

Queen Marie (with a sharp and vexed tone): I think I should know best what words are suited in the descriptions of my friends. And you haven't answered my question.

The Chronicler (conciliatory): Indeed, you do. That's why I am attempting to find the truth from your mouth, rather than through speculation.

Queen Marie: You interrupted me. Where was I?

The Chronicler: The time when you and Barbu were on his estate, surrounded by a bunch of people, after you had gifted him a copy of *Daniel Deronda*.

Queen Marie: Oh, yes. He avoided looking at me as long as the others were in our presence, but I could feel his gaze like the invisible eye of an omniscient writer watching every gesture of mine. What distinguishes a queen from other mortals is that when she is in public, she is under the microscope of countless eyes, she is a being made of her reflection in hundreds of eyes, so in the end, her being is a collection of reflections. I suppose this is what happens in the world of celebrities today; this is the reason these people are so fragile mentally and have a thirst for constant adulation without which they are nothing. One needs a strong character to resist the temptation to see oneself as some kind of god. I dare say I always resisted this temptation, maybe because I never took myself too seriously.

The Chronicler: Many people would be surprised to hear that. People who are familiar with your legend, in particular.

Queen Marie: People who are familiar with my legend don't know anything about me. Isn't a legend made of the very eyes who gaze at the object of their adoration, of the very hands who weave it?

The Chronicler: Are you saying that the object of adoration is beside the point?

Queen Marie: I'm saying that the object of adoration is a point nobody sees because everyone sees whatever they want to see. A pointless point.

The Chronicler: I'm more interested in you and Barbu.

Queen Marie: Yes. As I was saying, I could feel his eyes. But the way they felt was so very different from everybody else's eyes. The others' eyes always felt like a violation, as if trying to uncover something that was remote from them, and with their indiscreet gazes they could penetrate that remoteness, tear apart the veil and take out that alien thing and make it theirs. But Barbu's eyes were penetrating and tender at the same time. They had the intensity of the male who wants to possess a woman, but the male was someone who respected the royal family and would never have forgotten his duty and obligations, and so he did everything he could to control his gaze. I knew what he felt for me, but I couldn't tell if he had any idea of my own feelings for him. I thought that maybe I should give him some hints. And so, when we managed to be alone for a few minutes, horse riding again, I asked him if he'd had time to open the book I'd sent him. His tone was one of faked surprise—"Oh, yes, the novel!"—so I knew that it must have been on his mind. He thanked me for it in a very formal way—"It was very kind of you to think of me"—with a coolness that made the incipient smile on my lips freeze. Very kind? What was I? His nurse? Who did he think he was? "A lot less kind than you may think," I answered with ice-cold aloofness and without the hint of a smile. He was surprised by my brusqueness, and with the corner of my eye I saw how his entire upper body, not just his head, turned in my direction. I expected to hear his reply, while the words "Who does he think he is?" kept running in my head. But no answer came from him, and his silence was even more insulting than my previous unfriendly remark. We kept riding next to each other, and his prolonged silence, which was rather disrespectful, grew heavier and heavier, until it enveloped us both like a mantle. Suddenly, I noticed that we were surrounded by white globes of dandelion puff that floated above our heads like enormous snowflakes. "It's snowing," I said laughing, turning my head to face him. On his forehead rested a huge dandelion snowflake, giving him the appearance of a fabulous animal, which, in combination with his somber and dignified posture on the horse, made him look silly. I laughed even harder. "You turned into a unicorn," I said. His upper lip moved slightly, attempting a smile, but his eyes looked serious. I moved closer to him and extended my hand toward his forehead, and, as I did that, his expression changed. His vague smile vanished entirely, his eyes showed panic, and his body stiffened. I took the ethereal puff in the palm of my hand, and, blowing it away with a forceful breath of air, I said, "See? You attract the elements. If you keep staying here, you'll turn into a snowman." I was very close to him, my horse and his touching each other. "Then, maybe it's better for us to go," he whispered. I looked him straight in the eye. "Don't you enjoy my company, Prince Ştirbey?" For the second time, he gave no answer. We kept riding next to each other, and I felt how my anger was coming back. For a few minutes all we could hear was the sound of the rustling leaves under the horses' hooves. "Do you treat your other friends just as impolitely or do you reserve this special treatment for me?" He signaled to his horse to stop, and obediently, the animal did. "Your Royal Highness," he began, then, paused. I was having trouble making my horse stay still, because it was a horse I'd never ridden before, and, while I was struggling with the animal, he went on. "You know I don't treat anyone else the way I treat you." "I do?" (The horse had stilled.) I arched my brows as high as I could and looked him in the eye again. (The horse whinnied.) He sustained my gaze, his face utterly serious. "Yes. You do." The horse whinnied again, and I said, "Let's go!"

When we returned to the house, there were about five minutes during which we managed to be alone, as the others were either napping or picnicking outside. We both stood in the library, I by the fireplace and he by one of the large windows, enveloped in the stale odor of old books, as the silence around us was occasionally interrupted by fragments of voices from the outside. He stood with his back facing me—an impertinence!—as if he had forgotten about me, but this allowed me to examine him at length. His body was perfectly proportioned, and his profile—which I couldn't help compare with Nando's—was so esthetically harmonious I felt like placing my fingers on it and drawing its lines with them. His straight nose, thick black hair, flawlessly arched brow and jaw were an invitation to touch and outline them. When the impulse to get closer and touch him became so strong I began to step in his direction, the door was pushed aside and Nadeja, Nando and a few others entered, all of them talking at the same time, a chorus of mingled, chaotic voices that broke the spell and woke him up from his reverie.

That night, before going to bed, I took some charcoal and drew his portrait, the way I remembered him standing by the window. I didn't have to erase anything, his face was born in a few seconds before my eyes. But after I finished, I felt guilty, as if I had committed a crime, and was afraid that someone could find it and discover my secret. It was, of course, silly, as everyone knew I liked to draw portraits of those around me—my family, the servants, peasants I saw on various occasions. Still, I hid the drawing and began to concoct plans about giving it to him. The next day I was in a state of intense nervousness, thinking about the best opportunity when I could be alone with him again and give it to him. There was no opportunity, of course. In fact, he avoided looking me in the eye the whole day.

It was a long time before he saw that drawing, months later, on December 26th at Sinaia. After the children went to bed and only us adults were left around the Christmas tree in the Music Room, when it was time for Barbu to open his presents, Nadeja suddenly stood up and excused herself, invoking a migraine. Barbu saw her to the door, gallantly kissed her hand, then returned to his place and tore off the wrapping paper under which was hiding the folder with the drawing. As he was about to open it, the servant approached him with a glass of wine, which he took, then turned to face Nando, who had asked him a question. I watched how his lips—whose shape I had drawn many more times during the months following my first drawing—moved in response to the question, and as they did, he dropped the folder onto the coffee table next to him. He was now entirely absorbed in the conversation with Nando, discussing "the peasant question" and the necessity of an agrarian reform, a subject I would have been normally interested in, but all I could hear was the blood pulsing in my temples. I took the wine glass from the platter next to me, and raising the glass to my lips, I kept watching Barbu's, without hearing a sound. It was the third glass I had that night, and I could no longer concentrate, my senses saturated with the muffled, cotton-like sensation I had in my ears. An overwhelming desire to trample all conventions took hold of me, and I longed to strip naked, right then and there, and to tell dear, beer-gut, *urechi-clăpăuge* Ferdinand: "You never had this body. It's all his." Then, I would grab Barbu's hand, force him to stand next to me, place his arm around my waist, and press his body against mine in an ecstatic embrace that would leave him moaning and me screaming with pleasure until Ferdinand begged me to stop.

"What are you thinking of?" Nando suddenly asked. "You should go to bed, your eyelids are drooping."

Carmen Sylva: I knew it! I knew it! I told Karl that that poor Nando was *încornorat* (a cuckold) and that his closest aid and confidant was, in fact, the man who was sleeping in his bed behind his back, but he, no! Mind your business, he kept saying, it's out of our hands. (To Queen Marie): Every time I confronted you, you played the innocent, offended victim.

Queen Marie: You've always been jealous because I had what you never had: the passionate love of a man.

Carmen Sylva (spiteful tone, dismissive laughter): Oh, my poor dear! You think that because Karl was a man of duty, and because I didn't spend my life before a mirror, like you, we didn't enjoy our intimacy together. You couldn't be more wrong. Any biographer can see from our letters how eagerly we waited to see each other after a separation. You, on the other hand, having to share your bed with a dimwit, I can't blame you too much. But I do blame you for marrying him.

Queen Marie: You finally said it! What you've been thinking all along. You hate me because you think I stole him from that woman—as if it were my fault.

The Chronicler: Can we, please, go back to you and Barbu? Did you make love with him that time?

Queen Marie: You should remember from *Daniel Deronda* that, at the time, "making love" meant "speaking about love." And yes, we did make love.

The Chronicler: That very night?

Queen Marie: Yes, we did. Talked about it. That is, made it.

The Chronicler: You talked about it, or you made it?

Queen Marie: Talked. Made. Yes, we did.

The Chronicler: You are starting to sound like me.

Queen Marie: Oh, don't flatter yourself, my dear!

Carmen Sylva: Aren't you going to tell us when and where you did it?

Queen Marie: For an old woman with such a high moral sense, you sound rather curious and impatient. Curiously impatient.

The Chronicler: We want details!

Queen Marie: What language do you want them in?

The Chronicler: What do you mean, "What language"?

Queen Marie: I mean that Barbu and I spoke French.

Carmen Sylva: We speak French too.

Queen Marie (smiling): Not *his* French.

Carmen Sylva (sarcastically): Very clever! How clever you are and how you dwarf us all with your beauty and unparalleled wit!

The Chronicler: But you can still speak English and give us the quotes in French.

Queen Marie: I could, but I won't. Maybe I want to keep just for me the original and to give you the copy—that is, the translation.

The Chronicler: Was it then that he called you for the first time "My Marie"? Or did he say "Ma Marie"? Wait, no! He must have used English because all his letters to you, the letters written during thirty years, ended in ILYMM, his coded abbreviation for "I love you, my Marie." This means that your love language was English, not French.

Queen Marie: It was then that he uttered my name for the first time. I never imagined that one could get such pleasure from hearing one's name and from being looked at. But with Barbu, it was enough for him to lay his eyes on me, or say my name, and I felt a kind of joy that can't compare with any other. He looked me in the eye, and then, he held me, and I stood there, in my white dress with pink embroidery feeling how my cheeks were becoming red-hot under his gaze. He held me closer, and I felt that my cheeks were burning. When he was so close I could feel his breath on me, a dizzying sensation took hold of me, and I said I needed to sit down because I wasn't feeling well. Instead, he pressed his body against mine and kissed me.

Carmen Sylva (same sarcastic tone as before): Was his tongue speaking French when he kissed you?

The Chronicler: Don't listen to her! Go on!

Queen Marie: My romance with Barbu cured me of the repulsion I'd had of physical intimacy, which was due to Nando's excruciating lack of skills in handling a woman. When we got married, he was terribly in love with me, while I simply had a young and very naïve girl's crush on him, without being aware of what happened between a man and a woman behind closed doors. What a shock it was to see this respectable and shy prince transform himself into a hairy beast at night, who seemed to want to devour me! At the beginning he was insatiable, he was all over me at least three times a day, but with the years, after the birth of Carol and Elisabeta, he began to look for pleasure in other beds. Barbu taught me that physical love could be pleasurable for a woman too. But, after it ran its course, our love turned into friendship, a steady, loyal and unique friendship.

The Chronicler: And yet, he kept signing his letters "ILYMM."

Queen Marie: Barbu was a very loyal man. He never stopped loving me, but he felt that he owed the same loyalty to his family too, his wife and daughters.

My friendship with Colonel Boyle was very different. Although his origins were rather modest and his fortune was the result of his extraordinary skills, he was the only man with whom I felt perfect equality—maybe because he never considered me his superior, as everyone else did.

The Chronicler: Let's tell our readers that he was born in Canada and made his fortune during the gold rush when he became the owner of several gold mines. He was known as "the King of Klondike." In Romania, he represented for a while the Royal Dutch Shell Company. Later, he was named President of the Committee for the Distribution of Aid in Russia.

Queen Marie: Yes, it was during that time that I met him. This man who came from nowhere, in the sense that he had no pedigree, had a way of talking and acting in my presence as if none of my titles and lineage mattered.

The Chronicler: And you were seduced by that, of course.

Queen Marie: What I was seduced by was his honesty and straightforwardness. From the very first time I saw him I understood that ours will be a lifelong friendship because we were kindred souls. It is also true that I was seduced by the enormous strength he emanated. He was very tall and muscular, in a way that made me think of a Viking. He put his entire strength and goodwill at my feet offering to stand guard by my door and act as a filter for the numerous men and women who came to see me with all kinds of problems, thus eating my time away. He made the above offer with the passion of a troubadour of yore declaring his allegiance to his lady.

During the war I lived for a while in the small town of Bicaz, famous for its beautiful lake and gorges, and there, I prepared for Boyle a small peasant-like cottage where he and I met everyday, sometimes twice a day for an entire summer. Every night I went to see him, sometimes with a companion, most often alone, and, after discussing the most pressing questions of the day, we would eat a bowl of soup, then he would walk me home under the stars. On the rare occasions when I didn't go and see him, I stayed home with Barbu, reading *Dorian Gray* and drinking a cup of hot chocolate I had prepared myself. Barbu and Boyle had a very cordial relationship, based on which I imagined that Barbu must be fine with my visits to Boyle, until one day I received a poignant letter from him, in which he complained that I no longer trusted him, and he no longer was for me the friend he once was. I answered with a long letter, which I wrote crying, or rather, sobbing: how could he imagine that such a thing would ever happen? That the day would come when he would be no longer my most trusted friend and companion? But as I wrote it, I understood what Barbu never said in his letter: that someone else was between us, another man, who was now the one I trusted with my most important and delicate missions, such as talking to Carol and Nando. I realized that I had to navigate a fine balance between the two, and that our heart is a complex mechanism that can hold in it more than one love.

I had some type of love even for Nando, whom I never loved in the erotic sense of the word, if by "love" we understand a bond between two people grounded in mutual interests and affection. But, God, how he annoyed me with his constant indecision, with his incapacity to accomplish what he'd started! I'm afraid kings are not educated to be men—during the war, people kept repeating the repartee of the Count of St. Aulaire, France's special envoy to Bucharest, that the only man in Romania was me. Indeed, even the Romanians looked at me as the country's center of manliness and resistance to the German occupation. I shivered thinking that, given the influence Barbu and I had on Nando, we could have destroyed him if we had had evil intentions and not his best interest at heart! Boyle was Nando's precise opposite, a man driven by a desire to accomplish and finish everything he started, he was manliness incarnate, the absolute expression of what a man should be! It is true that his honesty and abrasive frankness sometimes inspired in him unorthodox methods that made him akin to a beast charmer, but we understood each other perfectly—like me, he was driven by a selfless desire to help others, something that a Latin people like the Romanians, with their cynical view of things, cannot comprehend; that's why they imagined he must have had some ulterior and hidden goals. I love my Romanians, but, as the Romanian saying goes, *nu te îmbăta cu apă rece,* one shouldn't get drunk on cold water, that is, one should look at the facts as they are: the Romanians are a cynical, most unsentimental people, while we, the English and the Anglo-Saxons in general, have a childlike enthusiasm for what is good and moral.

The Chronicler: You spent the entire summer of 1918 together with Boyle and your youngest daughter, Ileana, who was not even ten, like three musketeers, helping the poor of the neighboring villages. The three of you had identified several families that became your favorite, and paid them almost daily visits, fixing their homes, helping when their children got sick, bringing them food, and, at the end of the day, sitting on the terrace with them, smoking. I can see the three of you on a wooden terrace, Colonel Boyle in his uniform, you and Ileana in Romanian national costumes, and two or three old women with faces wrinkled like those of witches, seated next to you, puffing happily from the cigarettes you brought. And you too, smoking, with a detached smile, under Boyle's tender gaze.

You refuse to say it, but you were, at the very least, infatuated with Boyle, and he with you. You spent all your free time with him, to the point that there were days when you refused to see Barbu, which is what prompted that tragic letter from him. It is unlikely that two passionate adults, such as you and Boyle, would have no more than a platonic relationship, given that you were constantly in each other's company. Why you refuse to acknowledge that you were lovers is a mystery to me. Do you want to protect in this way the legend of you and Barbu? Do you hope, maybe, that the pain you caused him because of your affair with Boyle would be canceled if you refuse to acknowledge its existence even in posterity? Or, maybe, just maybe, was your love for Boyle even greater than the one for Barbu, and your silence is simply the veil with which you want to cover its mystery in eternity?

Queen Marie (silent): …

CHAPTER 8

IN WHICH I INTRODUCE MY FIRST-BORN, CROWN PRINCE CAROL

Queen Marie: I fell pregnant within days of my marriage, and I soon began to feel sluggish and nauseated by everything I ate. I, always healthy and full of energy, found myself lying in bed for hours, and couldn't comprehend what was wrong with me until a lady in waiting enlightened me about my condition. Laugh if you will, but it was not uncommon at the time for young women of my class to be completely innocent when they married. My mother had raised us in such ignorance of daily life that I had only some vague knowledge about how babies came into the world, and by this, I mean both the process and the result. After my lady in waiting, all smiles, informed me that I was with child, she spread the news to the rest of the household, and everybody, Uncle in particular, was very excited. For a while, they contended themselves to congratulate me in private—the servants, the politicians, Uncle and Aunty's staff—, but one day, while I attended a public event with Nando, a congenial minister whose beer gut was spilling over his waist in spite of the constraining tuxedo, congratulated me in front of everybody, and I felt how blood rushed violently to my face. Where I came from a woman's delicate condition was discussed only in whispers, never publicly. I felt so embarrassed I began to cry in front of everybody. Feeling self-conscious himself because of my tears, Nando took my hand in his and attempted to calm me down while the others whispered and smiled with *double entendre*. I felt so humiliated that I stood up and left in tears. This was only the first of many other similar scenes that followed. Eventually, I got used to the crude, Latin way of doing things, and thinking back on those times, I think it is probably healthier to acknowledge a woman's pregnancy than to pretend you don't notice her protruding stomach even if it's right under your nose.

The Chronicler: I won't hide it from you: I find your son, Carol, the best argument against monarchy as a form of government. A man raised by a couple who believed in duty more than in anything else, yet their offspring ended up abdicating not once, but four times! (Although at least one of the times he was careful to avoid the word "abdication" in the documents he signed, calling it a "transfer of duties" to his son, or something like that.) He brought back the country to the very instability the Romanians tried to avoid when they crowned a foreign dynasty. This worked as long as the dynasty remained foreign, and failed miserably as soon as the Crown Prince, raised a hundred percent as a Romanian, began to act like a Romanian politician by surrounding himself with a corrupted camarilla. He was as small as you were great.

Queen Marie: There is no need to rub it in. More than anyone else, I was the one who was the main target of his pathological jealousy. After Nando's death in 1927 and the proclamation of Carol as King, he took away from me all my official prerogatives, my office, my team, my most loyal man, and he replaced them with his spies. He couldn't stand that I was much more popular than him. At first, I thought it was some kind of misunderstanding, but the misunderstandings kept piling up. Sitta, whom he had married in Spring 1921, and who gave birth to Mihai on October 25th the same year, had already conquered the hearts of the Romanians with her quiet dignity and charming dimples, which Mihai and, later, Mihai's first-born, also inherited. As soon as he realized how popular Sitta was, Carol did everything he could to compromise her in the eyes of the nation, going so far as to spread fake rumors about her, a strategy he also used against his sister, Ileana, and, of course, me.

At first, Sitta's complaints about Carol rubbed me the wrong way: I was torn between sympathy and annoyance. She had just arrived in the country, was already pregnant, and was still getting acquainted with our customs and life at the Palace. One day she asked for a private meeting with me. She was clearly embarrassed and kept clutching at her pearls with one hand, while fidgeting with her teacup with the other, not daring to look me in the eye. In the end, sensing that her confession was of a sexual nature, I put my hand over hers in an encouraging gesture and said:

"My dear, you can tell me anything. After six children, I think I can take it."

She sighed and confessed that she was at a loss about how to deal with the Crown Prince, whose passion was so overbearing that he followed her throughout the day, forcing her to fulfill her conjugal duties at the most inappropriate times and in the most inappropriate places, as often as three times a day, on couches and chairs, a few steps away from the servants, who listened behind the doors and whose knowing smiles were so insulting she was ashamed to even leave her room. I recognized in her description the behavior of young Nando in the first years of our marriage, his violent, almost frightening passion, and in her tone, the same disgust that had been mine. I felt sorry for her, but at the same time, I knew that the advice I had to give her had to take into account my son's feelings. Wiping her tears with my own handkerchief, I told her that this is how all men are; that, apparently, this is how Mother Nature intended it, and that all we women could do was to use to our advantage a situation that was meant to favor men. Her sighs dwindled, and, wiping her nose, she asked whether this could hurt the baby. I laughed and confessed that when I was her age, I too feared the same thing, but that she had nothing to worry about, the child was safe.

Well, two months later, both mother and child almost died at birth. Mihai was born prematurely, and the birth was so traumatizing the doctors advised Sitta not to engage in any marital activity for months, which, now that I think of it, must have sealed the end of their marriage. Two years later, their marriage was so shaky they both took turns coming to me to complain about the other. Eventually, I came to resent both, although I admit that, at the beginning, I tended to take Carol's side. Yes, Sitta was charming and, God only knows I understood her, but she could have tried a little harder to … well, she could have tried a little harder. I know I sound old-fashioned, but what I mean is that although Carol was the one at fault, it takes two to tango. If Sitta had been closer to him, he might have resisted the vulgar charms of that other woman, the red-haired Jewess.

The Chronicler: In the summer of 1923, when the Royal Family was in residence at Sinaia, Carol met his wife's namesake: the woman who would destroy your life's work, Elena (also known as Magda) Lupescu, whom Carol and pretty much everybody else called *"Duduia,"* a word whose literal meaning is "lady," but which is no longer in usage, unless one wanted to refer to a bygone period. In time, the meaning of the word has been turned upside-down, and now one can only use it ironically, "We know what kind of lady …," wink-wink. It's not so much an allusion to a woman's sexuality, as it is to her vulgarity.

Queen Marie: A word I find perfectly fitting for the description of this woman. Elena Lupescu was one of the most vulgar women I have ever met. Of course, at the time, *duduia* was simply a synonym for the French "madame," but still, even then, there was something déclassé about its sound in my son's mouth. I could bet it was precisely because of her vulgarity that he had fallen for her, he was that kind of man, my son. And yet, he was a brilliant man. Historians agree that he was the most cultivated member of the entire Royal Family, and, certainly, the closest to the Romanian people, as he was the first Romanian-born offspring. I don't know what historians make of the man who is responsible for Carol's mindset, but I blame him for the ideas he put into Carol's head from the age of twelve when King Carol I, enamored as he was with the Swiss for their supposed forward thinking, decided to put a Swiss instructor in charge of our son's education.

The Chronicler: Oh, yes, Arnold Möehrlen, the thirty-year-old neurotic, melancholy teacher, a progressive—I think this is the best word to describe him—republican with impeccable French, *tobă de carte*, as they say in the language the Crown Prince and I share, whose hobbies, stamp collecting and natural sciences, in vogue at the time and appreciated by the Royal House, were no doubt a major factor in the decision to hire him. As was his morality, a quality much in demand at any Royal House, and in particular at the House of Romania, a country with very relaxed moral values—as Queen Victoria had justly opined—where the need to protect the morals of the young princes was all the more necessary. Young Arnold had a stellar reputation because no one was aware of any women in his life.

Queen Marie: This is what happens when a mother is refused the right to raise and educate her own child. From the point of view of the King and of the government, Carol belonged to the nation and had to be educated in a special way. Little by little, Arnold and Carol grew inseparable, spending all their time together, taking trips abroad and all over the country. You can only imagine the enormous influence that such proximity can have over the mind and soul of an adolescent. Arnold's gloom soon began to extend over the manners of our son, to the point that whenever they were together in our presence, Carol no longer smiled and appeared constantly irritated, as if ready to lash out at us. It took us a while to realize that the instructor was not only a convinced republican, he was also a socialist who kept telling Carol that the era of the kings was gone, that being a prince was shameful, and that he should rebel against us, his masters and oppressors.

The Chronicler: Ha, ha! Which proves that nothing is new under the sun, and Prince Harry isn't the first woke prince in history! But this Arnold did teach Carol some useful things. In their extended journeys, they visited all the factories in the entire country, in particular those producing candy, cigarettes and chocolate, items Arnold was fond of. From this point of view, Carol did have a truly progressive education: he knew the country better than most Romanians, and he knew his people, including those from the *mahalale* at the outskirts of the capital, ghettos populated by Gypsies and dirt-poor daredevils. There is no doubt in my mind that some of his best accomplishments were due to the education received from Arnold. The Royal Foundation Prince Carol, created the year Mihai was born, was responsible for the opening of thousands of libraries in all the country's small towns and villages, meant to alphabetize a population of illiterate peasants, as well as for the opening of the so-called *"cămine culturale,"* cultural hubs whose purpose was to both educate and entertain the peasants, and which have not only survived the abolition of the monarchy, but were later appropriated by the Communists and presented as their creation.

Queen Marie: Yes, Carol had many gifts, and his mind was one of them. I wouldn't credit Arnold, though, with the above accomplishments. Carol would have done the same thing with or without him. He had a model in the work of his parents and that of the country's first king. Another important accomplishment of his and which can definitely not be attributed to Arnold was the creation of the first boy scout organization, which was meant to instill in young boys the sentiments of honor, loyalty for the king and faith in God. Carol was still a teenager when he did this, and I remember how proud I was of my son then, my son in whom I believed more than in myself. He was, like all males in our family, a military man: he loved uniforms and he loved to give orders and be in command. As he was himself adored by the army, in particular the officers associated with the Royal House, he often received uniforms from them, which he tried on in the solitude of his bedroom, parading and yelling at imaginary soldiers.

The Chronicler: I remember an interview with King Mihai in which the King talks spitefully about his father's obsession with military uniforms and medals, calling him a megalomaniac and mocking him for having invented some ridiculously fancy military uniforms enhanced with revived Middle-Age symbols (a fascination, I'm afraid, he inherited from you). Indeed, here we are far from Arnold's influence. It seems to me that what Arnold managed to destroy in Carol was the respect a prince owes his parents and Souverains, as well as the very concept of duty without which no royal house can survive. The Swiss republican extinguished in the prince the notions of respect for the institution of monarchy and duty for his country, but he could not obliterate his innate characteristics, among them the big ego he inherited from you, Your Majesty. As I mentioned, he wasn't the only, nor the first, member of the Royal Family to recuperate medieval paraphernalia. Speaking of old accoutrements, have you seen the investiture of the Prince of Wales in 1969 at the age of eighteen? Not only was he dressed in some kind of old cape, but he also had a coronet on his head, and had to kneel in front of his mother, Queen Elizabeth, who proclaimed him her "liegeman." Not surprisingly, Prince William, who has inherited the title of Prince of Wales after the Queen's death, does not want to revive this ostentatious ritual at a time when his country is going through a period of austerity. In your case, however, the ego was balanced by your sense of obligation first and foremost toward your country of adoption, and by your British upbringing, which is repulsed by corruption and unfairness. But Carol was no British princess, he was a Romanian man, a Romanian man in a position of power, who happened to be endowed with a huge reproductive organ, and any Romanian man in this position would have considered that the satisfaction of said organ takes precedence over anything else. Carol was, of course, no exception.

Queen Marie: I will let the historians judge how big my ego was. As for Carol, he was also a sensitive young boy, much more sensitive than it would appear to an outsider, and I cannot stress enough how nefarious Arnold's influence had been over this young boy. One day, when he was fifteen, he showed us a letter received from Arnold, who used to occasionally hand him missives. Nando and I were shocked. It was … a love letter. The letter talked about the passionate feelings the young boy stirred in the adult's chest, particularly when the boy kneeled by his bed to say his prayer:

> If you could hear my heart beat whenever I see you so quietly and pensively open your delicate mouth each night, and, with your eyes closed and your body offered in complete surrender to the Lord, utter His prayer, so serene and innocent, so detached from everything material around you, as if I didn't even exist! In that moment, when your being is so detached from mine and so united with the Holy Ghost, all I want is to cross the enormous threshold that separates us, this wall interposed between us. I want to touch your immaterial soul

and, placing my pale lips upon your cold eyelids,
to make your sky-blue eyes look straight into my
hazel eyes.

The decision was taken immediately to remove this dangerous man from the proximity to our son.

The Chronicler: Ha, ha! I suppose we now know the reason why Arnold had such an impeccable moral reputation as a man with no amorous liaisons. But you are right, your son, Carol, was much more sensitive than future gossip—the *mauvaises langues* that referred to him with the same insulting expression used in relation to Britain's King Edward VII, "the playboy king"—made him appear. He was, like you, an incurable romantic fed with stories of impossible, tragic love, but unlike you, he did not have the power to sacrifice his heart for the higher reasons of State. He was, in other words, a typical man who led his life driven by the reason of his mighty Penis, all the while fooling himself that it was his heart that steered him. To his young mistress, Elena—

Queen Marie: Magda.

The Chronicler: To his young mistress, Elena Lupescu, not to be confused with his wife, Princess Elena, he used to recite lines from his favorite poet, Alfred de Musset, promising her eternal love, as they met in secret in the house he'd bought for her:

> *Du mal qu'un amour ignoré*
> *Nous fait souffrir,*
> *J'en porte l'âme déchirée*
> *Jusqu'à mourir.*

> *("Chanson de Fortunio")*

The anguish which a love untold
Makes us endure,
My heart has torn, my heart will hold
Till death, I'm sure.[17]

("Song of Fortunio")

Initially, they used to meet in the house of a navy officer, friend of Prince Carol and rival of Elena Lupescu's husband, an officer she married the same year Prince Carol contracted his first marriage, the marriage to Zizi Lambrino. I have a feeling that our readers are now getting impatient: slow down, please! Are you saying that Duduia—let's call her by the name she herself used to sign her letters with—was not only married when she met Carol, she also had a lover? Indeed, this is what I am saying. And are you saying that before marrying Princess Elena of Greece, Prince Carol had already been married? Yes, this is, indeed, the case.

In 1918, while the world was still in the grips of the Great War and the Romanian soldiers were in trenches, the Romanian Crown Prince left the battlefield and ran away to Odessa where he secretly married the commoner Zizi Lambrino. By the way, if the name Zizi sounds vaguely familiar to our readers, it's because there is another Zizi that has caused a scandal in the Royal Family, this one linked to you, my dear Queen: Zizi Cantacuzino, with whom you have been accused of having more than a flirt in your youth. Also, our Francophone readers may find it a bit ironic and amusing that the bearers of a name used by French little boys to refer to their penis were the cause of such scandals.

Queen Marie: Oh, for God's sake, try to stick to the main narrative! What's the point of going into all this?

---

17. English version published in 1881 by *Potter's American Monthly*. Translator unknown. https://allpoetry.com/Song-Of-Fortunio

The Chronicler: Very well, then, let's return to Zizi Lambrino. Although months before your son's disappearance you noticed that he was sad and often cried in secret but refused to reveal anything when questioned, the news of his escapade on September 15th, 1918, came to you as a total shock. In fact, maybe I should let you recount how you reacted.

Queen Marie: At first, I thought that something must have happened to him. I considered all the possibilities: could he have been taken prisoner? But when I realized that he must have eloped with the young woman he was in love with I felt sick. How could he do this to us when his country and family needed him most?

He'd left three letters: one for his sister, Lisabeta, one for the young woman's brother and one for the King. In the latter he justified his desertion from the army by saying that he was not allowed to do his duty as a soldier in the way he thought best, and so, it was better for him to leave. Not a word about the girl that was the real cause of his departure.

The Chronicler: What a coward! A deserter and a coward at the same time! Beating around the bush and claiming he was doing this to better serve his country! Not having the courage to acknowledge he was doing this for a woman!

Queen Marie: He was a young man in love, a man that was being taken advantage of by a calculating, cynical woman.

The Chronicler: He was an irresponsible man who sacrificed his duty to his penis. A year later he was already over her. But I'll grant you this: it was not only his penis, it was also his confused romanticism. Like you, he was a romantic, but while you were in search of a hero, he was the kind of upper-class man who idealizes women from the people.

Queen Marie: His gesture triggered a violent reaction in the Romanian people who, until then, had considered him their greatest hope for the country. He used to be their beautiful, mighty Prince—now they wanted his head.

The Chronicler: For once, I can't blame them.

Queen Marie: The conflict in which I suddenly found myself because of my son, a conflict between me and the Romanians who wanted Carol's head, transformed me into a lioness who defends her cub at any price. A lioness or a mother hen, I am not sure which. The government wanted to strip Carol of his right to the throne, and I could not accept it. I had long discussions with Boyle and Barbu, both of whom tried to help me by judging the situation with a detached and impassionate eye, although I could tell that Barbu was getting a bit impatient. Boyle was a very direct man, he never used subterfuge, he was always frank, which I loved but, at the same time, I could see that it didn't necessarily endear him or made him popular. At any rate, we tried together to come up with a strategy to save Carol.

Five days later I received a letter from Carol in which he told me about his plan of going to the French frontline where he would gather an army with which he would fight for Transylvania. Because he knew it was a risky idea, he claimed he had to bring his lover with him.

The Chronicler: What a bunch of malarkey! What BS! Again, he refused to take responsibility for his actions, for the fact that he deserted from the Romanian army in times of war simply to be with a woman, a woman that, moreover, the Romanian constitution didn't approve of.

Queen Marie: Easy for you to be a judge! As for myself, I did my best to understand my son's foolish behavior, and decided, together with Nando, to go meet Carol in a small town near the Eastern border. When we met, he was as pale as the moon that shined over us. We walked hand in hand under the bright, cruel moon, and he told me his story. I quickly understood that he had acted under the influence of some cynical individuals who pretended to want to help him, and, blinded by love, he fooled himself that he was behaving heroically.

The Chronicler: Indeed, he framed both his love and his desertion as an act of heroism.

Queen Marie: I told Carol that he should tell his lover that he had to return to his duty while the war was still going on, and then, as soon as the war ended, he could renounce all his privileges and go back to her. I could tell that my words had an impact on him, but he was silent. We separated, and I was left under the bright moon, which seemed to mock my suffering with its beauty.

The next day, Carol came to see me. He was coughing like a sick person, his face drawn and pale, his eyes teary. He said that he was ready to accept our decision. He said it like one who had accepted his death sentence, and I felt sorry for him. My poor boy, he was torn apart by suffering! I explained to him that few love stories, no matter how powerful, last a lifetime, but he was unmoved.

As for my dear Romanians, they were all very angry, asking for Carol's removal from the succession line and his replacement with Nicky. Luckily, I know that in Romania no miracle lasts longer than three days, as they say. Nando, as usual, was on the verge of a breakdown, and again, we had a fiery discussion, although this time we did our best to keep as calm as possible under the circumstances. I blamed him for never doing what he intended to do, and he blamed me for always doing more than I was supposed to, thus placing him in the awkward position of having to approve what I did.

After the discussion with Nando, I took my eldest daughters, Lisabeta and Mignon, and we went to see Carol at the Horaiţa Monastery, where he was executing his punishment. The surroundings were very peaceful, and Carol's two rooms comfortable, but the meeting was sad, and Lisabeta couldn't stop crying. In the end, it was Boyle who, after a long discussion with Barbu, went twice to see Carol, four hours at a time, to convince him of the right thing to do. Carol reluctantly accepted to sacrifice his love for the sake of the country, but only for the duration of the war, until the country was out of the current impasse. Few Romanians realize that our dynasty was saved—albeit not for long—by these two men, Boyle and Barbu.

Boyle offered to talk to Carol's girl and her family, and Nando and I accepted. It took less than ten minutes for Boyle to understand whom he was dealing with. He confirmed what we suspected: that these were scheming and devious people who would do anything to keep our son in the girl's claws. In fact, everybody who met the girl thought that she was an irresponsible young woman who simply didn't care that she was causing a constitutional crisis in the country. When, later that day, I told Carol for the first time what I thought of *her* and that he was a fool to destroy his future for such a woman, he answered with a pathetic and comical pride that I shouldn't talk like that about his wife. I burst out laughing. Poor boy! What a grotesque situation! My first-born, the successor to the throne, the man in whom not only his family but also the entire country had placed their highest hopes—to throw away his destiny for a vulgar adventurer!

When, on the 15th of September I went to see him together with my three daughters for his 25th birthday, all his sisters were in tears, and I could barely hold mine. As usual, he seemed to be suffering, with deep, violet circles under his eyes and a melancholy air. I implied that she wasn't, surely, suffering for him like he for her—which was a mistake because it made him mad. After he calmed down, we agreed on a plan: he had, *he absolutely had* to go fight as a soldier on the Allies' side, and, at the end of the war, if he still wanted Zizi, he was free to tell the entire world that he renounced everything for her. He could even see her once more before leaving, if he promised he wouldn't try to take her with him. This plan had the effect of reassuring and pacifying him.

But it took several more weeks of talks between Boyle and Barbu, on the one hand, and Carol, on the other, for the latter to accept the plan the two had come up with: that he would consent to the annulment of his marriage as the only way to save our dynasty, and that he would accept the King's assignment to go fight as the leader of the 1st Battalion (*Batalionul Vânători*) without bidding the girl goodbye— something that contradicted my promise to him, but Barbu begged me to be strong, to leave aside my feelings as a mother and to act like a queen.

The Chronicler: And so, to conclude: the marriage was annulled by the Royal Family, and the offspring that resulted from Carol's union with Zizi, a boy christened Carol Mircea, was never accepted by the royals. At twenty-five, Crown Prince Carol already had behind him an annulled marriage and a punishment of two months spent in the Monastery of Horaiţa for desertion from the army. What a difference between his behavior and that of his legitimate son, Mihai, who, at merely twenty-two, left to reign alone after his father's last abdication, would change the course of WWII through a coup against the fascist dictator Ion Antonescu, asking the Romanian army to join forces with the Allies against the Nazis! But about that, in due course.

For now, let's return to the story of Crown Prince Carol and Duduia. As I was saying, initially, they used to meet at the house of a navy officer, who was Duduia's lover at the time she met the Prince. There are, of course, many versions of the encounter, but the most plausible is the scene in the officer's living room where he had given a reception in honor of the Crown Prince. When, at the end, Prince Carol, charmed by the flirtatious redhead, offered to accompany Duduia home, the officer, jealous, threw a repartee for the history books in Duduia's direction: "Don't forget to take your pajamas! They are on the second shelf from the top."

We don't know what Duduia answered. What we do know is that in all the versions of their first encounter, Duduia comes across as very available. Much more available than the American, twice-divorced Wallis Simpson, with whom she has been compared, and certainly less attractive. The irony is that the relationship between Carol and Duduia solidified in the fall of 1925 when he had to go to England to attend the burial of Queen Alexandra, the wife of King Edward VII, with whom Carol has been compared.

Queen Marie: Yes, dear, beautiful Tante Alix, the elusive goddess of my childhood, on whom I had a secret crush, was no longer with us. Carol left in November with the Orient Express, and the nightmare started. On December 12th we received the letter in which he informed us that he was renouncing his dynastic rights and all the privileges that came with them, that he was doing it fully aware of the consequences, and that he promised not to set foot again in Romania for the next ten years. In a separate letter to his father he informed him that his decision had been caused by the oppressive way he was being treated by the Liberal government led by Brătianu. He never acknowledged he renounced his rights because of a woman. Brătianu told me that Carol was also furious with Barbu and that he was planning to modify the 1923 Constitution when he became king, intending to allow, among other things, morganatic marriages. This is the reason, by the way, why my other son, Nicky, who was also romantically attached to a Romanian divorcée, Ioana Doletti, was a supporter of Carol, and together with him, plotted Carol's return to Romania and the coup that would dethrone Carol's own son, little Mihai. But I am getting ahead of myself. It is December 1925, and Nando is still alive.

We begged Carol to change his mind. He was inflexible. He sent us another letter reiterating his request. I spent that Christmas like a woman who had just signed her death certificate. I couldn't believe that the work of a lifetime, *my* life and *my* work, was being destroyed by the very offspring of my womb. Brătianu tried to convince him to officially admit that he had left the country and his duties for a woman, suggesting that only after this admission could they discuss his return. Carol refused, and on December 28th, sobbing like a child, he signed the legal document through which he renounced his succession to the throne.

If this had happened in Britain, this would have been the end of it. Not so in Romania. From Italy, my son began to plot his return to the country he had himself abandoned, thus causing a division into those pro (the so-called "carlists") and those against him. Manifestoes were being circulated among army officers who were loyal to him, with the insinuation that Barbu and myself, jealous of his popularity, had concocted a plan to steer my son away from the throne. All these intrigues and lies made me sick to my stomach: my son, in whom I had believed more than in myself, was lost. My son was turning the army against me, the army, which until then, had venerated me. From Italy, where Carol stayed for a while, and later from France, we were being sent reports about his new "Court"— the controversial individuals he received at his hotel and the scandals he and *that woman* were involved in. I was ashamed for him. He began to give interviews to the foreign press in which he expounded his political views and in which he claimed that his having left the country was an act of protest against the Romanian Prime Minister, which, of course, wasn't true.

The Chronicler: I can't help noticing the difference between what was expected of the British and the Romanian Royal Families. In Romania, both Kings Carol I and Ferdinand, as well as Prince Carol, were very much involved in politics, in spite of their Constitutional limitations. Your son didn't even make a secret of it, and, when the opportunity presented itself, dissolved the political parties, unleashing a short-lived autocratic regime. On the other hand, in Britain, the slightest remark that could be construed as "political" sent everybody, anti-monarchists and courtiers alike, into a frenzy. When King Edward VIII, in his several months of reign, made a banal comment while visiting some coal mines that something had to be done about the lives of those people, the entire political establishment went apoplectic. How was it possible for a King to get political? "Get political"? The poor man had made a general statement about the overall condition of some of his subjects. He didn't ask them what party they were from. This is an aspect most people don't seem to understand: the interdiction of refraining from politics imposed upon the royals doesn't mean they shouldn't be allowed to voice any opinions whatsoever; rather, it means that they cannot get involved in party politics. Yet, in Britain, this is taken so seriously it almost means no opinion on anything. One begins to understand why Queen Elizabeth II was so revered, or why the Chinese emperors, who never spoke in public, were seen as Divine cyphers.

Queen Marie: Whatever one may say about Carol, he never had any problem making his opinions known. He was making them known even while in exile. And then, when he became King, we were drowning in his opinions, they were everywhere.

But I interrupted my story: as soon as Carol renounced his succession, Nando disinherited him and passed on everything to Mihai. The same year, in late fall, together with two of my children, Nicky and Ileana, I went on my American tour, of which we shall speak in a separate chapter, and which I had to cut short due to the news of the King's illness. On July 20th 1927, he died, and Mihai was declared King at barely five years old. Since he was a minor, a regency of three people was formed, which included Prince Nicky and two other individuals, who were there mostly in name. Meanwhile, Carol and Duduia, who were in France at the time, went to London—yes, he had the nerve to go to my country of birth and embarrass me in front of my relatives. There, the two runaways proudly strutted around at various *mondain* occasions that culminated with their grandiose appearance at the theater, where they were welcomed with thunderous greetings and cheers, and where Duduia could show off her furs and jewelry. They were under constant surveillance by the Scotland Yard—this is how we knew that Carol and his team had manufactured manifestoes addressed to "the People of Greater Romania," from which one could find out that he wanted to return and continue "the work of our two great Kings." The manifesto ended cynically with a blessing and a wish to the country: "Long live Romania! May God shield Her from the shedding of brotherly blood!"

Carol was asked by Britain's Minister of Interior to leave the country—my homeland!—a disgrace I could never have imagined. To see my own son chased from my country of birth because of his disgraceful behavior! *Oh, Carol, Carol, you chose your mother's beloved homeland to plot against your own son!* You and your brother Nicky schemed against your mother!

The Chronicler: Indeed, when former Prince Carol, now a civilian called Carol Caraiman after a famous mountain peak, secretly arrived in Romania's capital under cover of the night after four-and-a-half years of self-imposed exile, his brother, Prince Nicholas was the only member of the family who was in on it. This "mediocre" young man, as Carol used to call him, whose agenda paralleled that of his older brother because he too was in love with—

Queen Marie: "In love"?! *In love*?! Even if this were love, why is it that only men relinquish their duties to follow women? Questionable women, I should add. Why doesn't this happen the other way around? Has anyone ever thought of *my* life, having to live a lifetime with a man I was never in love with— though we became, thank God, allies and friends in the course of our marriage. Has anyone ever thought of *my heart*? The heart that had to give up all the loves of my life?

The Chronicler: Whatever you want to call it, love or lust, it made the two young men bond together and rebel against their mother, the same mother Carol had worshipped as a child and who was now replaced by Duduia. For one thing is clear: a man who calls his woman "Duduia" cannot have only erotic feelings for her; a man who swears his woman eternal love more than thirteen years after they first met is tied to her by more than just the flesh. And when the woman turns out to be as domineering as a mother, one has to wonder whether she is, more than anything else, a substitute for the mother.

Queen Marie: Pretty soon you are going to say that the mother is responsible for the son's behavior! And then, you seem to take for granted *that woman's* statements! I assume you are referring to the entry in her journal done on the *Nahlin* one summer day in 1938, when she claims that Carol fell to his knees before her and swore her eternal love.

The Chronicler: We should probably explain to our readers what the *Nahlin* was—the famous "love boat" that linked two couples and the destinies of two countries, not to mention the irony of bringing you closer to the man who could have been your husband, George V of Great Britain, by placing you both in the position of aggrieved parents of their irresponsible first-borns who shamed them. When did you hear for the first time about King George's troubles with his son, Edward?

Queen Marie: It was sometime in the early 1930s, I don't remember exactly when. But I knew from George's letters that he was very unhappy with his son, just as I was with mine, and for similar reasons. Edward too was living with a divorced woman—in his case, a twice-divorced American woman of dubious extraction, Wallis Simpson. When George died in January 1936, Edward showed himself at the Palace's window with his mistress, who was still married to her second husband. It was an unheard-of breach of protocol that shocked everyone.

It was on the *Nahlin* that the fate of Great Britain was decided when the newly-proclaimed King Edward VIII chose to take his mistress with him in the summer of 1936 on a tour of Eastern Europe on the Adriatic to visit countries that were either Nazi sympathizers or dictatorial regimes: in Greece, they met with King George, the former husband of my daughter Lisabeta, who had recently divorced him and returned home; in Hungary, Admiral Horthy gave the couple a royal welcome, and so did President Ataturk of Turkey, while in Yugoslavia, the official motorcade is said to have frightened the local peasants, scattering them away with its dangerous speed.

For diplomatic reasons, King Edward had decided to use the *Nahlin* rather than the royal yacht *Victoria and Albert*. The *Nahlin*, a yacht built in 1930 in Glasgow at the order of the richest aristocrat of the time, Lady Henrietta Yule, was truly luxurious, boasting six guestrooms with bathrooms, an office, a ladies' sitting room, a gym and a library, from where the King removed several shelves of books and replaced them with alcohol. When Carol bought the yacht a year later, he was no doubt aware of its past, and sentimental as he was, liked to imagine that the karma of the love story between another king and his mistress may rub off on him and his own mistress.

The Chronicler: Indeed, Carol was both sentimental and sexually promiscuous, an unusual combination. Like you, he was a romantic, a reader of tragic love stories; Duduia too was a lover of French romances, and she sprinkled her love letters to Carol with formulas from French novels. But the word "mistress" you are using is slightly misleading. By 1930 when Carol returned to Romania, both he and Duduia had divorced their previous partners. He had divorced Princess Elena of Greece in 1928 while he was still in exile, and when he returned, he was forced by Iuliu Maniu, the leader of the

National Peasant's Party, to promise that he would remarry her and grant her the title of Queen. But Duduia was very jealous, she wanted Elena out of the country, and so, eventually, King Carol forced his former wife to leave the country. By the way, do you know what Duduia and Carol used to call Elena in their private correspondence?

Queen Marie: I heard that they used to mockingly refer to her as "of Greece."

The Chronicler: Yes. Or simply: "Of." As in: "What is *Of* up to?" Of course, Carol didn't keep the promise given to Maniu, and Elena had to, eventually, take refuge in Italy where she bought the (now-famous) villa Sparta. During most of his childhood, little Mihai could only see his mother twice a year for, at most, a couple of months. For this, he never forgave his father.

Queen Marie: For a long time, I was heartbroken because of my son's conduct. Heartbroken because he destroyed my life's work. I felt ashamed when meeting relatives from abroad, I, once the envy of many of them, now having to carry this chip on my shoulder.

But looking at it a hundred years later, with the dispassion brought by the passage of time, and witnessing now the current scandals of the British Royal Family, or of the Norwegian Royal Family, I can't help thinking of it all as a pattern, a *familial* and familiar drama that gets passed on from generation to generation. If you look at it in this way, it becomes almost entertaining. For, in light of the drama of today's British Royal Family and of its spectacular display on the world's stage, the story of my Carol becomes some kind of an archetype.

Every time I see Prince Harry throw a stone at his brother from across the ocean, my heart sinks because I know how painful this must be for his entire family, including Harry himself. You can tell from Harry's facial expressions that he isn't happy. You can tell that he knows he is in the wrong.

He is the one who created a situation in which a journalist could ask his brother, "Your Royal Highness, is your family racist?"—which prompted this answer from William, "We are very much *not* a racist family." Harry knows that he has done something horribly unfair by putting his brother in such a situation, but he cannot admit it even to himself, because to do so would mean questioning the entire edifice of lies he and his wife have built their new life on. And yet, he must still love his brother. A closeness like theirs never dies entirely. Hence, his tragic circumstances. He is truly a tragic prince.

Carmen Sylva: He will become a tragic figure only when that wife of his shakes him off like a piece of dirt on her shoe.

Queen Marie: I see that you too, like so many royal commentators, live with the secret hope that she will divorce him. But she never will. When two people have such huge egos, they need each other because they see themselves in the other's eyes. I too lived for many years with the illusion that my first-born, Carol, will one day see the light, and divorce that horrible woman. But the more the years passed, the more he was attached to her. They died as a couple, and it is only in death that they were separated by their heirs, who decided to bring Carol's coffin back to Romania and bury him with the rest of the royal family.

The Chronicler: Today, some historians see their attachment as a great love story and claim that she was vilified only because she was a Jewess.

Queen Marie: Isn't this like saying that Meghan Markle was vilified because she is "black"? Doesn't this mean that we must ignore all their other characteristics and actions and focus exclusively on their race? Doesn't this mean that we must ignore their vulgarity and pretend they are some abstract categories instead?

Carmen Sylva: Did you see Meghan in that interview with that other Hollywood star, what's her name? Ellen Something, one of those hard to pronounce names, Detartrate or Degenerate or something like that. How that Ellen asked her to put a pacifier in her mouth and other humiliating things, which in their world pass for comedy? Vulgarity incarnated.

The Chronicler: Well, in her defense, one cannot claim that vulgarity never stained the Royal Family prior to that. You must know that Prince Philip couldn't even stand being in the same room with Sarah, Duchess of York, former wife of now-disgraced Prince Andrew.

Carmen Sylva: Have you heard the latest? Have you heard of Queen Margrethe of Denmark's demotion of her youngest son's children? All the royal commentators are talking about it, with some comparing Prince Joachim to Prince Harry the spare. The Queen knows that it is against the monarchy's interests to continue to accept that one of her sons, Prince Joachim, lives in another country, getting all the perks of a princely life and none of the responsibilities. Years ago, Joachim, who, like Harry, suffers of second son syndrome and couldn't accept living in the shadow of his brother, asked to be allowed to live in France with his second wife, Marie, who is French, and who bears an uncanny resemblance to his brother's wife, Mary. This, together with the fact that Joachim's two sons from his first marriage, Nikolai and Felix, are now working as fashion models, were the reason behind the Queen's decision. If members of her family were making a living by taking advantage of their birth rights, instead of, for instance, serving in the army, they might as well renounce their titles. It should be said, though, that she only took their styles away from them, that is, they can no longer call themselves highnesses, but they still have their count and countess titles. "Serve" is the key word here. This is what members of a royal family are supposed to do—serve their country. This is what Meghan couldn't understand. She couldn't understand it because she would have had to comprehend something foreign to her mindset: that we are not simply ourselves, but links in a chain that long precedes us, and which has survived in the institution of royalty. In a Royal Family, it is to this institution that all our actions and desires should be subsumed. By contrast, the biggest title of glory for a Hollywood princess is to play the role of savior and give uplifting speeches. "That's what I do. I like to save," the Duchess from Montecito said in that interview with Opera-or-whatever-her-name-is, showing us her "rescued" chickens. To give uplifting speeches full of well-meaning clichés: what an American invention!

Queen Marie: I wouldn't say that to give uplifting speeches is an American invention. I too have given plenty of uplifting speeches to the Romanian army, and there was nothing "American" about them.

Carmen Sylva: My dear, I too gave plenty of uplifting speeches in my life. But I am talking about something entirely different, about this new bizarre American mindset in which people feel obligated to dress up all their actions. This "activist"-minded person pretending that everything she does serves a higher purpose, when, in fact, it only serves the cult of her personality. It is precisely because these people do not believe in serving anything higher than themselves, because they do not believe in a higher order of things, that they have created this language of pretense. It is some kind of ersatz religion they have created precisely because they have no God.

CHAPTER 9

WAR AND DEATH

Queen Marie: When my little Mircea was taken from us, Barbu, my faithful and loyal Barbu, was there, as always, holding my hand, as I held Mircea's. My little Muki, as I called him, Mircea Vodă, my Sun Child, my little chick, the sixth and last of my children, a child with brown eyes, neither mine nor Nando's. I always wanted to have a child with brown eyes. Always? No, not always, rather since I met Barbu. Those of you who are reading this in order to get a bit of piquanterie of royal life, hoping for a full confession—you won't have it. I am not saying that Mircea was Barbu's. Or that he wasn't. Mircea was my child. A naughty child full of life, who is now gone forever. Forever. I will never see him again.

After it happened, I stood by his bed for hours, without crying, listening to the chorus of prayers around me, as if through thick cotton, until they took me away. Then, in the middle of the night, I returned and looked at his dear face. Strange, I recognized it and didn't, at the same time. His face had the eerie artificiality of a mask, imposing upon his features a gravity that contrasted with his tender age, as if he knew something the rest of us will never know. *What did my Mircea know?* What knowledge, forbidden to us, mortals, was his, and where was my little chick now? He was gone to some distant, foreign lands, while the country and Cotroceni Palace were bombarded by the Germans. I had the feeling that I was living a nightmare that would never end. Was this really happening?

Was my Mircea gone and the country on the precipice of a catastrophe? Maybe my child had to be sacrificed in order for the country to survive. Maybe a sacrifice is always needed for something to endure, as in the legend of Manole. My child for the country.

For a whole month I'd watched, helpless, the agony of the tiny body fighting a monstrous disease, I, a knot of pain, attempting to rid myself of it by helping our wounded soldiers from my hospitals. I was *Mama Regina*, Mother Queen, as they called me, dressed in my white uniform, carrying flowers, sweets, cigarettes and icons, which they all welcomed. I felt no pride whatsoever when these young men, who'd lost their limbs on the battlefield and who were in terrible pain, told me, as they kissed my hand, that it was all worth it if I was to become "the Empress of all Romanians," that is, the Queen of Transylvania too, for which they were fighting. On the contrary, I had the feeling of a horrible injustice. Why would these young, once healthy, wholesome men, accept to be mutilated like this? What world was this in which human, sentient bodies were butchered like meat? I went to my hospitals every day, holding the soldiers' hands, bringing them as much relief as I could, losing my own pain in theirs, sometimes crying with them, hoping for a miracle when I left the hospital and returned home. But the miracle never happened. I walked among the wounded soldiers as if in a dream, as if through a meandering, unending labyrinth, comforting them with my words or feeding them from a wooden spoon, while soldiers from nearby beds called me, "Mother Queen, Mother Queen," their wailings of pain, or sighs of gratitude at my sight gnawing at my heart, and I, separated from my own body, my heart away, next to Mircea's, touching their wounds with my grieving soul, could feel almost physically their love for me, and I knew that I was theirs, the way a lover belongs to the beloved. It is because of this connection that it was so hard for me to imagine leaving this country—which was presented to me more and more like the only possible outcome. Leaving this land was for me like uprooting my very self. And yet, we had to think of this possibility, we had to think of a way out. I absolutely refused to consider signing a peace treaty with the Germans; my British self refused to envision this humiliation, and so we came up with a plan that I called *"La Grande Aventure"*: getting out of the country via Russia. It was a horrific, impossible plan, yet the only honorable way out.

The soldiers were all familiar with my predicament and had tears in their eyes when they sent their wishes of recovery for "the little prince." This suffering created an unbreakable bond between me and the army—I knew that I'd won their hearts, that I was no longer the young, frivolous blond princess, but the Mother of the Country, the highest honor one can receive in a Latin country. Mircea was the only one among my children with whom I spoke only Romanian, and this too seemed to symbolize that I was tied to my country through him, tied with my flesh, blood, vowels and consonants. Now, my flesh and blood were buried in the garden of Cotroceni Palace.

After the Germans threw one hundred and sixty bombs around our home at Buftea—the home, at the edge of Bucharest, lent to us by the Ştirbey family—and it was decided that we, the royal family and our servants, had to run away and take the road of exile, I scribbled a desperate note "to whomever would take possession" of Cotroceni Palace and asked them to take care of the little grave, which I was forced to abandon. We took the train toward Iaşi without knowing where exactly we were going to live. When I asked Nando where I was supposed to go it was clear that he hadn't even thought about it. His passivity and lack of foresight had become truly unbearable. In times of war his character was a liability for the whole country—he wasn't even capable of giving orders. I begged him to let Carol go to the battlefront and show his face because the soldiers and the country needed to see the Crown Prince, who should have been a role model. I pleaded with him for weeks until he finally agreed. He should have realized that he, as King, was even more needed among his soldiers than the Crown Prince, but it was only weeks after Carol's departure that Nando bothered to follow him. As for the rest of the family, starting with me, the Queen, they were put on a train and left to fend for themselves. Never did I imagine that the day would come when I would be homeless—I, the children and my closest servants. During all this time, not a single word from Nando, nor from Mother, who was in Germany and from whom I hadn't heard since the beginning of the war. Like beggars, we moved from station to station, looking for a place, until, eventually, we arrived in Iaşi and were given the headquarters of the *Corps d'Armée*, a big and ugly building that belonged to the army. There, in just two days, my most faithful servants unpacked everything, and I did my best to hide the place's depressing ugliness by decorating it as best I could with the few things, rugs and furniture I had brought with me. I ached everywhere and missed Barbu terribly, but I avoided complaining because I knew that I had to set the tone, and if I started to feel sorry for myself, all was lost. Eventually, I received a long letter from Barbu, but, still, no word from Nando. In moments like these I wished to be a man so I could be King and take the fate of the country in my hands because watching how it was being taken over by the enemy while the King and his ministers were arguing with each other was truly heartbreaking. Of our country only Moldova and a part of Dobrogea were left. I continued to live in a never-ending nightmare, the sun brighter than ever, while the war, which until then had been a fiction to read about in novels, was raging around us. The sun shines, and somewhere people are killing each other.

The Chronicler: Do you know that this is precisely how Stefan Zweig describes the beginning of the war? A superbly bright, sunny day with people drinking their coffee, listening to music or strolling languidly under the canopies of trees, while hundreds of kilometers away the war has started? Soon, the war will reach them too, and their peaceful, tranquil lives will be turned into the unthinkable itself.

Queen Marie: Only a few months earlier I'd been a happy woman, my son was alive and there was no war. It shall never stop amazing me how our lives can suffer such dramatic changes in such a short time, how the hand writing in my journal, the hand that used to play with Mircea, and the hand that held his own dead hand, are the same. What a strange thing: that one day all this unbearable suffering will be simply a memory, the *past*, and even I will be no more! No more suffering.

The Chronicler: But even more amazing than this is that now your hand is *my* hand. That the entire history of the world is a chain of hands in which Being itself keeps taking new forms, each entirely unaware of its future existence. We can have glimpses of the past, but of the future we know nothing. Your hand is now my hand, and I tremble when I think that once I wore your crown on my head.

Carmen Sylva: So, you too believe in reincarnation!

The Chronicler: Not at all! What are you talking about?

Carmen Sylva: Maybe you should read what you just wrote.

The Chronicler: I wasn't talking about reincarnation. I was—

Queen Marie: *I* was talking about my son, about death, war and suffering, and you interrupted me to share your fantasies about wearing my crown on your head. I was just about to tell you about my exile in Iaşi, about our despair because all that was left of our country was a strip of land, and more and more voices were telling us that we should take the road of exile, that is, we should do the unthinkable—*leave Romania!* But where shall we go? I kept asking. And this is how the idea that we should leave for Russia began to creep in. We were so desperate that we were seriously considering it. Dear God, this was less than a year before the Russian Royal Family was executed by the Bolsheviks! Can you imagine what our fate would have been if we had gone to Russia? In the midst of all that insanity, a group of agitators came up with the idea that I should take advantage of my special relation with Nicky—the Tsar, that is—and go to him and beg him to save our country. This idea had the support neither of the King nor of the Prime Minister, but this group was adamant and kept on. One day, they sent Maruka Cantacuzino, Enescu's future wife, who until then, had been a close friend. What happened between Maruka and me that day is one of the saddest memories I have from that period! Faced with my resistance, she began to accuse me that I valued myself more than Romania, and that, in the end, I remained the young, frivolous British princess who had arrived on these shores thirty-four years earlier.

"You don't want to place yourself in an embarrassing situation, I get it. Your pride and your precious self are more important in the end than anything else, including your country. But maybe it's not your country, after all. What do you care? If I were you, I would crawl in front of the Tsar, I would lick his shoes and kiss the ground under them, anything, I would do anything to save my country."

Her words cut deep into my flesh, and she knew it. Of everything she could accuse me of, the accusation that I didn't love my country, and that, after all, this was not my country, was the most painful. Tears began to stream down my cheeks and my breath changed. I could no longer breathe—I kept inhaling, but something in my upper chest seemed to stop the air from entering it. I was suffocating. Eventually, Maruka stopped speaking and looked at me, worried, then, with a trembling voice, she called for the doctor. As soon as he understood what was going on, the doctor calmed us down, claiming that it was nothing serious—just "*angstneurose*," a concept developed by Dr. Freud. "The cure is simple:

inhale deeply and count so you can give equal time to your inhalations and exhalations!"

After the doctor left, Maruka hugged me apologetically and began to cry too. We made up, but her words lingered in the air. In fact, the same scene repeated itself in a different version—a different protagonist and a different medium, but the same idea. Several weeks later, she wrote a letter to Nando accusing him of, basically, the same: that he isn't putting country first, that the population is disappointed and has lost confidence in him, that all honest people are very worried. She, clearly, has some other people behind herself, I can smell a new group of schemers, probably the same group that insisted I go to Russia. And this from Maruka, one of our closest friends. It is true that she has always been very eccentric, probably the most eccentric person I know, behaving like a queen and demanding that the servants treat her as one. At her salons— where one can always listen to the most divine music—she sits quite literally on a throne, while I sit on the couch, like everybody else. Our friends have noticed the incongruity, but I think it's funny.

The other day, a tiny and funny man called Saharov, who is Nando's Chief of *Etat Majeur*, came for an audience, and he too reiterated in his broken and hilarious French, the need for us to go to Russia: *"you go with king ... you smile. Tsar say yes."*

I found his speech amusing, but eventually, those who did go to Russia were Crown Prince Carol and Brătianu. The government wanted to shoot two birds with one stone: announce the engagement of Prince Carol with one of the Romanov girls and use my influence and Russian relatives to obtain help in the war from the Tsar. The strange thing is that the Russians want this marriage even more than we do—what am I missing here? What could they possibly gain from us? Of course, now that a few months later, all of them, including that poor lovely girl, are no longer, I wonder whether they too were preparing for exile, maybe in our little country, while we were planning for exile in theirs.

When Carol and Brătianu returned from Russia, they brought with them several train cars full of life-saving gifts: undergarments, so necessary for our soldiers, tobacco, smoked fish, soap, bread, gloves, stockings, socks, sweets, and sunflower seeds that the Romanian peasants love to chew on. If we survived this war, it's mainly thanks to my Russian relatives, who sent us such gifts periodically. Another time, they sent us even more, when my sister Ducky came to visit.

The Chronicler: Funny, with the exception of sunflower seeds, all the other items were the kinds of gifts the Romanians were in great need of and used to receive from their relatives abroad during Communism. We had a saying, "If only we had more food, it would be exactly as in the war." We were referring to the second great war, of course, the one you didn't live to see.

Queen Marie: I am glad I was gone by the time WWII started. I couldn't have tolerated another war. Too much suffering. We no longer had a home, and my youngest son was resting under the earth hundreds of kilometers away from me. I kept myself busy, going to hospitals every day, keeping my mind occupied, knowing that if I let myself ponder the horror of my circumstances, I would collapse and break into a thousand pieces. *Mircea, what distant planet are you on, my Mircea?*

One day, as I was visiting a hospital to distribute my usual gifts—cigarettes and sweets, without which I never went anywhere—a wounded officer who had, apparently, lost his reason, began to wail like an old woman, and then he held his head in his hands, covering his ears, as if trying to stop them from hearing something unbearable. I suddenly felt such kinship with that poor man and the unspeakable horror of his suffering, I felt that he was the only human on this planet who could understand me, so I took his hands in mine and, holding them tight, I began to sob uncontrollably. Surprised, he stopped wailing, and this, in turn, put an end to my tears. We looked at each other for a few long minutes, silent, two broken souls in a broken world. Then, I got up and bid him goodbye. "Don't leave me!" he cried, but I could no longer stay, and I left, followed by the monotonous howling that he'd resumed.

Another time I stopped in a nearby village to distribute sugar and *opinci*—those laced, boat-shaped shoes that Romanian peasants wear—to the women and children, who were all very grateful. One of the women said in a touching and plaintive tone, the kind of tone only the most dejected people have, and which comes from abject hopelessness, that she could only give me a chicken in exchange. I told her I didn't need her chicken because I was the Queen. Full of joy, the woman became very excited and said that she knew I had to be someone important, maybe a general's wife, but couldn't imagine I was their Mistress herself. Then, she kissed my hands with the piousness specific to Romanian women and wished me a long and blessed life.

Among the many peasants I used to visit I had a few favorite old women with whom I sometimes sat down on the *prispă* (wooden terrace), and we smoked together. Sometimes they told me about the other peasants in the village, who were now jealous of the special attention they were getting. It was quite funny to see these babushkas with head scarves enjoying their cigarettes. Sometimes I offered them my framed portrait, and they hung it on a nail, crossing themselves before it. I sometimes thought that Romanian politicians would do well to come visit some of the huts these poor people lived in— they would have learned a lot.

The only thing that was the same was Barbu. Like a silent

rock, he was always there when I needed him, listening to my complaints, giving me advice, holding me when I cried, never asking for anything in return. He was the only human being I could still trust entirely. He didn't shy away from criticizing me, and sometimes our passionate discussions ended with me in tears. Other times we analyzed our impossible situation, that of being caught between the German enemy and the Bolsheviks, we looked at things from all possible sides, asking again and again what could be done and how to get out of it, until we felt caught in a maddening vertigo and we were physically nauseous. Our extraordinary situation had led me to abandon all diplomacy and I no longer held my words back with almost anyone: when you have one foot in the grave and nothing to lose, you might as well bring it all to light. I did the same with Nando, being honest in a cruel, unvarnished way, and our conversations often ended in screaming matches.

Since we took the road of exile, my other friends, including my personal assistant, who until then had been loyal as a dog, had become embroiled in all kinds of intrigues. I was surrounded by constant gossip, unverifiable rumors, people who stabbed each other's backs—mine included—politicians who, even now, were more concerned with settling personal accounts than the fate of the country. As for Nando, he was so weak he changed his mind every time he spoke with someone else. Any schemer could get under his skin. Aside from this, he had the bad habit of constantly interrupting his interlocutors, so he was never able to listen properly to the advice he was being given. Like all insecure people, he imagined countless offenses and thought of revenge but was too fragile and inconsistent to even come up with a revenge plan. Thinking back to the shy, clumsy young man I had gotten engaged to thirty-four years earlier, I could see that all his faults were already there, but I was too naïve and ignorant at the time. In fact, whenever I think of that poor young girl, I feel like hugging and warning her: Don't go there! That place is not for you! You are a creature of sun and light, you need peace and joy around you, you aren't made for intrigues and dirty deals with politicians. Too late now. I must lie in the bed I made for myself.

In order not to lose my mind I had to come up with all kinds of strategies. Seeing the funny side of all situations is one of them. Like, the other day, when my son Nicky was driving us around Iași in his car, which we called Bambino, we were forced to return because one of the city's main roads, muddy and full of potholes, was blocked by a fat pig. A fat pig in the middle of the road, like some kind of guardian of a precious castle—but there was no castle! I began to laugh hysterically, it was all so absurd. Speaking of pigs, do you know what I received for my birthday that year? Usually, I was gifted jewelry, but presents change in times of war: my youngest daughter, Ileana, brought me some ducks, and my oldest children a pig. Yes, a pig! Nando gave me money. All the above was meant, of course, to be donated to the military.

The Chronicler: Well, more than a hundred years later, the situation of the roads in Romania hasn't changed much. It is the country with the smallest network of highways in the European Union, in spite of the millions of euros taken from the same union for their construction. Now, as then, by the same corrupt politicians.

Queen Marie: Oh, how many times I wanted to have the power to tell these politicians off! But I was no king, and, in fact, even a king has limited powers. How many times I found myself in a verbal duel with Brătianu, the Prime Minister, who wouldn't stop insinuating that he had much more power than I did, and that, if necessary, he wouldn't refrain from using it! What exhausted me the most was having to deal with this; I was forced by circumstances to get involved in politics, when my inner nature had always been repulsed by it. I am by nature carefree, of a sunny disposition, and yes, maybe a little frivolous. I love beautiful dresses, expensive jewelry—which reminds me that most of my jewels, together with Romania's national treasure had been captured by the Bolsheviks after we sent them to the Tsar for safekeeping during the retreat of our army from Bucharest. In fact, it was to compensate for the loss of my jewels to the Bolsheviks that Nando bought the 478-karat sapphire set by Cartier in the sautoir I wore when I posed for the famous portrait of me by Philip de László.

I love being admired. But I am also deeply hurt by injustice, hurt to my very core, and I appreciate loyalty over everything else, and so, as the Queen of the Romanians, I feel that it is my duty to fight until my dying breath for this country. For the life of me, I don't understand how the Romanians themselves cannot put aside their differences and petty enmities to save their country. Rather than act, the Romanians prefer to sit passively, accusing each other, hoping that God will save them at the last minute—but I know that God only helps you if you help yourself. I feel like shaking them from their centuries-old stupor, Wake up, wake up before it's too late! When they do act, all they do is bicker and fight with each other, placing party affiliation and personal interests above loyalty to the country. In this sense, one could say that the poor King, weak as he is, is the only patriot in this country. The army adores him, and whenever we appear in public, we are welcomed with cheers and ovations. The worse the country's situation gets, the more we are being showed warmth and affection. It's as if the people can't stand the idea that their King and Queen could be taken away from them, and they want to show us their love and loyalty. The last time we made a public appearance in a salon, the cheers were so sublimely loud and intense, the love so palpable that Nando stopped exercising any control over his feelings and let his tears run down his cheeks. At least, people say, the King had the courage to sacrifice something:

he sacrificed his love for his country of birth and his German family to honor his duty as King of Romania. Couldn't Romanian politicians learn something from him? The King and I spend our time trying to unite the two major parties and convince them to put their differences aside for the good of the country, but it all falls on deaf ears. I am so disgusted with this country's politicians that I sometimes feel like running away, just disappearing somewhere where no one can see me. Yes, sometimes all I want is to lie down, to stop feeling and thinking, and just die.

But do you know what gives me the most pain? When the Romanians chop down their woods; they have this bad habit of destroying their woods in the most irrational way, and it kills me.

The Chronicler: Do you know that even today the destruction of Romania's woods is one of the most contentious points in the country's politics? One of the most dangerous jobs to have today is that of ranger because the thieves who want to steal wood are beating them to a pulp. Romanian wood is feeding the machinery of Western manufacturers such as Ikea, which pretends it doesn't know how the wood is being harvested.

But speaking of disgust, funny how life and the uncontrollable game of chance can take us from totally different points and, eventually, bring us to the same conclusion. Just a few months ago I decided that I could no longer stand life in the United States, and that, once again, I preferred to start life anew by facing the unknown in my middle age. Just as I was once disgusted with the country whose queen you were unfortunate enough to be, I am now disgusted with my adoptive country. And yes, just like you, I wanted to disappear, because I couldn't even feel that I belonged to the same species as my compatriots.

Queen Marie: And yet, personally, I always had an affinity with the American people. More than an affinity, in fact; I found most Americans I met truly charming, and I always connected with them. During the war, the American minister, Vopicka, was extremely helpful; he and his friends were scrupulously efficient and pragmatic in their distribution of goods to the military and our hospitals. One of my best friends, the American dancer Loie Füller, insisted that I come to America because it would welcome me with open arms and help me rebuild my country, which turned out to be true.

The Chronicler: We shall tell the story of your visit to America on another occasion. Now, about the theft of the Romanian national treasure and of your jewels, which you mentioned earlier. To this day, every director of the Romanian National Bank takes an oath that someday they will repatriate the stolen gold, but whenever they address the Russian government, the Russians just laugh at them: "They've been lost." But maybe this is the moment to discuss the abdication of the Tsar in 1917, and how it came to that. I know that your view of it doesn't put the blame entirely on the Bolsheviks. That the conduct of the Tsar himself may have played a role in the tragic events that followed.

Queen Marie: Not the conduct of Nicky himself—this is what we called the Tsar—but, rather, of his wife, Alix. But because he was so devoted to her and didn't realize how unpopular she was, he satisfied all her absurd demands, including those concerning Rasputin, and eventually, their ties to this man led to their demise. It was such an incredible situation, with no parallel in history: this woman, the Tsarina, I mean, through her arrogant conduct, managed to make herself hated by everybody, rich and poor alike, aristocrats and peasants. Even the members of her own family hated her.

The Chronicler: When you say, "her arrogant conduct," what exactly do you mean?

Queen Marie: The way she behaved, forcing the Tsar to hire her favorite people, who were unqualified for their positions, and doing this over everybody's heads, as if she alone was in possession of all the answers. Not caring about anyone else's opinion. Acting like an absolute autocrat and making Nicky adopt her opinions and attitude. And then, the power Rasputin was allowed to have and his overwhelming influence over her led to the removal of many capable people and to the gradual dissent and rebellion within all the social classes. Having interacted with her and having experienced firsthand the asperities of her personality, I understand very well why everybody hated her, and I wonder how she must have felt. I assume she saw herself as some kind of martyr, because this is the only way one could cope with such a situation, but what I don't understand is why she never tried to change her ways.

The Chronicler: Well, eventually, she did become a martyr. When the Bolsheviks killed her and the entire Royal Family, including the children.

Queen Marie: You are moving too fast. For a while it seemed that the monarchy could survive under a different monarch. When Nicky abdicated and was taken prisoner, he did it in favor of his brother Mikhail, but he too was in a very insecure situation, so at some point it appeared that the Great Duke Kiril, the husband of my sister, Ducky, could become Tsar. That would have been an amazing turn of events—my, sister, the Empress of Russia! But this possibility evaporated fast, as the Bolsheviks continued to gain strength, and months later I stopped having any news from Ducky. The rumors that came from Russia—officers being cut to pieces by their soldiers— were horrific, and anything seemed possible. Anything terrible, that is. The months when I had no news from my sister were full of anguish, but this was not the only reason I was interested in keeping friends there. As long as we had people favorable to us there, I could continue to receive gifts and provisions for our army, without which its survival was in question. I was beginning to tell you about that winter in

1917, one of the harshest on record. No matter how many furs we had on, we were still shivering. I had a chronic sore throat, I would develop a fever, stay in bed for a few days, then, forced to leave it, I would be out, apparently cured. And then, the fever would be back, and the cycle would start all over again. Same thing for Barbu, who, used as he was to come see me daily to discuss the horrible situation the country was in, and to try to find a solution, was sometimes obliged to lie abed, yet he would often come see me against his doctor's advice, and afterward, get even sicker. One day, as he rose from the table, his body could no longer cope with this brutal treatment, and he fainted. He knew how much his presence meant for me and did the impossible to be by my side as much as possible. In the evening, we always found the time to sit by the fire and read. Usually, I was the one reading out loud from one of my recently published books, and when Barbu wasn't there, I read with my children. I remember that at the time I was reading *The Wheels of Chance* by H. G. Wells with Mignon and Lisabeta, and *Alice in Wonderland* with Ileana. I had just received the Romanian edition of *My Country* in Iorga's translation, and I read from it (Speaking of this translation, which was highly praised, it should be said that Iorga, smart as he was, didn't pay much attention to style, and it is because a team—made of myself and my daughters, Lisabeta and Mignon—kept revising it night after night that the ultimate result was so good). Barbu was full of praise, and I know he meant it because he never lies. How lucky I am to have such a devoted man by my side, I thought. There is nothing more important to me than loyalty. Some of my contemporaries mistook this feature of my character for vanity, but they are wrong. The fact is that I am a very straightforward, honest person, and I expect others to be the same. And as a queen in a country full of schemers, I can't work unless I have around me a team of people I can trust. This is why when my personal assistant and administrator of the Crown, who, until our exile to Iași, had been the most devoted man I ever employed, began to act in a disloyal way, receiving my orders with hostility and questioning them not in a constructive way but simply out of a desire to oppose my wishes, I spoke with him frankly and told him exactly what I thought. I cannot let a boil fester, and I believe that people who do so end up chewing on their resentment until they choke. I prefer to address the problem honestly, to lay out everything in the open, and then we can try to solve it. I told my administrator that I had always respected him enough to be straight with him, and that I thought that the woman who was now his partner had a negative influence on him, because she was at the root of his change of attitude.

The Chronicler: Today, if you were to do that, you'd be called a misogynist because you are blaming the woman.

Queen Marie: *N'importe quoi !* As if women are never to be blamed! What kind of world is this in which blaming one particular woman amounts to blaming all the women? Besides, one doesn't need a survey to understand that, as a category, women are more prone to gossip because of the way they live. When one stays at home and has less access to the world, one is more inclined to imagine stories about a world out of reach. Men have the option of settling scores between them by fighting, whether in a duel or on the battlefield. Women settle scores by spreading rumors about each other. And in my household, the rumor mill was running to such an extent that I had to ask Barbu to step in and act as a peacemaker. God, how many times my ladies in waiting fought like wild cats, using the kind of language street women do!

The Chronicler: Clearly, the life at a Romanian Court is not the life at a British Court. I am sure the servants at King George V's Court were much more civil. Today, the servants who work in a British palace are called "the staff." These days, in fact, the British servants and courtiers are being accused by a woman who grew up in Hollywood and imported all her class-specific entitlement with her, of "not helping" her find a shrink to cope with the difficult lifestyle of a princess. More specifically, she went to the Department of Human Resources of the Palace to ask for help, and then she complained she didn't get it, when, in fact, that department is for the staff, not for the princes. She forgot that her husband was the patron of the biggest mental health charity in the country. Now, the courtiers and the staff are fighting back by accusing the princess of bullying them to the point of having developed PTSD. Some of them also claim that all her complaints are part of a plan she had from the beginning to return to the US and capitalize on her royal titles. Hence, the necessity of creating a narrative that she had no option but to leave Great Britain.

Queen Marie: Oh, dear, are we back again talking about "the American princess"? I think she has a certain charm, even though she, clearly, has no understanding of the monarchic system. But all this drama around her, why do you think that is?

The Chronicler: Every time a public person expresses an opinion it creates drama. And we are talking here about a person who has a lot of opinions, even though it appears that she can't tell the difference between an archetype and a stereotype, as proven by her Spotify podcast, "Archetypes." In America, if you are a woman who went to a good private school, the way she did, you also feel obligated to prove your feminist credentials, especially if you are friends with Gloria Steinem, or want to show you are friends with her by calling her "Glo" when you give interviews. And how do you prove this? By invoking stereotypes against women (which, in your great wisdom, you call "archetypes"). Curiously enough, she didn't count among these stereotypes the idea that women who have just given birth suffer from "baby brain," which is what she accused her sister-in-law of having after she gave birth to

Prince Louis. But she mentions the "spinster" as a supposed stereotype. My dear Queen, I don't know about you, but I have never heard a man call a woman a "spinster." Ever. In fact, the last and only time I heard someone use the word was by the feminist and human rights activist, Amal Clooney, who, in a speech meant to celebrate her husband, said—somewhat self-ironically—that before she met him, she'd been resigned to die a spinster. "Spinster" is a concept of the past, which is what this American princess is constantly fighting, while she accepted to be a part of, and to serve one of the oldest institutions of the Western world.

Queen Marie: I see your point, but, honestly, I don't care. Let's go back to *your*, that is, *my* country. When you live in a country in which people are constantly gossiping and plotting, you never know which of your friends will betray and stab you in the back. For instance, one of our men, an aristocrat no less, whom Nando had decorated, plotted against our army. How can one deal with such betrayal? I had to constantly waste my energy listening to everybody's complaints and sort out the webs they weaved against their political enemies, myself included. After I created the network of military hospitals "Queen Marie," they attempted to steal them from me. I was the one who went from hospital to hospital making sure they had what was needed, I was the one putting in heroic efforts to obtain provisions from my relatives abroad, and then they rewarded me by taking the hospitals from me and giving them to one of those corrupt individuals who made certain that all the gifts and goods went into his pockets.

The Chronicler: I see that the glorious Romanian tradition of pocketing the common goods goes way back! It is the mentality of the Romanian civil servant that the higher the position one is in, the more entitled he is to take advantage of it. Otherwise, his friends would accuse him of being stupid.

Queen Marie: One day I exploded. I began to scream that I would leave and let them marinate in their stinky Romanian pig trough. Barbu managed to calm me down, as always.

The Chronicler: I noticed that, twice, in your war diaries, after commenting on Barbu's absolute devotion and loyalty to both you and Nando, you insert, in italics, the Romanian expression "*a fost odată ca niciodată*," the equivalent of *once upon a time*, which could be literally translated as "it was once, as if it had never been." Interestingly, this is very similar to the Arabic version of the fairytale phrasing that could be roughly translated as "it was like this, it wasn't like this." Like in Romanian, an affirmation followed by its negation.

Queen Marie: I wasn't aware of the Arabic turn of phrase. I am sure you must have a theory about that.

The Chronicler: Not really a theory, just an observation: that, unlike Westerners, the Orientals—and the Romanians *were* Orientals until recently—don't believe in unidirectional power, also known as Progress. In the Orient, everything is double-edged, any up has its down, and an affirmation is by necessity followed by a negation. Remember the legend of Manole where everything built by day is being destroyed by an unknown force at night? *A fost odată ca niciodată.* You wrote these words after mentioning Barbu to make it clear that something *did* happen between the two of you. The adverb *once* (*odată*) projects the story into the atemporality of the fairytale. It happened once, but now it's all over, gone. *Ca niciodată.* It seems to me that by the time of the war your love story was over, at least from your point of view, maybe because you replaced Barbu with Boyle. What was left was Barbu's unwavering and total devotion to the Crown. The kind of devotion that only medieval chevaliers or troubadours used to have, something very rare in Romanian culture because it is a quality closely associated with that of *honor*. And honor is a sentiment that can develop properly only in an aristocratic culture. It is the word that appears over and over in your war diaries, particularly in that devastating part from March 2nd, 1918 onward, when the country seemed to have been lost to the Germans and the peace treaty that you call dishonorable and humiliating appeared unavoidable.

Queen Marie: March 1918: the darkest period of my entire life, with the exception of the death of my little Mircea, of course—although even his death didn't bring us to the peak of despair that the possible loss of our country did, and this maybe because we, I, at least, felt responsible for the lives of our subjects. The death of my son touched me alone, but the death of our country was something I had no right to preside over. I don't wish anyone to experience the feeling of hopelessness and sheer impossibility I was subjected to in those days when I felt I was losing my very reason.

The Chronicler: Let's start with March 2nd when Nando came to you sobbing after receiving a telegram from Vienna in which he was asked once again to accept the shameful peace with the Germans, to consent to their advancement toward Odessa via Romania, give them the country's postal system, its telegraph communications and all its railways. (Just as a parenthesis: there are those who say that if we had accepted that shameful peace, today's Romania may have trains that run on time rather than trains that never arrive at their destination.)

Queen Marie: Nando looked like a madman and told me he had no choice but to sign. I replied that anything was preferable to putting his signature on such a shameful document. Anything: capitulation, captivity, prison—anything. I tried to give him my own confidence, to empathically transfer my own feelings to him, because I knew how weak he was, and I knew that after talking to me he would talk to one of his generals, the "realists," like general Averescu, who would tell him that he had to sign because otherwise our army would be decimated, and that signing was the only way to save the country. I asked Barbu, who was just as desperate as I was, what we could do to save Nando from himself, to give him the courage he needed to withstand the pressure from all the generals and the politicians who wanted him to sign. I knew Barbu would do anything he could to inspire some courage in Nando, but, goodness, this husband of mine was so weak and so incapable of confronting the people around him! *If only I were a man*, I thought! Alas, I was only a powerless woman. Having to witness all this from the outside, I experienced an anguish I'd never known before.

It so happens that on March 2nd, the day when my anguish attained its peak, I met the man who would later play a major part in my life: Colonel Boyle. From the start, I saw in him a fascinating Englishman (though he was a Canadian, properly speaking), the type of adventurer who fears nothing and no one, and who, at the time, was working on our behalf in Russia. More about this extraordinary man later.

The next day, that is, on March 3rd, the Crown Council was to take place, and so I made sure to see Nando right before. What followed was our most violent encounter ever. I told him words I never imagined I would tell anyone, least of all him—but they had to be said. I told him that he was an idiot to sell his soul, and with it, his country and family's honor to a general he didn't even trust, I told him that he was a fool to let himself be used by others more powerful than him, because he lacked character. He became so angry he started screaming at me at the top of his lungs, and, as usual when he was angry, his face turned white as paper. I thought he was going to faint, or else become physically violent—I have no doubt that if he'd been a commoner, he'd have hit me. But I no longer cared, I confronted him like a lioness, I knew that the truth of a whole nation spoke through me. I told him terrible words, unfair words, but which were nevertheless true, words one says only once in a lifetime. I always thought that if we were to go down—and, the way things stood, the disaster couldn't be avoided—we should, at least, do it with dignity, we should die as heroes, not slaves. In the end, Nando calmed down, but he looked like a broken man. Tearful, he said that he felt he was going mad with so much pressure from all directions, the Germans on one side, the Russians on the other, and then, our government, which didn't want to assume any responsibility and put everything on his shoulders. I felt pity for him and managed to convince him to go get a cup of coffee before meeting the council. Then, Barbu showed up and I explained the entire situation, giving him a summary of what had just happened. As always, Barbu kept calm—he never lost his temper and tried to be objective. He said that I was unfair to Nando, while I repeated my remark that we had not a single real man in the whole country, and that my misfortune was that I had to be queen over a nation of cowards, starting with the King. There, I said it!

During the Crown Council, Nando, under the influence of our discussion no doubt, asked the others to carefully weigh the conditions of the peace treaty and only after painstaking consideration to come back to him with a proposal. When Barbu and I heard that he didn't sign, we became giddy with excitement. There was still hope! Everything was not lost. For a few hours I experienced an irrational state of exhilaration, hoping against hope that we had a way out. A way out! Then … General Averescu showed up. In a few words: he said that he was embarrassed to show his face before me, but he had to let me know that "they" were ready to accept all the shameful peace conditions because they had no choice. I told him that I was ashamed for him, that he was no man because a man could not accept defeat without a single gunshot. He replied that a fight could only lead to a massacre of our army, which we had to avoid at all costs. I answered back that he seemed to want to save our army by enslaving it to the Germans. We went back and forth like this for a while, I, extremely agitated, he, of a devilish calm, but full of resentment, no doubt. In the end, I accepted defeat and fell on the couch, exhausted, a vanquished queen and a broken woman.

After dinner, Nando, Barbu, Carol and I analyzed the situation from all angles once again until we felt that our brains would explode, then we went to bed.

On the 4th of March, after another Crown Council, Nando came out entirely crushed. I didn't even ask him how it went—I knew it. How could he accept such humiliation? How could he not fight until the end? I don't know why, it could be the blood of the ancestors running through my veins, but I cannot accept defeat. Nando, I can already see him resigned to his new life. He'll get used to it fast: he'll have his garden, his dog, that's all he needs. He can get used to being a slave. I can't. I must fight till the end, even though the end has already been decided.

The Chronicler: When you mention the King in this part of your diary, there are several lines that have been crossed out and darkened in ink. I assume you did that to protect both of you from the eyes of posterity. I assume the words you put on paper were so harsh you were afraid they may darken both of you in our judgment, and so, you erased them.

Queen Marie: You may assume anything you want. The next day, the same scene took place between me and Nando, though in an even worse version. He'd been told that I was turning his men against him, and I answered as calmly as I could, accusing him of weakness and cowardice. If you had the strength to resist all these cowards, I told him, you'd remain in history as *Ferdinand le loyal*, but as things are, you'd go down as a weak man through whose veins runs the blood of a slave. I also told him that it was about time for the Romanian people to be informed of what was going on because they had a right to know, but, as usual, he said that it was the government's duty to do that. Later that day, I went to visit some of my hospitals and offer my usual gifts, but I felt no pleasure any longer: everything had become anguish, as if my entire life was but a long, slow road toward death. In the evening, I went to Maruka, who was hosting a party for our foreign friends, American, British and French, who were getting ready to leave, as per the Germans' request. Not even trying to hide my tears, I said goodbye to the French general, Berthelot, who hugged me to his chest like a big bear. To Anderson, the American Colonel, who was one of my best friends and was leaving tons of provisions behind him, all under my care, I had said goodbye in a private meeting. The meeting had been particularly touching, since, like most Anglo-Saxons, he was reluctant to express his feelings in words, but I could feel his love and devotion in an almost palpable way. We sat side by side holding hands, and, at the end, he knelt and kissed the hem of my dress.

At the same party I decorated a few of my most loyal friends, some of whom were weeping, knowing that their departure abandoned us to slavery, and, at the end, they all cheered "hip-hip-hooray!" That evening, Maruka's daughter, who was only nineteen, kneeled before me, kissing my feet, and, with the innocence of her age, asked me to save our country by accepting to be the leader of a movement that will oppose both the government and the King. I told her that that was treason and was out of the question. I blessed her and added that maybe her words were madness, but I knew they were born out of patriotism, which was more than I could say about her other compatriots. But, as the King's wife, I had the duty to follow him.

The next day and then the next day again, the nightmare continued. Will this ever end? Lately, Nando had been avoiding me, clearly, because he knew he was guilty of having capitulated so easily to the shameful conditions of our enemies and was ashamed of me. I spoke with Barbu, who, like me, was very worried, and we decided to throw a party for our foreign friends to see if we could find out anything new. But the party was a long agony: I was split in two: a charming, smiling hostess on the outside and a desperate woman inside. I felt like a man whose coat had been caught in a machine that dragged him closer and closer to an inexorable death.

Every time I looked at Nando I saw a man on his way to dishonor, a man digging his own grave. He acted like a man under a monstrous spell, walking with a hunched back, as if the humiliation had caught up with him. His posture was the outward sign of his inner capitulation. I kept telling him that he could still free himself from dishonor, that the army was with him, but in vain. Barbu looked at me with a mixture of admiration and pity, not understanding that my English blood absolutely refused to accept defeat as long as there was the slightest possibility of success.

On March 8th another indignity was added to our list of miseries, and this time it didn't even come from the Germans but was the result of the disgusting cowardice of our government. Having been forced by the Germans to let them use our territory on their way to Odessa, our government allowed them to do so before the Allies were able to retreat, thus causing the latter to be caught by the enemy in a trap. This disgusted me to such a degree that it made me sick and kept me in bed an entire morning, something entirely contrary to my habits. The same day, General Berthelot, who was still in the country, went to see Nando at my request, but left very disappointed, not having managed to convince him of anything. That night, together with Carol, I spent hours desperately concocting plans, among which Carol's idea that he should go to the front and lead our soldiers in the fight against the enemy.

The Chronicler: I see here his romantic enthusiasm, which he inherited from you. Didn't he say he wanted to go fight wearing his medal, "Queen Maria"? As if his attire was of the essence.

Queen Marie: These kinds of details matter immensely when it comes to people's morale. We were also trying to make Nando issue some kind of statement about the offended honor of our friends and our lack of hospitality, to put it mildly, and we almost succeeded, but then … *l'Homme du malheur* arrived and made him change his mind once again.

The Chronicler: For obvious reasons, you refuse to give his name, but my guess would be that you are talking about General Averescu, considering that the Germans later demanded that any new government had to include him.

Queen Marie: There are many strange things Averescu did during that period: for instance, he sent to us a funny, immensely rich tiny Jewish man, who put all his riches at our disposal and exhorted Nando to order for himself a golden cape incrusted with precious stones, something incredibly inappropriate in times of war when people were starving. Later, we found out that this man was a very shady character, so it makes me wonder why Averescu sent him to us. Did he want to compromise us?

The Chronicler: Before we get sidetracked again: you mentioned Odessa earlier. Colonel Boyle had returned the same day, March 8th, from Odessa, hadn't he?

Queen Marie: Indeed, he had. He'd been there to help our prisoners.

The Chronicler: Also speaking of Odessa, I'd be curious to know what your relationship with the Ukrainians was at the time.

Queen Marie: In January 1918 I met four young Ukrainians whom I thought very charming and idealistic. Their country had just declared itself independent from the Russians and professed a desire to live in peace with us. The leader of the group looked very Romanian and spoke many languages, and, although he represented the democratic spirit of the modern times and was therefore not a monarchist, we both took a liking to each other. Like us, the Ukrainians were victims of the hordes of Russian troops who raped and destroyed everything where they passed, and we felt that we had to unite our forces to face a common enemy. The only problem with their ideals was that they wanted to make peace, and that would have left us alone. In fact, only a month later, they signed the peace treaty with Germany and promised to export all their wheat there. And then, in March, instigated by the Austrians, they demanded a big chunk of Bessarabia.

The Chronicler: You said that Colonel Boyle had returned on March 8th from Odessa, where he'd helped our prisoners. But I seem to remember that this was not the first time.

Queen Marie: Indeed, a month later he returned from another trip there with a number of our prisoners whom he'd managed to liberate. The stories he narrated about their escape and the adventures he'd gone through were so incredible that he made you think of one of those heroes of yore that feared nothing. To begin with, he was incredibly tall and strong, a giant of a man with rough, albeit noble features.

The Chronicler: Yes, I saw a photo of him in your diary. He is standing among a group of Romanians, towering over them, a head and a half taller, his broad shoulders and stocky body making the other men look like delicate schoolgirls. His features are also broad and masculine, inspiring a confidence he must have aroused in you too. In your diary you declare over and over again that Boyle was the man in whose hands you would gladly put Romania's fate, that you had absolute trust in him. Just like in Barbu.

Queen Marie: Yes, just like in Barbu. Coincidentally, it was around this time that a group of Romanian instigators tried to eliminate Barbu from my life, claiming that, because his sister was married to Prime Minister Ionel Brătianu, who, like many of his compatriots, was pro-German, he too must be pro-German. Poor deluded people! In fact, this assertion couldn't be further from the truth. Barbu, like me, was a strong supporter of the Allies, and the King had the most devoted and loyal subject in him. But, as always, jealous and petty opportunists tried to take advantage of a political situation to get rid of someone they couldn't stand for personal reasons, namely that he meant so much to me!

The Chronicler: Yes. Having lived in circumstances of extreme political upheaval, in both Romania and the United States, I can confirm that one of the first consequences of such times is that opportunists are the most eager to raise their heads and turn in their favor a context that is otherwise messy and confusing for most people. All extreme political ideologies end up creating the perfect platform for this universal type of human.

Queen Marie: This type of human may be, indeed, universal, but he is particularly present in Romania. This could be explained by the history of its people who have learned to be skeptical of any authority and learned *să se incline de unde bate vântul*, to follow the direction of the wind without any guiding principles or a belief in a higher cause.

The Chronicler: Indeed. Even though I lived there for fewer years than you, as someone born in that country, having spent there my most formative years, I know only too well my fellow countrymen. No principles. Amoral. Very likely because of their religion, Orthodoxy. A metaphysical religion with no concern for the here and now.

Queen Marie: My Romanians, to whom I devoted my life, were ready to get rid of me if another master could replace me in a way they deemed more advantageous to them. Speaking of advantageous replacements, the "hero of Mărășești," the general who was credited with one of the greatest military victories in Romanian history, decided to leave his wife for a much richer and younger one because, in his words, a hero owed it to himself and to his country to be rich.

The Chronicler: One thing you can't accuse the Romanians of is lack of humor. As for their lack of principles: adaptation is the ideology of the destitute. Honor is a luxury. The ideology of those who needn't work. The aristocrats. As you point out in your diary, the Romanians have no honor and no principles. A bunch of cowards, you say.

Queen Marie: You're unfair. I wrote that on one of the worst days of my life, in what may have been the darkest period of my life. I was simply venting.

The Chronicler: But I wasn't blaming you. I agree with you. Your verdict about the Romanians is true and precise. And your verdict about yourself is also true, even as you, carefully and modestly, say that your opinion about yourself may be too high: you were a healthy, honest center around which the rest of the country, made of poor fools, gravitated.

Queen Marie: Are you trying to mock me while pretending to praise me?

The Chronicler: Not at all. I truly believe that you saw not only others, but also yourself, in the most realist way possible. Besides, you are capable of self-irony: often, you refer to yourself with deprecating humor. When the Romanians pay homage to their queen in an exaggerated way by kissing her hands on both sides, then her feet, when they praise her excessively and you are expected to answer, you answer in a "queenish" way—*queenish*, not queenly. Later, when the war ends and everybody praises you to the skies, you shake off the praise mockingly—they "buttered me up," you say, which in Romanian is *a tămâia*, i.e., "covered you in incense." You are "Everyone's Mother," as the Romanians call you, you never leave home without cigarettes, sugar, tobacco and other essential goods that you share with the poorest of the poor, you spend your days clothing them in the most literal way, yet you never think of yourself as a "White Savior." It is a paradox, but it was your Aunt, Queen Elisabeta, who saw herself as such, even though she grew up under much more austere circumstances than you, and your background would have been much more favorable to such mythologizing.

Queen Marie (whispering): Careful … She could hear us.

The Chronicler: Nah, I think she's asleep.

Queen Marie: Well, to continue my story. On March 9th, I went to the train station to accompany our foreign friends who were leaving the country, and Colonel Boyle was among them. As I was taking my leave, I told him: "Everybody is abandoning me. They all swear me allegiance, but in the end, they all leave." He looked me in the eye, holding my gaze for longer than it should have been appropriate, and, clasping my hand in his with steel-like firmness: "But I won't."

It was sometime in the month of October that the Allies had started to win more and more battles, the French kept advancing, the Turks overturned their government, and the Bulgarians demanded peace. Our country's fate, which, until then, had seemed horrific, began to look much better. Caught between glorious hope and terrible dread, I couldn't quite believe that my day was about to come, that there was, finally, light at the end of the tunnel. I remember how once, in the Iaşi *Mitropolie*—God, how I hated this city!—, as I was seated on my throne contemplating the faithful during the religious service, I experienced a sensation of unbridled power surging inside me, and I let myself be overtaken by a feeling of formidable spite toward all my enemies who had made my life miserable during those past years. When I confessed this to my friend Boyle, who was back again, he looked me in the eye and, taking my hand in his: *"Your Majesty, you knew how to lose, now show that you know how to win!"*

On the 9th of November the Allies crossed the Danube into our country and our soldiers reentered the war. William the

Kaiser and the Crown Prince abdicated, which should have pleased me because they had done everything they could to destroy us, yet the news displeased me. I am a lioness when I need to defend my people, but when my enemy is down, I can't help feeling pity for him. His downfall didn't trigger my joy. Maybe it was class solidarity, but I was saddened by Germany's fate. How will this affect my mother, who lives there? I couldn't help thinking of the game that Fate keeps playing with us. Two months earlier we were enslaved by the Germans and their tyrannic emperor. Now, their emperor was gone, and their country had ceased to exist. Our country, on the other hand, was on its way to fulfill its age-long dream, the dream of a Greater Romania, in which Bukovina and Transylvania would unite with the Homeland, something that hadn't been done since Mihai the Brave.

On November 17th—coincidentally, Barbu's birthday—a delegation of Bukovinans came to see me and brought me a letter in which the desire of their people that I be their queen is expressed in a language that is so dear to me, the poetic language specific to the Romanians from that province.

The Chronicler: Let's see if we can translate it here in English for the benefit of our readers:

> Our Lady,
> From beyond the black and yellow pillars of a Sorrowful Land, tearful eyes have long been gazing longingly toward the Happy Land on whose throne sat Queen Maria, the Comforter of distress. Today, when these pillars are no longer lodged in Moldova's heart, Bukovina is sending us to let you know how deep her gratitude is and how great her happiness to know herself protected by the kindest mother that has ever sat on a country's throne.
> May You live long, Your Majesty!

I assume the black and yellow pillars refer to someone's flag. Which flag is that?

Queen Marie: The Habsburgs', of course.

The Chronicler: What I find fascinating is how your image as a queen is conflated with that of the Virgin Mary—"the Comforter of distress," "the kindest mother." A Westerner would be tempted to say that they idealized you, but that would be much too simplistic an explanation. I know how Romanian peasants think. They project everything onto an immemorial background, so, for them, individuals are archetypes. A great queen, or a great king, ends up being as much reality as legend. Stefan the Great becomes Stefan the Saint, and Queen Maria, Everybody's Mother, hence the Virgin Mary.

Queen Marie: On November 29th, Bukovina declared itself part of Romania under the reign of Ferdinand the 1st. The next day we began our glorious journey back to the country's capital, and each time the train stopped at a station, the excitement of the crowd and of the soldiers, the deafening cheers, the patriotic songs and the billowing flags were magnificent. "The Empress of all the Romanians!" they shouted, and tears ran down my cheeks, still incredulous that it was finally happening. I was wearing my uniform, a new coat with an English cut, with a gray astrakhan hat laced under my chin, and on my back a scarf borrowed from Barbu. I wrapped myself in a long, double mantle, and mounted my enormous horse, Jumbo, with Nando on my right side, Nick on my left, and General Berthelot on Nando's right side, all on horseback. Thus, we rode in a delirium of excitement along Calea Victoriei, which was lined with French and Romanian soldiers. It was as if even the houses and the stones were screaming in ecstasy—after two years of suffering, the population was so happy to greet us and to celebrate the country's golden dream! Our procession advanced until we reached Mihai the Brave Square where the parades take place every May 10th and we watched the soldiers pass before us. Then, we dismounted, and Nando and I entered an open carriage, which took us to the *Mitropolie*. There, I barely had ten minutes to change into a gala dress, a copper-colored velour dress with golden embroidery. During the church ceremony, as I watched the French and Romanian soldiers, I experienced the same vengeful satisfaction as in the Iași *Mitropolie*, but then, I remembered Boyle's words and controlled myself. Finally, we took an open car toward Cotroceni, and this is when my emotions overwhelmed me. I was, finally, coming home, home to my Mircea and his final resting place, the place of all my "*dor.*"[18] As we carved our way through the crowds, excited people climbed onto our vehicle and surrounded it, almost propelling it into the air like a flying carpet.

The Chronicler: Like King Mihai's car when he returned from exile in 1992. His car was so battered afterward that it had to be totaled.

Queen Marie: I found Cotroceni Palace almost unchanged. Only a few furniture items had been moved, but, apparently, nothing stolen. Shortly after my return, I fell bedridden with the infamous Spanish flu for three whole weeks. I had never been so ill. I had a splitting headache, I was nauseous, feverish and extremely weak, suffered from terrible insomnia and hallucinations that were driving me insane. Any sound, smell, color or taste was like torture. Everybody around me was worried, and Barbu, of course, more than anyone else. He took care of me with his usual devotion and, little by little, I began to feel better. What I didn't know at the time was that during my illness several other of my friends had been suffering from the same condition but were less lucky and didn't survive.

The Chronicler: As we are having this conversation, I too am recovering from Covid. A light form, but, still, very unpleas-

18. Deep longing or nostalgia (Rom.)

ant. The way our postmodern world dealt with this pandemic was something to behold. We had several lockdowns when no one was allowed to leave one's home. It seemed as if the entire human race had moved from the streets into their screens from where people were calling and talking to each other, like two-dimensional copies of their former, plumper selves. I saw cities become ghost towns; I saw Pope Francis hold Sunday mass in the empty St. Peter Plaza with the heroism of a saintly alien or an alien saint, his ghostly figure dressed in a long white robe flanked by young, athletic men in dark suits, his benediction floating above the deserted square like a mirage in search of an addressee.

Queen Marie: You, people of today, are too afraid of death. You have transformed death into something alien, when, in fact, it is part of life.

When I got out of bed three weeks later, the world had changed. The country was shaken by workers' strikes, and the law for the peasants' land allotment had been passed by Nando. It was a necessary law that compensated Romanian peasantry for its role in the war, and I approved of it; still, I couldn't help but mourn the end of a way of life and of a class, that of the landowners called "*latifundiari*."

The Chronicler: As a famous Romanian writer once said, Time was becoming impatient.

Chapter 10

In which I Invite the Reader to Accompany Me on My American Tour

Queen Marie: Every life follows a meandering trajectory that seems random and devoid of meaning. Death alone, with its absolute finality, brings closure and bestows sense and clarity upon what until then had been merely primitive enjoyment of life's organic expression. As long as we exist in the flesh—or, as the Romanians say, *în carne și oase*, in the flesh and the bones—life is simply a visceral form of existence. It is after one's death that one's body and mind are replaced by the survivors' memory of them, and what was previously random gathers coherence and meaning according to an order assigned by a third party. One could very well say that history's chroniclers are purveyors of meaning, scriveners who turn shapeless lives into meaningful stories. Then, on the red thread that holds a life together, one can find surprising recurrences and spectacular patterns. In my life and in the history of Romania's Royal House, one such recurrence was the number 18.

On October 18th, 2019, seventy-one years after her enforced exile by the Communists, and thirty-seven years after her death, Queen Mother Elena returned to Romania to rest by the side of her son. Almost thirty years earlier, on January 18th, 1990, having arrived for the first time in her country of birth, together with her sister, Princess Sophia, Crown Princess Margareta, King Mihai's eldest daughter, jumped from the plane's metallic steps onto the Romanian soil, which she touched for the first time. You, travelers of today, tourists of the quotidian, no longer understand the meaning of exile and separation, no longer understand what it means to touch *for the first time*, to step on the holy land of your ancestors. The forbidden kingdom. A kingdom not of milk and honey, but of hemlock and bitterness. Still, your kingdom. Can you begin to understand what it means to *long* for a realm you've never been to? The kingdom your father spoke of at the dinner table and family reunions? To *belong* to a land you've never seen? Maybe in order to understand this, one needs to have roots deep down in that earth, roots one can grow even when one is away from that land. This is what a Royal Family is: a tree whose gnarly roots embrace a country's past generations, a tree that carries the sap from the center of the earth all the way up to the future. Margareta was embarrassed to do in public what old women do in that part of the world: kiss the earth— she was at the airport, after all. But they say that when, in the mid-nineties, her father, King Mihai, visited Bukovina, which had been taken by the Soviets in 1940—after which Carol left the country for good, forced to hide in the royal train, as he was being chased by gangs of vengeful *legionari*—Mihai knelt and kissed the raped and butchered land.

And, of course, there is September 18th, 1923, the birthdate of Princess Anne of Bourbon-Parma, Mihai's future wife, and July 18th, 1938, the date of my death. Between these two dates stands another 18, this one in October 1926, when I was beginning my American tour from New York all the way to the state of Washington on the West Coast, and even a small portion of Canada, a total of 15,000 kilometers in forty-four days, not a small feat for those days.

The Chronicler: Yes, America. A country fascinated by royalty. The other great republic, France, has simply displaced its aristocratic nostalgia onto other areas, but the United States is, in its anti-metaphysical ethos and hatred of the past, the very incarnation of anti-monarchic sentiment—which is, of course, the very reason why it is so obsessed with royals. We all desire the thing that is most remote from us.

Now, America has its own, transplanted, royals: the Sussexes. On January 8th, 2020, the Duke and Duchess of Sussex announced that they were planning to step back from their position as senior royals and split their time between North America and the UK, while "continuing to fully support her Majesty, the Queen." Five days after the Sussexes' "abdication," the Queen summoned all the four Royal Households to Sandringham estate in what was dubbed the "Sandringham summit" for private talks with Prince Charles, Prince William and Prince Harry. The Sussexes' request for half-in/half-out was rejected. Almost three years later, in a Netflix "docuseries" for which the Sussexes were allegedly paid a hundred million dollars and in which they were followed by a camera inside their own home in California, the public was regaled with dozens of private photos from the couple who couldn't stop complaining about the violation of their privacy by the media, including a photograph of the marriage proposal in which Harry could be seen on one knee with a ring in one hand. Unless the Netflix cameraman was present on such a momentous occasion (which begs the question: was this show in the works already *before* their marriage?), one has to logically assume that the photograph was taken by the woman to whom the proposal was being addressed. Did she ask him, "Honey, wait a second, I need to take my camera to take a shot while you are still on your knees"? The other question triggered by this photograph in which Harry appears kneeling on the grass concerns the version of the marriage proposal delivered by the future Duchess of Sussex during the much-publicized TV interview of the couple's engagement in 2017, when she claimed that the proposal took place in the kitchen while she was roasting a chicken. Was their kitchen floor made of grass?

In March 2021 took place the infamous Oprah interview in which the couple explained the reasons for their departure from Britain to America: racism. As proof of British racism, Oprah showed five negative tabloid covers, one of which was Australian and two American. Not a word about the thousands of positive articles that were published in Britain before and immediately after the couple's marriage. As everyone knows, the best way to escape British racism is to come to Trump's America.

Whenever Prince Harry talks about the media's treatment of him and his wife, he conflates mainstream media with social media, as if they were the same thing, implying that his treatment is the result of an orchestrated hate campaign. In reality, it was only after his attacks on the media that journalists from mainstream papers began to respond in kind, the Sussexes' lawsuit for "breach of privacy" against the *Daily Mail* as a result of its publication of Meghan Markle's letter to her father—a letter given to the paper by the letter's recipient—being ground zero in this fight. As far as social media is concerned, the hatred for the Sussexes, whether fair or unfair, represents the loud and chaotic voices of everybody under the sun. Contrary to the Sussexes' narrative, it is neither sexism, nor misogyny, and not even British racism that is the main culprit for this global negativity. A 2019 study of the negative criticism received by the Duchess concluded that eighty percent of it came from women, most of them American.

It may be because I am an immigrant myself, but for me this is the story of an immigrant: an American who immigrates to Great Britain. What does an immigrant—*any* immigrant—do when she arrives in her new country? She tries to *learn* as much as she can about her new environment, especially when she has been accepted into one of the oldest and most prestigious institutions of that country. Any person who immigrates to a new country and is accepted into a prestigious institution, an institution that, in this case, happens to be older than the immigrant's country of birth, would show some humility. One would expect such a person to use words like "I am honored" and "I want to learn"—but no, such words are not part of the vocabulary of Hollywood princesses, who reject the offers of help offered by the various members of the Royal Family, only to later complain that they've received no help. They use words like "to carve a progressive new role" and "forces of change," as if the British monarchy were an NGO that needed the latest trendy makeover.

Carmen Sylva: This American obsession: to modernize! Phew! Just the other day I read an article about how the Americans have all kinds of "activities" inside their temples and churches. Why go to a temple or a church if you are going to turn them into an entertainment club? The whole point of being religious is to connect with something *out of this world*. It is the same with a monarchy. To "modernize" a monarchy is an oxymoron. If you want a "modern" monarchy, what you really want is the Kardashians in a Palace.

Queen Marie (to herself): Where has this crazy bird sprung from again? (Out loud): Who are the Kardashians?

The Chronicler: A family on American TV.

Queen Marie (to Carmen Sylva): Since when are you watching American TV?

Carmen Sylva (indignant): I never watch American TV! I occasionally watch German or Romanian or even Swedish TV in order not to forget the language of my ancestors and brush up on my language skills in Swedish. I wouldn't watch American TV if they paid me! But I do read the papers. Modernize! Phew!

Queen Marie: Well, personally, I liked the Americans' desire to modernize everything! This and their efficiency and pragmatism are what I liked most about them.

Carmen Sylva: Yes, in 1926. But, if you ask me, there are things that shouldn't be modernized. There are institutions whose very purpose is the connection to the past and tradition, but for an American, the past itself is a dirty word, something one has to expectorate like some kind of mucus stuck in one's throat. (To herself): I can't believe I used the word "mucus"! I hope no one will tell Karl. (To Queen Marie): My intuition tells me that Meghan Markle found the British ways and the customs of the Royal House so outlandish to her American sensibility that she couldn't adapt to them. Do you remember how shy you were when you first came to Romania?

Queen Marie: I was seventeen! Meghan was twenty years older!

The Chronicler: Precisely! A mature woman who couldn't see how absurd it is to give an interview in which, you, the member of one of the most privileged families in the world, are complaining that no one has asked you "how you are," and that, instead of "thriving," you are just "surviving." Not only is the British taxpayer financing your lavish lifestyle, but he also has to inquire about your fragile mental health!

Carmen Sylva: Good Lord! Speaking of uplifting nonsense, did you see Meghan when she wrote inspirational messages on bananas ("You are strong") for abused prostitutes, while wearing a splendid designer dress for the event. (Yes, bananas offered to prostitutes!) Of course, people are wondering: why is Prince Harry going along with this, he who grew up in a royal household and who understands very well how it works? Hasn't he explained all this to his wife?

Queen Marie: To see where Prince Harry is coming from, one has to understand the very peculiar position of the second-born in a royal family, also known as "the spare," a position with no equivalent in any other institution of the modern world. In the same way that no one can understand the unique position of a Monarch, no one can fathom the unusual situation of the second-born child. To try to grasp this, let's do an imaginary exercise: think of your own relation with your sibling, the brother or sister you grew up with, played with, quarreled with, maybe bathed with in the same bathtub—the person to whom you were probably the closest in the entire world until you became adults. Since your most tender age, you have been told that your sibling is special, and you have seen him (or her) being treated in a special way, by your own parents, the servants, the courtiers, and the general public, who emphasize that your sibling will be Sovereign one day and that day you will have to call him (or her) "Your Majesty." Few people in the world would not feel resentment, no matter how generous, how full of love for that sibling or how well disposed they might be. Until his engagement, the Duke of Sussex was known as a charming man who loved his brother, even though those close to him had always known that he had inherited not only Diana's charisma, but also her emotional instability, narcissism and tendency for mischief. It is clear from the requests he'd made to the Queen after his engagement that he'd felt slighted by his family; it is clear that he and his wife wanted to show that they were at least as, if not more, relevant and glamorous than the Cambridges, and when their requests were denied by the Queen, the Prince's resentment only increased.

The Chronicler: There is nothing more dangerous than the wounded pride of a narcissist! Empires have fallen and wars have started because of this. In the Netflix show, the resentful Prince used the works "speak truth to power," presumably referring to his father, as if he, the Prince, were a McDonald's employee, and his father (now King), the manager. Leaving aside the comical aspect of the situation, Harry knew very well that "power" (i.e., his father, the King, and his brother, the heir to the throne) couldn't answer because a royal house never answers. "Power," in this case, is powerless. King Charles is in an impossible situation: he is both a king, whose realm is being threatened by his own son, and a father, and no matter how mad he might be as a king, he loves his son and cannot accept that he's lost him forever. According to some insiders, knowing how fragile Harry's mental state is, the King is afraid that, now that his son has lost his country, his family and most of his friends, if his relationship with his wife underwent a crisis someday, he would not have the power to withstand it. The irony is that it is Harry and not Meghan, who claimed being suicidal, who suffers from mental health issues. The King is truly in an impossible spot and Harry knows it. With each of his public appearances, he thrusts the knife even deeper into the King's heart, while at the same time, playing the favorite American society game, which, now that he must make his own living, he has learned to perfection: victimhood.

The last public appearance of Harry and Meghan as working members of the Royal Family was painstakingly planned and directed for maximum effect—they got out of the car, both dressed in that mesmerizing bright red, Harry, striking in his black-and-red military outfit with those yellow embroidery-like things on his sleeves; and Meghan, straight as a pole, tall, beautiful, radiant, a red apparition with long, raven-black hair, next to a fierce-looking Prince. The public—photographers and a few "average citizens" who had welcomed them with screams of joy, let out a collective gasp of awe, and then, for a few minutes, one could hear only the thick silence interrupted by the blinding flash of the photographers. This scene had been planned by both as the *scène d'adieu*, or, for those with a memory, as a parallel to Diana's "revenge dress."

Of the many ways one could tell the Balzacian story of the Sussexes and the Windsors, my favorite is the telling of a Romanian, Virgiliu Pop, whose *Letopiset* (*Chronicle*) about various contemporary celebrities, politicians and topical global situations, is written in the language of 18th-century

Moldovan chronicles. These chronicles were written by historians in a language now archaic to document the lives and deeds of the period's princes and kings. I appropriated, with the author's permission, the paragraph about the House of Windsor, translated it into English, then, expanded it into my own chronicle:

*

A naughty one is this Harry, the English Bey. It was not enough for him and his woman, Meghan, to call their dog a shameless name (*Pula*, the most vulgar word for the male organ in Romanian); they also had to call their babe after a cat, Archie. It is said that he and his woman went to see the mighty Opera, a much-praised chronicler who lives in the Land of the Great Circus, the birthplace also of Meghan, to cast worldwide dishonor upon his blood kin. And they called his kin names, accusing them in the tongue of opera and circus of the thing called "racism," but which two years later, when talking to an English chronicler, Tom Bradby, Harry denied having said. And denying, he shamed other chroniclers for warping his and his woman's words, neglecting to illuminate why they had accepted a trophy from the same Land as a reward for their valiant virtue against said racism of his own kin.

In the Land of the Great Circus, Harry acquired the inscrutable secret of script and gave to print a tell-tale chronicle that he called *The Bowels Keeper*, through which he willed to reveal much, in the manner of Esau. And so, Harry reckons that his father, Charles Bey, and his mother of blessed memory, Lady Diana, having united in holy matrimony, she remained heavy with his brother William; and the latter, being the first born, was fated to rule over the English in the city of London. And being fearful for the life of this one, for harm brought to his princely bowels, the parents reasoned to once more unite in holy matrimony fashioning a brother to him—from whom to take be it a lung, be it the heart, if those of William were to be harmed—so they fashioned poor Harry, who good for nothing he is, save for being the keeper of his brother's bowels.

In *The Bowels Keeper*, Harry tells us of the suffering he endured because of his regal brother, how he always had to contend with a smaller bed, a smaller castle, even a smaller, frost-bitten male organ. No, not a castle, an outrageously tiny cottage, his woman said talking to Opera, who shook her head in mindful sympathy, because she had visited them on the grounds of the great Castle where the first-born lived. So tiny that Harry had to bend his head in order not to hit the ceiling, and when his brother punched him in anger, he fell on the dog bowl, thus causing harm to his bowels and much danger to the life of his brother inasmuch as his own bowels were meant to serve the latter. His discretion does not allow him to reveal what the fight was about, save that it was because of the woman, Meghan. Could the fight have been caused by what the private counselor to William and Catherine, who had also been that of Harry and Meghan, called Meghan's "bullying" of her maids, who then complained to the first-born, who, thereafter, went, enraged, to his brother? No, most certainly not, says Harry. Whoever says anything against his woman is motivated by this thing which in the New Land they call "racism." His own mother, the very blond and blue-eyed Diana, blessed be her memory, was a victim of racism too because she died while being courted by a brown man, says Harry, and if his now-woman is a victim of the same prejudice, this only proves that she is his own saintly mother coming back from her grave to save him. Save him from what or whom? Well, from the chroniclers—the same folk guilty of having killed his mother. Thy mother died because she went riding without a proper saddle, Harry. My mother is a saint—sanctified by the very people who killed her. I am her only rightful son, unlike my brother who used to be her likeness, but he is now getting older and bald. I, her rightful son, have seen mine woman, when I took her to my mother's grave, on all fours, on the tombstone, channeling energy and guidance from my mother of gracious memory in the manner of other saintly women. For it is a custom in the Land of Opera and Circus for women of repute, whom they call "celebrities," such as one Madonna, may the Grace of God be upon her, and one Gwyneth, may the Force be with her, to channel such energy, the former, who only drinks holy water shipped to her from the divine City of Jerusalem, getting forever young and hungry for the blood of young men, and the latter harboring magnetic waves in her nether area where she is said to hide eggs dipped in her primal juices, which eggs she then sells to the public impregnated with her spirit. And so it is in this noble tradition that Meghan, Duchess of Sussex, finds communion with Saint Diana of Gracious Memory. The dianesque spirit that runs through her veins has been acknowledged by another virtuous woman from the same Land whom they call Beyoncé, who sent Meghan a missive revealing that she (Meghan) has been elected as a healer to put an end to hundreds of years of black magic—which, in the language of Those Who Have Been Awakened, she phrases as "to break generational curses that need to be healed." Meghan herself read the message to the public with the same frank face she had when asserting that people had rejoiced at her marriage in the same manner they had rejoiced at the liberation of the warrior of great esteem, Mandela. She read it aloud during the six-hour play commissioned by the Sussexes, which can be watched at the Netflix Theater.

I only wanted to protect mine woman and offspring from evil tongues, says Harry, and this is the reason we departed for the Land of Opera and Circus. The best way to protect them was to command the above-mentioned play, a play scripted by the grandest chroniclers of that Land, who move about in private golden carriages and are in constant need of new, righteous blood to satisfy their anti-monarchic appetites, from which satisfaction thou too, Harry, have taken thy rightful share. For thou and thine woman and offspring inhabit a magnificent mansion in the desert equipped with sixteen chambers devoted to bodily ablutions, from where on occasion thou raise thy ginger head to speak to the simple folk about the earth's destruction in the manner of Greta-of-Sad-Visage.

Can't thou see, Harry, that thy family's motto was right and that the more thou open thy blabbering mouth the more thou are disliked? Leave him alone, thy followers say, he is only living an independent life. Who makes a living, Harry, by bad-mouthing his own family? What kind of "healing" is this in which thy most dearest are being darted such keen pangs? I am not a bowels keeper, I am a man of mine own bowels, thou say. Thou are *the man*, thine woman says, and thou quote her in thy chronicle. What hurt pride are thou feeding, Harry, thou silly boy, to make such words public? I am not a bowels keeper, I am a man who killed twenty-five foes of my country. Unlike my brother, who shall be King.

I am doing the work, says Harry in the tongue of Those Who Have Been Awakened, and my family is not. I am surrounded by twelve counselors of the spirit who, in the same tongue, are called "life coaches"—for in the Land of Opera and Circus life itself is an enterprise that needs careful guidance with proper payment. It is under the guidance of these counselors and of mine woman that I found my voice—against the motto of my family, "If thou grumble, thou'll go under." "Speak, Harry," said they, for this is the only way to heal from the wound of thy mother's passing. "Go to the bankers and talk about thy blessed and gracious mother, for this is the only way thou can cure thyself." "I am still healing," thine woman had said at the end of her talk with *The Cut*—healing from what? From being taken by the hand by the future King and accompanied to the altar? From the most majestic wedding in history offered to thee by the folk of Saxon Land, which thou have, so spitefully, called "a circus"? Do you see, dear reader, that the Sussexes are on a mission to heal both themselves and the entire earth? Healers, they are. And so, let us pray that poor Harry shall be in good health henceforth, for no one knows when the time shall come for his bowels to be of use to his brother.

*

Carmen Sylva: Well, you need to work some more on the archaic quality of the style, but you are right about the jealousy of royal siblings. I should add that this jealousy isn't confined only to the Spare. When I visited my relatives and Karl's relatives in Germany as a queen, I was shocked to see how jealous they all were of us. Carlo, Nando's younger brother, in particular, was so jealous of his brother that he couldn't help spread lies and gossip about him.

Queen Marie (ignoring Queen Elisabeta's words and addressing the Chronicler): Laugh all you want at these progressive people, but don't forget, my dear, that in my days I was myself considered a progressive Queen! Yes, yes, you may smile, or even laugh, if you will, but read Constance Lily Morris's account of my American tour; or read the many articles written about me in the American press at the time, or in the French press. Some of them were critical of my decision to embark on such a long journey without my husband, the King. When faced with such questions from nosy, meddling reporters, I just dismissed them with a handwave, for I have always been a very independent woman.

Yes, there was that boorish businessman who got up to the podium and began to lecture me and the entire audience about the greatness of Republicanism and how a Monarchy could never accomplish this and that—truly, such graceless behavior I was ashamed for him, but what could I have done? I pretended I was a good sport and applauded, like everybody else.

When I was in North Dakota, I invited two farmers, their wives and children to hop on the train I traveled with and join me for a discussion at each stop, well, more like a friendly chat, about farming and their daily lives. I was curious to know how they lived, and, particularly, to learn from them how they dealt with the problems they encountered in agriculture, how they built their amazing transportation system and their flour mills. I explained that I too came from a farming country, a country similar in many ways to the American Northwest and I intended to take their progressiveness to my own people— yes, this is the very word I used, "progressiveness." In fact, I invited all the American businessmen to come to Romania and invest, something that was quite revolutionary at the time!

The Chronicler: Hmm ... I doubt today's progressives would approve of your invitation to the business community to come and invest in Romania. Today, I'm afraid that would sound more like unchecked capitalism.

Queen Marie: *N'importe quoi !*[19]

The Chronicler: I'm telling you! The descendants of all those simple, dignified and upstanding people from the Northwest would not be pleased. Neither would they approve of your wearing the feather, beaded headdresses given to you by the Sioux Native Americans. Nowadays, they call it "cultural appropriation."

Queen Marie: *They gave them to me!* How is that appropriation?

The Chronicler: (laughs)

Queen Marie: I think the Americans of today would do well to learn from the ways of these brave, ancient peoples.

---

19. Whatever! Nonsense! (Fr.)

The Chronicler: This is called "exoticizing."

Queen Marie (laughing): *Mais qu'est-ce que tu dis ?*[20] *Vraiment ! On ne peut plus parler avec les nouvelles générations !* Let me tell you how it happened. The Indians placed me on a buffalo robe which was spread on the ground, and then six chiefs carried me very ceremoniously into their tepee where they initiated me by pricking my finger while they chanted all kinds of cryptic, enigmatic litanies. The ruling chief who carried me was famous for having killed another Indian called Sitting Bull. They gave me the title of "Winyan Kipanpi Win," meaning "The Woman Who Was Waited for," and they also called me "War Woman of the Sioux Indians."

The Chronicler: First of all, they are not Indians.

Queen Marie: Yes, they are Indians. I know better than you whom I met.

The Chronicler: Nowadays they are called Native Americans. Second: do you really believe that you are the woman the Native Americans have waited for?

Queen Marie: *Ma chère, je ne crois rien, moi. Je te raconte simplement ce qui s'est passé.*[21] I came home with delightful presents, among them the feather headdress, which I gave to little Mikey, who was five years old at the time.

The Chronicler: Yes, I've seen pictures. He looks very cute, but to give such a symbolic item to a small child …

Queen Marie: A small child who would be King within a few months of my return.

The Chronicler: King Mihai must have been very attached to that gift because there are several photos of him wearing it. Many years later, when he worked as a stockbroker in New York, he brought a cowboy costume to eight-year-old Princess Margareta. I think it was a Christmas present, and the fact

20. What are you talking about? Really, one can no longer talk with the new generations! (Fr.)

21. My dear, I don't believe anything! I am simply telling you what happened. (Fr.)

that he bought it when she was close to the age he was when he received his feather headdress makes me think he was somehow trying to relive that enjoyment through the joy of his first-born. I've seen photos of her by the Christmas tree, with a large Texan hat and two pistols, her face lit up by a huge grin.

Queen Marie: I was offered a myriad of gifts by my American hosts: cows, horses, a plow, a harvesting machine, a sewing machine, a Red Indian doll in war dress, several war bonnets with eagle feathers, a bullet-proof armored town-car, and my favorite: the naming of a mountain after me.

The Chronicler (to herself): Hmm ... and you wonder whom your son took after. He, who named himself after the tallest Romanian mountain peak.

Queen Marie: I have been tremendously impressed and enchanted by the love shown to me by the simple people, especially the farmers who came to see me on our train. A farmer wrote to me claiming that he had the most wonderful egg-laying hen in America and wanted to offer it to me, but he "wa'n't going to risk his hen on no train," and so he asked for my address to send it to me. Yes, the Americans showered me with love, compliments and praise like no other nation.

The Chronicler: Yes, of course they did. Of all people, republicans are probably the most susceptible to be impressed by royalty. Same thing when it comes to people proud to be friends with aristocrats or impressed by nobility: the more they advertise their "relatability," the more they long for a privileged status.

Queen Marie: There is, undoubtedly, some truth to what you're saying, but I beg to disagree with your core argument. In this case, I think the Americans were simply curious to see the representative of a faraway country, a mysterious land known to them solely through the mist of romantic legends. I too had the same curiosity about America. I read articles by American journalists who were very excited to meet "the embodiment"—that is, I—of "perhaps the most romantic land in Europe."

The Chronicler: Exactly. And why do you think these people had such a, frankly, laughable notion about my birthplace? To be clear: I am not saying that another country is more worthy of this characterization. I think the very notion of a "romantic land" is ridiculous. I once had an American boyfriend who forbade me to go to Paris because, in his eyes, Paris was the most romantic city in the world, and a woman alone there was the equivalent of an invitation to have an affair. It didn't cross his mind that for me Paris was simply a place—and a very prosaic one at that—where I could eat croissants and cheese to my heart's content.

All countries have some version of a creation myth, the myth of their origin, and this myth documents the nation's continuity, which is often at odds with the country's present. In Romania's case, the myth of origin is that of the union between the valiant Geto-Dacians, on the one hand, and the Roman conquerors, on the other. The birth certificate of the Romanian people consecrates the union between East and West, a union that has been tested many times throughout history. Like most offspring of mixed origin, the Romanians have their eyes obsessively fixed on the "superior" element of the mésalliance, the Romans, who have been statuefied, so to speak, throughout the entire country—pretty much every Romanian town has a statue of Romulus and Remus, the twin brothers who founded the city of Rome—trying to emulate them, and in so doing, to reject the "lower," more shameful part of themselves: the Oriental. Yet it is this very Oriental that has captured the Westerners' imagination, yours included, my dear Marie, from Pierre Loti, to Bram Stoker, to the French and the Americans who read them. All those photos of you in the Romanian national costume are, how should I put it?

They are on par with the photographs of you wearing the feather headdress of the Sioux Native Americans. As my fellow countrymen would say: "White Savior complex."

Queen Marie: Hmm … Aren't you becoming a little too … what's that word? Woke? You forget that *I am Romanian*, and therefore it is only natural that I wear the national costume. You seem to negate your own logic—aren't you the one who claims that we aren't defined by our place of birth and we can always "grow new roots," as Princess Mary of Denmark has said? Sometimes the most truthful explanation is a lot simpler than the complicated and twisted reasons people find behind the actions of a public figure. Maybe in this case, the real reason is this: I wear the Romanian national costume because among its dozens of versions there are some of exquisite beauty and I am someone forever in love with Beauty. Sometimes, it may take a British Princess to make the Romanians see the beauty of their traditions, and sometimes it may take a Romanian Queen to help the Americans see the many-sided aspects of America. Speaking of which, I enjoyed the American propensity for everything large, especially when it came to landscapes, yes, I enjoyed the long rides on those gigantic boulevards and through endless woods stretching to the horizon, and even more, I enjoyed their huge department stores in comparison with which even the Parisian stores seem a bit provincial.

And then, why not say it: I look quite charming in the traditional Romanian costume. On my American tour I received great compliments when I wore it for a reception held in my train car while in North Dakota. It was an ankle-length white robe embroidered in pale rose and gold over which I threw a linen coat with blue and gold needlework at the shoulders. On my feet I had Transylvanian red leather boots, and on my head, the traditional *maramă*. The Americans were quite taken with my outfit, and their papers published several articles about Romanian crafts and needlework. There, just take a look:

> The costumes of the peasants of Romania, whether they are of Transylvania, Bessarabia, Bukovina or yet the roving Tzigani, enchant one with their wonderful sense of color and sometimes miraculous needlework which make of these extraordinary national costumes a most prolific source of inspiration. We are all familiar with the various photographs of Queen Marie of Romania wearing the traditional costume of the simple peasant folk, but there are many who have never visualized the exquisite color combinations […]. They are really costumes to delight the soul and satisfy the sense of coquetry of the most blasée élégante. The needlework and embroidery done upon these national costumes are simply prodigious. […] The aprons which the peasants wear would make a book of very agreeable reading. They are often completely covered with the most lovely designs which are beautifully symmetrical and then embroidered and covered with beautiful sequins. […] The kerchief too is one of the most becoming and charming of headdresses, and one finds that the piquancy of the ruddy-faced girls is vastly enhanced by this graceful and becoming mode. Queen Marie is especially partial to it. Her auburn beauty is enhanced by the soft folds of this kerchief.

The Chronicler: The Romanians themselves are ashamed of the Oriental in them, and no distance is far enough from him; they are running to the four corners of the earth, and today they have one of the largest diasporas on the planet. But the harder they are struggling to kill their inner Oriental, the higher he raises his obnoxious head. They want to be Westerners and are resentful that whatever they do, the latter see them as Easterners. And what a terrible irony that their very name lends itself to the ambiguity of their double origin: these descendants of Rome are being taken for Roma people, the *tziganes* that you, my dear Queen, were so fond of. Poor Romanians: eternally caught between the Romans and the Romani. The Romanians look at themselves with the eyes of Westerners, forever unhappy with their lot, prone to an inferiority complex specific to peoples that have been ruled by others—a complex I have encountered also in those who come from former colonies. All such nations suffer from a type of nationalism that most Westerners, particularly the Americans, who are incapable of looking at themselves with the eyes of others, cannot understand. All colonized people—and the Romanians have the psychology of a colonized nation—have *otherness* as an integral part of their identity. The Americans, on the other hand, are a nation born through the excision of this otherness, which they have safely left in Europe when they moved across the pond. Because America's birth certificate is the conflict between a former motherland—or fatherland, whatever you want to call it—(the Center) and the conquest of a new land (the Margin), the Americans have forged their identity through a constant battle between the margin(alized) and the center. The American pioneer—the degree zero of American identity—is that human being who feels the imperious need to go farther West and to unlock yet another margin. This pioneer never died: like everything in history, it has simply morphed and hides under other masks, it has moved from the rugged terrain of the Wild West to the ivory tower of the college campus and today is best represented by the academic who keeps uncovering yet another marginalized category, another minority. This is also, by the way, why the lawyer is such a mythical figure in the collective imagination of the American people and such an important presence in the fight between good and evil: what is a lawyer if not someone in charge of *framing* our reality and of *defining our borders*?

Queen Marie: Speaking of your compatriots, *ma chère*— here, the Queen lit one of those long cigarettes one sees only in black-and-white old movies, took a drag and then blew out a cloud of smoke—I highly recommend you take a break from them and come to renew yourself at the sources of your origin.

Chapter 11

The Child-King

Queen Marie: When my American tour took place, my grandson, Mihai, or Mikey, as I used to call him, or Mihăiță, his pet name, was five years old. Soon after my return, Nando died. His death was officially recorded on July 20th, 1927, but it really occurred on the 18th, the exact same day as my own death would, eleven years later. With my son, Carol, in exile, Mihai was declared King at the age of five.

The Chronicler: How did this happen? What was the sequence of events?

Queen Marie: Remember how Carol went into exile with his lover, Elena, also called Magda, Lupescu?

The Chronicler: Yes.

Queen Marie: On the 28th of December, 1925, while in Italy, he signed a document prepared by the Brătianu government, according to which he renounced all his rights as a Crown Prince and member of the Royal Family. He also renounced his parental rights and promised not to return to Romania before ten years had passed, and then, to return only with the Monarch's agreement. He signed the act, crying. After Nando's death, since Mihai was a minor, a Regency was formed of three individuals: Carol's brother Nicky, the Patriarch and the President of the High Court.

When on July 19th Mihai was awoken by his nanny with the words "Your Majesty," he replied, puzzled: "Why are you calling me this? Has my name changed?" It was just a nickname, he was told. But after he was given a more detailed explanation, the boy became quite nervous and asked if he was still allowed to play. Then, he went to meet the three members of the Regency, who took the oath of allegiance to him, and he had a hard time trying not to burst into laughter seeing how serious they all were.

As the child assumed his new position, his mother would often tell him: "Collect yourself!" She was always by his side, holding his hand and motioning to him whom to greet and how. When he arrived at Parliament and was introduced as "His Majesty the King," and the deputies saw a blue-eyed little boy with curly blond hair, all dressed in white, holding tightly his mother's hand, a collective gasp was heard. As instructed by his mother, the boy performed the military salute, and the room answered with appreciative applause.

The Chronicler: There are all kinds of anecdotes about the Child-King. In one of them he told the priest when he went to take communion with his mother that he never drank wine so early in the morning.

The child grew up in complete isolation, playing all by himself within the walls of Peleş Castle, raised by a mother who, her Greek origin notwithstanding, had had an Anglophone upbringing. She educated him according to a rigid and puritan system in which all the child's instincts and desires were submitted to rigorous self-control and discipline: the Kensington system named after Kensington Palace. The teaching took place in one-on-one sessions with various private instructors. Some historians speculate that one reason for the child's solitude was his birth defect, a speech impediment diagnosed by one of them as *palatoschisis*. Yet, according to the same historians, there are no medical records of such a diagnosis, and the King's descendants are unaware of such a finding.

Queen Marie: You know very well that at the time people

were a lot less eager to see everything as medical disorders, the way they do today. We just thought that this was his way of speaking. Initially, we were all smitten with him: so cute, charming and, apparently, intelligent. But by the time he was seven, he had become fat, entirely apathetic, lacking interest in anything, and not particularly bright.

The Chronicler: That's not quite true. The child did have some interests, more specifically, in anything dealing with mechanics and cars. When he was six, he was already learning to drive, seated in the lap of his driver in King Ferdinand's Rolls Royce. He was also trilingual, able to speak Romanian, English and German.

Queen Marie: Yes, the two of us only spoke English, and, for a while, he used to come every day to have breakfast with me. But by the time his father returned from exile, nothing was left of the once-charming boy. The discipline instilled by his mother was so rigid it completely annihilated his personality. We became like two strangers.

The Chronicler: Wait … About his father.

Queen Marie: Yes, his father. One night of June 1930, my eldest son, who had abandoned everything five years earlier for a vulgar woman who was suspected by the Romanian Secret Services of working for the Bolsheviks, my son, Carol, returned. He returned in spite of the promise he'd signed, breaking his word, yet was received with enthusiasm by the Romanian Parliament, which proceeded to invalidate the act that had taken away from him all his rights five years earlier. Eager to meet his son, who couldn't even remember his father, Carol sent his brother Nicky for him. When Mihai entered the room, he saw a mustached, intimidating man seated astride on a chair, which he left to take him in his arms and hold him tightly: a stranger who laid claims on him and for whom the boy felt nothing, except maybe fear.

Meanwhile, Sitta had automatically become queen again,

once Carol's abdication had been invalidated.

The Chronicler: Sitta?!

Queen Marie: Yes, Sitta—Elena, my daughter-in-law. The Romanian politicians wanted to convince her to accept the annulment of her divorce from Carol for the good of the country. They almost convinced her, but, in the end, the politicians' foolish desire to return to a state of affairs from before Carol's departure was sabotaged by Carol himself. Lupeasca, his mistress, had settled nearby—she'd literally rented a villa next to Peleş Castle—and from there was making demands. She wanted "Of" out of the picture, her title of queen removed and she, out of the country.

The Chronicler: Yes, I remember that she used to mockingly call Elena "Of." As in "of Greece," but also because in Romanian the word "*of*" (literally, an interjection) is a synonym for "sorrow" or "pain."

Queen Marie: It was Lupeasca with her intrigues that convinced Carol to hire policemen for Sitta's constant surveillance, and eventually, to chase her out of the country and force her to go into exile in Florence. It was also her who persuaded him to isloate my most trusted men, including Barbu, and to strip me of my royal perogatives. Eventually, I moved to Balcic.

The Chronicler: With Sitta gone, Carol took control of his son's education, first, by replacing all the teachers she had hired; then, he initiated an educational experiment that would remain famous in Romania's history: the so-called "Palatin Class," in which eleven to twenty gifted students from all the social classes were brought to the Palace every day to have courses with his son—children of peasants, officers, factory directors, and from all the country's regions, including two representatives of the German and Hungarian minorities. A sort of "diversity" program *avant la lettre*,[22] if you will. Once

22. Before its time (Fr.)

a year they took field trips, and at the end of the year Mihai was examined by his teachers in his father's presence, a process meant to eliminate the teachers' temptation of giving the child higher grades than he deserved. At school he was known by the pompous title his father had given him after having dethroned him: "*the Great Voevod of Alba Iulia*"—which was somewhat of a misnomer, insofar as "*voevod*" is supposed to mean "Reigning Prince."

Queen Marie: Mihai was a good student, especially in sciences. But he continued to be unhappy.

The Chronicler: Apparently, once, he threatened to commit suicide by throwing himself from the second floor of the Palace. He hated "Duduia," his stepmother, and he missed his mother, whom he was only allowed to see once a year during summer vacation.

Queen Marie: Little by little, I became persona non grata in my son's eyes, and so did all of his siblings, Ileana in particular, who was very popular, and therefore a threat to his own popularity. After Ileana married Anton of Habsburg and became pregnant, I wanted her to give birth in Romania to make sure that her offspring would keep his place in the line of succession, but Carol outmaneuvered me, and from that point on we were at war. Mihai was now a teenager and still a disappointment, although he was no longer fat and had become very handsome. But he seemed too indolent and intellectually slow, and I was worried about the future of the dynasty.

The Chronicler: Carol, on the other hand, was very sharp, and had started a process of modernization and industrialization of the entire country. He built cultural hubs in all the villages, promoting literacy among the illiterate peasantry; he was very involved in the creation of publishing houses and supported the younger, talented writers; he encouraged folklorists to collect ballads and other pieces of folklore from around the country; and he believed that the country's economic development was essential for its political stability. But his modernizing and progressive project was counterbalanced and ill served by what was known as the "Camarilla," the corrupted network of politicians and influence peddlers surrounding "Duduia" and himself. And then, of course, there was the infamous *Garda de Fier*—the Iron Guard—with which he had to deal, a fascist, nationalist-Orthodox political movement led by Corneliu Zelea-Codreanu. Is it true that Codreanu used to ride a white horse, dressed all in white, holding an icon and a sword?

Queen Marie: Yes. Ironically, he may have modeled himself on my son's own fashion style. Carol, who was somewhat grandiose, used to ride a white horse too and had appropriated medieval Romanian paraphernalia—at public events he wore an imperial casque with feathers, gallons and decorations.

The Chronicler: Well, I know a certain Romanian queen who did something similar with a medieval crown. But speaking of the Iron Guard, in 1933 Carol outlawed it and, as a result, the country's Prime Minister was murdered by the *legionari* (the Guard members). Angered, they even plotted the assassination of the King and of the Crown Prince, who barely escaped alive, alerted by the Secret Services.

Queen Marie: And yet, even under these circumstances, Carol failed to instruct Mihai about the country's messy political situation. He used to take him almost everywhere, yet he wouldn't allow him to read the papers. The poor boy was so unprepared for what was to follow!

The Chronicler: On February 10th, 1938, a new government led by the Patriarch Miron Cristea comes to power, through which Carol hopes he could control the infiltration of the Orthodox clergy by the *legionari*. On February 27th he signs into law a new Constitution that annuls the previous anti-Semitic laws and gives women the right to vote while, at the same time, limiting democratic institutions and giving the Monarch almost absolute powers. On March 30th he dissolves all political parties, which he replaces with The Front of the National Renaissance, a party meant to "fight extremism." At the end of the year, he takes a trip together with Mihai to Paris, London, Brussels, and … to Hitler's famous retreat, during a tour meant to strengthen the country's ties with the Allies, while trying very hard not to make an enemy of Hitler either.

Queen Marie: You forgot to mention an event that took place the same year during the month of July: my death.

The Chronicler: I didn't forget, I just thought this wasn't the right moment.

Queen Marie: Is there a "right moment" to die?

The Chronicler: What do you want me to say? That you died prematurely because your son, the King, failed to give you adequate care—which, according to some historians, was intentional? That you died away from the love of your life, Barbu, who had been forced by the same jealous son to leave Romania? That you asked to be dressed in white and the mourners at the funeral procession in violet, not black, as it is customary, and that, after your death, a strong perfume of violets filled your room, or so they say? That young Mihai, who was obligated to follow your coffin, was very emotional? That your legend followed you in death, as it had followed you in life?

Queen Marie: I simply want you to remember. We all want to be remembered. Remembrance is the affirmation of our existence. It means we lived.

The Chronicler: I think our readers are more curious to find out how the meeting between Carol, Mihai and Hitler went. In fact, King Mihai later recalled how he wasn't allowed to attend the meeting, how, in fact, he waited outside while his father met with Hitler. From this visit, Mihai was left mostly with a feeling of awe at the view seen from the top of the cliff where Hitler's vulture nest was located. But there was another visit he paid Hitler three years later at the age of twenty, when he was King. At the request of Ion Antonescu, who led the Romanian government, Mihai and his mother went to see Hitler, this time at his Berlin residency. Elena too was seeing him for the second time. This time, the two of them had access to the real Führer, as the latter raised his voice while declaiming in his usual manner, his glassy eyes sparkling in a way that sent shivers down the young King's spine. The Führer was not particularly impressed with the King, whose "lack of good manners" he criticized later. Well, who could compete with Hitler's refined manners, really?

Queen Marie: I don't know when Hitler made that comment, but he had some concrete reasons to be angry with Mihai, as with Carol, by the way. After Carol and Mihai saw him in November 1938, when Carol returned home, the leader of the Iron Guard, Corneliu Zelea-Codreanu, was assassinated at the order of the Police's Prefect, and this political murder, together with that of other *legionari*, infuriated Hitler, who believed that Carol must have been aware of this plan during their meeting.

The Chronicler: Indeed, as a result, Hitler sent into Romania hundreds of German spies supporting the Iron Guard, thus starting a war between the latter and the state's institutions and causing a bloodbath that lasted throughout 1939. By then, WWII had started. Through the Molotov-Ribbentrop agreement, Germany had agreed to let the USSR take Bessarabia from the Romanians. Thus, Romania was threatened from all sides: to the West, by Hungary, who claimed Transylvania, to the South-East, by Bulgaria, who wanted the Cadrilater back, and to the East and North-East by the Russians. Carol knew that the country, too small to set its own course, had to choose between Nazism and Communism. Despite his German blood, like you, he was an Anglophile, and he did what most Romanians would have done in order to survive: played chess with both sides, hoping that he could postpone the fatal denouement.

On September 21ˢᵗ, 1939, the Romanian Prime Minister is assassinated by the *legionari* as revenge for Codreanu's death. Carol's answer is the nomination of a new government that will answer in kind, that is, with the murder of over 250 *legionari* in the entire country.

On June 27ᵗʰ, 1940, Mihai passes his *baccalauréat*, his father, the King, in attendance. That day, after midnight, the Russians give Romania an ultimatum: Stalin demands Bessarabia and the North of Bukovina, and the Romanians have 24 hours to answer. Just like that. As I am writing these lines, eighty-two years later, the Russians, under Putin's command, have invaded Ukraine, threatening also Moldova, Poland, Finland and even Sweden. The West is in shock—as if this had never happened before. As if this were not a very Russian story.

The King is stunned. As if in a daze, he remembers the years of the previous war when you, Marie, were caught in a similar predicament. The impossible itself. How could the Romanian army fight on three military lines? The King meets the Crown Council, and the generals are clear: the army cannot do this. Like you a quarter of a century earlier, he refuses to accept Romanian fatalism, against which his spirit rebels. He'd never believed that History repeats itself, but it seemed that History was, if not a circle, a spiral akin to the shape of a tornado that swept everything in its path. Of the twenty-six members of the Crown Council, twenty vote to accept the Russian annexation. The King protests and calls this a day of national shame. In his diary he writes that this has been the darkest day of his life, that something has broken inside him, and he can't even look at himself in the mirror. As the Romanian soldiers return from Bessarabia, they are subjected by the Russians to attacks and degrading humiliations, and Carol feels, like you before him, that he is losing his mind. He cannot accept this dishonor. Why isn't Hitler helping him, after all his concessions to him? He is trying to get in touch with him—good luck with that! Thinking that it may appease the Führer, his government puts on the table anti-Semitic laws and decides to eliminate all the Jews from public functions.

During the night of August 29th-30th, Nazi Germany and Mussolini's Italy decide, through the so-called Vienna Diktat, that Romania shall award half of Transylvania to Hungary. Carol spends another white night, feeling, again, that he is going insane, and considers abdicating. He hears gunshots near the palace and voices demanding his abdication. Mihai, who is with him, takes a gun and promises he'll defend his father, if need be. The King's counselors advise him to create another government—is this his 18th one? I lost count—led by General Ion Antonescu. Barely in his new function, Antonescu asks Carol to sign a document that would give him, the General, increased powers, and, desperate, his thinking muddled by exhaustion, Carol signs, dissolves the Parliament and cancels the 1938 Constitution. He regrets it as soon as he signs the act, and with good reason: the first thing the empowered General does is to ask for the King's abdication.

Six days later the situation will have escalated to a point where Carol will be obligated to leave the country, which he will bequeath to his eighteen-year-old son, whom he had, up to then, kept uninformed and, as much as possible, away from political matters. The Palace had been under fire during the entire night of the 5th/6th September. The King is desperately trying to convince his son, who has just finished high school, to take over his prerogatives because he has no other choice but to abdicate—a word, however, that he will be careful to avoid in official documents. The Crown Prince refuses. How can his father ask him this? How can he consider leaving him alone with the General who has betrayed his King, surrounded, within the country, by *legionari* who cannot wait to take revenge, and outside, by the Bolsheviks, the Nazis and the Hungarians? A lamb encircled by wolves. Ready for slaughter. His youthful, candid face does call to mind a fresh, innocent lamb, in spite of the fact that his tall, robust stature is very masculine. The young Prince is exceedingly handsome—he has chiseled features, brown hair and blue eyes, and when he smiles, he sports two dimples, just like his mother. All the young girls are in love with him. The young Prince is not yet a man, yet he is being asked to man-up and deal with it! Eventually, he says yes. What else could he have done?

The next day Mihai is King. Taking advantage of the new King's inexperience and confusion, General Antonescu places before his nose a document through which the General assumes absolute powers. Mihai signs. Two days later, at night, he drives his father and his mistress to the train station, where they hug goodbye. It is the last time father and son will have seen each other. (Years later, Mihai will refuse to attend his father's funeral in Portugal, where the latter is exiled.) Throughout Carol's entire journey on Romanian territory, his train is being shot at by the *legionari,* so much so that he is forced to hide under the seats. Meanwhile, the General, realizing the helplessness of the young King, decides to ask for the return of Carol's former wife—Elena, Mihai's mother. When she arrives, Mihai welcomes her at the same train station where he has recently taken his father. A legendary photograph has immortalized the moment the Queen Mother (the title given to her by Antonescu) gently caresses her son's face with her hand. The cunning General knows what to give the Romanian people to tickle their national pride, so he organizes a resplendent reception for Elena, who has always been popular. Mother and son ride in a sumptuous carriage drawn by magnificent horses, she with a discreet veil covering her face, he in military uniform. Followed by the crowd's loud cheers, they are taken to religious celebrations where, suffused by the daze and smell of incense that always accompanies the kneeling *legionari*, they drink in the assembly's adoration. Henceforth, the Queen Mother and her son are the objects of the people's adulation, and at the General's counsel, are often seen in public, eating in restaurants or shopping, thereby accosted by members of the adoring public who want to shake hands with them and, just like today when representatives of the House of Windsor show up, let out screams of unbridled excitement. In a Germanified country, mother and son speak only English. The young King spends most of his time in a dolce far niente, until, eventually, he decides to hire and bring to the Palace a team of scholars and professors who would teach him constitutional law, history and public speaking. With his speech defect, he certainly needs the latter. Meanwhile, the country falls deeper and deeper into the hands of the *legionari*, a situation that culminates with the brutal murder of Mihai's former teacher, the historian and scholar Nicolae Iorga. Antonescu has no longer any qualms about putting on the green shirt of the *legionari* in broad daylight, before he decides that they have become too dangerous for the country's institutions and, in January 1941, after their violent riots and pogroms, dissolves and outlaws all the political entities associated with them. However, faithful to Hitler, Antonescu continues his anti-Semitic policies and approves the Führer's plan to engage the Romanian army in an offensive against the Soviet Union by conquering Odessa and regaining Bessarabia and the North of the Bukovina.

One day, the King—who is now nineteen—finds out that his country is at war with the Russians. Although, in theory, he is the leader of the army, no one has bothered to inform him. Enough already! His pride hurt, he swears to get revenge on this General who can't stop humiliating and treating him like a little boy. He invents a special code that only he and his mother can understand. Under Antonescu's orders, the Romanian army occupies Odessa, but loses in the process 100,000 soldiers, and bestially murders thousands of Jewish prisoners. The King and the Queen Mother attempt to have a discussion with the General about the Jewish question, blaming him for the Odessa massacre and trying to convince him to, at least, delay the deportation of the Jews. Secretly, the Queen Mother hides hundreds of Jews to prevent their deportation. Little by little, the King gets the idea that maybe he could outsmart the General and find a way to change the course of Romania's history, bringing her back to its old Allies. He refuses to follow some of the General's decisions, always in his silent, stubborn way, always with the demeanor of one who is a bit slow-witted. The General truly believes that this young, naïve young man *is* slow-witted—something that will end up costing him. Secretly, the young King begins to take flying lessons, and to meet people that don't see eye to eye with the General. A small opposition group is gradually forming around the King. He is now a very handsome twenty-year-old man.

Queen Marie: Our beautiful, good-hearted Mihai. It was around this time that he bought the mansion from Săvârşin in Western Transylvania, which was decorated and furnished by his mother, and which, after his forced abdication, was nationalized by the Communists, then in the early 2000s, given back to him.

The Chronicler: Indeed. Now, his daughter, Margareta, lives there part of the year. A couple of years ago I had the chance of visiting the estate's grounds and its beautiful wide garden.

Queen Marie: Poor Mihai! He was still counting on the British. He had no idea that they had decided to abandon Romania to the Soviets. The Allies, who wanted him to mount a coup d'état against Antonescu, were soon bombing the capital. Even the house near the Palace where the King now lived had its windows shattered from a nearby bomb.

Under the bombs that fell everywhere, the population was still hopeful: like Mihai, they were hoping that once the Germans were defeated, the Soviets would be kept at bay. Meanwhile, the latter reconquered Odessa and entered Bessarabia. The Allies were ready to give Transylvania back to Romania, but not Bessarabia and Bukovina. They were also asking for the Romanians to allow the Russians to move freely on their territory. Mihai's conspiratorial group took the pulse of the army and sent its plan to the British and the Americans for approval.

The Chronicler: Antonescu knows nothing. Mihai still hopes that he can win Antonescu over to his side and drives to meet him in private. As it happens, the General is about to leave for a meeting with Hitler, and catching a glimpse of young Mihai, makes no effort to stop and talk to him. The General leaves spitefully, letting the frustrated King stew in his own juices. The King won't forget.

Queen Marie: Our beautiful, young Mihai! He was only twenty-two.

The Chronicler: Beautiful, young, silent, clumsy, indolent, apathetic Mihai moves ever closer to the *point culminant*. The plan of the coup d'état—which, in the interviews he will give decades later, he will refuse to call as such, saying that, as King, he couldn't lead a coup d'état in the state whose chief he was— is now perfected to its last details. The date is set for the 26th of August, but as it happens, on the 22nd he finds out that the General will go to inspect the battlefield on the 24th, so the date needs either to be postponed, or else, moved to the 23rd. And so, it is decided: the 23rd—who could have predicted that this date would become the most hideous misappropriation in the history of the country and end up being synonymous with the Communist Party itself?

Queen Marie: The 23rd of August. Tell our readers what happened on that most fateful day!

The Chronicler: The King summons the General to the Palace. The General arrives fifteen minutes late. The King asks him questions about the situation on the battlefield. He wants to make sure that the General's position hasn't changed. Indeed, the General confirms that the Romanian army will fight next to the Nazis until the bitter end. Having found out what he needed to know, the King gets up in silence and leaves the room. He lights a cigarette and thinks. He puts out the cigarette and, with his hand, signals the agreed-upon code. The four officers who are next to him enter the room as the King orders: "In the name of the King, you are arrested!"

Queen Marie: The King is twenty-two.

The Chronicler: The General is immobilized by the officers. He cannot believe his ears. After the first moment of bewilderment, he begins to spit at the officers in anger. The officers take him by force and imprison him in a huge safe deposit box where King Carol used to keep his most treasured stamp collections. (Later, without the King's permission, the Soviets will kidnap the General and execute him.) That night, the King informs the army of the latest developments, and orders them to fight henceforth alongside the Allies. For twenty-four hours, in the initial confusion, the Romanian army is at war with both camps, the Germans and the Russians, but after the King's orders are received everywhere, the 180-degree turn is done without a single desertion or protest. Historians claim that the King's decision shortened WWII by six months and saved the lives of almost 200,000 people.

Queen Marie: The King was twenty-two.

The Chronicler: August 23rd should have remained in history as King's Day. Instead, after the Soviets forced the King to abdicate, the Communists, who came to power under their protection, didn't contend themselves with the banishment of the Royal Family. For the duration of their regime, half a century, they taught generations of students that August 23rd is the day when the Romanian army, under the leadership of the Communist Party, switched from supporting the Nazis to the Allied Forces. This day became the national day, that is, the day when Communist propaganda was at its highest, and all you could hear on TV was "*Marele Conducător*," "*Clasele muncitoare, intelectualii si ţăranii au scuturat jugul*," etc. This is how August 23rd came to be the most hated day in the history of the country. Even today, more than thirty years after the fall of Communism, most Romanians still believe that August 23rd is the day when the Communists changed the course of the war. The erasure of the Royal Family, the family that built modern Romania had to be total, and, like all erasures, it culminated in the very appropriation of its most heroic act. A diabolical reversal.

Queen Marie: It is time that we told the story of the abdication.

The Chronicler: In 1945, after the Soviets instated the Communist government under the leadership of Petru Groza—whose mansion, by the way, I used to pass by as a child whenever my father took me to the park on Sundays—the King wrote a memorandum in which he explained point by point why this government was undemocratic and sent it to the Americans and the Russians. The Russian general to whom he'd given personally the document replied drily that this was an act of hostility toward his country, and the King answered even more drily, "Too bad," henceforth refusing to put his signature on any governmental laws. The King was—as incredible as this may sound—on strike! The first time in history when such an act of protest, a tool in the arsenal of oppressed workers, was used by the one alleged to incarnate power and privilege, but who was, in this case, precisely the opposite. For it was around the same time that the King's mother was informed that if her son had refused to accept Groza as Prime Minister he would have been kidnapped by the Soviets and brought to Moscow, where he, very likely, would have suffered the same fate as General Antonescu. And so, one can only imagine how the King's refusal to collaborate with Groza was seen by the Soviets. The royal strike lasted for five months during which time the Soviets hired a Romanian officer to murder the King, but the officer committed suicide.

After the fraudulent Parliamentary elections from November 1946 and their recognition by the Soviets, the Americans and the British refuse to take action. The West wasn't going to start another war with Stalin in order to defend Romania, Churchill is quoted to have said. When the King opens the Parliament on December 1st the same year, at the end of his speech, the group of politicians resulting from the elections gives voice to some of the most absurd cheers ever to have graced an assembly: "Long live Stalin! Long live Mihai!" And yet, this grotesque marriage—a Communist government with a King—lasts for another year.

In 1947, whatever was left of the traditional parties is dissolved and their leaders arrested, tortured and murdered. On May 10th the King is awarded by the American government the Chief Commander Degree of the Legion of Merit Medal for the 23rd of August coup d'état. The same year, in October, Mihai receives the invitation to attend the wedding of Britain's Prince Elizabeth with Prince Philip of Greece. At Mihai's request, the Groza government approves his trip to London. The King leaves the country after having been accompanied to the airport by several members of the government, Groza included, all with big smiles on their faces. They are convinced that this is the last time they will have seen the King.

In London, Mihai and the Queen Mother are staying at the Claridge Hotel. Mihai has private meetings with various dignitaries to whom he attempts to explain Romania's situation, but all of them, including Britain's Minister of Foreign Affairs, while sympathetic, end up apologizing: there is nothing they can do. One night, Mihai is invited to a party. There, he is introduced to one of his many cousins, Anne de Bourbon-Parma, who has worked as an ambulance volunteer during the war. Years later, Anne, with her frank charm, will tell the story of their first meeting in an interview: seeing the King in his military uniform, she involuntarily stands at attention, clacking her heels like a soldier, even though she is wearing an evening gown. The King tells her to stand at ease, and they both laugh. During their one-week courtship in London, they take walks together and go to the movies, which the King, who has grown up in a palace, is doing for the first time in his life. "He was fascinated by the smallest things, like buying a movie ticket, because he had never done this," Anne says laughing. It is the beginning of an education that will last a lifetime, after the King will have lost his kingdom.

The King asks Anne to marry him less than a week after their meeting. Initially, she says no, but eventually she agrees, though it is not clear whether she agrees in London or later, in Geneva. After the royal wedding of Princess Elizabeth, where, in the reels that have been kept, Mihai and his mother can be seen walking behind the newlyweds in their splendid attire, the King returns home to the utmost shock of the Romanian government. Per the Constitution, he asks the government to approve his marriage to Anne. Hoping that they will force him to abdicate, the government representatives refuse, under the pretext that the country doesn't have the money for the wedding.

On December 29th, the King is asked to grant an audience to Groza in order to discuss "a family matter." The King, who is spending the winter holidays at Sinaia with his mother, assumes that the Prime Minister wants to discuss his marriage to Anne, and departs for the capital the next day. The meeting takes place at Elisabeta Palace on Kiseleff Street, which will become the King's official residence after he will have returned from exile half a century later. The Palace will still be owned by the Romanian state, which has nationalized it after the King's forced abdication, allowing the former Monarch to reoccupy it in 2001. Between these two dates, 1947 and 2001, lies the gaping maw of Communism and its aftermath, a mass grave full of decomposing corpses.

As the King enters the house—a large house, rather than a "palace"—on that fatal December day, does he have any idea of what is in store for him? Does he know that this is the last time he will have set foot in it until the cut-off thread of his life will be reattached to Romania half a century later? The room where the meeting with the Prime Minister and the General Secretary of the Communist Party takes place is on the first floor. There, the Queen Mother and her son welcome the two politicians, who kiss her hand with excessive politeness, according to the tradition of male gallantry. Then, Groza takes out a file and, with a mischievous grin, informs the King that the Romanian people have decided that the monarchic system was no longer viable and he will have to renounce his position. The King's first reaction is one of puzzlement. Then, very fast, he understands that he has been caught in a trap. He retorts that no one has, in fact, consulted the Romanian people, that he, the King, is beloved by the people who need him now more than ever. In turn, the Prime Minister replies that a mysterious "they" have decided to abolish the monarchy, and that if he agrees, he will have a nice life abroad with a fat stipend from the government. The King answers that he has no need of such a stipend and that his rightful place is in Romania with his people. At that point, the Prime Minister's tone changes. If the King refuses, he will bear the responsibility for the consequences. A thousand students have been arrested during their demonstrations of support on the King's birthday, and they will be executed. Their blood will be on his hands. The King ponders the situation. Anger suffocates him. He wants to scream *No*, he who never raises his voice. But he knows what "they" are capable of. He reads the document that Groza has put in his hands, and which begins with the customary "We, Mihai I, King of Romania …" He takes his pen and signs.

*

The King and the Queen Mother will leave Romania on January 3rd, 1948, with several suitcases and three cars. The Communist authorities will search all their belongings, cutting in half even the apples they were planning to snack on to make sure nothing was hidden in them, and will confiscate the Queen's jewelry. After the royals' departure, the Secret Services will spread the rumor that the King left the country with a train full of gold and countless objects of priceless value. The no-longer King who was once incapable of buying a movie ticket, will become private citizen Michael de Roumanie, learning to make a living first in Great Britain where, together with his wife, Anne, he will work as a farmer, selling chicken eggs at the market; then, in Switzerland, as a pilot, and finally, as a stockbroker in New York. He will die on December 5th 2017 in his modest home in Switzerland, and will be granted a national funeral in Romania, attended by members of all the European royal houses. The car carrying his coffin will be followed by another car enclosing the steel crown that once belonged to Carol I and which he, Mihai, never wore. He, the once-upon-a-time Child-King will be buried next to his ancestors at the Curtea de Argeş necropolis, matrix of the legend of Manole and of the doing and undoing of being.

Chapter 12

Fata Morgana

Queen Marie: If one were to divide people in two categories, dreamers and realists, I would definitely count myself among the former. All my life I dreamed of an ideal house, which I chased with the passion of a man with a parched throat desperate to quench his thirst. I knew, of course, that there is no such thing as a dream house, that it was merely a Fata Morgana, yet it was my life's quest, and now that I can look at my life with the dispassionate eye of the one who's lived it, I understand that this desire belonged to Maria-the-Artist. All great artists create with their eyes fixed on an ideal, which they attempt to replicate in their works, all the while knowing that this is impossible, that, in fact, this is the Impossible itself; yet it is this very knowledge that pushes them forward to pursue an illusory dream. If one were to ask me for a definition of the artist, I would say that an artist is someone who longs for a Fata Morgana, all the while knowing that she doesn't exist. I tried to find this shadow in my writings, and, in real life, I tried to find her in the houses I created.

I built my Fata Morgana in the small town of Balcic in the Dobrogea province, which, alas, now belongs to the Bulgarians. This part of the country is one of my most beloved because it is so unlike the rest of Europe one has the feeling that one is on some other planet at the ends of the earth, maybe in *A Thousand and One Nights*. The land is arid and the sun unsparing, the houses are primitive and made of clay; yet, the poverty of the land and of the people has nothing depressing about it, on the contrary, it projects a mysterious aura onto everything, lending a magic quality to the passersby, who seem to descend from the pages of an Arabian fairytale. The Turks are fascinating with their colorful turbans, and their women make me think of some strange, fabulous birds, clothed as they are in long, dark blue or black dresses. The local population is very mixed: besides the Turks, there are blue-eyed Russians with reddish beards and crimson shirts, *Lipoveni* (an ethnic group related to the Russians), Bulgarians and, of course, dark-eyed Romanians. They often pass me by, having no idea who I am, yet admiring my thoroughbred horse, they who are big experts in horses. Their horses too are beautiful, though not quite as beautiful as mine, and we exchange smiles and glances of connoisseurs. Even today, the town of Mangalia in the Dobrogea province is still the place where one can find some of the most impressive thoroughbreds in Eastern Europe.

The Chronicler: Mangalia! Mangalia! Oh, my dear Queen, if you knew what memories you've brought back! The last time I saw Mangalia I must have been around ten years old. In fact, this may have been the last time I saw the Black Sea, where Mangalia is a port. I can hear the thud of the waves against the shore, I can see the pelicans and the cormorants drawing large circles in the infinite, cloudless sky, and I can imagine the thin, arrow-like minarets of the mosques whose whiteness and simplicity have inspired your Fata Morgana.

Queen Marie: Indeed, of all architectural styles, the combination of the Romanian *brâncovenesc* style and the Arabic mosque-like architecture is dearest to my heart. How strange and ironic that Mangalia is for us a meeting point across centuries and continents in the white pages of your book, it too a Fata Morgana! And speaking of the Black Sea, have you ever been to Constanţa?

The Chronicler: Sure, I have! More than once, also in my childhood. This is the largest Romanian city on the Black Sea, incidentally, the place where the Latin poet, Ovid, was exiled. Tomis—its name in antiquity. Constanţa comes from Constantiniana, a feminization of Constantin, the Emperor of the Eastern Roman Empire, after whom was named Constantinople (today, Istanbul). I remember how once, during the bleakest period in Communism, I was vacationing there, and the local state-owned boutiques, which usually carried tiny Ovid sculptures, were peppered with signs informing us that they were "out of pickles and Ovids."

Queen Marie: Carmen Sylva too was in love with Constanţa, and she even had a pavilion made for her right on the seafront cliff where she used to sit in a large chair all night long, waiting for the fishermen's return. The sailors were familiar with the snow-white silhouette of the gray-haired queen and were proud of her love for their land. I was the one who made her discover Ovid's Island, where the poet used to come to lament his exile and compose his immortal verses. There is no doubt that one of the major reasons for Carmen Sylva's attraction to Constanţa was the feeling that Ovid's ghost hovered above it, and above her.

Carmen Sylva: I even have a short story, "Snake Island," about Ovid. "There once was a Roman poet called Ovid"— that's how it begins. Not many people know that this land— now Dobrogea—was called at the time Moesia. It was my husband, King Carol, that took Dobrogea from the Turks after our Independence war in 1877, and it was afterward that the Turkish Kunstendje became Constanţa. During Ovid's time, this territory was mainly sand and swamps with very few inhabitants, a morose, mute piece of land to which, for the first time, he gave a voice. Often, a land needs someone from afar to be given a voice. The most beautiful song often springs from the throat of a migrating bird. On this soil where, today, one sees elegant women moving to and fro, listening to the marching bands that play military melodies, almost two thousand years ago wandered poor, lonely, sad Ovid. Because he had no one to talk to he had become friends with a little snake named Colubra, which spent its time tied around the poet's neck or arm. The author of "The Metamorphoses" believed that his pet snake must have been a cursed princess on whom a spell had been put.

One night he dreamed that Colubra told him to go to Snake Island in the Danube Delta and witness true metamorphoses not just write about them. He followed her advice, but, as soon as he set foot on the island, he noticed that his pet had vanished. However, he forgot about her immediately because an unusual sight opened before his eyes: a charming garden with bountiful fruit trees on whose branches rare birds sang magnificent songs, marvelous fountains from which water sprang high up in the air, green grass with forget-me-nots and red poppies polished by soft sunrays, stairs of white marble slowly descending toward the turquoise sea. Before Ovid had been able to pull himself together, he noticed an enchanting young woman advancing toward him. The woman took him by the hand, and said, "I am Colubra, and you are now on Snake Island, where all the men who lied in their previous existence are exiled. Once in a thousand years we come back to our human existence, the island regains its vitality, and everything is in bloom. But among the living, only one man can see us, a most unfortunate man who cannot speak, for if he does, he will be punished for the tiniest lie and be transformed into a snake for thousands of years to come."

At sunset, Colubra looked into the poet's eyes and said, "You need to leave now. Better to remain with a beautiful dream than experience an ugly reality." But Ovid refused, and soon, an old, white-bearded man named Caron appeared with a boat, and all the island's strange creatures gathered around him, pleading to be taken on his boat. "Who has spoken the truth in the last thousand years?" Caron asked, and when the creatures answered, "I have," they were instantaneously metamorphosed into snakes. Colubra too had answered positively, and she too was now a tiny snake that wrapped itself around the poet's neck. Frightened, Ovid asked the sailors with whom he'd traveled to take him back. Since then, Snake Island turned itself only once more into the celestial garden the Roman poet had once seen, but no one had been able to see the divine metamorphosis, no one save for another exiled Poet.

Queen Marie (to the Chronicler): As you can see, Queen Elisabeta thinks of herself as a new Ovid, a misunderstood, lonely soul, a martyr on the altar of tragic beauty. In defense of the queen, however, I should add that when I came to Romania, I too identified with the exiled poet. How well I understood his *sfâșietoare* melancholia, here at the ends of the earth! What's the English word I'm looking for? "Heartbreaking" is not quite it; "poignant" is a weak and banal approximation. The word comes from "*a sfâșia*," to tear to pieces. Strange, I just realized that it must have the same root as *fâșie*, "strip," as in "a strip of land."

The Chronicler: How ironic, once again, that you are looking for your (English) words, while I am often at a loss when it comes to the Romanian language! That I too have come to the other end of the earth, here in the land of California, named after a fictional island ruled by Queen Kalafia, whose name was very likely derived from the Arabic "Khalif." How ironic that you are me and I am you in this California-Dobrogea, Dobronia-Calibrogea! Both lands equally beautiful, both sanctuaries for refugees and exiles, so alike even in their elongated geographical shape and arid landscape.

Queen Marie: There is something devastatingly beautiful about Dobrogea and its inhabitants, about its patient, quiet, dark-skinned men. The Turks welcome you with their traditional gesture: a hand placed first on the heart, then on the forehead. They are friendly, but their faces are impenetrable, they never betray any wonderment. Their women are seated, silent and apparently shy, at a respectful distance, but if you approach them, they become chatty and gregarious in their incomprehensible language. Their children too are charming, dressed as they are in their Turkish harem pants, especially the girls with their long hair braided in many tresses. There is something majestic about this desert-like land sprinkled with boulders and cliffs, the salty air merging with the turquoise waters and the azure sky, the silver brightness of the moonlit nights sheltering myriads of seagulls that cross the sky like spectral visions, something so eerie that I took the decision to erect my Fata Morgana on these lands.

The *Lipoveni* are among the most striking people I have ever met. The bearded, red-haired men, dressed in their crimson shirts, make me think of some enormous red poppies, and their women too wear brightly colored dresses. I'll never forget a journey when our yacht stopped in the middle of the lake: it was at twilight and we could see the tall minaret of a white, ghost-like mosque in the distance, behind the pale hills. The Danube was suddenly full of boats that were quickly advancing toward us, carrying thousands of locals in their Sunday best with armloads of flowers, while above us, the sun was exploding, and from its liquid body, streams of red and orange merged with the sky's blue.

All of a sudden, a boat stood out among the rest with a tall man in a priestly dark garb standing by the bow, his golden hair descending in waves past his shoulders, so bright that it obscured the sun's own brightness, truly a divine apparition. The man carried a big wooden cross and seemed to have sprung out of the very waters, like a mythical Christ, half-fish, half-man. He climbed onto our yacht's deck, followed by two peasants in crimson shirts who sang some kind of church songs, and he handed us the cross to kiss it. As he did so, he spoke in Russian with a soft and melodious voice. I will never forget him and his companions, all three from another world, like three Magi brought to us by fate to give us their blessings. Like the three wise men, they brought us frankincense, represented by the incense spread from one of the peasants' censer, myrrh, in the form of a vial carried by the other peasant, and the most precious gift of all, gold, metaphorically embodied by the mysterious man's golden locks.

The Chronicler: These Russian mystics still exist. Just the other day I saw in the news that some weirdo with long sandy hair, who fancied himself as a second Christ, was arrested in Russia at Putin's directives, no doubt.

Queen Marie: I have always been fascinated by unorthodox forms of spirituality, and for me, such men are no "weirdos." It is rather sad that they have no place in today's societies. Dobrogea and the Danube Delta have many such men who seem to have come from another planet. One really has the feeling of having arrived at the ends of the earth where everything we know about normal life is being challenged. There, I have seen islands whose inhabitants can barely be distinguished from vegetal or animal forms of existence, old shepherds sitting still for hours, like mute tree roots, Sphinx-like in their enigmatic presence, forever morose and silent, manifesting their disapproval at our arrival through their dark eyes and frowning foreheads. Clothed in pelts and long woolen coats that resemble the very animals whose guardians they are, they have become akin to these animals and to the surrounding wilderness. Statue-like, supporting their tall bodies on some long walking sticks, staves, I suppose they are, or as they call them in Romanian, *toiag*, pronounced *to-jag*, one of those words impossible to pronounce by a foreigner, they let their detached, impenetrable gaze float over the unwelcome guests that we are. They respond in monosyllables when we address them, as if they had forgotten how to use speech, as if they had become one with the landscape whose peace we have disturbed. By contrast, their sheep are very gentle and often eat from our hands. At night, these wild shepherds gather around enormous bonfires and proceed to sing songs whose melancholy sadness reaches our yacht in fragmentary bursts, filling me with longing for another life, a simpler, freer, quiet, anonymous life I will never know.

Every now and then, we leave our yacht and continue our journey by car through unknown villages with Turkish names such as Caramurat, Bairam-Derde, Anadolkioi, Casapkioi, names whose unusual sounds gave them the attractive allure of magical fairylands.

We often visit monasteries where we are greeted by nuns whose enthusiasm at our sight stands in stark contrast with the shepherds' grumpiness. One such monastery comes to mind, a monastery with a strange-sounding name, Cilic-Dere, where, after a long journey through winding, dusty sideroads, we are welcomed by Russian and Romanian nuns who offer us the traditional rose preserves accompanied by cold water from their well, followed by Turkish coffee served in tiny porcelain cups. The monastery's grounds include a modest church whose inner walls have been painted in striking colors by the nuns themselves. I have always preferred these simple churches, often made of wood, to the fancy, opulent constructions the clergy favors. We leave the monastery, our arms full of presents—roses and dahlias, embroidered napkins and an icon of the Virgin Mary—and, driving back, we come across peasant houses decorated in our honor with countless, enormous bouquets of marigold; even the telegraph poles are decked out in yellow and orange, the entire village like a wheel of fire resplendent under the magnificent sun.

The Chronicler: Caramurat-Bairam-Derde-Anadolkioi-Casapkioi ... They do sound like a poem, or rather, *o poemă*, an ode, one might say. As does the entire book in which you depict them, *The Country that I Love*, which is the closest literary equivalent to George Enescu's musical masterpiece, *The Romanian Rhapsody*. A Romanian rhapsody written by a former British Princess in which the ideal beauty is Oriental. Your Fata Morgana has Scheherazade's magic: dressed in white, her face covered with an Oriental veil, she is *of* here, but not *from* here. She is your California—the untamed East merging with the Wild West.

One can see in almost all your stories the theme of a Christ-like child of light in which Paganism and Christianity are intertwined, just like the shapes of your Scottish milk thistle and Romanian *ciulin*. Whether visual (light) or aural (the divine music of a thousand harps), the quest for the Impossible is always there, hidden behind your desire for a white abode, a mythical, almost sacred, Heideggerian dwelling clothed in Beckettian whiteness. Light and whiteness—the unbreakable thread of your life, uniting the search for divine peacefulness with your affinity for Oriental architecture, the kind of whitewashed humble dwellings one sees in Greek or Arabic landscapes against the bluest of skies and the equally azure sea. Nowhere is this desire more present than in "The Sun Child," whose protagonist is a young girl with golden hair blessed by the sun (clearly, an alter ego of yours), and whose words are like the pearls a legendary queen has threaded on silk. In this story, you are both the humble girl with golden hair and the legendary queen who needs her help. Like all great artists, you can split yourself in two and you are both the object and the subject of your quest—you are your own creation.

Queen Marie: The Sun Child was blessed—or maybe cursed—with a heart and body that captured within themselves the pain of all the mortals, which she preserved in tiny vials. The vials were full of people's tears, which, through the power given to her by the sun, she could transform into precious stones, and the tears-stones began to tell stories, the sad stories of the people who'd lived them.

The Chronicler: Do you know that many years ago I too wrote a story in which tears were transformed into stones? I think it ended with "forever gathering tears and turning them into stones." But they were not precious stones, just heavy, banal stones. Fluidity reified.

Queen Marie: I think the transformation in my story is very different from the one in yours. While in your story there is no redeeming value for the stones, in my tale, both tears and stones are sparkling, they are endowed with the transgressive gift of enchantment that suffering can bring to us as it cleanses and purifies us.

The Chronicler: Another Christ-like character and theme—for, in the end, the Daughter of the Sun dies, suffocated by the countless vials that end up covering her tiny body; her heart is broken by too much pain, and when it breaks, all the sunlight hidden inside it at birth rushes out, cascading in an avalanche of blinding light, just like the girl's hair.

Queen Marie (pensive): Your words about my being my own creation and splitting myself in two … I never thought about it, but I think you are right. In asking to have my body buried at Curtea de Argeş and my heart at Balcic, I wanted my royal self in the family vault, and my true, artist self in the home that was my own creation, my Fata Morgana.

The Chronicler: Nothing resembles a book more than a house, that's why the Creator of the universe is often compared to an Architect. In *Solenoid*, the Romanian novelist Mircea Cartarescu imagines his dream house as a ship with countless labyrinthine rooms through which he wanders, never knowing where they will take him. The house, built on a vacant lot, is *white as snow*, of a whiteness that can only be equated with pure silence, the silence from before the creation of the world. "Beautiful as a pearl," he says. A pearl is white, translucent, divine in its round, self-sufficient existence. In Romanian, a pearl can also be called a *mărgăritar*, from "*margareta*," "daisy." Your Balcic Castle is a white pearl, a pearl that encloses your own pearl-shaped heart in its eternal silence.

Now, your heart is in the Golden Room of Pelişor Castle, the same room where it beat for the last time on July 18th, 1938, and which I visited for the first time just two weeks ago. On another occasion I had seen the gray, wrinkled heart on TV, after it was taken out of its original box by the Communists and obscenely exposed to the light of day.

Queen Marie: So, you are back. Back to the ancestral homeland.

The Chronicler: So, I'm back.

Queen Marie: You need to come visit us at Curtea de Argeş, which is, simultaneously, a white pearl, a cathedral, a monastery, a burial plot, a vault, and an extraordinary myth of creation—the Fata Morgana of an entire people. It too built on a sacrifice. As any lasting creation. This, I learned from my people. My Romanians. But you haven't told us what you thought of my Golden Room in Pelişor.

The Chronicler: What I thought of it? First of all, I found Pelişor much more endearing than Peleş. I could tell that while Peleş was King Carol's creation. Pelişor—or small Peleş, for those who don't understand Romanian—is yours. It is truly a home with small cozy rooms. Even the Golden Room is relatively small, and, in spite of its opulence, it doesn't have the vulgar vibe massive gold usually gives, because the paneled wood is wrapped in gold, and so the gold appears darker, copper-like. The design on the walls is that of a field of milk thistle in relief to remind you of your beloved Scotland, although the south of Romania, the Bărăgan plain, is also famous for its *ciulini*. On the right side of the room, in the forefront, stand two thrones wrapped in gold with the same thistle design. Next to them, a little farther back, is a tall gray metallic stove, on whose sides climb, like ivy, the same golden leaves of milk thistle, creating a striking effect, as if the stove were clothed in golden lace. The ceiling is even more impressive, with the wooden beams forming a square inside of which one can see a large Celtic cross above an enormous sun, symbol of Life and of the Infinite—all the motifs in the room designed by you. In the center of the room, on a pedestal, rests a flag, British on its visible side, Romanian, on the hidden side. On the flag, the box inside of which, like in fairytales, there is another box, and in this, another even smaller box enclosing your heart. The entire room exudes a melancholy, crepuscular amber light, as if the sun from one of your fables had poured its heart out and the room itself were merely the background of a glorious sunset.

Queen Marie: Pelișor Golden Room has a twin room at Cotroceni Palace, which became Nando's residence in 1889, and our official residence as a couple a few years later. I put all my creative energy into this house, my first one as a married woman, a palace that has gone through many restorations and styles over the years, starting with the one done by the French architect, Paul Gauttereau, before my moving in. Everything that is Romanian in this palace is as a result of my efforts.

The Chronicler: As is often the case, in order for the Romanians to take an interest in something that was theirs, a foreign eye was needed, an eye saturated with shapes coming from faraway lands. We need distance to see better what is our own, and what is our own becomes more brilliant and richer when looked at with *othered* eyes.

Queen Marie: All I did was follow my instinct, and my instinct always pulled me toward the heart of things. But maybe in order to get to the heart of things we need to be closer to God, and in order to be closer to God, we need distance from His creation.

The first thing I did at Cotroceni was to transform my Louis XV private salon into an Art Nouveau Golden Room. I imagined this room, like the one in Pelișor, as a living thing, a creation of such beauty that, when looking at it, your heart would immediately leap up, as if pulled by unseen strings toward the realm of the divine and the infinite—for this is what gold is for me: not an expensive metal, but the symbol of divinity, a symbol that allows me to partake of the infinite. The salon's walls were of green plaster covered in gold sheet, and, like Pelişor's Golden Room, they were etched with roses and filigree-rich leaves interspersed with undulating ribbons that cascaded in amber-like waves. The ceiling was of paneled wood disposed in rectangles, while the ground was covered in shimmering turquoise ceramic tiles bearing such a resemblance to the sea that our little Mignon liked to pretend she was drowning in their splendor. The entrance was a vaulted opening next to which could be seen several chairs of golden wood. A golden throne incised with Celtic motifs and hand-painted lilies that copied my own watercolors was created for me, and, next to it, a four-poster couch and an armchair with gray-blue sateen upholstery displaying light pink flowers and gold embroidery. Behind the couch, a beautiful old icon I'd acquired from Constantinople, and behind the throne, another, chimney-like rectangular structure made of the same golden wood with Celtic patterns engraved in the upper part and with a round opening in the middle. On top of it were displayed various knickknacks from my travels around the world: a cock, a cat, and numerous frogs of jade and other semiprecious stones, at the back of which flashed the reddish rays of an enormous sun that decorated the slanted wall. Another area of the wall displayed my life-size portrait illuminated by a very large wreath-shaped green chandelier with scintillating precious stones. It was truly a divine, dream-like room.

The Chronicler: A dream-like room destroyed, like so many other buildings, objects and monuments, by the Communists. All that is left of it are a few inadequate photos and descriptions. But maybe it's only fitting for dreams to remain in their unreachable, camera obscura world, for the Absolute never to be represented, and for us to strive toward it with extended palms, like beggars. Beggars of the Absolute.

Queen Marie: This time I won't contradict you. I was a queen on this earth, but a beggar of the Absolute.

The Chronicler: Do you know what the Communists did with Cotroceni Palace and its Golden Room after they nationalized them? They transformed the palace into the Pioneers' Palace, and your Golden Room into a hall where they taught Communist propaganda. An extraordinarily perverse reversal. While medieval philosophers took cheap metals, and, through an alchemical process, transformed them into gold, the Communists took gold and turned it into trash. A devilish counter-alchemy.

The other room that bears your mark, just as much as the Golden Room but in the opposite way, is your bedroom, also called the Silver Room or the Celtic Church Bedroom. I can see the impulses that have given birth to these two very different rooms: in both cases, an ascendent movement, a desire to elevate your soul toward the divine, but while in the Golden Room the predominant feeling is one of awe, in your bedroom one can sense a desire for peace, the peaceful serenity one experiences within the confines of a church.

Queen Marie: I have been thinking about what must have inspired me to imagine such interiors. I believe that, my love of beauty aside, there was something in the air, as we lived in uncertain times, and those with an innate desire of freedom, writers and artists, were forced to project it onto fairytale spaces in which they lost themselves. As in my other rooms, I used in my bedroom many Celtic symbols seen through modern eyes, which at the time meant Art Nouveau style. My bed's woodwork included engravings of fabulous animals and unusual shapes, such as a Celtic cross. Other Celtic motifs resembling interlocked braids were drawn on the Gothic-like white arches and the solid columns supporting them, both arches and columns giving the large room the appearance of a medieval cathedral.

The Chronicler: I was a bit surprised by the heaviness and clutter of this room, which, in spite of its church-like atmosphere, had so many objects—dozens of vases, little ornaments, and a large sculpture of a man on horseback placed on one of those tall white columns, not to mention another enormous column on whose upper platform you rest your arm in one of your photos, dressed in a white gown sewn with precious stones, and sporting a tiara, it too in the shape of a Celtic-like braid, a calculated, radiant goddess in a room meant to symbolize religious detachment.

Queen Marie: In that case, all artistic endeavors are "calculated."

The Chronicler: Yes, in a sense, all artistic creations are "calculated," if by "calculated" one means artificially made. But, at least, your photograph was tastefully calculated. I can think of some very calculated royal photographs whose taste is much more dubious, if not quite laughable. Just the other day I saw the cover of *Time* magazine with the royal couple from Montecito, California: both air-brushed, looking into the future like the visionaries they are, or like … hmm, the couple from Grant Wood's "American Gothic." The only thing missing was the pitchfork. Two princes in search of a kingdom.

Queen Marie: I thought they had already found their kingdom. But why do you keep moving away from our topic? We were talking about art and artists. *My* art. My paintings, my interior design, my stories. How many times did my children tell me that I should put pen to paper and write down the many tales I used to tell them at bedtime! "Mother, you should write these fables!"

*

Once, there was a little boy called Peter, who was so poor he only owned the shirt on his back. He lived in a village with a tiny wooden church and, like the other villagers, he dreamed of a bigger, more sumptuous church with a tiled roof, a church white as snow, which would sparkle under the sun and whose inside walls would be painted in bright colors that would be pleasing to God. At the edge of the village there was a well at the bottom of which lived an unknown creature to whom the peasants had taken the habit of bringing presents, especially on saints' days or high holidays in order to appease it and in the hope that their gifts would bring them something in exchange. They didn't have much to give—fruit, donuts or, sometimes, little pebbles—and didn't ask for much. Mostly, they asked for a cure for an ailing loved one, or for a nicer house of worship. Peter's mother was herself very ill and didn't seem long for this world, and the boy would have done anything to keep her alive. Anything? Well, almost.

On Christmas Eve, the boy took to the road, bringing with him his most precious possessions, which he'd received from the local priest: a candle and five matches. He intended to go to church in the nearby village and pray for his mother, but, as he passed by the magic well, he heard a voice coming from deep down: "Please help me, little boy, please help me! Give me your candle and matches so I can get out of here! I am here, all alone in the dark, a boy just like you. Please give me your candle and matches!"

Peter was counting on using the candle and matches for his prayer, which he hoped would cure his ailing mother, and tried to explain to the disembodied voice that he couldn't satisfy its request. But the voice grew more desperate, and Peter, who was good-hearted, began to cry together with the boy in the well. What was he to do? He couldn't go away and leave the boy alone in the well, but he couldn't sacrifice the only thing capable of saving his mother either. Eventually, he threw the candle and matches into the well, and out came a beautiful young boy with golden hair, and, as he rose from the well, the celestial sound of a thousand harps filled the air. The golden boy told Peter that his mother was cured and then asked him to go to the wooden church.

When Peter arrived at the church, he saw a globe of blinding light that was coming from his tiny candle, which had miraculously arrived there too, and the church had become so gloriously beautiful it seemed otherworldly. He stood there, bathed in the pool of divine light, and his soul was filled with the music of the spheres.

*

The Chronicler: But your greatest story is, without a doubt, "The Dreamer of Dreams," a story about a painter who loses his mind after dreaming of a fascinating pair of eyes. After the dream, he becomes restless and leaves the court of the emperor, whose favorite he was, in search of the eyes, without which he can no longer paint. The painter is, clearly, your alter ego, and his search for the Impossible is your own, but I wonder whether you were aware that Fiona Macleod, whom you quote fifteen times in the epigraphs of your chapters, was the female pseudonym of William Sharp, who wrote a romance novel under it, then, like Fernando Pessoa years later, created a whole persona for his pseudonym and exchanged correspondence under it?

Queen Marie: *Ma chère*, it should be your task to determine whether or not I was aware of it. What I can tell you is that, like her, I dream with open eyes, and that like her, I devoted my life to following a path, mesmerized by the enchanting sound of the unseen brook from where Beauty itself springs. "The fountain of all dreams!" Like her and my other idol, Rabindranath Tagore, I wanted to catch a golden dream, and so I imagined that, in his journeys, the painter in my story meets a woman seated on a golden throne, dressed in a golden robe, a Sphinx-like, enigmatic creature, a creature with no eyes! The painter desperately desires to catch a glimpse never before caught by any other eyes, but the eyeless creature refuses to let herself be pinned down, she is an elusive Fata Morgana, a golden dream akin to the golden room where my heart now rests—captive in a golden box.

And so, the painter left the eyeless ghost, following his path, forever searching for the eyes he longed for, until he met a beautiful young woman. Were these the eyes he so longed for? He thought they were, but when she turned to face him, he cried in bitter disappointment, for he knew that these were not the eyes. He walked and walked until he reached an ice palace where the Ice Queen lived wandering through a desert of whiteness where countless broken hearts had been exiled. The Queen's white fingers were stained with blood dripping from the poor, broken hearts, and by the end of the chapter, her long white hair had turned into a veil sweeping the ice floor of the palace, her face surrounded by an aura made of fireflies.

The Chronicler: Ice and fire: two opposite elements like a white and red thread that crosses your writings, as does mine. Your search for the Promised Land is mine—the Promised Land, which in this story takes the shape of "a marvelous apparition of light and beauty." One can see that you are both the painter *and* his Fata Morgana, the subject and the object of his search. The one who gazes and the one gazed upon.

Queen Marie: But the Ice Queen turned out to not be the wished-for one, and so the painter kept on until he arrived in the middle of a colony of nomad Gypsies where he was greeted by an old witch with dark, wrinkled skin, dressed in rags barely held together by a bright red girdle, who took the young man by the hand and led him to an island from where an enchanting violin song came in cascading waves.

The young man felt that he was getting closer and closer to the point where the thirst of his desire would be finally quenched when he spotted the creature holding the violin. She was like an apparition from another world, so slim you could see through her, with long, red-brown hair and sea-green eyes, and when he saw her, he knew he had arrived at the end of the road. He had reached the Promised Land, here, among the Gypsies, these swarthy nomads whose hot blood pushed the men to draw knives when you least expected it, and whose young women displayed unparalleled beauty: tall and straight, with necklaces made of empty shells around their long necks, and white pipes in the corners of their sensual mouths. He could tell that the divine apparition whose features were the answer to his prayers and who seemed to have come from another world was like a diamond treasured by the colony of Gypsies and by the old witch, who took care of her with the possessiveness of a jealous mother. He began to spend time with the young woman, who seemed unaware of his feelings for her, and unbeknownst to her, he painted her marvelous face. When he showed the portrait to the old woman, she declared that never before had a human likeness been reproduced with such a degree of accuracy. The portrait seemed so real one expected the young woman to begin moving and fly away. Her eyes looked in the distance toward a faraway realm seen by them only—the eyes that our painter had searched for his entire life. Moved to tears, the old woman encouraged him to go to the young woman and kiss her to prove his love. As the young man sat down next to his beloved, he looked into her enchanting eyes and, with desperate longing, touched her lips with his, he touched them with such passion, as if he were attempting to drink her very soul. And then ... a miracle happened: the young woman who, until then, had averted her eyes, turned them, gazing into his eyes, and, as she did this, she began to respond to his passionate kiss. Her eyes sparkled like stars, and she herself seemed more like a luminous planet than a human being—her name was Stella (*star*). In that kiss, the past, present and future merged, melting together—an alchemy that brought their two separate beings to a state of heavenly harmony, making them one.

But, alas, when he woke up in the morning, he saw that his sweet love had a death-like pallor and realized that he was holding a dead body. The young woman had died, burned by the fire of his passion.

The Chronicler: I confess that at this point in the story I had a hard time containing my laughter. "She died of passionate kissing."

Queen Marie: How sad that you've become so cynical! Have you never known passion?

The Chronicler: It doesn't matter what *I*'ve known—*you* are the one who matters here. Have *you*?

Queen Marie: Yes, I have lived great passion more than once in my life, and if you haven't, I pity you.

The Chronicler: If you lived it more than once, then I'm afraid you experienced just some plain, prosaic, run-of-the-mill infatuation. According to your own stories, true, passionate love should kill you. I thought you believed in the Absolute.

Queen Marie: I do. But, in the end, I too am no more than a woman. I lived in the world, among real humans, humans made of flesh and bones. One can experience great passion more than once, especially if one is from the race of those who experience everything with great intensity. Great artists are made of a different raw material than the rest of humanity.

The Chronicler: Which reminds me of your story, so let's get back to it!

Queen Marie: Our painter was, of course, devastated with pain, and so, after a while, he decided to go back to the court of the emperor he'd left many years earlier to finish the frieze he'd started, now that he knew what the eyes looked like. "I found the face of my dreams and held it for an instant," he said. "I was a dreamer of dreams, and couldn't hold on to my visions, which had brought me to the Promised Land." The moral of the story is that we only know happiness for the briefest of instants, and when we pluck the Absolute's blue flower, which should only be touched by our soul, we kill it with our own thirst.

The Chronicler: I often wondered after I read this story what your love life was *truly* like, because you couldn't have written such a story had you not experienced it in some way.

Queen Marie: My loves are discussed in a different chapter.

The Chronicler: Are you saying that your loves weren't an aspect of your search for a Promised Land or a Fata Morgana?

Queen Marie: It is not up to me to categorize my loves—that is the task of my biographers, or, in this case, yours. One lives one's loves and that's it. All I can tell you is that when I did love, I did it with my whole being, and those who loved me were, likewise, entirely devoted to me.

The Chronicler: Were they devoted to *you* only, or were they also in awe of your crown?

Queen Marie: I thought you knew better than to ask such inelegant questions. Who we are and, especially, whom we fall in love with, cannot be entirely separated from our dreamlife, and our dreamlife is, often, a reflection of our social status. The dreams of a queen are not the same as the dreams of a peasant. However, the dreams of artists everywhere are, more or less, the same, no matter the artist's background. An artist can only fall in love with someone they admire, someone the artist can look up to. And if the artist happens to be a queen, it is hard to find people one would look up to. That individual would have to be exceptional, a hero of some kind—as you know, heroes are the closest equivalent to gods.

The Chronicler: That hero for you was Boyle. And heroes, as we know from fairytales, usually fall in love with princesses and queens, who are the closest equivalent to goddesses.

Queen Marie: Maybe. You are very indiscreet, my dear. It is a bad quality.

The Chronicler: Isn't indiscretion the very essence of writing? As a writer, you should know.

Queen Marie: It is the essence of *bad* writing.

The Chronicler: Only if you think of "indiscretion" in the popular sense of the word. But insofar as authentic writing is a revelation of some kind, all great writing is indiscreet.

Queen Marie: And I suppose you think of yourself as a "great" writer, which would give you license to probe all the hidden chambers of my soul, drag my secrets to the light of day and show them to the mob that you so despise. Maybe even expect some literary prize for it.

The Chronicler: All writers who have a true vocation hope that they are great. Otherwise, what's the point of writing? Some writers, who compare themselves to craftsmen, think of themselves as workers who polish sentences the way a jeweler does a golden piece. But I do not think of writing in this way, even though I love beautiful jewels. For me, writing is like descending into a never-ending dark well from which you may never return. Deep down in the well, your face blurred by the murky water. Your inversed double, as in the myth of Fata Morgana, in which one sees images and their upside-down double. Writing this chronicle, my dear queens, was like a descent into a well—all three of us links in the olden, rusty chain from which hangs the water bucket. You, especially you, Marie, seem so real, so alive, that I am overtaken by an immense feeling of melancholy, the same melancholy I feel when I read a dead writer's diary or correspondence because of the intense presence conjured up by the dead person's inner life and thoughts, by the conflicts she once had with people who are now long gone, conflicts that for her were more real than this keyboard is for me right now. This presence, contradicted by the dust and ashes to which she is now reduced, reminds me that one day I too will be dust and ashes, and that these thoughts right now, which are my aliveness, make me no more than a link in a long chain of dead souls. And I know that these thoughts of mine now in the reader's head, these lines linking me to this chain mean that I am already dead, dead like you, with whom I now bury myself, right here, in this chronicle, which is my very tombstone.

Epilogue

Queen Marie: May 6th, 2023—the enthronement of King Charles. We see the King entering the Abbey dressed in his crimson velvet, ermine-caped robe of state, under which one can spot his black pump slippers with metal buckles, modeled on a pair worn by his grandfather, George VI, the King's long red train carried by four pages in crimson attire, one of whom is his grandson and future king, another George in a series of kingly Georges; in front of the King, the Queen Consort, all in white, she too in a robe of state that has been personalized with engraved rescue dogs and embroidered names of family members, her train carried by her own grandsons, all clothed in black; following the King, his heir, William, in his lavish black robe of the Order of the Garter with the order's insignia on one side and a golden chain on his chest pinned with white frills on each side; next to him, his wife, Catherine, she too in the Garter robe, hers even more dramatic, an electric blue with crimson margins, wearing a diamond-leaved headpiece, which has a replica in the smaller ornament worn by her mini-me, Charlotte, all in white, holding the hand of her younger brother, mischievous five-year-old Louis. They walk the length of the Abbey's long hallway with the congregation on both sides, they, the royals, those meant to be watched, the "privileged," but also the *entrapped*, entrapped in the golden cage of their destiny.

Carmen Sylva: Are you saying that Prince Harry was right to call his father and brother "trapped" and to claim that he's found his freedom?

The Chronicler (interjecting herself, not without a certain impropriety, between the two queens): Well, he was not entirely wrong to call his family members "trapped," but as far as his own freedom is concerned, shall we mention once again how he makes his living? That he is becoming a billionaire by doing the only thing he knows how to do, talk about his family? Compare this to the way King Mihai of Romania made a living after his forced abdication. After the Coronation, Dior posted a message on Twitter in which they announced that Harry had worn a Dior-made suit at this extraordinary event. A walking advertisement, he was present for two hours, having arrived spouseless, walking around clumsily and talking to the only royals still speaking to him, his cousins Beatrice and Eugenie, daughters of disgraced Prince Andrew, and seated next to them in the third row, sign of his demotion, behind Princess Anne's extremely high red feather that partially covered his face.

Queen Marie: By "those meant to be watched" I meant the objects of people's fantasies, those that the people turn into idols but also into monsters. Those who personify moral notions in fairytales. Once upon a time there was a good king, who was at war with his neighbor, the evil king. In folktales, characters symbolize *principles*—good against evil, beauty against ugliness, strength against weakness, truth against lie, justice against injustice. The characters themselves are meant to impersonate these principles because these stories were created in a *symbolic* world. This is the world of royalty: a world of symbols. A world of poetry and beauty, to which my heart—my heart buried in my dream house at Balcic—is devoted forever.

The Chronicler: But today, very few people see the symbolic order of this vanished world. All they see is privilege.

Queen Marie: Through its ritual, King Charles's crowning reminded us of the old world of symbols in which the divine appears personified in the person of the king. I watched him and saw his overwhelmed, grave expression, the face of a man perfectly aware of the moment and humbled by it. Hidden by a screen decorated with a green-leafed tree with as many leaves as there are countries in the Commonwealth, and embroidered with their names, he was anointed with the holy oil poured from an aquila-shaped golden ampulla while in the background one could hear the choir sang "Zadok the Priest" ("God save the King!" "God save the King!") and emerged from behind the screen, purified, in his white hemp monastic shirt, like a peasant, kneeling, vulnerable.

Thus renewed, "the First Son of God," now wrapped in a robe of silk and gold and seated on a throne, the King is presented with symbols of military honor and chivalry: spurs "to advocate for those in need" and a diamond-studded sword offered by the leader of the House of Commons, an impressive woman that reminds one of a fierce Viking. The recipient is exhorted to "not use the sword in vain" but put it in the service of justice, to "stop the growth of iniquity," "help and defend widows and orphans," and "punish and reform what is amiss." A symbolic exchange ensues in which he exchanges the sword for a tiny velvet crimson purse with golden coins.

The Chronicler: All this while in the background we can hear a Byzantine choir sing a monotone Orthodox chant that lifts my soul and takes me back to my origins, which are also the spiritual origins of the King's father, Prince Philip, the Greek.

Queen Marie: Prince William places around the King's neck a long golden stole, then helps other aides lay a golden flower-embroidered mantle on his shoulders. The Archbishop of Canterbury exhorts: "Receive this robe. May the Lord clothe you with the robe of righteousness and with the garments of salvation." Other religious leaders of different faiths present the King with a series of symbolic gifts: two golden bracelets "of sincerity of wisdom"; a golden orb with a cross atop ("Receive this orb set onto the cross and remember always that the kingdoms of this world are to become the Kingdom of Our God and of His Christ); a ring ("symbol of the kingly dignity and of the covenant between king and people"); a white glove, which the King puts on ("Receive this glove that you may hold authority with gentleness and grace, trusting not in your own power, but in the mercy of God"); a royal scepter ("the end sign of kingly power and justice," "the rod of equity and mercy").

The Chronicler: And these images: the 3,000-diamond-studded crown weighing three kilos placed on the King's head by the Archbishop of Canterbury, so heavy that he needs help to rise from the throne; a similar crown placed on the head of Queen Camilla, who watches, a visible expression of dread on her face, the crown above her, and instinctively moves her head aside, as if to avoid a blow. What a destiny! Who would have thought that she would be crowned queen some day?

Prince William kneeling in front of the crowned King, pledging allegiance—"I, William, Prince of Wales, pledge my loyalty to you, and faith and truth I will bear unto you as your liegeman of life and limb. So help me God!"—then, arisen, touching the crown in a symbolic gesture, and finally, kissing his father's left cheek. The latter, visibly touched, murmurs: "Thank you, William!"

They begin the slow, long procession through the hall of the Abbey, the crowned King in his robe of estate—no, this is not a typo, this is a different robe than the robe of state in which he'd arrived, this one is made of imperial purple velvet—holding the orb in one hand and the scepter in the other. Outside, the King and Queen are helped into the golden state carriage, a 200-year-old carriage made entirely of gold and weighing several tons—and don't be jealous, because it is very uncomfortable. They are followed by a long procession of soldiers on horseback, the horses superb, their manes sparkling with electric-blue decorations made from recycled bottles, contrasting with the soldiers' crimson military garments. The royals are expected to appear on the famous balcony of Buckingham Palace, the last act in a centuries-old religious play.

*

I went to Windsor two weeks after the Coronation of King Charles. It was a peaceful early Monday afternoon, and the medieval high walls could be seen as soon as one left the train station. The castle was fenced in by a construction-site barrier. As one took the main path, one arrived at a crossing where one had to decide whether to first visit St. George's Chapel or the castle itself. I decided to first see the chapel. I had seen images from it dozens of times on the small screen of my computer in my home in Santa Cruz, California, away from the world of Europe's queens and kings, away from the world for so long, not knowing whether I would ever be able to come back to it alive or sane, or whether I would remain forever enclosed in my home where a chronic illness had confined me for the past several years forcing me to gaze at the world through the keyhole that was my computer screen.

I entered the chapel whose threshold had been crossed so many times by the princesses and princes I had dreamed about in the sad bed of my never-ending misery, and tears began to stream down my face. I was alive and I was back in the old world where I belonged! I had survived my own death and could now bear witness to the uplifting beauty distilled within the chapel's walls. The quire's stone vaulting was peppered with three-leaved clovers, each enclosed within a circle linked to another one by a diamond-shaped geometrical figure. Every now and then, two such rhombuses met to create the badge of some royal highness or other. The walls themselves were paneled with intricate constructions of wooden mini-chapels, a series of meta St. Georges, harking back to some medieval fable. At the top of each mini-chapel, one could see a cross, and atop, a crown. The infinite mirroring of a story-inside-a-story that was Europe's royal history was set before my eyes in its most literal form.

In a discreet side chapel I spotted the burial site of the late Queen. The gravestone under which also rest her parents and her husband was sober and simple, listing only their first names—George VI and Elizabeth, separated by a garter star from Elizabeth II and Philip, as if the ultimate simplicity, that of being known only by one's given name, was a privilege of the highest rank.

I exited the chapel and entered the castle, and as I entered it my body arched into the unearthly evanescence of a transreal leap, a sky-high leap from the white pages of a book—*this very book*—splattered with the ink of its characters, kings and queens that had roamed through the castle's centuries-old walls, into the very reality that had inspired the book in the first place. I had lived with these characters for so long, arguing with them on the page, and now, I could finally release them from the dark recesses of my brain into the bright world where they belonged.

The End

California, USA, 2019—Transylvania, Romania, 2023

Acknowledgments and Bibliography

Badea-Păun, Gabriel. *Carmen Sylva. Uimitoarea Regină Elisabeta a României*. Translated from the French by Irina-Margareta Nistor. Bucharest: Editura Humanitas, 2012, 2008, 2003.

Carol I al României. *Jurnal*. Trans. from the German and edited by Vasile Docea. Bucharest: Polirom, 2020.

Cioroianu, Adrian. *Elisabeta. Carmen Sylva*. Bucharest: Editura Curtea Veche Publishing, 2019.

--- & Alexandru Groza. *Elena a României*. Bucharest: Editura Curtea Veche Publishing, 2018.

Ifland, Alta. "Two Kings, Two Mistresses and a Luxury Yacht." *Royal Central UK*. 2020.

---. "Fata Morgana." *The Creative Process*. Special issue guest-edited by Helene Cardona. June, 2025. https://www.creativeprocess.info/cardona2/alta-ifland

Loti, Pierre. *Carmen Sylva and Sketches from the Orient*. University of California Libraries, 1912.

Mandache, Diana. *Balcicul Reginei Maria*. Bucharest: Editura Curtea Veche, 2014.

---. *Cotroceniul Regal*. Bucharest: Curtea Veche Publishing, 2015.

---. *Later Chapters of My Life. The Lost Memoir of Queen Marie of Romania*. Sutton Publishing Limited, 2004.

Morris, Constance Lily (Rothschild). *On Tour with Queen Marie*. New York: Robert M. McBride & Comp., 1927.

Niculescu, Tatiana. *Regele si Duduia. Carol II si Elena Lupescu dincolo de bârfe si clișee*. Bucharest: Humanitas, 2019.

---. *Regina Maria. Ultima Dorintă*. Bucharest: Humanitas, 2015, 2016, 2018.

---. *Mihai I, ultimul rege al românilor*. Bucharest: Humanitas, 2016.

Pakula, Hannah. *The Last Romantic. A Biography of Queen Marie of Romania*. New York: Simon and Schuster, 1984.

---. *An Uncommon Woman. The Empress Frederick: Daughter of Queen Victoria, Wife of the Crown Prince of Prussia, Mother of Kaiser Wilhelm*. New York: Simon & Schuster, 1995.

Pop, Virgiliu. *Facebook.com/Letopiseț*.

Principele Radu al României. *Povestea Palatului Elisabeta*. Bucharest: Curtea Veche Publishing, 2021.

Queen of Romania, Marie. *The Story of My Life*. Vols. 1-3. London: Cassell, 1934-35.

Regina României, Maria. *Gânduri pentru vremuri grele*. Intro. by Tatiana Niculescu. Trans. by Anca Barbulescu. Bucharest: Humanitas, 2020.

---. *Jurnal de război*. Trans. by Anca Barbulescu. Edited by Lucian Boia. Vols. 1-3. Bucharest: Humanitas, 2014-2015.

---. *Povestea vieții mele*. Trans. by Margarita Miller-Verghi. Vols. 1-3. Bucharest: Editura Rao, 2013.

---. *Povesti*. Vols. 1-2. Bucharest: Editura Saeculum, 2015.

---. *Însemnări zilnice*. Iasi: Editura Polirom, 2013.

---. *Tara pe care o iubesc* (*The Country that I Love: An Exile's Memories*). Translated by Maria Berza. Bucharest: Humanitas, 2006.

Sylva, Carmen. *Povestile unei Regine*. Bucharest: Editura Curtea Veche Publishing, 2012.

---. *Fluturi sărutându-se*. Bucharest: Editura Curtea Veche Publishing, 2013.

---. *Letters and poems*. Introduction and notes by Henry Howard Harper. Boston: The Bibliophile Society, 1920, 2 volumes.

---. *A Real Queen's Fairy Tales*. Trans. from the German by Edith Hopkirk. Chicago: Davis and Company, 1901, pp. 211-229.

---. Ed. Silvia Irina Zimmermann. *Gedanken einer Königin/Les Pensées d'une Reine*. Stuttgart: Ed. Ibidem-Verlag, 2012.

Woolf, Virginia. "Royalty." *Time and Tide*. Dec. 1, 1934. Reprinted in *The Moment and Other Essays*. Michigan: Hogarth Press, 1952.

Zimmermann, Silvia Irina & Romanița Constantinescu, Editors. *Corespondența Perechii Regale Carol I-Elisabeta*. Vols. I & II. Bucharest: Humanitas, 2020.

Zimmermann, Silvia Irina, Editor. *The Child of the Sun: Royal Fairy Tales and Essays by the Queens of Romania, Elisabeth (Carmen Sylva, 1843–1916) and Marie (1875–1938)* (Series of the Carmen Sylva Fürstlich Wiedisches Archive). Stuttgart: ibidem-Verlag, 2020.

---. *Reginele scriitoare ale României, Elisabeta (Carmen Sylva) şi Maria.* Ediţie îngrijită, introducere, note şi bibliografie de Silvia Irina Zimmermann. Colecţia "Istorie cu blazon." Bucureşti: Editura Corint, 2021.

---. "Portretul perechii princiare moştenitoare Ferdinand şi Maria din viziunea Reginei Elisabeta a României în scrisori personale şi texte pentru publicul larg."*Revista Bibliotecii Academiei Române*, Anul 1, Nr. 2, 2016, pp. 11-35. [A]

OTHER SOURCES:

Florescu, John. *Războiul regelui.* Documentary about King Mihai. 2016.

---. *Maria—Inima României.* Documentary about Queen Marie. 2020.

Florescu, John & Trevor Poots. *Regele Mihai: Drumul către casă.* Documentary about King Mihai. 2021.

"Interviurile lui Vitalie"/An Interview with Nicolae Medforth-Mills. 10/15/2019. stirileprotv.ro/stiri/interviurile-lui-vitalie/fostul-principe-nicolae-interviu-exclusiv-ce-spune-despre-relatia-cu-bunicul-sau.html

"Living History presents an interview with King Michael of Romania." Feb. 11-12, 1992. History Program at Duke University. youtube.com/watch?v=L0YDS5VJGqk

Ora Regelui: "La masa regilor"—un film despre ospitalitatea regala (TVR1): youtube.com/watch?v=afbb4slzBwo

"Inima reginei" (TVR1): youtube.com/watch?v=q4NHNxD2-Lc

Rotaru, Marilena. *YouTube* archives.

"Gloria Steinem challenges Meghan Markle 'Princess' Stereotype:" www.youtube.com/watch?v=afbb4slzBwo

The author wishes to thank Cristina Bejan, Dagmar Lowe and Roger Greenwald for their editorial suggestions.

About the Author

Born in Communist Romania, Alta Ifland came to the US as a political refugee in 1991, where she obtained a PhD in French language and literature. After a brief period in academia, she published two collections of prose poems (*Voix de Glace/Voice of Ice* and *The Snail's Song*) and two books of short stories (*Elegy for a Fabulous World*, 2010 finalist, Northern California Book Award, and *Death-in-a-Box*, 2010 Subito Press Fiction Prize of the University of Colorado). Ifland's novels, *The Wife Who Wasn't* and *Speaking to No. 4* were published by New Europe Books in 2021 and 2022. After 30 years of life in the US—Florida, Arizona and California—Ifland now lives in France.